About the author

Sharon Booth writes uplifting women's fiction — love, laughter, and happy ever after. Happy endings are guaranteed for her main characters, though she likes to make them work for it.
Sharon is a member of the Society of Authors and the Romantic Novelists' Association, and an Authorpreneur member of the Alliance of Independent Authors. She has been a KDP All-Star Author on several occasions.
She loves Doctor Who, adores Cary Grant movies, and admits to being shamefully prone to crushes on fictional heroes.
Sharon grew up in the East Riding of Yorkshire, and the Yorkshire coast and countryside feature strongly in her novels. Her stories are set in pretty villages and quirky market towns, by the sea or in the countryside, and feature lots of humour, romance, and friendship.
If you love stories with gorgeous, *kind* heroes, and heroines who have far more important things on their minds than buying shoes, then you'll love her books.

Books by Sharon Booth

There Must Be an Angel
A Kiss from a Rose
Once Upon a Long Ago

This Other Eden
Being Emerald
The Skimmerdale Collection

Resisting Mr Rochester
Saving Mr Scrooge

Baxter's Christmas Wish
The Other Side of Christmas

New Doctor at Chestnut House
Christmas at the Country Practice
Fresh Starts at Folly Farm
A Merry Bramblewick Christmas
Summer at the Country Practice
Christmas at Cuckoo Nest Cottage
The Bramblewick Collection

Belle, Book and Christmas Candle
My Favourite Witch
To Catch a Witch
The Witches of Castle Clair Complete Collection

Once Upon a
Long Ago

Sharon Booth

Green Ginger Publishing

First published in 2016 by:
Fabrian Books
Kent, England
Published in 2020 by:
Green Ginger Publishing
Yorkshire, England

Cover design by Berni Stevens. www.bernistevensdesign.com

ISBN: 978-1-9993602-6-9

To Dan, Lisa, Phil, Jamie and Jemma.

I love you more than I could ever say.

xxx

Chapter 1

Will had always loved the smell of the stables. The scent of horse, mixed with leather, hay — and peppermint, because he never entered a loosebox without a packet of Polos in his hand — had always brought him comfort.

Sometimes, when life at home was getting too much to bear, he would head out across the yard, make his way into a loosebox, sit on an upturned bucket, and just *be*. The horses never seemed to mind. He'd been friends with most of them since he was a child, and they were used to him. They would continue pulling on their hay nets, occasionally pausing to nudge him or breathe softly into his ear, not seeming to find it unusual that a young man, who lived in such a grand house, preferred to sit in a stable, saying nothing, thinking, dreaming.

Right now, he was with Pilot, his father's ancient hunter. Pilot was well over thirty and hadn't been ridden for years, but his eyes were still bright, and he was alert enough to remember that Will was the one who provided the mints.

As the horse pushed his greying muzzle into his pockets, seeking the Polos with eager determination, Will smiled.

'Go on, then. Just one.' Retrieving the packet, he fed a mint to the delighted gelding. 'I reckon you deserve it today. Just you and me now, eh?'

'Thought I'd find you here.'

Bernie, the estate manager, closed the bottom half of the loosebox door behind him, carefully sliding the bolt into place.

Will rubbed Pilot's nose and rested his forehead against the horse's broad white blaze. 'Where else would I be, Bernie?' he asked, suddenly overcome with weariness.

'In bed, if you'd any sense. How long is it since you got any sleep?'

'Plenty of time for that when everything's organised. I had to break the news to old Pilot here.'

Bernie raised an eyebrow, and Will knew he was probably thinking that the horse wouldn't give a damn. Never mind horses, there weren't many people who would mourn the Thirteenth Baronet Kearton, whose rudeness and arrogance had won him few friends. He knew Bernie wouldn't be hypocritical enough to pretend to be sorry that the old man was gone. Will wasn't sure how he felt about it himself. He was too exhausted to try to analyse his feelings at that moment.

'How did he take it?' Bernie asked.

Will turned to face his estate manager with a wry smile. 'Surprisingly well. Hasn't put him off his mints, anyway.'

'Well, let's be honest, he hasn't seen him for years. Not one for sentiment, Sir Paul. When he couldn't ride any more, he lost all interest in the poor bugger. If something had no use to him, he didn't waste time with it, did he?'

Will shrugged and walked over to the stable door. He folded his arms on the lower half and leaned out, staring across the yard. 'What on earth do I do now, Bernie?'

Bernie put his arm around him. 'What you've been doing for the last year: carry on with your plans to make this house pay. At least you don't have to worry about your dad any longer. You've had a tough time since his stroke, but you're free now, Will. You can do all the things you've wanted to do for so long, and save Kearton Hall before it's too late.'

'What if it's too late already?'

Bernie shrugged. 'Well, we'll go down fighting. You're not on your own with this, you know. You'll always have me, and Woody, and the rest of the staff and tenants. We're all on your side. Always have been. And the villagers will support you. You don't realise how well thought of you are.'

Will smiled. 'Thank you, Bernie. That's very kind of you.'

'I'm not being kind. I'm telling you the truth. The way you've carried everything this last year, having all the responsibility for this place and caring for the old man, it's been amazing. Taken its toll on you, though. You look buggered. And you've had no social life, at all.'

Will said nothing, and Bernie squeezed his shoulder. 'Reckon now your dad's shuffled off the mortal coil, it might be time to think about yourself a bit, eh?'

'I wish Lexi was here,' murmured Will. He longed to see her. He needed one of her hugs.

He pictured her face, her turquoise eyes warm with compassion for his loss, even though she hadn't thought much of his father and hadn't exactly hidden her feelings. She was an extremely honest person. It was another reason he loved her so much.

'Aye, sod's law that she's away the very weekend Sir Paul pops his clogs.' Bernie sighed. 'You could ring her, tell her what's happened. She'd come back early, I'm sure of it.'

'No, no, let her enjoy her weekend away. She's probably sleeping off a hangover after the wedding.'

Will straightened and turned back to Pilot, giving him one last Polo before he ushered Bernie out of the loosebox and locked the door behind them.

They headed into the yard, where they stopped and stared toward the grand, Elizabethan house that loomed in front of them. For hundreds of years, the place had been in Boden-Kean hands, with successive baronets caring for it, keeping it safe to pass onto the next generation.

In the measure of a day it had become his turn, his responsibility. With the burden pressing down on him, he knew it was going to take every ounce of determination to keep it going.

He thought about Lexi. With her by his side, he'd have the strength to do anything. He'd waited a long time for her. He understood she wasn't ready to have a relationship with anyone, let alone someone as plain and awkward as himself, but maybe things were changing at last. Maybe, with his father gone and a different mood at the Hall, she would start to see him in a new light.

It was all he could hope for.

****

So it was true. I'd really done it.

I'd been half-hoping that the large amount of alcohol I'd knocked back the previous night had played havoc with my memory, and that reality had merged with wine-soaked lustful dreams and confused me.

Sadly, as I finally plucked up the courage to open one eye and peer cautiously around the room, my suspicions were confirmed. I was definitely not at number twelve Tippet's Yard. And the breathing I could hear quite distinctly was not that of my little stepsister, Amy, who sometimes crept up the flight of stairs to my attic bedroom and climbed into bed beside me, but someone much larger, and inappropriately close by.

I lay quite still, hardly daring to breathe as I considered my situation. If I moved, I would almost certainly wake him, and that would lead to one of those ultra-embarrassing moments that I'd read about in books, and seen in situation comedies, but had never imagined in a million years that I'd experience for myself.

What did you say to a complete stranger who'd spent hours the previous night exploring every inch of your quivering body? And boy, he'd done more exploring than Captain Cook, if memory served me right.

Risking a slight turn of the head, I viewed the man who'd been my first one-night stand. He was gorgeous. Even fast asleep with his blond hair all messed up and his face squashed against the pillow, I could see the good looks that had turned my head so much the previous night that I'd abandoned my cousin's wedding reception and headed up to the man's hotel room, while my hormones battled against every bit of common sense I possessed.

I supposed I should feel ashamed. After all, I'd allowed myself to be chatted up and seduced by a stranger, and I couldn't even blame the drink. The evening had barely got started when I'd spotted him in the hotel reception, and more-or-less abandoned my family in the function room to sit with him in the bar.

Obviously, I was very sorry that I'd left Pandora's and Fuchsia's wedding, because it meant so much to them, and they'd made gorgeous brides, and I was extremely fond of them both … but he was only the third person I'd ever slept with, and I needed *something* interesting to tell my grandchildren. If I ever had any grandchildren that is. Not that their sex life was something I supposed any doting granny ought to discuss with her grandchildren, but you know what I mean.

Beside me, the man — did he even tell me his name? — shifted and emitted a grunt.

I stared at him, my stomach churning. For a moment, he was still, and I thought he was safely asleep. Except, suddenly, his eyes flew open, and I found myself gazing into a pair of deep blue pools of utter gorgeousness.

My stomach somersaulted, and I realised with sudden dismay that I desperately needed the loo and, horrifyingly, I was stark naked under the duvet and wouldn't be able to get to the bathroom without him seeing my body. That may have been fine last night when I was in a state of heightened arousal, but him seeing me in the cold light of day filled me with dread.

The man frowned for a moment then gave me a lazy smile. 'Morning, gorgeous. Still here then?'

What did that mean? Was I supposed to have left in the night, or something? What was the etiquette for a one-night stand? I had no idea. I only knew I needed a wee, and soon.

I'd seen people in a similar situation in films, many times, and they always seemed to have a handy sheet to wrap around themselves as they edged their way out of the bed. If there *had* been a sheet, other than the one we were lying on, it had been cast off and thrown somewhere I couldn't see it, and as far as I could tell there was no way out of this predicament that didn't involve total humiliation.

I suddenly realised that I hadn't even replied to him. I cleared my throat, nerves making it dry. 'Um, morning, er—'

Hell, what was his name? He must have told me. Even high on passion, I wouldn't have slept with a man without knowing what he was called, surely?

He grinned. 'Nat.'

'Sorry?'

'My name. It's Nat.'

Yes, that was it! It all flooded back. He'd told me last night, and I'd immediately thought of my stepmother's Uncle Joe, who described mean people as being "as tight as a gnat's arse", and had wanted to laugh. How had I forgotten that?

'And you're Lexi?'

'Yes. Well done.'

He yawned and stretched, and in the blink of an eye he was out of bed and heading for the bathroom, apparently totally unfazed that he didn't have a stitch of clothing on. Well, he was probably used to this sort of thing. At least it gave me a chance to get dressed without him seeing me.

Waiting 'til he closed the bathroom door, I dived out of bed and frantically gathered up my clothing, almost strangling myself as I rushed to make myself decent before he came back into the room.

He strolled out of the bathroom, just as I collapsed onto the bed in relief, my dress still unbuttoned but my bits thankfully covered. 'You're dressed. That's a shame.'

Breathlessly I gasped, 'I need the loo.' I shot past him into the bathroom and locked myself in.

'Help! What do I do now?' I whispered to myself and, thankfully, obeyed when the little voice in my head replied with, *Have a wee, for goodness sake!*

As I washed my hands, I stared at my reflection in dismay. I had big black smudges under my eyes, and the makeup had rubbed off my skin, leaving me deathly pale. I hoped I hadn't got foundation and blusher all over the posh pillowcases.

Washing my face, I removed all smudges and wished I'd thought to grab my handbag, so I could at least have combed my hair before facing the man — Nat — again. I ran my fingers through my matted, red hair, in a vain attempt to tidy it a little, and pulled a face at myself in the mirror. Next time I had a one-night stand I'd be more prepared. I'd carry a toothbrush, a comb, and some face wipes at the very least. Not that there'd be a next time, of course. I wasn't that kind of girl.

As I returned to the bedroom, I was astonished to see him sitting up in bed. I'd expected to find him dressed and urging me to get out of his room. Instead, he gave me a wicked grin and patted the bed beside him.

'Er, I should be going,' I muttered uncertainly.

He raised an eyebrow. 'Really? But we've barely been introduced. Besides, I can't let you go with such a bad impression of me.'

I sat tentatively on the edge of the bed. 'Bad impression?'

'I'd had quite a bit to drink last night. I wasn't on form, and I'd hate you to think that was the best I could do. I'm wide awake now and I'm sure we could have a lot of fun.'

I stared at him. He wasn't on form? Was he joking? I thought about the nights of so-called passion I'd shared with Derry and Robbie — not at the same time, of course; I definitely wasn't *that* sort of girl. I'd thoroughly enjoyed myself with both of them, but Nat had taken things to a whole new level. And he said he hadn't been at his best? Jeez, what the hell was he capable of?

He patted the bed again and I hesitated.

The wedding would have gone on until the early hours, and we didn't have to vacate our rooms 'til lunchtime, so everyone was probably having a lie-in, or busy with babies anyway. No one would have a clue that I wasn't in my own room.

Nat grinned at me and a familiar tingling spread through me, suddenly making the outcome inevitable. I pulled off my dress and jumped back into bed.

Oh, well. In for a penny and all that …

Chapter Two

Newly showered and changed, I locked my room and headed next door to Dad and Eliza's suite. I couldn't pretend I was looking forward to going in. I'd heard the wailing coming from there for the last fifteen minutes and didn't relish walking into chaos. It had been nice to have a bit of peace and quiet.

Opening the door, I found Eliza sitting on the edge of the bed with Mikey draped over her shoulder, her eyes half-closed as she gently rubbed his back.

Dad was pacing up and down, rocking Hannah in his arms whilst trying to avoid my step-sister Amy as she cantered around the room, riding her imaginary pony, Twinkle. He smiled, delighted to see me — Dad, I mean, not Twinkle. That would have been worrying.

'Great, you're up. Here, do your big sister duty and look after Hannah.' He plopped the baby into my arms, but as he dropped, exhausted, onto the bed, Eliza promptly handed him Mikey and jumped up before he could give him back.

'I've got the packing to do,' she said, as he started to protest. 'We have to be out of here in less than two hours and look at the mess. First things first though. Who wants a coffee?'

'Better make it strong and black,' said Dad. 'Otherwise I'll be asleep in five minutes.'

I plonked myself on the sofa and cooed at Hannah, who stared at me in a very accusing fashion, as if she was perfectly well aware of how irresponsibly I'd behaved the previous night.

Amy cantered over and peered at me, her hands clutching imaginary reins. 'Mummy took me and Twinkle to your room, but you didn't answer,' she said. 'Where were you?'

'I, er—'

'I told you, Amy. She was still asleep. Coffee, Lexi.' Eliza put the cup beside me on the small table and gave me a knowing look. 'I must say, she's looking very refreshed today, isn't she, Gabriel? Positively glowing in fact. Good night?'

My face burned as she grinned at me. Luckily, Dad was too exhausted to listen properly. He was far too absorbed in trying to shut my little half-brother up.

Suddenly, Mikey gave a very satisfying burp and the wailing stopped immediately.

'Thank God for that,' Dad said. 'Now he may finally sleep.'

Mikey gave him a crooked smile, and I laughed when Dad visibly melted. He kissed my brother's forehead and carried him to the travel cot, where he laid him carefully on the mattress and stood watching him for a moment.

Hannah waved her fist at me, as if to ask what I was waiting for, so I carried her over to the cot and lay her next to her twin. Dad and I held our breath for a moment, but the two of them soon snuggled up together, and within seconds their eyes closed.

'Blessed relief,' whispered Dad, collapsing on the bed.

'Your drink,' said Eliza, holding out a cup.

He groaned and reluctantly struggled to sit up. He took the cup from her and gulped down a mouthful of hot coffee.

'I suppose we'd better get as much packed as we can while the twins are asleep.' Eliza glanced around at the toys, nappies, clothes, and various toiletries in despair. 'How can such tiny people make so much mess?'

'I have no idea. I'm too old for this lark.' Dad sighed.

'Well, you wouldn't listen,' I said smugly. 'I warned you it would be too much for you at your age, but you didn't take any notice. Now see what you're landed with.'

'Be fair,' Dad said. 'How were we supposed to know we'd end up with double trouble?'

'Serves you right for bonking at Beltane. You know perfectly well it's a time of fertility. You were asking for trouble.'

'According to Rhiannon, *every* solstice is a time of fertility. Anyway, I told you, they weren't conceived at Beltane,' said Eliza, sitting down beside me and stifling a yawn.

'Yeah, right. Beltane on the first of May, and the twins arrive on February the twelfth. Coincidence? I think not.'

'Twins are nearly always early, not late,' said Dad. 'Ours were no exception. I may not accept all Rhiannon's beliefs, but I'm not stupid enough to take any risks. Thank God I didn't, or we could have ended up with quads. Amy, please stop cantering round the room, darling. If you knock the twins' cot and wake them up, I may just cry. Eliza, is there any chance at all that I can have a nap? I'm absolutely shattered.'

'No chance,' she said, then her expression softened. 'You do look tired, and you were up with them more than I was last night. How about Amy and I help Lexi pack and leave you in peace? Just for half an hour though. I really do have to get to work on this room.'

Dad put his cup on the bedside table and blew her a kiss. 'You're an angel,' he murmured, then closed his eyes and lay back on the bed before she could change her mind.

'Come on then, girls,' Eliza said, standing. 'Let's leave him to sleep.'

We headed quietly out of the room, and Amy immediately cantered ahead, clicking her tongue and flicking imaginary reins.

'Should I be worried?' said Eliza. 'She's getting quite obsessed with this Twinkle.'

'Be glad it's only ponies,' I advised. 'In a couple of years, it'll be some God-awful popstar, and then you'll really have something to worry about.'

'You sound about forty sometimes.' She nudged me, a knowing look on her face. 'So, go on then, tell me all about it.'

I fumbled in my pocket for my key card, my face burning. 'All about what?'

'Where you were last night. The good thing about breastfeeding is that, while everyone else is getting sloshed, I'm fully alert and able to spot things that others miss — like my stepdaughter deep in conversation with a rather handsome blond man in the bar.'

'You're kidding,' I said. 'Who else knows?'

She gave me an apologetic look. 'Rose.'

Wonderful. Of all the people to find out my dirty little secret, it had to be Eliza's best friend and business partner, Rose.

'Well, I guess I'm going to have to have words with her, aren't I?' I sighed. Rose wasn't the most discreet of people.

I pushed open the door, and Eliza called to Amy, who was guiding Twinkle over imaginary jumps further down the corridor. She steered him carefully around and cantered him back to my room, rewarding his clear round and excellent behaviour with a loving pat on the neck.

'Amy, can you do me a favour?' I asked, not wanting her to be party to the conversation that I absolutely knew was coming. 'Get that bag and start putting all my makeup and stuff away from the bathroom please.'

She halted Twinkle and eyed me suspiciously. 'What's in it for me?'

'A pound?'

She tutted and prepared to canter away.

'Okay, a fiver,' I said.

She grinned and headed into the bathroom. Honestly, kids today are a disgrace — no wonder the world's going to rack and ruin.

I turned to Eliza. 'How come Rose knows?' I demanded. 'Thought she'd be too busy getting sloshed on vodka to notice.'

Eliza grinned. 'She and Flynn made a deal to take it in turns to stay sober at social events so one of them is able to see to Violet. It was her turn yesterday and she was furious about it, more so because Flynn wouldn't change it, which she thought was rather mean. Personally, I think he did us all a favour, including Rose. The downside is, she was with me when I spotted you with the handsome stranger. Who was he anyway? He wasn't a guest at the wedding, was he?'

I shook my head. 'He's in Yorkshire on business. Just staying at the hotel for a couple of nights. His name's Nat, and that's all I really know about him. Except that — well — he's rather gorgeous.'

'And you did the deed?'

'At least three times,' I confirmed.

'You're so lucky. It's been ages since … Sorry, I know you don't like to think of your dad that way. I'll shut up.'

'I'm not six, Eliza,' I pointed out. 'The twins' arrival tipped me off that you weren't just roommates. Are things not good between you?'

She smiled. 'Oh yes, fine. We're just so tired. It's hard enough caring for one baby, but two ... Things will get back on track eventually. Don't worry.'

'Maybe I should babysit more,' I suggested, feeling a sudden anxiety.

'Don't be silly. You have them once a week as it is, and you've got your job to do and your studies to finish. You do more than enough. Honestly, Lexi, we're okay. Think no more about it.'

I nodded but resolved to help out a bit more. Dad and Eliza had been totally loved up, more-or-less since they'd first met. My parents' marriage had been a disaster, and Dad was in a pretty bad state when Eliza had turned up in the village, reeling from her husband Harry's betrayal with the voluptuous Melody Bird. She'd totally transformed his life, and I didn't want anything to spoil that.

'So, you don't even know his surname?'

'What?' I blinked, realising she was talking to me. 'Er, no. God, I bet you think I'm awful, having sex with a man whose surname I don't even know.'

'It was a one-off,' she said. 'It's not as if you make a habit of it, is it?' She frowned. 'Amy's taking an awfully long time, isn't she? I'm just going to see what she's up to.'

Just as she stood to go, the bathroom door flew open, and we stared in horror as Amy trotted out looking like an extra from *Priscilla, Queen of the Desert*. Wearing thick grey eyeshadow, she had lipstick smeared all over her mouth and huge circles of blusher on each cheek.

'What on earth have you done?' Eliza gasped. 'Right, madam, back into the bathroom, and let's wash that muck off before

Gabriel sees it.'

She glanced back as my phone began to ring. 'Bet that's your dad telling me the twins are awake,' she said with a sigh.

I shook my head. 'Rhiannon,' I said, frowning at the screen. 'What the heck does she want?'

Rhiannon was the landlady of The Hare and Moon pub in the village, and a good friend of the family, but she rarely had cause to ring me.

'Lexi, is that you? I'm so sorry to trouble you, darling, but I thought you should know before you get home. I think Will could use a friendly face, and he did say not to trouble you, or disturb the wedding, but you're coming home today anyway, aren't you? I thought maybe you could get yourself straight to the Hall? You know Will, he's being awfully stoic about everything, but, well, everyone needs someone at a time like this, don't you agree?'

'A time like what? I have no idea what you're talking about.' I shrugged when Eliza mouthed, *what's wrong?*

'Of course. Stupid of me. It's Sir Paul, darling. He died on Friday night — another massive stroke — and of course, Will's been all alone, what with half of the village being at the wedding. Well, not totally alone, obviously. Bernie and Mrs Woodrow were with him, and I popped up there to see him, but I'm sure he'd appreciate a visit from you. You *are* his best friend, after all.'

'No! Poor Will. I'll be home as soon as I can, and I'll go straight away. Thanks for letting me know, Rhiannon.'

'I'd have told you when it happened, but he insisted ... I'll see you soon, Lexi. Take care.'

'What's happened?' asked Eliza from the bathroom doorway, where she distractedly rubbed Amy's face with a wet flannel.

'Sir Paul died on Friday night,' I said, imagining Will in that house all weekend while I'd been ... God, I felt sick.

'Gosh. How awful! Poor Will.'

'I should have stayed with him. We knew Sir Paul wasn't well.'

'But you didn't know he was about to die!'

'But I should have realised that Will was concerned. He'd have come to the wedding otherwise, wouldn't he?'

'Darling, Sir Paul's been ill for months now. You couldn't possibly have predicted that things would get so much worse this weekend. You mustn't blame yourself.'

'Will must be devastated,' I murmured. Even though his father had always treated him with contempt, I knew Will loved him. It wasn't in his nature to harbour grudges or resentment.

'Bless him. Of course you must go to him,' she said. 'Come on, Amy. We'd better get packed. We have to go home. I'm sorry about your makeup, Lexi. She's made an awful mess of it. I'll replace it, of course.'

'It doesn't matter. It's the least of my worries,' I said.

She hugged me before ushering Amy out of the room.

I glanced around, dazed, then dragged my bag from the top of the wardrobe. Nothing else mattered right now, except getting home and comforting Will.

Sometimes, during the last year, it had felt as if we'd drifted apart a bit. Sir Paul had been bed-bound for months, and Will had taken on complete responsibility for the estate, as well as taking care of his father who, despite being unable to walk or even speak properly, had somehow still managed to intimidate and harangue him. Having been on the receiving end of one of his piercing glares, it didn't surprise me. I hadn't seen as much of Will as I used to, and I'd missed him. He was such a good mate, and he was going to be feeling the pressure, since the situation placed him in sole charge of the place.

Well, I'd be there to help him. I wouldn't let him down.

****

Just a couple of hours later, I parked the car, shot across the small staff car park and through the private entrance to the west wing of Kearton Hall.

Woody, the housekeeper, cook, and surrogate mother to Will, was in the kitchen, her eyes red with crying.

'Are you all right?' I asked, slightly surprised to see her so grief-stricken. She was hardly Sir Paul's biggest fan.

She hugged me. 'That poor boy. That poor boy,' she murmured, and I realised she'd been crying for Will, which made much more sense.

'Where is he?' I said.

'He's in the Great Hall, love. I think he's struggling to take it all in, bless him. I'm so glad you're here. I've got to pop home to see to my Bobby. Will you take care of him 'til I get back?'

'Of course, Woody. Don't worry about it. I'm staying put all day.'

I found Will in the Great Hall, leaning against the fireplace which was almost as tall as he was. He looked tired but managed a smile, and his eyes warmed when I held out my arms to him.

'You're back.' Relief weighted his voice, and I held him to me, tears pricking my eyes.

All around the hall his ancestors glared down at us. Will always said he felt as if they were watching him, judging him, and for the first time I knew what he meant. The burden of responsibility for the ancestral home was suddenly all his, and it seemed almost as if they were daring him to fail. Well, they could bugger off. It had been Sir Paul who'd put the future of Kearton Hall in danger, not his son. The Fourteenth Baronet Kearton was more than up to the job.

Bloody hell!

'You're Sir William!' I breathed, as I stepped back from him and stared at him in awe. 'Blimey, should I curtsy?'

'I'm so glad you're here!' He laughed and hugged me again. 'I'm not officially Sir William, yet, though. Not that it's important. It's so good to have you back, Lexi. You always make everything seem all right.'

'Everything *will* be all right, Will,' I said. 'Just give it time. I'm ever so sorry about your dad, though. Were you with him?'

He shook his head. 'Woody found him. I'd only left him alone for half an hour. It was almost as if he waited for me to leave.'

'You look knackered. Why don't you go back to bed?'

'There's so much to do. I'm meeting the funeral director in Helmston tomorrow, and the vicar came to see me yesterday, to pay his respects. We're going to discuss the service in a couple of days. It will be at St Hilda's, of course, followed by a private internment later. Hymns!'

'Pardon?'

'I must think about hymns. I don't believe Father was particularly religious, but even so ... What hymns does one have at a funeral? There's *The Lord is My Shepherd*. That's a given, isn't it?'

'Will, you're exhausted. You need sleep.'

He shook his head again. 'I must think about food.'

'Are you hungry?'

'I mean for the wake.'

'I'm sure Woody and I can come up with something,' I said. 'Right, come on. I think a cup of tea is called for.'

I put my hands on his shoulders, steered him into the Outer Hall, and through the door marked private, into the part of the Hall that wasn't open to the public. On reaching the kitchen, I pushed him into a chair.

Buttons, his chocolate Labrador, trotted over from his bed and rested his head on his knees, and Will stroked his silky head while I put the kettle on and sorted out two mugs.

'Is there anything I can help with?' I asked, dropping two teabags into the mugs, then heading to the fridge for milk. 'Have you told everyone who needs telling? Are there any relatives?'

'I've let my cousins know, more out of courtesy than anything. He never saw anyone for years, and I don't think they liked him much. Father's only brother died a few years ago, but I spoke to his wife, and she's letting Mother know.'

I swung round to face him. 'Your mother? You think she'll come back?'

He looked wretched. 'I don't know. Maybe. What do you think?'

How would I know? Will and I had hardly struck gold with our mothers. Mine had wrecked my dad's life, then cleared off to Paris. I tried not to think about her much. It was easier that way. As for Will's mother ... Elisabeth had cleared off to New York when Will was only three years old. She and Sir Paul had apparently spent the first few years of their child's life bickering, while she fought for a divorce and he did all he could to avoid shelling out cash to her.

Finally, he'd offered to fund her a new life in New York, on the condition that she left Will behind for him to raise. She'd agreed, and as far as I could tell, she'd hopped over to America without so much as a backward glance at her son. She hadn't bothered to keep in touch with him at all, not even sending a birthday card. I only knew what I knew through Bernie and Woody. Will rarely mentioned her and had never said a bad word about her, but then, that was Will all over. He never said a bad word about anybody.

I handed him his tea and sat in the chair next to his. 'I suppose it's possible,' I said carefully, not wanting to raise his hopes. 'We'll just have to wait and see. We'll find out soon enough, I suppose.'

We sipped our tea, and he leaned back in his chair and closed his eyes. I watched him, my heart aching for him. He looked shattered, and I knew he'd be full of anxiety, desperate to do the right thing by everyone, not least his father. I thought about all the people he'd become responsible for — all the staff and tenants of the Kearton Estate.

Will had tried so hard to make Kearton Hall pay its way, but it had been a huge battle to get Sir Paul to agree to anything, as he frequently reminded us that the place was first and foremost his home. The upkeep of the estate was massive, and Will often said that we were running to stand still. Lately, his expressions had shown that we were starting to go backwards. I wondered how bad things really were. I'd an awful feeling we were about to find out.

'I'm so sorry.' Will's eyes flew open and he leaned forward, all concern. 'I never asked about the wedding. How did it go?'

Bless him, he was always thinking about other people.

I smiled. 'It was fabulous. The brides were beautiful, and the service was lovely. Archie and Flynn did them proud. The cake was gorgeous — I've brought you some back. Everyone was asking about you. You were missed.'

'People are so kind, aren't they? I'm glad it went well.'

He put down his tea and leaned back in the chair. As Buttons sighed and lay down at his feet, I watched them, sipping my tea in silence. Eventually, Will's breathing became slower, deeper.

Even Buttons gave a little snore, and I smiled and placed my empty cup in the sink. I would fix Will something to eat when he woke up.

In the meantime, I'd find Bernie and see if anything needed doing urgently. Will had always been so good to me. It was time to return the favour.

Chapter 3

'You mean, all the kids are actually asleep?' Charlie sounded aghast. 'What did you do? Drug 'em?'

I grinned to myself as Eliza said, rather huffily, 'Certainly not. They do sleep sometimes, you know.'

Charlie looked deeply suspicious. 'Hmm. If you say so. But he *is* a doctor,' he pointed out, nodding at Dad. 'Bet it would be easy for him to get his hands on sleeping pills. Crush 'em up. Drop 'em in the food. Bob's your uncle, Fanny's your aunt, as they say.'

'I hope you're not suggesting I would drug my own children,' Dad said indignantly. 'Anyway, we're wasting time talking. Let's eat quickly, before the little … darlings wake up again.'

Joe needed no further invitation. He dug his fork into the chicken pie with indecent haste. 'I've been looking forward to this all day,' he admitted. 'Absolutely bloody starving. Can't believe you've had time to bake, Eliza. You're a wonder woman.'

I stole a glance at Eliza, who was — as I'd expected — scarlet with embarrassment.

'Actually,' she admitted, 'it's shop bought. Sorry. I had to make a quick dash to Sainsbury's today. I had nothing in, and I really didn't have the time or energy to make a pie from scratch. Or anything else for that matter.'

'Oh.' Joe, and Charlie looked a bit disappointed. Joe shrugged. 'Well, never mind. Who needs homemade? And I expect you'll get back into it all when the twins are a bit bigger.'

'I can't even imagine it,' she confessed, looking momentarily bleak.

'Is it all getting too much for you?' Joe reached over and squeezed her hand. 'Do you need any help? You know me and Charlie are always here for you.'

Joe had taken care of Eliza ever since her mother died. Her real father had abandoned them before she was even born, so Joe, although actually her uncle, was more like her dad.

'It's fine,' Eliza said, smiling gratefully at him. 'I'm coping.'

'Especially when they're asleep,' I said. 'We all cope better then.'

Charlie, Joe's partner, laughed. 'Can't be much fun for you, my little Gingernut. Stuck up there in the attic, like Paddington Bear.'

I shrugged. 'It's not so bad. At least it's an escape from Amy and her endless trotting hoof sound effects.'

'Does she still have that imaginary pony?' Joe shook his head. 'Maybe you should think about getting her some riding lessons. Surely, your mate Georgia or Pandora would teach her?'

Georgia ran the White Rose Riding School, and my cousin Pandora was a riding instructor there. I supposed either one of them could teach Amy to ride, though they'd both failed to persuade me to learn. I loved horses, as I loved all animals, but I wouldn't actually sit on one. They were too scary by half. The thought of little Amy sitting on one filled me with dread.

'She's too young,' I said.

'Not really,' said Dad. 'Plenty of seven-year-olds have riding lessons. Maybe we should think about booking her some as a Christmas present?'

Eliza shuddered. 'I don't think so. Anyway, we've got other priorities, don't you think?'

'Really?' Joe stabbed a roast potato and raised an eyebrow at her. 'What priorities?'

'We're putting the cottage up for sale,' she said. 'So really, we need every penny we have to buy something new.'

'Well, I can't say I'm surprised,' Charlie said, impaling a floret of cauliflower on his fork. 'The wonder is that you didn't do it before.'

Dad sighed. 'You're right, of course. We should have done it the minute we knew it was twins on the way. This place is far too small. I'm an idiot.'

'It wasn't just you,' Eliza pointed out. 'I didn't really want to move. I love this cottage, and we've been so happy here. It feels really sad to be thinking of leaving.'

I felt the same. The cottage was the first real home I'd ever known, and I felt happier there than I'd ever felt in the other houses we'd lived in. But then, maybe that was down to Eliza. She'd made Dad so happy, and she'd been like a real mother to me. She'd turned the cottage into a proper home. Maybe she could do the same wherever we lived.

I told her so as I cut into my vegetable pie and she almost burst into tears. I should have remembered her hormones.

'Oh, Lexi! That's such a lovely thing to say. You've made my day.'

Dad grinned. 'Well, she's quite right,' he said. 'We'll be happy wherever we are.'

'I wonder where you'll end up,' Joe said. 'Not many houses for sale in this village that would fit six people.'

'I'm more worried about who'll buy this place,' Dad confessed. 'I can't bear the thought of it ending up as a holiday cottage, but since it's fairly compact and so close to the beach, I've an awful feeling that it's outsiders who'll want it.'

'Well, we'll just refuse to sell it to them,' said Eliza. 'We'll only sell to people who want to actually live here all year round.'

'Good luck with that,' said Joe.

'It's a shame Robbie and Chrissie can't buy it,' I said. 'They're desperate to stay in the village and buy their own place, but I doubt they could afford it.'

'Not on the wages your stepmother and Rose pay Chrissie,' said Charlie, with a mischievous twinkle in his eye. 'Proper slave labour in that marshmallow factory. If William Wilberforce was alive today, he'd be campaigning against it.'

'Don't be cheeky,' said Eliza. 'We pay well above the minimum wage.'

She sighed suddenly, and Dad gave her a sympathetic look. 'You miss it, don't you?'

She nodded. 'I really do. It's funny. Just before the twins were born, I couldn't wait to leave. I was so looking forward to taking time off and spending my days caring for the babies. I loved it when I had Amy. It's different now, though. I suppose I miss the company. Rose and Chrissie are such fun to be around, and there's always someone popping in for a chat.'

'Sometimes, they even buy marshmallows,' said Joe, winking at her.

'They do! A lot! And then of course, Amy was so much easier to care for. Two are much harder work, and they seem a lot more demanding than she was.'

'I reckon they egg each other on,' said Charlie. 'Like competing with each other to see who can scream the loudest.'

'When do you plan to go back to work?' asked Joe.

'I'd like to go back now,' she admitted. 'They're six months old, after all. But with the house move looming ... And then there's the childcare issue. I need to find a decent childminder or nursery, and I'm not sure where we'll be living, so it's best to wait until we've moved into our new home and things have settled.'

'Big changes all round then,' said Joe. 'And what about Will?' he asked suddenly, watching me as I chewed broccoli in silence.

I swallowed and shrugged. 'What about him?'

'Well, how is he? Big responsibility for him, that. New Baronet Kearton, after all. And that big house to run all by himself.'

'Proper mausoleum, that is.' Charlie shuddered.

'No, it's not!' I snapped. 'It's absolutely beautiful.'

'Is it? Well, I suppose it looks nice from the outside,' he conceded, 'but honestly! I mean, all that dark wooden panelling, and them creepy portraits glaring down at you everywhere you go. And the creaking! Them stairs are scary as hell.'

'They're hundreds of years old,' I said. 'You'd creak a bit, if you were that age.'

'His knees creak loudly enough now,' Joe said. 'But seriously, how is Will? Let's not forget he's lost his father.'

'Some father,' said Eliza.

'Yeah, fair dos, he was a miserable old sod,' said Charlie. 'But you know Will. He'll still be feeling the loss. Must be grieving.'

'Any word from his mother?' asked Dad.

I shook my head. 'Not so much as a text. His aunt's not coming either. Says she's not well. He doesn't know if his cousins will turn up. He let them know straight after Sir Paul died, last Friday night, but never heard back from them. What a family.'

'Good God. The compassion! He's better off without them if you ask me,' said Joe.

'He's thrown himself into preparations for the funeral,' I said. 'He wants it to be perfect. He was going to spend a fortune on hiring caterers, but Woody and I talked him out of it. He's been over and over the service with the vicar. He's determined to do the old man proud.'

'Yes, well, that's probably because Sir Paul never seemed proud of *him* when he was alive,' said Dad with a sigh. 'Poor Will. He could never do anything right, could he? Who knows, this might be the making of him. He can be his own man at last. I think he'll surprise us all.'

'He won't surprise me,' I said. 'I always knew he could do it. I have every faith in him.' I saw them all exchange glances. 'What?' I said.

'Nothing, love,' said Joe. 'Just nice that you can see him for what he is.'

I looked at them all blankly. 'Well, of course I can. I know what Will is. He's my best friend, and he's kind and generous, and intelligent and determined. He'll make Kearton Hall work. You see if he doesn't.'

Eliza smiled. 'I quite agree,' she said. 'Now, who's for dessert?' She gave a sudden yelp.

'What's wrong?' said Dad.

'I forgot to defrost the Pavlova!' She sighed. 'Who's for a Lightweights yoghurt?'

****

Will closed the study door carefully behind him and stared up at the large portrait of his father on the wall. It was almost time. The service was due to start in thirty minutes, and then it would all be over. His father would be truly gone, and everything would be down to him.

He shivered. He'd always hated his father's study. When he was younger it had been a place of terror to him. If he'd been summoned there, it meant he'd done something to displease Sir Paul, and that meant being yelled at or given a good thrashing.

Physical abuse he could handle. It was the endless drip, drip of criticism that got to him. The constant put-downs and the certain knowledge that, once again, he was a disappointment to his father. He'd tried so hard, all his life, to live up to Sir Paul's expectations, but he knew he could never be the son he'd wanted.

The trouble was, Will was nothing like his father. Sir Paul had been outspoken, confident, and gregarious. It was well documented that he'd been a real lady's man when younger. Handsome and virile, he'd had half the women in the county hoping to become his wife.

Staring up at the portrait of him, Will wondered what had gone wrong in his own case. His mother, as far as he could remember, was beautiful, yet Will seemed to have inherited rogue genes from somewhere. He knew he lacked the good looks of the rest of his family.

Kinder people called him unusual. He had a long, rather pale face, deep set green eyes, and a broad nose. His best feature, he thought, was possibly his mouth, which was a bit of a waste since he rarely got to use it for kissing anyone. He didn't share his father's fine blond hair but possessed a thick mid-brown mop, which seemed to have a life of its own and was forever springing up and refusing to stay tidy. He was tall but didn't have the muscular build that his father had once had. Instead, he was what Bernie called lanky. He looked, and felt, awkward.

No wonder Lexi had never given him a second glance.

Woody cleared her throat. 'Sir William?'

'Please, just call me Will,' he pleaded. Sir William was a ridiculous thing to be called. Besides, it wasn't even official yet.

She nodded. 'Fair enough. You, er, have a visitor.'

'Really? Who is it?'

She looked quite disdainful. 'It's, er, it's—'

The door flew open behind him, and Will stared in amazement as a tall, handsome, blond man stalked into the room. 'Oh for God's sake, Woody, just spit it out. It's me, Will! How are you, cuz?'

Mrs Woodrow looked at the new arrival as if he was something that had just been dragged in by one of the estate cats.

'All right, Woody, that will be all,' said his cousin.

She ignored him and turned pointedly to Will.

'It's fine, Woody. Thank you.'

She sniffed, but nodded and left, closing the door quietly behind her.

'Well, this is a great welcome, I must say. You could at least pretend to be pleased to see me.'

Will stepped forward and embraced his cousin in genuine pleasure. 'I *am* pleased to see you, Nathaniel. Always. It's just been a long time, and you never replied to my email.'

Nathaniel shrugged him off, seeming embarrassed by the display of affection. 'Well, I wanted to make damn sure the old git had really croaked it. He *is* definitely dead? I don't want to start celebrating prematurely.'

Will closed his eyes. 'Don't, Nathaniel.'

'What? Don't tell me you're sorry to see him go? Bloody hell, Will, he must have mellowed a lot since I last left, if that's the case. He was vile to you, as I recall. I couldn't believe the way he treated you. My father always said he belonged in another century. I don't know why you stuck around here, to be frank. You should have hopped over to New York to live with your mother. That's what my mother always said anyway.'

'How could I? You know I had this place to see to. What would have happened to it if I'd just left? I needed to stay and learn the job.'

'The job!' Nathaniel laughed and sauntered over to his uncle's desk. He hesitated a moment before sinking down into the large comfortable chair behind it.

Will watched in awe. He had never sat in that chair and couldn't imagine that he ever would. His cousin had no fear or respect whatsoever.

'It's a bloody house, Will. No more, no less. Anyway, now the old goat's popped his clogs, you're free. Sell the bloody thing on and have a bit of fun, for God's sake.'

Will's mouth dropped open. 'You're joking, right? This house has been in our family for centuries! I can't just sell it on. It's my duty to preserve it, to improve it, hopefully, for future generations.'

His cousin grinned. 'Same old Will. So serious and responsible. It's like I never went away. And, by the way, drop the Nathaniel bit. No one calls me that any more. I'm Nat, okay?' He seemed to consider Will carefully for a moment. 'So, talking of future generations — is there a prospective Lady Boden-Kean on the horizon?'

Will flushed and shook his head. 'Not really.'

'*Not really*? So, there *is* someone, just not special enough?'

'She *is* special!' The words were out before he could stop them.

Nat smirked. 'Ah. Hit a nerve. Let me guess. You really like someone, but you haven't had the guts to ask her out.'

Will swallowed.

Nat laughed. 'See? You haven't changed a bit.'

'You'd be surprised. What about you? Are you here alone, or have you brought a lady friend?'

'Lady friend? You know, Will, you're absolutely priceless. I reckon you belong in a previous century, too. Christ, no chance. Had a bit of a bunk up with someone last Saturday night, at a hotel in Helmston. That was jolly good fun, but no involvement, thank you very much.'

'You've been staying in a hotel for over a week? Why didn't you come straight here?'

Nat sighed. 'No, not the whole time. After I got your email on the Friday night, I came up to Yorkshire, and then — well, I went back home. Sorry, Will. I just couldn't face it to be honest. I realised I needed to psyche myself up first, and only intended to stay at the hotel for one night and then come here to see you, but ... This place — well, it does kind of hang over us all, doesn't it? Anyway, after thinking it through I decided you needed my support, so here I am. And, I might add, this is entirely for you.

I'm not here to mourn your father's passing. He ruined my family's life. My father always resented the fact that it was your father who inherited. He insisted he could do so much more with the place than Uncle Paul, and it drove him mad that he wasn't allowed to help. He and Mother were always arguing about it. She wanted him to forget all about it, but he wouldn't. Always worried that your father would lose his beloved Hall. Reckon it killed him in the end.'

Will sighed. 'He probably had a point. Father wasn't very clear-headed or realistic when it came to the future of this house. Is Rebecca with you? Is your mother any better? I'm sorry she's ill.'

Nat shook his head. 'Rebecca's on holiday, and she won't cut that short for anyone,' he said, referring to his younger sister. 'As for Mother, she's not ill. She lied. She hated your father, and she hates this place just as much. She spoke to your mother, though. Told her the good news. Don't get your hopes up,' he added quickly. 'She's not coming back. Doesn't think it appropriate to come back for his funeral, given that they've been divorced so long. Said it would look like she was dancing on his grave. Not that she wouldn't like to, I suspect, but you know your mother.'

'No,' said Will quietly. 'I don't really.'

Nat stood up and pushed the chair back carelessly. 'No, well maybe not. But now he's gone that can change. You could visit her. She's got a really cool apartment in New York. We've visited her several times, which wasn't always fun, what with her and Mother sitting there like the Bitches of Eastwick, slagging our fathers off. Or she may come to visit you, now that the coast's clear.'

'I won't hold my breath,' said Will. 'Anyway, your room's all ready. I asked Woody to organise some fresh bedding for you, just in case you turned up. You need to hurry up and change. The funeral's in twenty minutes. Are you — are you staying long?'

Nat shrugged. 'Who knows? I'm, um, between jobs at the moment, so nothing to get back home for. It rather depends on what there is around here to keep my interest. I must admit it will be nice to be able to ride every day again. London's brilliant, and I don't blame Mother for selling the house and buying down there, but it's good to breathe the country air again. I presume there's something decent for me to ride?'

Will raised an eyebrow. 'We've still got a few horses,' he said.

'Have you? Excellent. Well, I'll have a ride out tomorrow. Have a look around the village and see what's what. If it's as dull as it ever was, I may head back to London, but if it's a bit livelier, I might stick around and help my cousin with his new responsibilities. Right, I'd better get my mourning gear on and play the grieving nephew. That will test my acting skills.'

Will gave a weak smile and led the way out of the study up to Nat's old room. He loved his cousin, despite his rudeness about Sir Paul. When they were young, Nat had spent many summers at the Hall, keeping Will company. They'd got up to all sorts of mischief, and Nat had led Will astray on several memorable occasions.

He remembered that his father had thoroughly disliked the boy, which was odd as they had so much in common. Bernie wasn't keen on him either, and Woody had always disapproved, saying he had no manners and no respect. For Will as a lonely little boy, though, Nat had been a tonic. Although he wasn't exactly tactful or sympathetic, Will was still glad to see him.

Even so, he couldn't help feeling a sense of foreboding at Nat's words. Having his cousin around again after so many years would be quite a challenge. Will wasn't sure that he could keep him in check, without Sir Paul around to rein him in. Nat needed careful management, and Will had an awful feeling that he wasn't up to the job.

Chapter 4

For a man who hadn't been particularly sociable for the last twenty years of his life, Sir Paul's funeral was well attended. The little church of St Hilda's was packed to the rafters. Almost all the villagers were there, as well as many of his old business associates, almost-forgotten friends, and a few very distant family members, who hadn't been near him for decades.

'Hoping to get something in the old bugger's will, no doubt,' whispered Nat to Will, as they stood at the front of the church, waiting for the first hymn to finish.

Will said nothing but stared at the coffin that bore his father's body. He felt almost as if he were in a coffin himself, with the weight of responsibility crushing down on him. There were many people at the service who lived in Kearton Hall properties and had jobs on the estate. No longer his father's responsibility, they were reliant on Will to keep the place running and ensure their security. It wasn't going to be easy.

The fortunes of the Boden-Kean family had been in decline for almost a hundred years. The house was much loved, but it absorbed money like blotting paper absorbed ink. Will had joined forces with his father's tenant farmers some years ago, and they'd worked hard to establish Kearton Hall Foods as a quality business, with a shop in the grounds, and contracts to supply shops in the local area. The rents from the tenancies, together with charging admission for the Hall's gardens, which had been lovingly restored by Will's grandfather during the nineteen-thirties, and opening a handful of rooms in the house up to the public one weekend a month, meant they were just about managing to keep going, but Will knew that they would have to do much more.

Looking at the magnificent coffin before him, he almost envied his father lying there at peace, with no worries or concerns to keep him awake at night. Will had been finding it increasingly difficult to sleep. His mind raced and his heart pounded as he lay in the oppressive darkness — considering the possibility that it might be himself who brought to an end fourteen direct generations of ownership of Kearton Hall, and ruined so many families' lives.

****

We were late for the funeral and I felt bloody awful about it. I'd been up to the house to see Will earlier in the morning, to check how he was coping. He looked a bit shaky, but had assured me he was fine, and no, he hadn't heard from his mother, aunt or cousins. I thought they were absolutely disgusting and wondered again how the hell Will had turned out so nice, when his relatives were such prats.

I'd rushed back home to shower and change an hour before the funeral, to find Eliza in meltdown. Joe and Charlie were babysitting the twins, and just as she'd picked Mikey up to hand him over, he'd thrown up all over her black dress. Wailing that she had nothing else to wear, she hadn't been comforted when Charlie suggested she wear blue, to match Sir Paul's blood.

'His varicose veins, more like,' Joe said, and they'd laughed together quite heartlessly, while Eliza almost burst into tears.

Dispatched to Ivy House to beg Rose for help, Dad had come back with a black skirt that was two sizes too big for her, so in the end Eliza had dug out some black trousers and a white shirt and had been moaning ever since that she looked like a waiter.

We'd arrived at the church just as the rest of the congregation

36

had begun to sing the first hymn, *Abide with Me*, and had crept in with some embarrassment, taking a seat at the very back and hoping no one had noticed our late arrival.

Dad's sister, Sophie, and her husband Archie were sitting a few pews in front of us, with my youngest cousin, Tallulah. Nobody could've missed Sophie — she wore a black hat the size of a satellite dish. I saw her whisper to Archie, who nodded and put his finger to his lips. Sophie tutted and turned back to face the front of the church. I grinned. Sometimes, my auntie was like a naughty schoolgirl. She didn't have much patience, but luckily, Archie was solid and responsible, and always managed to rein her in before she got too out of control.

As we sang the final line of *Abide with Me*, there was a relieved shuffling as everyone put down their hymnbooks and waited expectantly. The vicar motioned for us all to be seated, and I sank down in relief. My shoes were killing me. I rarely wore heels any more, and my poor feet had barely recovered from the wedding, when they'd been forced into five-inch heels. I spent most of my time lately in trainers, wellies, or boots and was sure I was getting a blister, which was all I needed.

Catching everyone murmur 'Amen', I sat up with a jerk and told myself to pay attention. Doing exactly that, I glanced around the church.

Flynn and Rose sat just in front of Sophie and Archie. Rose easily stuck out, with her distinctive pink-streaked hair. With Rose being Eliza's partner in Mallow Magic, and Flynn being Dad's partner at Ivy House Surgery, I saw quite a lot of them.

Rose's daughter, Fuchsia, had just married my cousin Pandora at the wedding we'd all attended, so I guess that made us sort of related. The newlyweds lived in the flat above Mallow Magic, since Rose and her other daughter, Cerise, had moved in with Flynn at Ivy House. There was no sign of Cerise, though. I guessed she was babysitting her half-sister, Violet.

On the opposite side of the church, Rhiannon sat with her son, Derry. They looked very much alike, with their dark brown curls, melting chocolate eyes, and heart-shaped faces. Rhiannon was stunning, and Derry was gorgeous, too, there was no denying it.

I'd gone out with him for a while, a few years ago. Well, I say gone out — actually, we'd mostly stayed in and shagged, because that had been the deal. Friends with benefits. It had been a beautiful arrangement, and one that had suited us both very well, until Derry got all possessive and wanted us to be in a proper relationship. That had put the kibosh on the whole thing pretty quickly, just as I'd warned him it would.

I didn't want a relationship. Not with anyone. It soon became apparent that we weren't suited as a couple, and we'd split up for good. He'd been pretty upset at first, but he'd eventually started seeing a decent sort of girl from Moreton Cross, so things had worked out for him in the end.

'Lexi!' Eliza hissed.

I blinked and struggled to my feet, realising everyone else had stood and were reaching for their hymn books again.

'Bugger,' I muttered and grabbed my book, rifling through the pages as the first notes of *The Lord is My Shepherd* began to reverberate through the church.

Dad calmly handed me his hymn book turned to the right page, and I glanced at him apologetically, but grinned when he winked at me.

As Bernie's deep baritone voice reverberated around the church, I scanned the pews for him. He was quite near the front, which was only fitting really, since he'd been estate manager at Kearton Hall for years and was probably the closest thing to a real father that Will had.

As the final note of the organ died away and we all sat down again, I strained my neck searching for Will. I just about made out his mop of thick brown hair in the front pews, which faced inwards, as he stared straight ahead toward the coffin, his face sombre.

I should have been closer to him really. I could hardly offer him moral support from all the way in the back. I hoped he was coping all right. Though, on closer inspection, he seemed awfully pale. Like he'd seen a ghost. Oops, hardly the most appropriate choice of words, given we were at a funeral. Well, white as a sheet then, or some other such cliché.

Beside him, I could just make out another man. Just as I was wondering who he was, Will bent his head, bringing a golden halo into full view as the early September sunlight shone through the church windows upon a head of blond hair.

'Shit!'

I wasn't aware I'd spoken aloud but I must have done, because Eliza turned to me immediately.

'What's wrong?'

Staring in shock at the two men who had risen and were standing by the coffin, I said nothing.

She followed my gaze, and I heard her gasp before she whispered to Dad, 'Who's that blond man with Will?'

'I think it's Nathaniel, Will's cousin. He's the son of Sir Paul's younger brother. Used to spend his summers at the Hall when they were younger. At least someone in his family has bothered to turn up. I see Elisabeth hasn't shown her face.'

Eliza turned back to me. 'Did you hear that?' she whispered. 'That's Will's cousin, Nathaniel.'

'Nat,' I said, feeling sick. 'I never caught his surname.'

'Boden-Kean,' supplied Eliza.

'Well, yes, I know that now!' I hissed. 'Jeez, how embarrassing.'

'Let's just hope he doesn't say anything in front of your father,' whispered Eliza.

I closed my eyes and said a silent prayer. Of all the people to bump bits with! And Nat obviously wasn't so grief-stricken that he was beyond picking up a total stranger for a night of passion.

I just hoped he was the discreet type. I didn't think Dad could cope with knowing that his daughter had been getting jiggy with a man whose surname she hadn't even thought to find out.

****

'So kind of you to come. Do make your way to the house. You'll be very welcome.'

I wondered how many times Will had repeated those words as he stood at the church door beside the vicar, shaking hands with every single person as they filed out into the sunshine.

Beside him, Nat stood with his hands in his pockets, kicking at a piece of turf and giving the occasional nod.

I didn't see how I could avoid them, though God knows I'd tried to come up with a plan. There was just no getting out of it. I could hardly ignore Will, especially not on a day when he needed me most, and his cousin seemed stuck to his side at the moment, which was bloody ironic, considering all the years he hadn't so much as bothered to text.

He looked up as Tally approached, and I saw him eyeing her rather appreciatively.

'Hello. Who are you then?' he asked with a distinct gleam in his eye.

Sophie's eyes sparked like flint. 'She's my daughter, Tallulah. It's nice to see you again, Nathaniel.' She held out her hand in greeting.

Nat shook it and nodded, saying nothing. There was an awkward silence for a moment, then Will hugged Sophie to him, twisting awkwardly to avoid smacking his head on her massive hat.

'Thank you so much for coming, Sophie. It's so lovely to see you. I'm terribly sorry I missed the wedding, though I understand it went very well. I'll pop and see Fuchsia and Pandora, as soon as they get back from honeymoon.'

Nat's eyes widened. 'Fuchsia and Pandora? Are they lesbians?'

Sophie glared at him. 'Well, I'd hardly call my son Pandora, would I?'

'What a hoot! Now that's one wedding I would have loved to see. Usually avoid the spectacles at all costs. Dull as ditch water, don't you think? Never been to a same-sex wedding, though. Which one wore the suit?'

As Sophie gritted her teeth, Archie pulled her away. 'Neither. Both wore beautiful dresses and looked stunning. I see you haven't changed a bit, Nathaniel.'

'You neither, Archie. And do call me Nat. I loathe Nathaniel.'

'Don't we all,' muttered Archie as he moved away.

Will's face had turned scarlet when I walked reluctantly to his side.

I winced as Nat's eyes widened in recognition, but luckily, Will didn't seem to notice.

'Nat, please don't upset people. Especially today,' Will muttered. 'Lexi, let me introduce you to my cousin. Nat, this is Lexi, my … Lexi works for me.'

Nat gave me a lazy grin. 'Does she indeed? Doing what, I wonder?'

I felt my face burn and wondered if I was as red as Will.

'Just about everything. She helped me get the shop up and running, she helps out in the café, she admits visitors, and she's researching the history of Kearton Hall, as we're thinking of writing a book about it.'

I stared at him. It was the first I'd heard about any book. When he offered an apologetic smile, though, I found myself smiling back. 'That's right. And when more of the Hall is opened up to the public, I'm going to give guided tours, too.'

'Are you indeed? I expect you'll be jolly good at guiding people in,' he drawled. 'Tell me, why would a young woman like you want to bury herself in that musty old museum? I'm sure you'd have a lot more fun elsewhere, and you look as if you're the type who'd be up for a bit of fun.'

'Lovely service, Will.'

Hearing Eliza's voice behind me, I closed my eyes gratefully. Thank God for that.

I moved along, away from the Boden-Kean boys, trying not to feel mean about abandoning Will. It was for his own good, after all. Imagine how embarrassing it would be if he found out that his cousin had shagged his best mate, and would it make things awkward at work? It had been a stupid one-night stand. It wasn't worth him knowing about.

'I don't think much to that brat,' said Sophie, putting her arm around me and glancing over her shoulder at Nat in disgust. 'Did you hear the way he spoke to me? Archie would have liked to punch him on the nose, wouldn't you, Archie?'

'I suspect,' Archie said with a sigh, 'that before the week is out, there'll be a whole queue of people who feel the same. Nat never was very polite.'

'Do you think he's staying then?' I asked.

Sophie pulled a face. 'God, I hope not. That's all Will needs. And where's Lady Elisabeth, might I ask? Some mother she turned out to be. Fancy not even bothering to come home and support your son in his hour of need. If that was my Oliver, I'd be here like a shot.'

'You'd never have left him in the first place, Mum,' said Tally truthfully, earning an affectionate squeeze from her mother. Oliver was Pandora's twin, and the apple of Sophie's eye, despite abandoning her to do his legal training in Bristol.

Rose and Flynn came rushing over to me — at least, Rose rushed, and Flynn was kind of dragged along by the arm behind her.

I steeled myself, all too aware that Rose wasn't always the most tactful person.

She practically hauled me away from Sophie and stared at me, a gleam of excitement in her eyes. 'Can you believe it? You shagged Nat Boden-Kean! I couldn't believe my eyes when I saw him standing there, and Meggie told us who he was. Jesus, Lexi, of all the blokes to f—'

'For heaven's sake, Rose, keep your voice down,' said Flynn, glancing round. 'I'm sure Lexi doesn't want all the details broadcasted to the village.'

'How come *you* know?' I demanded.

He rolled his eyes, and I sighed. 'Yeah, stupid question. Look, Rose, please keep it quiet, okay? I don't want Dad to find out, and I don't think Will needs to know, in the circumstances. He's got enough on his plate.'

For a moment her expression was sombre. 'You're right. It will break his heart.'

'Break his heart?' I laughed. 'I think that's a bit dramatic. Might be a bit awkward though. I mean, I do work for him, and no one likes to think of their employee having sex with a family member, do they?'

She giggled. 'Dunno. Our Fuchsia's had to cope with her boss having sex with her mother.'

'Yes, all right, Rose.' Flynn's ears turned pink, and she threw her arms around him.

'Aw, you've gone all embarrassed again. You do look sexy. Give me a kiss!'

He laughed and kissed her, and I took the opportunity to back away fast, only to bump into Eliza.

'Are you going back to the Hall?' she asked.

'Of course I am. Will needs me.'

She frowned. 'I don't know that it's such a good idea. What if he finds out? How will he take it?'

'God, Eliza, it's not that serious. I know it's awkward, but it won't kill him. He's a big boy now. Besides, if Nat was going to say anything, I'm sure he would have already, and I'm certainly not going to spill the beans. Let's get off to Kearton Hall. We need to help Woody, anyway.'

She nodded, and we went to round up Dad and Amy, passing Rhiannon on the way. She was standing by the church gate, watching me with a very odd expression on her face.

'You all right, Rhiannon?'

She put her hand on my shoulder. 'Lexi, be careful.'

'Be careful? Of what?'

'There are things you don't know. Things Will doesn't know. I'm afraid it's all going to get rather messy very soon, and he's going to need you. Please, don't be led astray. Don't be distracted by fool's gold. Seek out the real treasure, and always keep a clear head.'

'What do you mean?'

She shook her head. 'Just be careful. Promise?'

I shrugged. 'Promise.'

I had no idea what she was talking about, but that was Rhiannon all over. Eliza always said she had magical powers, but I think she was just a bit eccentric. She was rumoured to be the cousin of Sir Paul's first wife, coming from a titled family, and everyone knew the aristocracy were as mad as a box of frogs.

Except for Will, of course, although Will was always pointing out to me that baronets weren't part of the aristocracy. Well, having a title and owning a house like Kearton Hall made him aristocracy, as far as I was concerned, whatever the rule book said, and he was far from mad. Nat wasn't mad, either, but I had a sudden feeling that he could be very dangerous, and the thought sent an unexpected thrill through me. I shivered and followed Eliza to the car.

Chapter 5

The Great Hall was full to bursting with villagers from Farthingdale and Kearton Bay, all keen to pay their respects, or, in many cases thought Will, wanting to nose around the house — or a few of the ground floor rooms at any rate. Not that he minded that. Hopefully, when the house opened properly to the public, they'd be willing to come back and pay for the privilege.

Woody, Lexi, and Eliza had dressed the huge oak dining table, and it had been laden with food that was evidently much appreciated by the guests, judging by the rate at which it was disappearing. Hired waiters kept everyone's glasses topped up with drinks from the well-stocked bar that had been set up in the Inner Hall. There was a loud buzz in the air, as villagers exchanged gossip and speculated on what would happen to the Hall with Sir Paul gone, and where Elisabeth was, and why she hadn't come home to support her son. It seemed to be the general opinion that Will had had a rough deal all round, with little support from his family, and no one seemed convinced that Nat was a welcome arrival. Many in the villages apparently had long memories of a brattish child, and a terribly rude and arrogant teenager.

Catching snatches of the conversations, Will moved away from the crowd. He didn't need reminding that his mother hadn't so much as written to him, and he was aware of many people's feelings towards Nat. Finding a quiet spot, he sipped his wine while leaning against the fireplace, deep in thought, and almost dropped his glass when a hand was laid gently on his shoulder.

'Are you all right, darling?' Rhiannon looked up at him, her large, velvet brown eyes filled with concern for him, as always.

Will smiled. 'I will be. It will be better when today's out of the way, and I can start to sort things out.'

Rhiannon nodded. She clutched her glass to her chest, her lips tight. Will could feel the tension and didn't know what to make of it. It wasn't like her.

'What about you?' he asked. 'You seem a bit preoccupied.'

She hesitated. 'Will, you know I adore you, don't you?'

Well yes, he did, and the feeling was mutual. For a couple of amazing months, a few years ago, he and Rhiannon had been lovers. Rhiannon was fifteen years older than him, and had been a friend of his mother's, so it had been an unexpected development. She'd evidently taken pity on Will, sensing his unrequited devotion to Lexi, who'd been involved with her son Derry at the time. Will had been, to put it frankly, terrified, but Rhiannon was an amazing woman, and though it had been a short-lived affair, it'd had a depth and intensity to it that Will would be forever grateful to have experienced.

It had only ended when he realised that his love for Lexi was so powerful, so all-consuming, that no one else could come close. Rhiannon had been very understanding, and had never mentioned their relationship since, so he was astonished and not a little alarmed that she'd suddenly decided to tell him she adored him.

His forehead creased with worry at an unwanted thought. 'Rhiannon, you're not — you're not ill, are you?'

Rhiannon laughed and hugged him. 'My darling Will, thank you for caring, but no, I'm fine. Honestly. I just — Will, I want you to know that I'm not a bad person. You do believe that?'

'You're the kindest person I know. There's not an ounce of you that isn't good. Why on earth would you ask such a question?'

'Sometimes, things happen. We don't always realise at the time what we're doing. How much impact our actions can have on other people. I've always loved you, and your whole family. Your mother was my best friend. Your father was a poppet. I just want

46

you to be happy. I would hate for us to fall out. I never want to lose you.'

Will squeezed her arm. 'I really don't know what you're talking about, but I promise you, we'll never fall out. I love you, and you'll never lose me.'

Rhiannon's eyes gazed deep into his own, and the doubt he found in them baffled him.

Then she smiled. 'I hope so. You know, I remember the last time you and I were at a funeral together. Do you?'

Will nodded. 'Hannah's funeral. I remember.'

'And we both realised that it was time to part, because your heart lay elsewhere.'

Will gazed out of the window. He couldn't speak, all too aware of where the conversation was headed.

'Lexi was with Derry at the time, and I told you not to give up because they weren't meant for each other. I was right, wasn't I?'

He nodded silently.

'That was over four years ago. Now, what have you done about it since? Why is Lexi chatting to Meggie and Ben, and you're standing here alone, gazing out of a window?'

Will turned to face her. 'It's not time.'

'So, when will it be time?'

'That's up to her. You know how Lexi's parents' marriage affected her, and how she's shied away from any kind of involvement.'

'But it could be different with you.'

'Perhaps. I hope so. But she has to want this as much as I do. I don't want to be another man she has a casual fling with. I can't be. When — if — Lexi and I get together, it has to be for keeps, and that means I can't push her. She has to come to this in her own good time. I just hope that, one day, she'll realise what we could have together.'

'You've grown up so much this last year. You're so much more confident, mature. You're a remarkable man.'

He laughed, embarrassed. 'Hardly. And I'm not exactly God's gift in the looks department, am I?'

'You're quite beautiful,' she said, touching his cheek and smiling at him. 'Anyone who knows you will see that. A soul like yours can't hide its glory, Will. That much I do know. Well, if you're certain that you need to wait a little longer, I respect that. Normally, I wouldn't push you but ... Just be careful, won't you? Don't leave it too long. I wouldn't want anyone to steal her away from you while you wait.'

Will sighed. 'This is something Lexi has to figure out for herself. When she trusts in me, in us, it will be time. If not — well, I guess the estate will pass to my cousin's descendants, because there'll never be anyone else for me.'

He managed a smile, and Rhiannon squeezed his arm. 'You're a real treasure, darling. I'm quite sure she'll see that. Eventually.'

****

Sophie, apparently, loved funerals.

'Black's very slimming,' she pointed out, waving a hand over her own attire — a close fitting black dress, black tights, black court shoes, as well as her black flying saucer hat. She carried a black handbag and had a black coat draped over her arm. She was nothing if not thorough. 'And the thing is,' she added, 'unlike weddings, there's no covert competing going on. You know, no checking out other women's outfits, to see if they look better or worse than you. And no one dare make bitchy comments, because we're all supposed to be grieving.'

Dad shook his head. 'Do you ever wonder if you've got slightly skewed priorities, Sophie?'

She seemed a bit baffled. 'What do you mean?'

He grinned. 'Never mind.'

'Can you believe Nathaniel turning up?' Sophie asked him, her eyes wide. 'Haven't seen him for a few years.'

Rose, who was eavesdropping in the way Rose did, gave me a sly grin. 'I know,' she said. 'Fancy. But didn't you notice him at the hotel, Sophie?'

My face heated up quicker than my super-powered straighteners, and I glared at her, while Eliza cast a nervous glance in Dad's direction.

48

'He was at the hotel? You mean, when the wedding was going on?' Sophie looked puzzled. 'I didn't see him.'

'Oh, yeah. Well, he wasn't in the function room, obviously. He certainly wasn't one of our guests. Must have been staying there though. He was in the bar earlier, but then I saw him heading upstairs.' She looked very sweet and innocent, and I saw Eliza give her a gentle nudge.

'How did you notice that?' Sophie peered at her suspiciously. 'You wouldn't know him. He hasn't been near this village since you moved in — which may, or may not, be a coincidence.'

Rose shrugged. 'I always notice a good-looking man.'

'Charming,' said Flynn, in mock indignation.

'Well, that's odd,' Sophie said. 'Why would he be staying in a hotel, when Kearton Hall has all those empty bedrooms? Something funny about the whole thing, if you ask me. And did you see him earlier, trying to chat our Tally up? Soon gave him short shrift, didn't you, Tally?'

Tally rolled her eyes. 'I can't bear that sort. So full of himself. Who'd fall for those cheesy chat-up lines, for goodness sake?'

By then I was so hot, I felt as if I'd had my head grilled, and I was pretty sure someone would notice soon and comment, so I made my excuses and moved away from the group. I glanced around the room, hoping to spot Georgia, but there was still no sign of her. She was nearly always late for everything. There was always some horsey crisis she had to deal with before leaving the stables. It was a good thing she was so devoted to her job.

I considered heading over to Will, but as I spotted him Nat approached him, carrying a glass of something decidedly alcoholic. He handed the drink to Will, and I noticed, with some surprise, that Will appeared a bit woozy. Was he drunk? That wasn't like Will at all. Then again, to someone not used to it, a couple of drinks could have a weird effect on them.

Woody approached me, carrying a plate of mini cheesecakes. 'Want one?'

I shook my head. 'No, thanks. Do you need any help?'

'No, it's fine. People are helping themselves. I'm only offering these out to keep myself busy. I'll start doing the dishes soon.

How's it going, do you think?'

'Not too bad. Will seems a bit tipsy, but he's got every reason to need a stiff drink after everything he's been through.'

She sighed. 'It's what he's got to face that worries me more. Fancy Nathaniel turning up again after all this time. He always brings trouble.'

'Does he? Why?'

She pursed her lips. 'Not for me to say, really. Let's just hope he's not staying long. Can you believe Elisabeth didn't turn up? Does that woman never think of anyone but herself? As if she couldn't spare a few days for her only child. Bloody woman. I could slap her.'

I put my arm around her. 'Never mind, Woody. Will's always got us. And Bernie, of course. We'll keep him going.'

She nodded. 'You're right there, love. We'll be here for him. And God knows, with the family he's got, he'll need all the help we can give him.'

****

'I don't believe it. Are you pissed?'

Will blinked and tried to shake his head, then wished he hadn't. Nat stood before him, peering at him closely. 'You bloody are! I never thought I'd see the day when Saint William got rat-arsed. And at the old man's funeral, too. Shame on you, Will. Disgusting behaviour.'

Will tried desperately to clear his head. He couldn't possibly be drunk. He'd only had a couple of glasses of wine, and a couple of beers. Certainly not enough to make him feel as woozy as he did. He felt very disoriented and unsteady, and he wished he had someone to put his arm around for support.

He found himself searching for that distinctive red hair, and his hungry eyes quickly found Lexi. She was talking to Meggie and Ben again. Meggie, a short, well-rounded woman with a dark bob and sparkling brown eyes, was a receptionist at the surgery, working alongside Fuchsia. As Meggie laughed, he smiled to himself. Lexi was obviously being her usual sparky self. She made him laugh a lot, too. In fact, she could brighten his entire day with just one sentence, even when everything else around him was miserable.

Suddenly aware that Nat had followed his gaze and was also staring at Lexi, Will tried to focus on his cousin, but Nat was looking at him very strangely. For a moment, he was positive he'd given himself away, but then Nat took a sip of his drink and his face was casual again. He must have imagined it. He needed some air. His head felt very fuzzy indeed.

'Some coincidence,' said Nat.

Will blinked, trying to clear his vision, which was distinctly blurry. 'What is?'

'That redhead who works for you. I know her.'

Will blinked again. Had he just imagined it, or had his cousin said he knew Lexi? He must be mistaken. 'I don't see how. Unless — well, she lived in the village when you were here last, but that was years ago.'

'No, no. I mean recently. In Helmston, in fact. She was at the hotel I stayed at before I came here.' He took another sip, and Will had a sudden feeling of dread. 'Pretty girl, isn't she?' Nat said, nodding casually in her direction.

Will swallowed. 'Yes, yes, I suppose she is.'

'I don't know,' said Nat. 'I'm almost tempted to make a move on her, but I don't like to revisit the scene of the crime.'

Will said nothing, but he took another mouthful of beer and gulped it down.

'Although,' Nat said, 'she was bloody good. Remember that bunk-up I told you about? Well, she was some ride. What a night!'

The glass hit the floor and shattered into little pieces. A stream of beer snaked its way along the ancient, oak floorboards, and Will felt the colour drain from his face. Nat grabbed his arm to steady him as he swayed.

'Are you okay?' Lexi grabbed Will's other arm, her eyes anxious.

Beside her, people crowded around, clearly worried.

Flynn appeared at his side. Through a fog, Will heard him ask, 'Are you all right? Do you need to sit down?'

Nat tutted. 'He's had too much to drink. Probably gone over his two glass limit.' His tone was mocking. 'He just needs some air. I'll take him outside.'

'No, you won't. I'm fine.' Will wrenched his arm away from Nat's grasp, and his eyes met Lexi's. He saw shock and alarm in her expression, and felt a moment's satisfaction that he'd communicated his feelings to her.

Rhiannon took Will's arm. 'Come away, darling,' she murmured, and he found himself stumbling after her, allowing her to lead him from the room without a hint of protest.

She guided him outside, through the main entrance door in the south side of the Hall. Pushing him down onto the steps, she waited patiently, her arm around him, as he sat shivering, his head in his hands. When he eventually looked up, he gazed at her, full of pain that he couldn't allow to escape. He'd been too well instructed by his father to risk any tears.

She reached up and stroked his face, her fingers tracing the line where they should have fallen. 'It may have done you some good to cry,' she murmured.

'It's okay, I'm all right,' he said.

'But you're not, darling. Not really. And it's okay to admit that.'

'And what good would that do?' he demanded. 'Would it rewind the clock and make her not go to that hotel and fall into bed with my cousin, do you think?' His voice cracked, and he shook his head. 'I'm terribly sorry,' he said, sitting up straight and rubbing his face wearily. 'I shouldn't have snapped at you. It was unforgivable.'

'You didn't snap at me, Will. You don't have to apologise for anything. I can't say I'm impressed with Nat. He doesn't seem to have matured much. Look, whatever happened between him and Lexi, it doesn't mean that they're destined to spend the rest of their lives together. You know what she's like, and Nat certainly doesn't strike me as someone seeking a steady relationship.'

Will's jaw tightened. 'I just don't understand. Why did she go to bed with him? Why would she have sex with a total stranger? Doesn't she know she's worth so much more?'

'Oh, Will.' Rhiannon smiled at him with obvious affection.

'Sometimes, sex is all a woman wants. It isn't just men who occasionally feel the need to indulge in physical passion without any commitment. Women don't always want hearts and flowers. Sometimes, it really is just all about assuaging a need, a hormonal rush, a glint in a stranger's eye.' She sighed. 'We should go back inside. It's awfully chilly out here now.'

'I'm sorry. I should have thought.'

She shivered, and he wondered why he wasn't feeling the cold. Maybe it was the alcohol. He didn't understand what had happened. He'd never been affected so harshly before. He'd made a complete fool of himself.

'Please, go back inside,' he said. 'I'm going to be fine. I really don't know what happened there. I didn't think I'd drunk that much.'

Rhiannon frowned. 'Neither did I, darling. It's all very odd, isn't it?' An edge had crept into her voice, and a steely expression into her usually warm eyes.

Will wondered what she was thinking. He had a feeling there was something he was missing, but when he tried to make sense of it all, the thoughts evaporated. He should be ashamed of himself, getting drunk at his own father's wake. He could imagine what Sir Paul would think of it all, and as tears pricked his eyes suddenly, he blinked furiously, appalled at his lack of control.

He got to his feet. He would have a walk around the grounds, get some fresh air, make plans for the house. Keep busy. That's what they recommended for grief, wasn't it? Though, as he took the first step, Will wondered exactly who, and what, he was really grieving for.

****

Georgia was full of apologies. 'Really sorry I'm late. I wanted to make the service, but you know how it is with horses to look after, and with Pandora away ... Hey, what's up?'

I couldn't stop trembling.

Georgia put her arm around me. 'What's happened?'

'You just missed the floor show. Will got drunk and looked as if he was about to collapse.'

'Will, drunk? Bloody hell, trust me to miss that. Can't believe it. I suppose his old man's death has really hit him hard.'

'I don't think it was that.' I looked across at Rhiannon, who was murmuring something in Nat's ear.

He shook his head and shrugged, and she stepped back, glaring at him. When they looked across toward me, Rhiannon's expression was serious. Nat, on the other hand, seemed extremely pleased with himself.

I felt sick as he grinned and winked at me.

'Who's that bit of all right? What's going on?'

'That,' I said, 'is Will's cousin, Nathaniel Boden-Kean, also known as Nat.'

'Nat? You don't mean — Jesus!' Georgia peered across at him, frowning as he laughed.

Rhiannon grabbed his arm and resumed her argument with him.

'What's going on with those two?'

'I have no idea, but I've got a feeling that Will knows what happened in Helmston.'

'Right.' Georgia sighed. 'That explains Will's behaviour.'

'Does it?' Personally, I didn't see why. I knew it might have been a bit awkward, his having to think about his best mate bonking his cousin, but it didn't merit that look he'd given me. I tried to define the expression that had been in his eyes, but it was hard to label it. There was something I couldn't put my finger on, but it made me feel suddenly depressed beyond words. I'd never seen Will look at me like that before. It was horrible.

'So, that's the handsome stranger,' mused Georgia. 'I'd be careful with that one.'

'What do you mean?'

'He's a real looker, there's no denying it, but there's something about him I don't trust. He appears pretty arrogant to me. And why tell Will? Seems to me like he's out to hurt him, and what kind of man does that make him?'

'He probably didn't think he needed to keep it a secret,' I said, wondering why I felt the need to defend him, and wondering also why everyone was so concerned about Will finding out. It was hardly a sackable offence. It wasn't like it was in my employment contract that I had to abstain from sexual relations with all Boden-Keans. Or maybe it was? I'd never actually read the contract, so maybe there was a clause in there to that effect.

'So, will you be seeing him again?'

'No chance. I told you, it was just a one-night stand. I don't think he's the relationship type, somehow, and you know my views on all that.'

'Even now, when we're surrounded by all these loved-up couples? I dunno.' Georgia sighed. 'What, with your dad and Eliza, Rose and Flynn, Charlie and Joe, and Pandora and Fuchsia, it's been like living in a Richard Curtis film lately. I wouldn't mind a bit of it myself.'

'A bit of what?' I smiled.

'A bit of the other for a start,' admitted Georgia. 'But a nice bloke to come home to after a hard day at the stables would be nice. Even if all he wanted to do was heat up a pan of soup and watch the telly with me, it would be something.'

'Jeez, you've got low standards. Mind you, it seems to me that all relationships start with all the lovey-dovey stuff and end up with a pan of soup and *Coronation Street*. Happy ever afters only happen in fairy tales. Real life is a bitter disappointment. I think a quick bunk up is much more fun than all that hearts and flowers stuff.'

'Really? That's very liberal of you.'

I spun around and blushed to my hair roots as I came face to face with Nat. He seemed most amused, and I'd no doubt he'd heard every word I'd said.

I gulped. 'Er, Georgia, this is Nat Boden-Kean, Will's cousin. Nat, this is Georgia, my best friend.'

Georgia gave him a stony look, as he held out his hand, his eyes appraising her, and his lips curving in amusement as he noted her obvious disapproval.

'How do you do,' she muttered finally, shaking his hand briefly, then dropping it as if she'd just found out he was contaminated with a deadly virus.

'So, Georgia, do you work at the Hall, too?'

She shook her head. 'I run the White Rose Riding School on Cherry Tree Lane.'

'A riding school? You ride, then?'

'Well, obviously. It would be a bit of a difficult job if I didn't.' Her tone was cool, most unlike Georgia.

Nat held her gaze, his blue eyes twinkling, then he turned to me, a very naughty smile on his lips.

'I was just thinking … I'd really like to ask you out for a meal. Wine and dine you. Get to know you a little better. However, if you don't want all that stuff—'

Great. I'd really backed myself into a corner there. How could I admit that, when it came to him, I *did* want all that stuff? I hadn't even realised it myself 'til he'd just asked me out. He *had* asked me out, hadn't he? I tried to speak, but it came out kind of like a squeak.

Georgia stared at me in surprise.

Nat was obviously waiting for an answer.

'Thank you,' I said.

'For what?'

'For, er, asking me out.'

'Ah. And would you like me to wine and dine you? Or would you rather skip all that and go straight to the, er, what was it you called it? Ah, yes, the *quick bunk up*.'

'I — I would like to go out for dinner. Thank you.'

'Fine. I'll pick you up at seven on Monday. Where do you live?'

'Twelve, Tippet's Yard. It's off Kings' Row.'

'Yes, I know it. I'll be there.' He flashed us both a dazzling smile, then sauntered off toward Bernie and Eddie.

I gaped after him, suddenly overwhelmed. 'My God. I've got a date.'

'So you have,' said Georgia, her voice flat. 'Just do me a favour eh, Lexi? Be careful. That one's far too full of himself, if you ask me.'

Chapter 6

Woody handed me a cup of tea. 'Never seen Will in that state. Something very funny going on, if you ask me. I mean, I know he was upset about his dad, an' all, though God knows why, miserable old bugger, but he's far too polite to get drunk at his funeral. My Bobby is firmly of the opinion that his drink was spiked.'

I laughed. 'Who'd want to spike Will's drink? He just lost track of how much he was having, that's all. It was a very emotional day.'

'Aye. Sure it was,' she said, watching me with beady eyes. 'And since when did two glasses of wine and a couple of pints make Will behave like that? Everyone remarked on it. Who'd want to spike his drink, you ask? Well, there's a question. I can't imagine who'd be so mean-spirited and selfish, can you?'

I narrowed my eyes. There was no doubt in my mind as to whom she was referring. But Nat wouldn't do that to Will, especially at his own father's funeral. It was ridiculous.

Or was it?

Will had certainly behaved out of character, and he'd looked distinctly woozy. Still, I dismissed the idea. Nat may have been the mischievous sort, but he wouldn't be that spiteful. Will probably hadn't eaten all day, and he was already stressed. That was all there was to it.

I sipped my drink and helped myself to a digestive. 'So, how was Will yesterday?' I asked. 'Sleeping it off?'

'You must be joking. Up first thing, mucking out them flipping horses as usual, and then his lordship decided to get up and go out for a ride. "Course, he didn't offer to help in the stables first. No, just gets all the benefits and none of the work. Typical Nathaniel. He hasn't changed.'

'Seriously, why don't you like him? What was he like when he stayed here before?' Crunching my biscuit I eyed her curiously.

'Pretty much as he is now. A little brat, and that's being polite. You want to watch that one. There was a spiteful side to Nat, a dark side. He did some cruel things … Chalk and cheese, them two. I remember when they were kiddies. Anything Will had, Nathaniel wanted. Time and again, I recall Nat pinching Will's toys. I used to tell him off, but Will just used to smile and say it was all right, and if Nat wanted them he could have them. Placid as they come. Too nice for his own good, if you ask me. That sort get walked all over. Look how his bloody father treated him for a start.'

I nodded. 'But they were just kids then. Maybe Nat's changed?'

'I wouldn't count on it, but if you say so, who am I to judge? Saw you and him talking. Looked very cosy, if you don't mind me saying so.'

'He's asked me out for dinner tonight,' I admitted, rather uncomfortably.

She sniffed. 'Has he indeed? And is that what you want?'

I shrugged. 'Why not? Free meal, if nothing else. Besides, he's good company.'

'Really? Well, I'd be careful, if I were you. I dunno, some folk can't see the wood for the trees. Have you told Will about your date?'

I shook my head. 'Haven't seen him to tell him. I wasn't here yesterday, and I haven't caught sight of him yet today.'

'Do me a favour, lovey? Tell him. He deserves to know.'

I watched her, surprised to see anxiety in her eyes. Jeez, she really wasn't keen on Nat — she seemed genuinely worried about my date. 'I will. Honestly, I don't think it'll be a problem. It's only a meal, and it's not breaking any employment rules. At least, I don't think it is. I can't see Will finding it awkward, just 'cos his employee's going out with his cousin. He's not like that, is he?'

'No. All the same ...' She trailed off and smiled brightly, as the man himself entered the kitchen. 'There you are! I was just coming to look for you. Nice cup of tea and a couple of digestives here for you. Sit yourself down and rest a few moments.'

Will smiled and took the cup she offered. 'Thank you. I'm really ready for that.'

'What have you been doing?' I asked, as he sank into the armchair by the range and took a sip of tea. Buttons lay down beside him, and as Will fed him a digestive I felt a pang of loss, remembering the days when my own dog, Tessa, used to come to work with me and lie in front of that very range.

'I've been going through the archives,' he said. 'If we're going to write this book, we need to check every detail.'

'Were you serious about that?' I said. 'I thought it was just something you said.'

'I'm very serious about it. Well, to be fair, it will probably be more of a booklet than a book. If we're going to open the house up to the public full time it would be good to have a product for customers to buy that details the history of the place. I also think it would be interesting to find out all I can about my ancestors, from a personal point of view. With your interest in history I thought you might like to be involved.'

'Definitely! We can have a look today if you like?'

'I have a meeting with Archie and the accountant later,' he admitted. 'I can't say I'm looking forward to it. Perhaps tomorrow?'

'Sure,' I agreed, frowning when I caught Woody's eye and her meaningful stare. 'Er, Will, there's something I have to tell you,' I began, but broke off as the doorbell rang.

Woody put down the cleaning cloth and took off her pinny. 'Will that be Mr Crook and Mr Gregson now?' she asked.

Will glanced at his watch. 'Shouldn't be. We said ten-thirty, and they're usually very punctual. Well, perhaps there's a lot to get through. Doesn't bode well.' He sighed, as she scurried off to answer the door. 'I suppose I'd better find Nat. He wants to be in on this.'

'Will, about Nat,' I said.

He took another sip of tea and leaned forward to stroke Buttons' head. 'What about him?'

'He asked me out for dinner tonight, and I was wondering if that was okay with you?'

He broke off a piece of biscuit and fed it to the chocolate Labrador, who looked delighted, if a little surprised, to be given another one. Will was usually pretty strict with treats. 'Why shouldn't it be?'

'Just that, well, with me being your employee, and Nat being your cousin, I wasn't sure if it would be awkward.'

'Why should it be awkward?' He leaned back in the chair and stared into his tea. 'I may pay your wages, Lexi, but I don't own you. You can go out for dinner with whoever you like. If you choose Nat, that's up to you.'

'Thanks, Will. I didn't think you'd mind, but people seemed to think it might be a problem. Is everything okay, or is that a stupid question?'

He rubbed the back of his head. 'Fine. Just worrying about this meeting. Feel a bit nervous. It's the inheritance tax, for one thing. I mean, Archie and John Gregson have been preparing ever since Father's stroke, and Archie says it will be fine, but I don't know what the situation is, so...'

'It'll be all right.' I hoped so, anyway. Archie had been Sir Paul's solicitor for years, and I was certain he'd know what to do. It wasn't as if the death had been sudden, or unexpected, after all. 'Don't worry,' I soothed. 'I'm sure—'

I broke off as Woody returned with a big smile on her face, trailing Mr Gregson, the accountant, behind her.

'Come early in hopes of one of my fruit scones,' she announced, much to his evident embarrassment. 'Must have been psychic. I've not long taken some out of the oven.'

'Good morning,' said Will, standing up to shake the man's hand. He turned to me. 'If you'll excuse me, I need to find Nat before Archie arrives. I'll see you later, okay?'

I nodded, and he murmured something to Mr Gregson about

meeting them upstairs in the sitting room. As he left the kitchen, Woody raised an eyebrow at me, and I gave a slight shrug of the shoulders.

I'd done as she'd asked, and he'd been fine about it, just as I'd known he'd be. It was a mystery to me why people were so worried.

****

Will's mind was whirling as Archie and John droned on about his father's will, trust funds, insurance policies, and the future of Kearton Hall. At least he was trying to make sense of what they were saying, whereas Nat clearly couldn't be bothered, even though he'd insisted on attending the meeting. He just sulked in a chair, growling, 'Bloody rip-off,' every now and then, while fiddling incompetently with a Rubik's Cube.

'Basically,' said John, giving Nat a filthy look, 'the estate is in a better position than it would have been if the financial arrangements had all been left to Sir Paul. He — ahem — was never one for making provisions for the future. Fortunately, he followed our advice, regarding the creation of several trust funds and taking out a substantial life insurance policy in trust.'

'And, of course, there's no inheritance tax on agricultural land, and the estate has almost four thousand acres of farmland,' added Archie. 'Then there's the woodland—'

'Yes, yes, but even so,' said Nat, 'there *is* going to be a bill, right?'

'Well, yes,' said John, 'but there are ways and means, as we said. We think the first thing is to claim Conditional Exemption, and then set up a Maintenance Fund, as all monies going into that won't be liable for inheritance tax. The money can be used for maintaining and repairing the house itself, as well as the gardens, the wages—'

'We know,' snapped Nat. 'You've already told us three times. Conditional Exemption, blah blah blah. But it's the word *conditional* that I'm not keen on.'

'You have no need to fear that,' said John. 'It simply means that we have to fulfil certain obligations in order to avoid a tax bill.'

'Exactly. Obligations like opening this house to the public for a minimum number of days in the year and allowing the great unwashed to gawp at all our belongings.'

'Really, Nat,' said Archie, in disgust, 'is there any need?'

'I have to say, it's a massive relief,' Will said. 'I was imagining a much worse situation.'

'We can make this work, Will,' said Archie.

'Oh, can *we*?' said Nat. 'I wasn't aware you had a stake in the Hall, too.'

'As we've discussed before, there are alternatives. Handing the estate to a heritage organisation, or setting up a charitable trust, whereby you'd continue to live here, but—'

'—But the house would no longer belong to the family.' Will shook his head. 'I can't do that.'

'Should hope not,' said Nat. 'You'd be better off putting it on the open market. I'm telling you, Grant's Hotels would snap this place up. We'd make a killing.'

'You needn't worry, Nat,' said Archie coldly. 'You're not likely to starve. Sir Paul has left you and your sister a modest amount in a trust fund.'

'Very bloody modest,' said Nat gloomily.

'I have to say,' continued Archie firmly, 'it seems very generous of him, given that you rarely saw him, and that your own father had a substantial inheritance from the Twelfth Baronet.'

'Which he left to my mother,' said Nat.

'Who is, I'm sure, very generous towards you, and will no doubt pass the legacy to you in her own will.'

Nat opened his mouth to speak, but shut it again, much to Will's surprise. He'd been expecting a torrent of abuse, seeing as Nat had probably anticipated a hefty chunk of money from his uncle and had been left, in Nat's words, a pittance. Whatever the reason for his restraint, Will was glad of it. His head was throbbing.

'The point is,' said Nat, just as Will hoped he'd decided to go quietly, 'even without the inheritance tax bill, what about the future? I mean, you may have dodged a bullet here, Will, but you still have to pay for the upkeep of this house, and I can't see an easy time ahead, can you? It would have been different if you'd turned this place into a proper business, but it's hardly raking in the cash, is it? It's so bloody infuriating. My father could have made this place thrive, if your father hadn't been so bloody stubborn. You should have made Uncle Paul listen.'

'I tried to make him listen. If his own brother couldn't succeed, what chance did I have? And you know as well as I do that your father tried many times and failed,' said Will quietly.

'Don't you dare put the blame on Pa. God, no wonder he was so frustrated. He could see your father making a giant mess of it all, and you just let him do it. You always were too soft.'

'For goodness sake,' said Archie, 'arguing between yourselves isn't going to help. Will's hardly going to be putting his name on the council list, Nat. It's not that bad. You just need to decide which course of action you want to take.'

'Shut up, Nat,' Will said. 'I'm sorry, Archie. What do you think?'

'It depends what your priorities are, Will. What do *you* want to do with the estate?'

'Flog it,' said Nat. He stalked over to where Will sat on the sofa with one hand supporting his weary head, the other stroking the head of the devoted Buttons. 'Seriously, Will. Think about it. Your whole life has revolved around this place. Just think of the freedom if you got rid of it.'

Will searched his face, seeking any sign that his cousin was joking, but no, he was actually serious. 'How can you even suggest that? You really don't get it, do you? This place isn't mine to sell. I'm just the caretaker for the next generation.'

'You sound just like my bloody father. Anyway, I wouldn't worry about that,' said Nat, throwing himself down beside him on the sofa. 'The rate you're going, there isn't likely to be a next generation.'

Will bit his lip. 'Look, I may never have children, but what about you? The day may come when it's your heirs who inherit this house. Would you want me to sell their home? Their birthright?'

Nat shrugged.

'And even if you don't care about that, what about all the tenants we're responsible for? If we sell off their homes, they may be turfed out, or at the very least have their rents put up to unreasonable levels. You know the situation around here. Every house in the area is fair game for the holiday let market. And what about the people we employ? If this place became a hotel, what would happen to them? No. Whatever happens I won't sell this estate. I'm going to make it work. I'm going to turn it into a real tourist attraction.'

'So, you agree with mine and John's plan?' said Archie.

Will nodded.

'Fine,' said Archie. 'Let's be clear, though. If we submit a claim for Conditional Exemption to the tax office, we have to declare that we have no intention to sell, and we must be willing and able to open the Hall to the public, and allow access to its contents and land within a reasonable amount of time.'

'How reasonable?' said Will.

'Well, probably around six months. They're quite understanding. As long as we can demonstrate that we're moving forward with our plans and we're not trying to get out of our side of the bargain, they'd probably allow a little leeway on that. But I'd say six months was doable, wouldn't you?'

'Good-oh,' said Nat sarcastically. 'Good old Uncle Paul, leaving his family to deal with the flak and entertain the hoi polloi. Can you imagine it? Hordes of chavs wandering round the place. Ugh. If he'd dealt with the problems years ago, it might not have come to this. Really cared about the next generation, didn't he?'

Archie cleared his throat. 'On that subject, Will, I have a letter for you.'

'A letter? From whom?'

Archie rummaged in his briefcase, then held out an envelope. His hand shook, and he didn't quite meet Will's eyes. 'It's from your father.'

'My father?' Will took a deep breath and reached for the letter. 'Should I open it now?'

'I think so,' Archie confirmed, glancing at John, who gave him a sympathetic look.

Evidently, thought Will, the contents of the letter were also known to his father's accountant.

Nat narrowed his eyes. 'What's all this about?'

'Well, if you give me a moment, I'll be able to tell you,' said Will. He opened the envelope and drew out a sheet of thick, white paper. Unfolding it, he began to read, his heart speeding up as he took in the words on the page.

Nat tutted. 'Well? What does it say?'

Will looked up, and his eyes met Archie's. He wasn't a bit surprised to see the nervous and rather shamed expression on the solicitor's face.

'Well,' he murmured, 'that's something I didn't see coming.'

'What's going on?' Nat demanded.

Will folded the paper and put it in his inside pocket. Quiet for a moment, he tried to make sense of the new information that the letter contained before he gradually became aware that Nat was staring at him impatiently. 'Tell him, Archie. It will no doubt be common knowledge within days.'

Archie nodded. 'Very well. The letter explains that The Hare and Moon is no longer part of the Kearton Estate. Sir Paul gave it outright to Rhiannon Bone some years ago.'

Nat frowned. 'And just why would he do that?'

Archie's eyes flickered over to Will.

Will swallowed. 'It appears that my father had some sort of relationship with Rhiannon, many years ago,' he said, hardly believing the words as he spoke them.

'The randy old devil.' Nat pulled a disgusted face. 'Ugh! Doesn't surprise me, though. I remember her reputation, even when I was a kid. Still, bit extreme paying for sex with a pub, isn't it?'

'The fact is,' said Archie, 'the relationship resulted in the birth of a child. Derry Bone is Sir Paul's son, and Will's half-brother.' He looked apologetic. 'I'm sorry to be the one to break the news.'

There was a stunned silence for a moment. Nat gaped at him, but only for a second before he exploded. 'Well, the cunning, sly bitch! My God, she knew what she was doing, didn't she! That pub must be a goldmine, and she's been raking in the profits all this time. The conniving cow!'

Will's head spun as he digested the horrific truth that he'd slept with a woman who'd also slept with his father. That really didn't bear thinking about. Then something else occurred to him, and he turned to Archie. 'Did my mother know? Is that why she left me?'

Nat stopped ranting and stared at Archie. 'Did she? Is that what happened?'

Archie shook his head. 'I honestly don't know about that. I wasn't aware of the situation at the time. It was only when your father came to see me about ten years ago, regarding the transfer of deeds, that I discovered the truth. I'm sorry, Will.'

'And what about Derry? Does he know?'

'He will do now. Your father also left a letter for him, which I delivered this morning. It details the truth of his parentage, and informs him that he's been left a legacy in the will.'

'A legacy? How fucking much?' demanded Nat.

'It doesn't matter how much,' said Will.

Nat stared at him incredulously. 'Of course it matters! I'm going to go round there and tell them what a cheating, swindling pair they are.'

'Nat, shut up,' said Will. 'None of this is Derry's fault. Imagine how he's feeling right now — finding out who his father is, after all these years, and realising that I'm his half-brother. Trying to come to terms with all that must be awful for him. I doubt he's even thought about the money. Anyway, think of the money we've had spent on us all our lives — boarding school, horses, cars. What's he had? And he's missed out on having a father. You can't begrudge him a penny.'

'I bloody can. I wish I'd missed out on having a father, and if you'd any sense you'd wish the same,' muttered Nat. He folded his arms, his eyes dark with fury.

Archie picked up his briefcase. 'I think you need to think things over, take some time to take everything in. We'll meet up again on Monday and go over things in more detail when we've all calmed down. By the way, have you got those things I asked you for, Will?'

'What things?' demanded Nat.

Archie rolled his eyes. 'Just some legalities. Nothing for you to worry about.'

'I have to send statutory declarations and some certificates off to London,' said Will, handing Archie a large brown envelope.

'What for?'

'So that he can be registered as the Fourteenth Baronet Kearton,' said Archie. 'It's standard procedure.'

Nat tutted and folded his arms, and Archie shook his head in despair.

'Thank you for your time, Archie. You, too, John,' said Will, shaking their hands. Leaving Nat to his sulking, Will showed the two men to the door.

'Well, it seems to me you've more than got your hands full with that one,' said John. 'If you need any help or advice before our next meeting, you know where I am.'

'Same here,' said Archie. 'Don't let Nat push you around, Will. I know what he's like. Sorry to drop that bombshell on you, on top of everything else.'

'It's hardly your fault,' said Will. 'I expect it's been quite difficult for you, carrying that secret around all these years.'

'You're not kidding,' he admitted. 'Glad it's all out in the open now. That's the worst part over with.'

In spite of himself, Will couldn't help smiling. 'I wouldn't count on that, Archie. This is going to be all round the village soon enough. When Sophie finds out you kept such juicy gossip to yourself all this time, she won't be best pleased.'

Archie groaned. 'Oh, hell's bells, I never thought about that. She's going to throttle me!'

Chapter 7

I felt weirdly nervous. I never usually experienced butterflies before a first date, so it was a novel experience. I'd made a real effort and bought a new dress for the occasion. Not being much of a one for partying, I'd possessed only one decent dress, and as I'd been wearing that at the wedding, I could hardly wear it again for our date. I'd nipped into Helmston on Sunday afternoon and found a simple shift dress in a deep turquoise colour, which Eliza said matched my eyes beautifully.

I'd thought that we may go somewhere like The Kearton Arms, but Nat informed me we were going to Helmston, to the much grander Fox and Hounds. I'd never been there before, but I knew it had an excellent reputation for good food and plush surroundings. I felt very special as we took our seats, and I realised that we were lucky to have got a table at all. The restaurant in that place was usually booked up weeks ahead.

'How did you manage to get a table?' I said.

'Shagged the manageress,' he replied.

I laughed half-heartedly, not entirely sure whether or not he was joking.

He tutted. 'Kidding,' he assured me, picking up a menu.

I watched him curiously. He wasn't exactly chatty. In fact, he seemed positively miserable, and had barely spoken a word to me in the car.

'Is there something wrong?' I asked. I didn't think it was an unreasonable question, given that he'd been the one who'd asked me out and he was being very offhand all of a sudden.

He put down the menu and sighed. 'Sorry. I'm being unforgivably rude,' he acknowledged. 'I've had some rather shocking news today, that's all.'

'Anything you'd like to talk about?'

He hesitated, as if considering whether to confide in me. Then he obviously decided against it, flashed me a winning smile, and handed me a menu. 'Let's just forget it, shall we? Tonight is all about you. Let's order.'

The meal was fabulous, although I blanched when I saw the prices. Nat looked pretty appalled when I confessed to being a vegetarian and announced he'd never been out with "one of you lefty lettuce munchers" before. Charming.

As I tucked into my vegetable moussaka, and Nat ate his lobster with apparent satisfaction, I wasn't blind to the admiring glances he attracted from other women around the room, and I couldn't deny feeling a bit smug that he was with me.

Before long, he'd enthralled me with riveting talk about London life, my favourite subject — not.

My eyes began to glaze over, and I stifled a yawn. 'Sorry, what?'

'Would you like a coffee?'

I snapped back to attention and smiled. 'Yes please, I'd love one.' Glancing at my watch, I was surprised to find it was only nine o'clock. Would he take me somewhere else after there? Or would he deliver me straight home? Maybe he'd take me back to Kearton Hall for a nightcap? Will wouldn't mind, I was sure. He'd made it quite clear he had no problem with me seeing his cousin, which had been a huge relief.

'I'm sorry, what did you say?' I blinked in confusion. Surely, Nat hadn't just said what I thought he had?

'I said, we'll take it up to our room.'

I stared at him. 'What room?'

'The room that I booked for us.' He sounded a bit irritated. 'We're spending the night here.'

My stomach gave a sickening lurch. Is that what he thought I was? Someone who would just jump into bed with him, whenever he wanted? How dare he just assume that I'd stay with him overnight?

Uneasily, I remembered what I'd said at the funeral, right before he asked me out. I could hardly play the innocent all of a sudden, could I?

'I — I think you've got the wrong impression of me,' I said, trying to keep my voice steady. 'I'm not like that. You were my first one-night stand. I don't make a habit of it. Sorry.'

Nat tensed, and for a moment I thought I'd completely blown it as a mixture of annoyance and guilt washed through me. Had I led him on? Should I offer to pay for the meal to make amends? I didn't want to feel I owed him anything — certainly not a bloody bunk up in some hotel room. The moussaka had been good, but not that sodding good. If he thought that was all I was worth, he could shove it.

Visibly swallowing, he took my hand in his. 'I'm sorry if I've offended you,' he murmured. 'Of course I don't think you're easy. I just didn't want this night to end. Though, if you don't feel the same way, I'll take you home immediately and I won't bother you again. I'd hate for you to feel compromised in any way. You're far too lovely for that.'

I stared at him. Was he serious? His blue eyes twinkled back at me, and I found myself melting. His fingers stroked the inside of my wrist, and I felt suddenly shivery as an ominous tingle went through me. He was so gorgeous, and he had a truly delicious smile, and there was a glint in his eyes, and those fingers really knew what they were doing.

As he locked the bedroom door behind us, some fifteen minutes later, I thought I really ought to ring Eliza and tell her I wouldn't be home 'til the morning, but I knew she would ask a lot of questions and probably warn me off.

As Nat's lips found mine, I thought, maybe I'd send her a text instead. In an hour or so. Right now, I had other things on my mind.

****

'I can't believe you gave in like that! Is that all you think of

70

yourself? You should have told him to fuck off. Arrogant little shit.'

'It wasn't like that,' I protested, my face burning with embarrassment. I'd never seen Georgia so angry. I'd arrived at the stables expecting that we'd have a good gossip about all the saucy details of my night of passion with Nat, but Georgia hadn't reacted at all how I'd expected. As we sat cleaning tack, and I shared what had happened at The Fox and Hounds the previous night, her mouth tightened. She didn't seem to find any of it funny or exciting. Rather than giggling with me, she seemed furious — so much so, I was beginning to feel uncomfortable and wished I hadn't mentioned it.

'So what *was* it like?'She put down the bridle she'd been cleaning and stared up at me, her blue eyes flashing with anger. 'You have a one-night stand with this bloke. He winds Will up by telling him all about it. He then asks you out, and on your very first date he's booked a room for you both. Doesn't that ring any alarm bells with you, Lexi? 'Cos it sure as hell would with me.'

'He really likes me,' I said. I couldn't think of anything else to say. Put like that, I supposed Georgia had a point. Then again, she hadn't been there. She hadn't seen the expression in his eyes, heard the compliments he'd poured on me, felt his hands gently stroking my body, until I'd ceased to care about anything except being with him. My stomach flipped over just at the memory of it.

Georgia narrowed her eyes. 'Why are you gawping like that? Don't tell me you've gone and fallen for the jumped-up tosser? You barely know him.'

'Of course I haven't fallen for him. Don't be ridiculous. We had dinner and then — well, he's good at it. What can I say?'

'I'll bet he's good at it! Strikes me as the sort of bloke who's had plenty of practice with idiots like you.'

I glared at her. 'Charming. I come over here after work to give you a hand with cleaning tack, and this is what I get. What the hell's wrong with you?'

'Nothing's wrong with me, Lexi! It's you who's behaving like a stupid teenager. You hardly know him. He's just using you for sex, and you're too blind to see him for what he really is. Stop being a pushover and get a grip.'

I stopped soaping the saddle that I'd been cleaning and glowered at her. 'Well, thanks very much for that. I think you're jealous.'

Georgia's face turned scarlet. 'Jealous! Why the hell would I be jealous? I can't stand the man. You're being ridiculous.'

'I mean jealous that I'm having such a good time. Let's face it, when was the last time you actually went out on a date? All you care about is your horses. You know what? Clean your own sodding tack!'

I pushed the saddle off my knee onto the floor and stormed out of the tack room, leaving Georgia to continue the cleaning alone.

I couldn't understand why she'd reacted so badly. We'd been friends for years, and she'd never talked to me like that before. Georgia was someone I could rely on to understand. I felt quite bewildered, and more hurt than I'd admit. Well, stuff her. Stuff everyone. Nat was nowhere near as bad as people made out, and, anyway, what did it matter? I was only out for some fun. I was hardly likely to fall head over heels in love with him. Was I?

****

After a long day at work, then the row with Georgia, I couldn't say I was looking forward to going home that night. As I trudged wearily down the alley towards the tiny cottage, I could hear the wailing coming from the open window and pulled a face, but immediately felt mean. After all, Eliza had to cope with that racket all day. I didn't know how she stood it. I couldn't have done it — it had put me off having kids for life.

Rose was sitting in the living room when I walked in, bouncing a screaming Violet on her knee. The baby's cheeks were red and tear-stained, and she looked almost as upset as Rose herself, who wore an expression of absolute despair.

'Bloody teething,' she said, as I closed the door behind me. 'Honest to God, Lexi, I'm at my wits end with it. I'm knackered.'

'Where is everyone?' I asked, relieved that it wasn't the twins who were crying, for once.

'Your dad and Flynn are working late, catching up on paperwork, and Amy's having tea at Joe's. Eliza's just nipped to the shop. We ran out of teabags. There was panic all round.'

'Have you been at work?'

'Yeah, just 'til lunch time. I dunno, I used to think working part time would be a dream come true, but I'm bloody glad to get to the shop these days, to get away from madam here.' When she looked down at her wailing daughter, though, her expression softened. 'Bless you. They'll soon be through, and you'll be all smiles again. Bloody back teeth. Always the worst.'

I sank onto the sofa and stifled a yawn. 'How's Flynn coping?'

She grinned. 'He loves every minute of it. Even when she's screaming her head off, he never loses his temper.' She stroked Violet's head, and as the sobs softened to whimpers, and the baby closed her eyes and snuggled into her mother's arms, she sighed.

I glanced up at the door opening, and Eliza walked in, her face flushed and her eyes bright with excitement, and smiled. She seemed almost like her old self again — before the twins had worn her out.

She ruffled my hair. 'Had a good day, Lexi? You'll never believe what I've just heard!'

'What?' I said.

'You might know already.' She sat on the sofa beside me. 'I popped into Henderson's for teabags and a bag of Maltesers, and guess what Milly told me?'

Rose goggled. 'What? And did you get me any Maltesers?'

'No. You said you were sticking to the Lightweights' plan. Weigh-in tomorrow, remember? Anyway, never mind that. Apparently, it turns out that Sir Paul gave The Hare and Moon to Rhiannon ages ago and never told anyone.'

'Really? Why?' Rose turned to me. 'Did you know about this, Lexi?'

I shook my head. 'No. Will never mentioned it. Not that it's anything to do with me, anyway.'

'That's not all,' said Eliza. 'He only left Derry a small fortune in his will.'

'Eh? What the hell for?' Rose sounded stunned.

I gaped at Eliza. 'Are you sure? Is this just Milly Henderson making it up as she goes along again?'

'No,' she said. 'It's all round the village. Apparently, Derry was furious and had a massive row with Rhiannon, and Kerry was working in the pub kitchen and heard everything, and she told Mrs Roberts, who'd come in for lunch with her sister, and Mrs Roberts told Milly, and about a hundred other people, from what I can gather.'

'Why would Derry row with Rhiannon over being left a fortune? I'd be ecstatic. Oh.' Rose's eyes widened, and we all looked at each other.

Eliza nodded. 'Yep. Turns out that Sir Paul wasn't immune to Rhiannon's charms, either. Derry is another Boden-Kean boy.'

'Fuck me,' murmured Rose.

I thought about Nat's distracted manner last night at dinner, and how he'd said he'd had some shocking news that day. He wasn't kidding. Poor Derry. He must've been distraught at finding out who his father was, after all that time, and how did Will feel about it all? What a mess.

I blinked as the distinct sound of wailing drifted down the stairs.

Eliza's smile vanished, and she put her head in her hands. 'God, not again.'

'Sit there,' I said, squeezing her shoulder as I stood up. 'I'll see to them. You make a cup of tea and relax.'

As I headed upstairs, it occurred to me that Eliza and Dad hadn't been out together for ages, and Dad had been working longer and longer hours lately. No wonder they both looked so tired. I would have to do something about that. Their relationship wasn't going to suffer—not if I could help it.

Chapter 8

I usually got up pretty early, but I'd had a late night. Nat had taken me out for dinner again, then we'd gone for a stroll around a chilly Whitby, had a couple of drinks in a pub to warm us, and headed back to the Hall, where we'd tumbled into bed and Nat had soon thoroughly heated me up.

He'd confided in me that Derry was Sir Paul's son, and I'd admitted that the gossip had already worked its way round the village and reached my ears.

'Bloody unbelievable, isn't it?' he said, shaking his head. 'I mean, I remember Rhiannon Bone being talked about in the village when I used to stay here years ago. She's a real weirdo, isn't she? What would Uncle see in her?' He tutted. 'Well, stupid question, I suppose. She's pretty enough, in a gothic, witchy sort of way.'

'Pretty enough? She's stunning. Besides,' I said, feeling the need to defend a family friend, 'she's a good person. Kind. I'm sure there's more to all this than we know.'

'Are you saying she wouldn't have an affair with a married man?' he demanded.

I hesitated. I could hardly say that, given her track record. But Rhiannon had been friends with Will's mother. Surely, that would have made a difference?

'Let's not talk about that now,' I suggested. 'It will all sort itself out, one way or the other.'

'Huh, like the future of the Hall?' he said. 'If Will doesn't do something radical, there won't be a future.'

'Will's plans will work out,' I said. 'He knows what he's doing.'

'I don't think he does,' he said, entwining a length of my hair in his fingers. 'It's not as if he's really experienced with all this, is it? It's not as if he's got management qualifications, or a background in heritage. Not like some people, who make it their life's work. I mean, some people actually study this stuff, and do it for a living. There are people who spend their entire lives turning around the fortunes of country houses. Will's just a hapless homeowner with no clear vision. It's a terrible shame.'

I thought about it for a moment. Much as I hated to admit it, Nat was quite right. 'Maybe,' I said hesitantly, 'we could bring someone like that in?'

His eyes widened. 'What do you mean? Hire someone to take over the running of the estate?'

'Not the entire estate,' I said. 'Bernie's in charge of the grounds and land, after all. But the house itself, maybe.'

'Well, it's an idea,' mused Nat. 'You mean, like a House Manager?'

'I suppose so,' I said. 'What do you think?'

Nat kissed me on the nose. 'I think, my darling, you're an absolute genius. Wish I'd thought of that.'

It seemed my brainwave had turned him on. We got quite distracted after that, with the result that it was fairly late when he dropped me off at the top of Bay Street, and after facing Eliza's knowing looks and Dad's pleading that, in future, I should tell them if I was going to be in so late, it was even later by the time I got to bed.

After sleeping in until just forty minutes before I was due to start work, I headed off to the Hall, a bit hot and bothered, but determined to tell Will about my idea to employ a House Manager. It made perfect sense, and I was sure he'd agree.

****

Sitting on the sofa, Will tapped away at his laptop keyboard.

Nat seemed bemused. 'Why don't you use Uncle's study?' he asked. 'You never go in there. I'm sick of seeing all your paperwork and accounts lying around everywhere.'

Will stayed silent. He wouldn't admit to his cousin that the study made him nervous. Whenever he went in there, he could feel his father's presence. He knew that the old man would already be full of rage that he was determined to open the Hall on a full-time basis to the public, and the last thing he needed was to feel negative vibes attacking him in that room. The rest of the house didn't have the same effect on him, but the study was strictly off-limits.

Nat leaned over and peered at the computer screen. 'What are you looking at?' he asked. 'Isn't that Chatsworth?'

Will nodded. 'Just checking out other country houses, to see what they offer to attract visitors.'

'Bloody hell, Will. You're hardly the Duke of Devonshire. More like Baron Hard-up. You'll be eyeing up Buckingham Palace next. Get a grip.'

'I'm perfectly well aware of that,' said Will patiently. 'I'm just trying to get ideas, that's all. I've looked at lots of different houses, large and small. Some of them have done amazing things to keep going. I'm very impressed.'

'If you want to be impressed, take a look at this,' Nat said, snatching the laptop from Will's knees and typing a name in the search engine. 'There you go,' he said, passing it back and pointing at the screen with obvious satisfaction. 'Now that's impressive. You can't deny it.'

Will looked and tried to suppress his irritation. The website was for one Hollyfield Manor, a country house hotel set in glorious countryside in Somerset. It boasted luxury rooms, tennis courts, stables, a swimming pool, spa and gym, as well as a top-class restaurant and several bars.

'That was old Lady Bessingby's house. Remember her? Years ago, she stayed here as a guest of Uncle's. Bloody awful woman. Stank of lavender. Well, she finally shuffled off the mortal coil, and her nephew sold the whole shebang to this hotel chain. See what they've done to it. It's stunning. And Hollyfield was never as grand, nor as old as this place. Think about it, Will.'

'I don't need to think about it. I don't want the Hall to be turned into a hotel, and that's final. It's a home, and it's going to stay that way.'

'You're so bloody stubborn.' Nat stood and began to pace the room.

'I really could use you onside in this,' said Will. 'I need to turn this place into a proper business, and I'd appreciate your support.'

'I—' Nat broke off, as a gentle tapping came before Lexi peered round the living room door.

Will gave her a weak smile, but he couldn't help noticing that Nat seemed irritated by her appearance.

'Sorry. Not interrupting anything, am I?'

'Well, you are, actually. We're in the middle of something. Shouldn't you be working?' said Nat.

Will looked at him sharply. His cousin wasn't exactly known for his good manners, but he was being downright rude.

Lexi appeared uncomfortable by his lack of welcome, so Will waved her in.

'Come and sit down, Lexi. Thank goodness you're here. We were just about to have an argument, and now you've stopped it. Just in time.'

Lexi smiled at him and shut the door behind her, sitting beside him on the sofa, as Nat continued to stand in silence. She seemed puzzled by his off-hand attitude. 'I wanted to put something to you.'

'I'll bet you did,' Nat said.

Lexi flushed. 'Who's rattled your cage?' she demanded.

'Ah, she does have some spirit, then,' said Nat. 'I was beginning to wonder.'

Will ignored his cousin. 'We were just discussing the future of the Hall. I'm afraid we can't seem to agree on the best course of action.'

'You mean *you* can't agree,' Nat said. 'I've already told you what we should do.'

'And I've already said no,' said Will calmly. 'Nat wants me to sell the place, and let it be turned into a hotel. I want it to stay as our home.'

'What do you think?' demanded Nat.

Lexi glanced from one to the other.

Will put the laptop down. 'It's not fair asking Lexi to choose,' he said. 'She's far too polite to want to upset either one of us. You said you wanted to put something to me, Lexi?'

'I'm sure she's not so feeble that she can't express a bloody opinion,' snapped Nat. 'Or maybe she is. Who knows?'

Lexi's expression changed, and Will saw her famous temper rising. 'If you must know,' she said, 'I agree with Will.'

'Surprise, surprise,' said Nat. 'Of course you do. Who would disagree with Saint William?'

Lexi's eyes flashed. 'This is a family home and has been — well — forever. You can't sell it off, if there's even a remote chance it can be saved. You have to do everything possible to hang onto it. What would happen to all your tenants and employees if you sold it? Or perhaps you don't care about that?'

Will saw the muscle in Nat's jaw twitching. His cousin's eyes were full of contempt, and Will realised Lexi seemed rather taken aback at Nat's reaction.

Time for him to make a sharp exit. 'This is a discussion for another time. I'm going to The Hare and Moon. I want to see how Rhiannon and Derry are. It's time I showed my face there, showed there's no hard feelings.'

Nat eyes widened. 'No hard feelings? Are you for real? Don't you dare go near that place, or that woman. Sometimes, Will, I think you're from a different planet. Have you forgotten what she did to Aunt Elisabeth? How she betrayed her trust and drove her away? It's thanks to that woman you grew up without a mother.'

'We don't know that for sure,' Will pointed out. 'I'd like to hear Rhiannon's side of the story before I start blaming her for everything. Anyway, I'd like to see Derry, too. See how he's coping with all this.'

'With a wad of cash in his back pocket, I should think he's coping quite nicely, thank you very much.' Nat picked at the threads on one of the ancient cushions as if it was a casual buy from Helmston market. 'He's really got it made, hasn't he? His slapper of a mother shags your father, and now they've got a bloody good pub out of it, and a stash of cash, to boot. He must be laughing at us. What a bloody joke.'

Lexi scowled. 'Derry's not like that,' she said. 'He'll have been mortified about Sir Paul being his father. It's probably his worst nightmare. I was going to go and see him myself,' she admitted. 'I should have. Just been a bit preoccupied.'

Nat threw the cushion on the floor. 'For God's sake, am I the only one with any sense in this place? Just because you fucked him doesn't mean you have to defend him, you know. He's got everything he could wish for. He doesn't need you to go round there comforting him. Unless, of course, you're thinking of the cash.'

'Sometimes, Nat, you really piss me off.' Lexi glared at him. 'I don't give a damn about his money. Derry's a good friend. I can't believe you just said that to me.'

'Can't you? Will reached down and picked up the cushion, placing it carefully on his own chair, away from the careless hands of his cousin. He could believe it, only too well. 'What did you want to talk about, Lexi?'

She was still glaring at Nat. 'It doesn't matter. It can wait. I think I'll come with you to The Hare and Moon, if that's all right?'

Nat waved his hands in a gesture of defeat. 'Fine. You two go and commiserate with poor, dear Rhiannon and her illegitimate sprog. Just don't expect me to have anything to do with either of them. The entire village is disgusted with that woman, and rightly so, but if you two think you know better, then go and comfort her. Should have known you'd side with Saint William, Lexi. How noble you both are.'

He stormed out of the room, slamming the door behind him.

Lexi turned to Will. 'What the hell was that about?'

Will sighed. 'Nat wanting his own way,' he said, as he got to his feet. 'Forget it. Look, you don't have to come with me. If you'd rather find Nat, make it up with him…'

'I'm coming with you,' she said, standing. 'Nat can stew for a while. Besides, Rhiannon and Derry need us more.'

She slipped her arm through his and Will tensed. He knew he

should have been worrying about Rhiannon and Derry, but right now, all he could think about was how close Lexi was to him at that moment. And how very far away she remained.

****

Walking down Bay Street with Will was quite an experience. Unless a person was loading or unloading, cars weren't allowed in Old Town — the part of Kearton Bay that straddles the cliff side, all the way down to the beach. Apart from council and emergency vehicles, deliveries and taxis, the roads were strictly for pedestrians, which was a good thing, really, given the number of tourists that the village got, especially in summer.

The newer part of the village, Up Top, was more modern. Well, I say modern — I'm not talking about brand new housing estates, but mostly Victorian buildings. Old Town, however, was just that. It dated back to the sixteenth century, and there were still cottages surviving from that period; all thick, whitewashed walls, sagging red roofs, and crooked chimneys.

The main route down to the beach was Bay Street, a very long, very steep, winding road that started at The Kearton Arms pub at the end of Whitby Road, and finished at The Hare and Moon on the seafront. From there, it changed to King's Row and swept around in a horseshoe, back up the cliff side, before ending abruptly with a fence and warning signs where the cliff dropped away.

From there, you could either parachute down to the beach below or, more sensibly, turn left down Water's Edge, follow the winding passageway, where Mallow Magic was located, and come out back at the little stone bridge on Bay Street, which carried the road over the stream called Kearton Beck.

Bay Street was charming. I still loved walking down there, even after all those years, taking in the sights and sounds and smells of the place. Even on that cool, September afternoon, plenty of tourists milled about.

It only took the merest hint of sunshine for visitors to make their way to the Bay. The fish and chip shop had a queue snaking out of the door. People peered in through the windows of the Whitby Jet shop, eyeing up the various pieces of jewellery for sale. Even the dinosaur and fossil museum seemed pretty crowded.

Above the pungent smell of fish and chips coming from the chippy, I caught the salty tang of the sea. Seagulls cried and swooped overhead, desperate for their share of the food that was being eaten by contented tourists. The whole place was a hive of activity, and I felt the familiar delight and gratitude to be living in the village that held my heart.

As we passed by, locals nodded and smiled at us, calling out greetings. They seemed delighted to see Will out and about. Several approached him to offer their condolences, and it was touching to see how much they liked him, and quite sweet to see how embarrassed he got by all the attention.

It was amusing to hear the older villagers calling him *Sir William*. Will had asked the first couple to call him *Will*, but they'd looked shocked by his request, so he didn't ask again. The younger ones weren't so deferential, thank goodness. He was just plain Will to them, and I knew he'd be relieved about that.

We finally reached the bottom of the street, with the slipway down to the beach straight in front of us. In high season, tourists streamed out of the old lifeboat house museum, milled around the little boats that were moored on the front, or headed down to the sands, but that day the museum seemed empty and the beach was deserted. In spite of the sunshine, a cold wind blew in from the sea, and it definitely wasn't sunbathing or paddling weather.

To the left of us, The Hare and Moon stood perched on the edge of the sea wall, looking out over the coast, as it had for hundreds of years. A large, whitewashed structure, with the obligatory red, pan-tile roof, it was my second favourite building, after Kearton Hall.

Glancing at each other, Will and I both took a deep breath and climbed the steps up to the door. Pushing our way inside, through a small crowd of tourists clutching their bottles of local beer, we headed toward the front bar, which overlooked the slipway, and found Rhiannon serving a couple of cheerful pensioners in matching anoraks.

While we waited for her attention, I glanced around and realised there were no locals in the pub at all. I wondered if Rhiannon was aware of the gossip going around the village. I hadn't discussed it with Nat, or Will, but I knew from my own family that just about everyone seemed to know that she'd had an affair with Sir Paul, and that Derry had been conceived as a result. People were already making assumptions that she'd been responsible for the breakup of the Boden-Kean marriage, and were blaming her for the departure of Elisabeth.

While Rhiannon was probably used to gossip, the latest juice was different because it affected Derry too. If there was one thing that mattered to Rhiannon, it was her son. I wondered how it had impacted on their relationship, because it surely must have.

Spotting the two of us, she eyed us nervously. After whispering something to Kerry, her barmaid, who nodded, she opened the door marked *private* and beckoned for us to follow.

We trailed after her into the hallway behind the bar, and she shut the door behind us. There was a moment's silence as she stood stiffly, eyes wide, staring at Will with a pinched expression on her face. Then, as Will held out his arms to her, she crumpled in visible relief.

I waited patiently while he embraced the woman who may well have been responsible for him losing his mother. Will never ceased to amaze me. He was loyal and kind and wise beyond his years — the gentlest person I'd ever met. If I'd had a big brother, I would have wished for one like Will.

'Oh, Will, I'm so sorry,' Rhiannon murmured.

He shook his head. 'I know. It's all right. We'll talk. Can Jack and Kerry cope alone for a while?'

'I expect so. We're not exactly rushed off our feet.'

'Come on,' said Will. 'I'll make us a drink, and we'll try to sort this mess out, eh?'

Rhiannon nodded, seeming unable to speak for a moment. We headed up the stairs, and Will led her into the kitchen, where he proceeded to put the kettle on and take out some cups. Rhiannon sank into the chair and put her head in her hands.

I'd never known her seem so defeated. She was the eternal optimist. Things had obviously been pretty bad at The Hare and Moon since the truth had come out.

'Is Derry around?' I asked. I figured that Will and Rhiannon probably needed to be alone. Besides, it was Derry that I'd really come to see.

'He's in his room, I expect,' said Rhiannon. 'He usually is these days.'

'I think I'll see how he is,' I said.

She gave me a weak smile. 'Thank you, Lexi. Thank you both. I can't tell you how much it means to have you here.'

****

Derry was certainly in his room. Frankly, it looked as if he hadn't moved out of it all week. His floor was covered with dirty mugs — green mould growing in the dregs of his coffee — and plates and cutlery encrusted with days old food.

I found him lying on his bed, eyes closed, listening to music on his iPod. It was probably his attempt to shut out the world beyond the lyrics of Mumford and Sons, or whichever of his favourites he was currently playing.

My nose wrinkled against the smell of sour milk and dirty socks, as I nudged him.

His eyes flew open, and he yanked out his earphones, looking around as if embarrassed by what a mess his room was.

I sat on the bed beside him. 'Hello, you.'

'Lexi. Jesus, you could have warned me you were coming,' he muttered.

'Spur of the moment thing. Didn't know myself or I'd have made sure I got my inoculations,' I said, staring pointedly around the bedroom.

'Yeah, well, you know how it is.' After plumping his pillow, he sat up and sighed. 'So, how's things with you and posh boy? Has he proposed, yet?'

'Don't be stupid,' I said, not liking his sarcastic tone.

'You want to get a ring on your finger. Either that or get yourself knocked up. You, too, could own a place like this.'

'Derry! Don't be horrible. Anyway, I'm not here to talk about Nat. It doesn't matter.'

'Doesn't it? Actually, the fact that my ex-girlfriend is shagging my cousin feels quite weird. Not as weird as the fact that my brother was shagging my mother, but there you go.'

For a moment, I couldn't make sense of what he was saying. Then the fog lifted as I realised what he meant. I shook my head. 'Will and your mother? Don't be ridiculous!'

He grinned, seeming pleased by my shocked reaction. 'Disgusting, eh? Talk about incestuous relationships. My fucking head's in bits, trying to work out the merry-go-round of sexual partners in my so-called family.'

'You're wrong. You've got it mixed up, somehow. Will's never — I mean, he doesn't...'

I trailed off, not sure what to say. It had never occurred to me that Will had even had sex before, let alone with Rhiannon. He never mentioned it, never talked about women — any women. If anything, I'd wondered if maybe it wasn't women he was interested in, at all. He'd never given the tiniest hint that he liked anyone, male or female.

And Rhiannon? I mean, yeah, she was gorgeous and everything, but, come on, she was old enough to be his mother! Well, all right, not quite, but still. I felt a bit sick just thinking about it.

'You've got it wrong. You've misheard something. Added two and two together and made — I dunno — four-million-and-seventy-six, or something. Jeez.' It couldn't be true. Of course it couldn't.

'These walls may be thick, Lexi, but I'm not. Trust me. I could tell you some stories. Will was another of her conquests, and from what I heard, a bloody good time was had by all.'

'My God.' I could hardly take it all in. I hadn't had a clue. I was shocked at how much the thought of him and Rhiannon appalled me. I supposed it was because she was Derry's mother that it seemed so wrong. That, and the fact that she'd previously slept with his father. Ugh!

Poor Derry. No wonder he'd retreated to his room and his music. Even I wanted to shut those thoughts out, and it was nothing to do with me.

'God, Derry, I'm so sorry. You've had such an awful time of it.'

'Yeah. You could say that.' He scanned the room again and tutted. 'Christ, this is a shit tip. Embarrassing.'

'Your mother looks awful. She must have been dreading this day.'

'You think? Serves her right, if you ask me. No doubt she's down there in the bar right now, flirting with the next mug.'

I bit my thumbnail, wondering whether to confess. 'Will's with her. They're in the kitchen, talking. She was very upset. He wanted to help.'

Derry laughed bitterly. 'Bet he did. Help himself to second helpings, no doubt.'

'Will's not like that!' Though even as I said it, I felt a sudden confusion.

Wasn't he? What did I know, anyway? Obviously not much, or at least, not as much as I'd thought I did. Not about Will.

'They're all like that, Lexi.' Derry looked drained, exhausted. 'Every man in this village has either had her or wants to have her. They moon after her like pathetic little puppies. I must be the only bloke in Kearton Bay she hasn't shagged.'

'Don't be stupid! There's my dad, for a start,' I snapped. 'And Nat.'

'How do you know she hasn't had your dad?' he demanded. 'He's hardly likely to announce it over breakfast, is he? Now he's married, he's even higher on the danger list. As for Nat, well, give her a chance. She likes to keep it in the family.'

'Oh, Derry.' I hated to see him so bitter. I reached out to stroke his hair.

He flinched. 'Don't.'

I retreated, hurt at his reaction. He was different, no doubt about it. The whole event had obviously hit him hard. I didn't know what to say to make it better for him.

'I've got to get out of this place,' he said. 'I can't stand the gossip, the knowing stares, the pity. Can you imagine what it's like knowing that your father was an ancient, randy philanderer, and your mother is a slut? I can't stay here. I can't be around her.'

'Your mother loves you,' I said. 'She didn't mean to hurt you, Derry. You have to listen to her side of the story, give her a chance.'

His face set with determination. 'No more chances. I've had enough.'

'What are you going to do?'

He looked up at me, his eyes filled with defiance. 'The one thing I know will hurt her more than anything.'

I didn't like the expression in his eyes. It was arrogant, cruel. I suddenly realised, with some discomfort, that he reminded me of Nat. 'What are you on about?'

He smiled triumphantly. 'I'm going to track down my grandfather and write to him. No matter what she says, I'm sure he'll want to see me. Let her have a taste of her own medicine for a change. I don't want to be around her any longer than I have to be, Lexi. I want to get to know my family. My *real* family. And she's not going to stop me.'

Chapter 9

Despite it being a warm autumn day, with the sun shining brightly outside, the library was still surprisingly cold as I snuggled in the armchair the following morning. Sir Charles Boden-Kean, First Baronet Kearton, glared down at me from the wall, as if challenging me to explain what I was doing in his sanctum.

'Well, actually mate,' I muttered to the far-too-large portrait that hung above the fireplace, 'I'm trying to find some interesting facts about your bloody boring family. Some booklet this is gonna turn out to be.'

I sighed, wondering if there was a single ancestor of Will's that was worth writing about, as I skimmed through the story of Dorothy Boden-Kean, her patronage of fishermen's widows, and her efforts to provide education for their children. Very worthy and noble, but it was hardly likely to make Philippa Gregory lose sleep, was it? I needed to find someone interesting — someone whose life story would capture the imaginations of visitors, not put them in a coma.

I put the book back in its place and moved along the shelves, selecting one that looked promising. *The Boden-Keans of Yorkshire.* The family who'd lived here in this very house since Oliver Cromwell had ruled the country. The thought was quite awe-inspiring.

Taking the book with me, I settled into the armchair by the

fireplace and began to flick through the pages, hoping to find something — anything — that wasn't more likely to send me to sleep than stir my imagination.

When the library door opened, I glanced up and my stomach turned over when Will walked in. I looked back at the pages, feeling an unfamiliar sensation of anger against him.

Derry's revelations still smarted. I'd tried to convince myself that he'd got it wrong, but I knew deep down that he was telling the truth. It felt as if something big had happened, which was ridiculous, but I couldn't dismiss the feeling.

'Good morning, Lexi. I didn't know you were in here.'

He smiled at me, and I noticed how his green eyes crinkled at the corners, and the way his hair had flopped over his face again. As if he'd read my mind, he pushed his hand absently through his thick mop before leaning in close. 'Anything interesting?'

I bristled and shrugged at him. 'Hardly,' I muttered. 'I mean, it's your bloody family. Not likely to be anything riveting is there?' Although I tried to sound calm, I could sense a rage growing inside me as he brushed against me.

He seemed a bit taken aback. 'Have you still not made it up with Nat?' he asked, as he sat on the chair opposite mine and frowned at me. Buttons came running in and stood at my side, wagging his tail furiously. To my shame, I barely acknowledged him, and he turned away and headed back to Will. He sank onto the floor, head on his paws, his resentful stare filling me with guilt.

I glanced away from him and gave Will a defiant shrug. 'Nat and I are absolutely fine,' I said. 'Brilliant in fact. We're having a lot of fun. And I mean, *a lot*.'

He eyed me curiously for a moment, then stood up and headed to a bookcase, taking a book from the top shelf.

'I found this yesterday,' he said. 'Covers the history of smuggling in the village. Quite fascinating. I believe one of my ancestors had a great deal of involvement in it. It's one of our darkest family secrets.'

'Really?' I said. 'I'm not in the least bit surprised. I mean, you could never really trust the Boden-Keans, could you? You may think they were pillars of society, but who can say what was going on under that respectable facade? I reckon they were a bunch of crooks on the quiet. Probably how they got so rich.'

'Lexi, have I done something to offend you?' Will carried the book over and sat down opposite me again, his frown heavy. I felt mean. I hated being horrible to Will.

On the other hand...

'Why didn't you tell me?' I asked, my anger resurfacing as he sat there, all innocent, stroking a slightly mollified Buttons.

'Tell you what? Have I missed something?'

'No. It was me that missed something. All the bloody signs. I mean, what were you thinking?'

'I'm sorry?'

'You and Rhiannon! Rhiannon, of all people. Though, why I'm surprised, I don't know. It would be stranger if she didn't shag you, I suppose. God, I thought you were a bit pickier than that.'

'I see. Derry filled you in did he?' He stopped stroking Buttons and stared at me, his mouth set. 'So, you're casting judgement on me for my relationship with Rhiannon?'

'Relationship? Is that what you call it?' I gave a short laugh.

'Actually, yes. What did you think? That it was a one-night stand, or something? I don't do that sort of thing.'

I thought about my night of passion in the hotel room with Nat and blushed. 'So, did you love her?'

His eyes widened as if the question surprised him. 'I'm very fond of her. I always have been. I suppose I do love her, yes.'

I found that my fists were clenched. I put the book down and stood. 'Well, I hope you're happy that you've added to Derry's misery. And if it doesn't bother you that she shagged you, after shagging your own father, there's something a bit wrong with you if you ask me.'

'I didn't know about that, obviously,' he acknowledged. 'Although, it wasn't as if she went straight from his bed to mine. There was a good twenty-five years between the two events. And I didn't ask you, did I? I really don't see why you're getting so worked up about it. What do you want me to say?'

'I don't want you to say anything. What's it got to do with me?' I demanded.

'Well, quite.'

That did it. I glared at him. 'Actually, it *is* something to do with me, because I thought we were friends, and I thought friends told each other stuff like that. Kept it bloody quiet, didn't you? Ashamed or something?'

He watched me for a moment, then shook his head slightly. 'When it happened, I hardly saw you. You weren't working here until after the relationship had ended, and I'm not going to gossip about women I've slept with, Lexi. I don't think that would be a very gentlemanly thing to do.'

'Women? So, not just Rhiannon then? And there's me thinking you were a bloody monk. Just shows you.'

'I don't recall you mentioning your night with Nat,' he pointed out calmly. 'If he hadn't turned up at the funeral, would I ever have known about that? If he hadn't been my cousin, would you have mentioned your fling with a total stranger in a hotel?'

I felt my face begin to burn. 'That's a cheap shot, Will.'

'Really? Why? What's the difference?'

'The difference is—' I began, but stopped. Shit. What *was* the difference?

'The difference is she was with me, and you were with an old slapper,' came a voice from behind, and I groaned inwardly as Nat entered the room, his face white with anger. 'So, *you* slept with that tart, too? My God, Will, I understand your desperation to lose your virginity, but that's taking it too far. If I'd known how bad things were, I'd have hired you a prostitute for your birthday. Same difference really.'

'Stop it, Nat,' said Will, his voice deceptively quiet. Beside him, Buttons stiffened, and I knew that, like me, he recognised the tone of his master's voice.

'Stop it? You do realise that slut slept with your old man? Your own father! And she knew that when she jumped into bed with you. My God, she's absolutely shameless. Disgusting old whore. I'll bet you didn't touch the sides.'

Okay, so that was out of line. Nat wasn't exactly pure as the driven snow, so why was it okay for him to jump into bed with anyone he liked, but wrong for Rhiannon to do the same? Talk about double standards.

I was about to point that out, but Will leapt to his feet, and the two of them stood there, fury in their eyes.

'Don't you dare talk about her like that!' Will ordered. 'You're hardly a paragon of virtue, are you? Hypocrite.'

I didn't like the way things were going. I hadn't intended to hurt Will, and I certainly hadn't meant for Nat to find out. I wished I'd never brought the matter up.

Why had I? Because I'd felt really let down and hurt by him, that was why. Which didn't make sense. Okay, so he was my friend, but that didn't mean he had to tell me everything. I hadn't told him everything, had I? He was quite right about that.

I moved between them. 'Okay, boys, that's quite enough of that,' I said, trying to keep my voice light. 'Nat, Will doesn't have to justify his actions to us,' I continued, trying to ignore the little voice in my head that was shrieking *hypocrite* at me. 'And, Will, now that I've got your attention, can we just discuss an idea I've had about the Hall. I meant to tell you about it yesterday, remember?'

Nat's gaze flickered towards me. 'Before you rushed to console poor Rhiannon and Derry.'

'Shut up, Nat.' I pushed him into the chair I'd just vacated and turned to Will, who was still staring at his cousin. I grabbed his arm and forced him to look at me. 'I think you should bring in a House Manager.'

Will seemed to finally focus on me. 'House Manager?'

'Yep. You know Bernie is the estate manager, and he's responsible for the land and the farm, the properties, tenants, and the staff who work outside? Well, I think you should hire someone to do the same sort of job indoors. Someone who has experience with working in a stately home, and would be able to organise the Hall staff, as well as know how to make this house a tourist attraction, and how to utilise it best. Someone who could take the burden off your shoulders. What do you think? You need to be more business-like about the whole thing. I mean, we've got to do something, haven't we?'

I hoped neither of them could hear the desperation in my voice.

It wasn't just the Hall that had me appealing to him. I desperately wanted to defuse the situation between them that I'd created with my temper and my big mouth.

'I — I suppose so. I'll give it some thought. Thank you.'

'And there goes Lexi again, always on your side. Where *will* it end? You'll have a whole fucking harem before long.' Nat stood up and pushed past me, stalked out of the study, and slammed the door behind him.

Will looked at me for a moment.

I flushed. 'I'm sorry,' I murmured.

He didn't reply. He picked up his book and headed out of the room, Buttons following at his heels.

Shaking, I sank down into the armchair and clutched *The Boden-Keans of Yorkshire* to me.

Above me, Sir Charles smirked down.

'Oh, bugger off,' I said.

****

When Nat slept, he looked like an angel. His fine, blond hair fell across his face, and there was an air of peace and innocence about him. It was amazing, really, because when he woke up, that far-from-innocent gleam would appear in his eyes almost immediately. There was nothing angelic about Nat when he was conscious, that was for sure.

I yawned, thinking I really should get some sleep myself. It had been a long day, and I'd be busy tomorrow too. What time was it anyway?

I peered over Nat's shoulder at the alarm clock on his bedside table, but it was too dark to make out the dial. Instead, I rummaged in my bag, found my mobile phone and checked the time on that. Nearly midnight. I must sleep!

I turned onto my side and closed my eyes. Within seconds they flew open again, as I heard a distinct creaking sound coming from somewhere on the landing. I shivered, straining my ears for footsteps, but couldn't hear anything. I closed my eyes again, but the creaking restarted.

I sat up, pulled the duvet tight against my chest, and wondered
if I should investigate. It could have been Will, I supposed, but I
couldn't hear anyone walking around, just the occasional creak
of floorboards.

'What on earth are you doing?' Nat's voice cut through the
darkness. 'Get to sleep, for God's sake.'

'I can hear creaking,' I whispered. 'Listen.'

Within seconds, it happened again.

Nat laughed. 'Are you serious? You do know how old this
house is? It creaks and groans all night long.'

'I've never noticed before,' I said, uncomfortably aware that he
had a point. How had I not thought about that?

'You were too busy the other times you stayed over,' he said,
reaching out a hand to stroke my face. 'Then I wore you out so
much, you slept right through all the noise.'

'Hmm, if you say so,' I said.

'Seriously, there's nothing to worry about. This house is just
breathing, and after all the centuries it's been standing, let's be
grateful that it still manages it, eh?'

I nudged him, laughing, and he pulled me down towards him,
giving me a long, lingering kiss.

'I'm glad we're friends again,' he said.

'Yes, well, you're lucky I decided to forgive you, after that little
temper tantrum earlier,' I said.

He sighed and wrapped his arms around me, and I lay my head
on his chest, thinking I was actually feeling quite tired at last. I'd
probably be asleep in a minute or two.

'It's just that, well, Will and Rhiannon,' he said. 'I mean, *her*! Of
all people. It's quite disgusting, don't you think?'

I didn't really want to think about it at all.

'Let's just drop the subject,' I said. 'I think we both made it quite
plain how we felt.'

'Why does it bother you so much?' he said. 'I loathe the woman,
because as far as I can see, she was the one who drove Aunt
Elisabeth away, and left Will without a mother all those years,
but that didn't seem to matter to you yesterday.'

I hesitated. I wasn't actually sure. Some vague and unfamiliar feeling swirled around inside me every time I thought about Will with Rhiannon, but I couldn't put a name to it. It wasn't a feeling I wanted to investigate too closely.

'I've had time to think about it,' I said. 'Will's my mate, and she deprived him of his mother. Besides, how could she sleep with that old man, then his son? It's low, even for Rhiannon.'

I felt wracked with guilt as soon as I'd spoken the words. Rhiannon had always been lovely to me, and to everyone I knew. She was one of Eliza's best friends, and my dad was very fond of her too. I shouldn't have been speaking about her like that. I was beginning to sound like Sophie, who'd never been her biggest fan.

'Well, hopefully we made Will see how vile the situation is, and how she's to blame for his parents' divorce. Maybe he'll steer well clear of her from now on.'

'I wouldn't count on that,' I said. 'Will's far too loyal to abandon her now, especially when the villagers are pointing the finger at her, and when Derry's being so horrible to her. If anything, it will probably make him stick even closer to her.'

'Bloody hell,' said Nat. 'What's wrong with him?'

'He's just like that.' In spite of myself, I found myself smiling as I recalled Rhiannon's relieved expression when he'd held out his arms to her at the pub. She'd obviously been terribly afraid that he would turn his back on her, but it would never happen. If you could count on anyone's support, it was Will's. In spite of my feelings for Rhiannon, I was glad that he hadn't let her down when she needed him most. I felt quite proud of him, in fact, which just shows how contradictory I can be.

'You're really close to Will, aren't you?' said Nat suddenly.

I lifted my head and stared at the dark outline of his face. 'What an odd thing to say.'

'It's the way you are with him. When I first saw you together, I wondered if maybe you had a bit of a crush on him.'

'A crush! On Will?' I laughed and planted a light kiss on his forehead. 'Bless you. What made you think that?'

'I'm not sure. Just a feeling.'

There was no amusement in his voice, and I felt a bit uneasy suddenly, though I wasn't quite sure why. 'Nope. You're barking up the wrong tree. Me and Will are just friends. Good friends.'

'Like you and Georgia?'

'Georgia? Well, yes, I suppose so. They're my two best friends in the world. I tell them everything.'

'Doesn't Georgia have someone else she can talk to? Surely she's got a boyfriend, or something?'

'No.' I laughed. 'Georgia's too busy caring for her horses and ponies to make time for a man. I'm lucky she manages to fit time with me into her busy schedule.'

He nodded, stroking my hair in an absentminded fashion. 'All work and no play makes Georgia a very dull girl indeed.'

'She's not dull!' I felt an immediate need to defend her. 'She's great fun, and I'm sure she'd love a boyfriend. She's just not got the time to find one.'

'Probably like you,' he said. 'Wouldn't mind a casual shag now and then, but definitely no strings.'

'She's not like me,' I said, not sure I liked how he described me. 'Georgia's a romantic and would want all the hearts and flowers stuff, and the commitment. And is that how you see me? Someone just out for a casual shag?'

'Well, aren't you?' He smiled. 'I'm not insulting you, just stating facts, as told to me by you yourself, may I remind you.'

'I know.' I sighed. 'Still, I'm not a cheap slapper, you know.'

'I never thought you were,' he said.

'Really. I've only ever slept with three men in my life, and you're one of them. I don't just jump into bed with anyone. I do like to be in a relationship, just not an intense, committed relationship.'

'You don't have to justify yourself to me,' he said. 'I feel exactly the same.' He played with a strand of my hair, twisting it around his finger. 'I've never met anyone like you, Lexi. Most women want the whole works. You're not like that. It's all very easy with you. I guess you and I will never settle down.'

A sudden sadness swept over me at his words. There was something about the way he spoke — was it a twinge of regret? It felt as if something had just shifted, but I couldn't think what. For a split second, it seemed as if we were both acknowledging something — something that filled me with a deep, if fleeting, despair. As quickly as it came it had gone, and Nat was pulling me to him, evidently wide awake.

From somewhere far off, the house creaked and groaned, but it didn't worry me any longer. I was far too busy to care.

Chapter 10

William took a deep breath as he entered the kitchen the next morning and found Lexi sitting at the table, wearing nothing but an old baggy t-shirt of Nat's and a pair of his socks.

She had the grace to look embarrassed. 'I'm sorry, Will. I wasn't expecting you up this early, or I'd have dressed,' she mumbled, pushing her bowl of barely-touched cornflakes away.

Will turned away from the sight of her, all tangled hair and long legs. He busied himself making tea and toast, wishing it wasn't Woody's day off. 'Don't be silly. You're Nat's guest. You don't have to apologise to me,' he said. 'Would you like tea?'

'No thanks. Nat made me a cup before he went out.'

'He's gone out?' Will spun back to face her. 'Where to?'

'I've no bloody idea.' She prodded her spoon in the bowl, splashing milk onto the tablecloth in the process. 'He was up with the lark this morning and seemed full of the joys. Not like him at all. He's usually asleep 'til at least eleven.'

Not giving a reply, Will collected his tea and toast and sat at the table next to her. He broke off the crust to give to Buttons, who sat devotedly at his side as always.

'Tessa always liked the crusts,' said Lexi softly.

Will looked at her, feeling a wave of sympathy for her loss. 'How long is it now?'

'Seven months,' said Lexi. 'Poor, gorgeous dog.'

'At least you know you did the right thing. You wouldn't have wanted her to suffer. I'm sorry, that sounds so trite — I didn't mean it to. I do know how you feel, though. When Cinders died, I felt as if a part of me did, too. Luckily, I had her puppy here to keep me going. Didn't I, old fellow?' he said, reaching down to fondle the dog's silky, chocolate-coloured ears.

Lexi smiled and reached over to stroke Buttons' head. Her hand brushed against Will's, and he tensed as she caught it and held it.

'I just wanted to apologise,' she said, her face flushed.

Will removed his hand and cupped his mug of tea. 'It doesn't matter.'

'But it does matter. 'Course it does. I had no right to have a go at you for sleeping with Rhiannon. I mean, look at me and Nat. I don't know what came over me, honestly I don't. I feel so bad about it.'

'Forget it.' He gulped his tea, scalding his mouth in the process, and tried not to yelp. 'I have.'

She seemed to be watching him thoughtfully. 'You're always so kind, Will,' she said.

'Not always.' He wondered what she'd say if she knew some of the far-from-kind thoughts he'd been having recently.

'It's true. You always give people the benefit of the doubt, and you're so loyal to everyone. You're such a nice man.'

Will's heart sank. *Nice.* He didn't want her to see him as nice. Where was the passion in nice, for God's sake?

'I've given your suggestion some thought,' he said, changing the subject. 'I think you're right. I do need to start seeing this place as more of a business, and I need professional help.'

'That's great news! We've really got to get moving on this, haven't we? It would be good to have the house open properly in time for the Easter holidays. That's when all the crowds start arriving in the area, and I'm sure loads of them would want to visit. I'll stay here today, if that's okay with you, and get on with researching your ancestors. I do need to ask you a favour, though, Will.'

'Go ahead,' he said, wondering what more she could possibly ask of him.

'The twins and Amy. Eliza and Dad are really struggling. Please don't say anything but, well, they've been drifting apart lately and need time alone together. I was wondering, I know it's a big ask, but would you mind if I brought the kids here for the day on Sunday? I mean, if I do an extra shift on Saturday to make up for it? I just thought I could take them around the grounds, so if they cry it won't disturb anyone. Am I being very cheeky?'

Will smiled. 'It would be lovely to have them. Does Amy still have her imaginary pony? Perhaps she'd like a ride on Frosty? She taught me to ride and she's getting on a bit, but I expect she could cope with Amy plodding up and down. And you don't have to go off anywhere. I'd love to see the twins. It would be nice to have children in the house for a change, and, besides, you can't manage three of them alone. I'll be happy to help.'

'You don't have to do that. It's not your problem. Could one of the others do my shift in the farm shop on Sunday, do you think?'

'Of course. Nina's always asking for extra hours, so I can't see it being a problem. And I'd love to spend some time with the children. It would make a nice change from worrying about money.'

Lexi smiled at him, her eyes bright with laughter. 'You're a funny one. What other bloke would want kids around? Thanks, Will. I'll spend today working very hard, promise. I've made some notes. I must say, the Boden-Keans are surprisingly tame. I'm going to read up on the First Baronet today, around the Civil War period. Could be interesting.'

He grinned. 'I wouldn't count on it, although it was a terribly turbulent time for the Keartons. It was during that period that the house passed from the Kearton family to the Boden-Keans, and it's been ours ever since. I have a lot to live up to. It's no use doing what my ancestors have always done — selling chunks of the estate to pay the bills. Anyway, I certainly can't afford to lose the rents. I don't know...' He sighed, and Lexi squeezed his hand.

'We'll find a way through, Will. We won't lose Kearton Hall. I promise.'

He glanced down at his hand, held tightly in hers, and felt a tremor pass through him.

The back door flew open and Nat swaggered in, a grin on his face. 'Phew, what a fabulous ride. Masquerade goes like a bomb.'

He stared at them and his smile faded. 'Am I interrupting something?'

Lexi dropped Will's hand as Nat held out his arms to her. 'We were just talking about hiring a House Manager. What were you doing out so early, anyway? You usually sleep in until late morning.'

Will pushed his chair back. 'I'll just clear these dishes away,' he said, though he knew neither of them heard him.

Nat had wrapped his arms around Lexi and was nuzzling her neck, while she squirmed and giggled in a most nauseating fashion.

'I want to talk to you, Will,' said Nat.

Will halted, amazed that his cousin had even remembered he was there.

'Don't look so suspicious. I've been thinking about this House Manager thing, too. Didn't sleep much last night actually. Hate to make Lexi even more big-headed,' he said, grinning as she nudged him indignantly, 'but her idea made perfect sense, so I've drafted an advertisement. I'd like you to take a gander at it, and if you approve, I'll send it out. I'd like to help, really I would. Would you allow me to weed through the applicants? Take that burden off your shoulders, at least. Obviously, you'd sit in on the interviews when I've shortlisted them, and you'd have the final say in who we chose.'

'Really?' Will frowned. 'And what's brought on this change of heart?'

Nat sighed. 'I feel bad, the way I spoke to you. Let's face it, I've not exactly done much to help you have I? At least let me try to make amends by helping you find someone suitable.'

Will wasn't sure what to make of that. 'Well, I must say I'm surprised. I thought you were keen for me to sell, so I wasn't expecting you to help me.'

'It's good news though, isn't it?' Lexi looked from one to the other. 'I mean, it's good to have you both on the same side? And the sooner you hire someone, the sooner we can start to pull things together. Right?'

'Yes, of course. Thank you, Nat.' Will placed his plate and cup in the sink. Behind him, Lexi thanked Nat for being so thoughtful, and Will closed his eyes as the sound of them slobbering over each other followed. He twisted the tap to run the hot water.

'Cup of tea, Nat?' said Lexi. 'Will? Another drink?'

'No, thanks. I have work to do.' Another moment in their company was too much to ask.

'Go on. I've only seen you for five minutes,' Nat said. 'Let's have a drink together before we start the day.'

Will sighed and nodded. He finished the dishes before sitting at the table, while Lexi poured three mugs of tea.

'I was thinking, Lex,' Nat drawled, putting his feet up on the next chair to his. 'What about coming riding with me one day? Nothing better than a gallop through the fields first thing. She could borrow one of yours, couldn't she, Will? Think Masquerade may be a bit of a handful for you, but there's always Captain. I suppose Pilot's a bit past it now,' he mused.

Will glanced at Lexi, feeling sympathy as the colour drained from her face.

'I — I don't actually ride,' she murmured, handing Nat his tea.

Nat blinked. 'What do you mean, you don't ride? How can you not ride?'

'Not everyone does, believe it, or not, Nat,' said Will. 'It's not compulsory.' He took his mug from Lexi and gave her a sympathetic smile.

'But your best friend runs a riding school! You must be able to ride!'

'I never learned.' Lexi sat down and cradled her mug of tea in her hands, as if drawing comfort from its heat. 'Thing is, I didn't want to. I'm a bit scared.'

'Of horses?' Nat sounded horrified. 'My God, you're not serious?'

'I love horses,' she protested. 'I really do. I just don't like the idea of sitting all the way up there on their backs. It frightens me. I'm sorry.'

Nat was silent for a moment, then he shook his head and stood up. 'First, you admit you're a vegetarian, and now this. Well, there's only one solution. You have to learn.'

'What?' Lexi paled.

'She's just told you she's afraid of riding, Nat,' Will said. 'Leave her alone.'

'Nonsense. She just needs to sit on a horse, and she'll be fine. Come on. I'll tack up Pilot. Old bugger's so knackered he won't bolt or buck, or anything like that. Hasn't got the energy. I'll teach you. It'll be a laugh.'

'No way.' Will shook his head. 'You're the last person to teach her to ride.'

'Meaning what?'

'Meaning you're far too impatient. You're reckless and overconfident. You'd scare her to death. No, she needs someone patient to teach her. Someone who'd take it slowly.'

They were all quiet for a moment, then Lexi said faintly, 'Perhaps you could—'

Nat cut off her sentence before she could finish it. 'Fine. Georgia can teach her. Good idea. Come on, let's get ready and head over to the stables right now.'

'I can't, Nat. I have work to do.'

'I'm sure Will can spare you for a couple of hours.'

'No, because I want to do extra work today so I can take Sunday off to spend with the kids.'

'What bloody kids? Look, Lexi, this is important to me. Bad enough you're a bloody veggie, but this...'

'I know, but—'

'Tell her, Will. She seems more likely to listen to you.' Nat slumped back in his chair and folded his arms, frowning at his cousin.

Will shook his head. 'Nothing to do with me,' he said. 'This is Lexi's decision.'

Lexi looked from one to the other. 'Will, would you mind? Just for an hour?'

'If it's what you truly want,' he said. 'But is it? Don't let anyone force you. It's up to you.'

'For God's sake,' growled Nat. 'I'm hardly dragging her there in chains.'

'I'll be fine,' said Lexi. 'I suppose it's time I tried to overcome my fear, anyway. It may be good for me.'

'That's the spirit! Come on then, get yourself dressed,' said Nat, slapping her on the behind as she stood up.

Will took a sip of his tea, saying nothing. It was none of his business. He just hoped she knew what she was doing.

****

As Nat's sports car crunched up the gravel drive to the White Rose Riding School, I felt like a condemned man being taken to the gallows. I couldn't believe what I was about to do.

It wasn't just the riding thing I had to worry about, after all. Georgia and I hadn't spoken since our row, and I wasn't at all sure she'd be welcoming. I supposed that was one of the reasons I'd agreed to go there. It gave me an excuse to talk to her again, see if we could make it up. Although, to be fair, it wasn't exactly something we could discuss too openly, given that the subject of our row was sitting right beside me.

Nat rambled cheerily on about the first time he ever sat on a pony, when he was three years old, and how he'd won his first rosette when he was only four, and everyone had said he was a star in the making. I was too nervous to comment. My stomach was doing a clear round all on its own.

Pushing a wheelbarrow of dirty straw to the muck heap in the stable yard, Georgia paused at our approach. As I climbed out of the car, she lowered the barrow, surprise and a trace of suspicion evident in her face.

'Hello! Didn't know you were coming. I'm a bit busy at the moment. Haven't really got time to stand and chat.'

'I'm not here to chat,' I said. 'I'm here on business.'

'Really? And what possible business could you have at a riding school? I'm intrigued. Do tell.'

I swallowed. She stared at Nat, her eyes expressing her hostility. I took a deep breath. 'Would you give me riding lessons? Obviously, I'll pay the going rate.'

Georgia's eyes narrowed and she tilted her head, clearly thrown by my question. 'Riding lessons? But you hate horses!'

'I don't hate them,' I said truthfully. 'I'm just flipping scared stiff of them.'

'Well, okay. But you've been hanging round here for ages, and you've never entertained the idea. Why now?' Her gaze cut to Nat, her expression scornful. 'You're doing this for him.'

Nat had been surprisingly silent so far, but he seemed to shake himself awake at that point.

'I'm quite sure she has a mind of her own. I haven't forced her to do this, you know. I should have thought you'd be pleased, anyway. Or does it make you feel superior to her, knowing that you possess at least one talent that she doesn't have?'

'I beg your pardon?' Georgia drew herself up to her full five-feet-two-inches and glared at him as he stood beside the car, one arm draped casually along the top of the open door. 'What do you mean by that?'

'Well, I just think it's odd that, in all your years of friendship, you've never tried to help her with her phobia of riding. I do wonder what the reason for that could be.'

'Why would I force her to do something she doesn't want to do? That seems to be your forte, not mine.'

'I can assure you I don't have to force Lexi to do anything. It's not my style. But then, I've never needed to force women. They're usually all too eager to please.'

'You're disgusting,' snapped Georgia. 'I'm not making Lexi do something she's afraid of, just to please a chauvinistic, arrogant git like you. You can bugger off.'

'Fine. I'm sure there are other, more professionally-run, riding schools in the area. Your loss.'

He climbed back into the car.

'Georgia, can I have a word?' I asked. 'In private?'

She seemed to think it over for a moment before she shrugged. 'If you insist.'

I told a sulky Nat to give us five minutes and headed off to the tack room with my friend.

She didn't pull any punches. 'What the hell do you think you're doing, Lexi? You don't pander to demands from that jumped up little tosser! He's bad news. He's bullying you, forcing you to do something you don't want to do. Please, just forget all about riding. I know you don't want to learn.'

'I do,' I said. 'I really do want to learn.'

'Why? Why now?'

I sighed. 'Things aren't great between us, Georgia. I mean, the sex is fantastic, but there's nothing else going on.'

'I thought that's how you liked it,' said Georgia. 'Remember Derry?'

'Yeah.' I blushed. 'Now I understand where he was coming from, when he complained that there was nothing else to our relationship. I'm in the same boat as he was. It's not nice.'

'No. Guess not.' Georgia picked up a bridle and examined it. 'So, why riding? Isn't there something else that he's interested in, that you could join in with?'

I shook my head. 'To be honest, he doesn't seem to be interested in anything else. Sex and horses. That's it. He's a bit boring, actually.'

'Then, why are you with him? You do know you can't trust him? He's not the settling down type.'

'And I am?' I laughed. 'I don't want to settle down, Georgia. That's the whole point.'

'I don't understand what you're talking about. If he's so shallow and untrustworthy, what's the point of seeing him?'

'Because he's shallow and untrustworthy.' I avoided her gaze, aware that she'd never understand, and I didn't want to talk about it in detail. 'Look, I'm sorry I walked out on you that time, and I know you only have my best interests at heart. Please, just trust me. I'm not going to get my heart broken, and I'm not going to let him bully me. Promise.'

She scrutinised me for a moment, then sighed. 'Whatever. If you want to learn to ride, I'll be happy to give you lessons. I just think you shouldn't have to do something you're not comfortable with, just to keep Nat happy.'

'It's not like that.'

'Isn't it? So, what's he doing to help your relationship? Has he met your family? Does he show any interest in your hobbies or work?'

I almost laughed at the idea. Nat show an interest? I didn't think he even knew I had younger siblings, and he'd never shown the slightest inclination to meet Dad and Eliza. If I was being really honest with myself, I knew that having Dad and Nat in such close proximity would be unnerving. Without him having said a single word on the subject, I knew that Dad didn't approve of Nat. And then there was Amy to think about. She would no doubt irritate him with her endless questions and childish conversation.

He wasn't at all like his cousin, who'd won Amy over years ago and seemed able to communicate effectively with just about anyone, simply because he was actually interested in them. Young or old, rich or poor, Will always wanted to know about them, and was happy to talk to anyone. I wished Nat could be a bit more like him.

Georgia was watching me, and I cleared my throat nervously. 'I'm sure all that will come in time. In the meantime, one of us needs to make a move, so it may as well be me.'

'Fine. If that's what you want, who am I to argue?'

'Aw, thanks, Georgia. So, when should I start?'

'Not this week. I'm fully booked. How about next Wednesday? That's your half day, isn't it?'

'Great. Thanks, Georgia. I owe you one.'

Georgia gave me a rather unconvincing smile. 'You don't owe me anything, Lexi. Really you don't.'

Chapter 11

The kitchen was its usual scene of chaos. Dad hastily buttered toast while telling Amy to eat her cornflakes and keeping a wary eye on the toaster. Eliza was feeding Hannah as she grabbed the occasional bite of her own toast and listened out for Mikey, and I was making cups of tea for everyone and wondering what the hell I was letting myself in for.

'Are you absolutely certain Will doesn't mind you taking the children?' Dad asked for the millionth time.

'No, I told you. He said it was fine.'

'But all three? Are you sure he didn't think you just meant Amy?' Eliza's doubtful expression showed that she couldn't believe anyone would welcome the twins with open arms.

'Honestly, it will be fun. Stop worrying. I want you to have a day all to yourselves. What are you going to do?'

She looked blank. 'Gosh, I don't know. We hadn't really given it much thought. Give this place a thorough clean, I suppose, since we've got another viewing on Tuesday. The windows need doing, and I must wash the bedding, and the skirting boards are a disgrace.'

Dad leaned over and planted a kiss on her head. 'Forget all that,' he said. 'You and I are going to go for a walk round the Bay, searching for *For Sale* signs. Then we'll have a drive through the local villages to see if we spot any houses up for sale, before lunching in Helmston. I believe the Fox and Hounds does a lovely Sunday roast.'

'Are you serious?'

'Absolutely. I've already booked a table, so you needn't worry about that. And this afternoon, how about a walk around Whitby?'

'We could visit the abbey!' Her eyes shone.

'We will. And then home for an hour, or so, before the children get back.'

'And what shall we do while they're still out?' she enquired, a mischievous smile on her lips.

'I'm sure we'll think of something,' he said, taking hold of her hand. 'If I forget what to do, we'll ring Rose and Flynn for instructions.'

She burst out laughing and threw her arms around his neck.

'Yuk!' I said, but I was grinning — as much with relief as anything else.

Amy bashed her cornflakes with the spoon and peered up at me. 'Are we going to the big house?'

'That's right,' I said. 'So hurry up and finish your breakfast so we can get off.'

'Is there a ghost in that house?' she asked.

'Of course not. You've been there before,' I said. 'You liked it, didn't you?'

She considered that before answering, 'Some of it. Some of those statues are horrible. Will Mrs Woodrow be there again?'

'Yes, why?'

'She gave me chocolate biscuits last time. Will there be chocolate biscuits today?'

'I'm not sure, but I'm sure there'll be something.'

'Can I take Twinkle?'

I sighed. 'Not really. Why don't you leave him here this time? Will's got a pony called Frosty. Would you like to have a ride on her?'

Amy's eyes widened. 'Really? Can I?'

'Will may not agree—' began Eliza, but I cut her off.

'It was his idea. Asked me if she still had her imaginary pony and suggested she might like to ride a real one. And before you ask, yes, he's got loads of old riding hats. One of them's bound to fit her.'

Eliza smiled. 'Bless him. Fancy him remembering! He's so lovely, isn't he?'

'S'pose so.' I shrugged.

'No suppose about it,' said Dad. 'Can't imagine his cousin thinking of her like that. When are you going to bring him round, by the way? I should have thought we'd have met him properly by now, seeing as he's your boyfriend.'

'He's not my boyfriend,' I protested.

He raised an eyebrow. 'He's not? Well, you've spent enough nights sleeping over at his place. And how on earth he persuaded you to take up riding lessons I dread to think.'

'Don't.' I shuddered, wondering the same thing myself. What the hell had I been thinking?

'I hope you're not trying to turn yourself into someone else, just to please him,' said Eliza. 'Seriously, Lexi, I've been there, done that. It's a waste of time. If he doesn't love you for who you are, don't bother.'

'Love me?' I laughed at the thought. 'Nat doesn't love me! And thank God for it.'

Dad shook his head. 'I'll never understand you, Lexi. Really, I won't. You deserve to be loved.'

Eliza smiled. 'She'll come round to it in her own time, Gabriel,' she said. 'One day, she'll open her eyes, just like Sleeping Beauty, and see what's right in front of her.'

'What do you mean by that?' I demanded.

She winked at me and took a bite of her toast.

****

Will was waiting for us in the car park, Buttons by his side. He waved and rushed over as I pulled up, helped to unstrap the babies without even being asked, and lifted Hannah out, while assuring Amy that, yes, Mrs Woodrow was in, and he was absolutely certain there were chocolate biscuits and probably cake too, and that Frosty would be delighted to let her ride her, if she was positive Twinkle wouldn't mind.

I hoisted Mikey over my shoulder, draped the enormous bag that contained changes of clothes, bottles of milk, nappies, creams, baby wipes, toys and God knows what else, over my other arm, and kicked the back door of the Fiat 500 shut.

Will grinned at me and I frowned. 'What?'

'It's fun, isn't it? You, me, all these children...'

'Fun? I can think of other words to describe it. Crap!' I stared at him in horror, as a trail of baby sick spurted over his shoulder and down his back. 'God, I'm so sorry, Will.'

He laughed. 'Why? It's only a shirt. It can be changed. Come on, let's go and find those chocolate biscuits shall we, Amy?'

I followed him inside, watching in awe as he held Hannah gently, talking to her as if she understood every word he was saying. He was a natural.

Hannah looked over his shoulder at me, a huge grin on her face. Evidently, Will had won her over, just as he had Amy.

My stomach suddenly gave a very odd lurch. It was quite peculiar.

Woody *did* have chocolate biscuits, thank God, because if Amy had been let down in that department, I dread to think what would have happened. She poured her a glass of lemonade, fed her biscuits and angel cake, and cooed over Hannah and Michael, while Will rushed upstairs to change his shirt, and I sank into the armchair by the range and wondered how the hell Eliza coped all day, every day. No wonder she was tired and snappy.

One thing offering to help when I'd got a spare hour or so, but quite another to know that you're stuck with them all the time, and when they cry there's no one to hand them back to. It was going to be a long day.

Woody bounced Mikey on her knee, taking no heed of my warning that he could erupt at any second. She was just entertaining him with a rendition of *Round and Round the Garden*, while he stared at her with enormous eyes and an expression of astonishment on his face, when the door opened and Nat strolled in.

He took in the chaotic scene in the kitchen and stopped dead. 'What the fuck—?'

'Do you mind?' Woody glared at him. 'Children present.'

'I can see that, Woody. Whose children? Jesus, it's like a bloody crèche in here. What's happened?'

'This is Hannah, and that's Amy, and that one's Michael, or Mikey, as we call him,' I said, nodding at each child in turn.

'Is that supposed to mean something?' he asked, stepping gingerly over the nappy bag and plonking himself on the arm of my chair.

I knew he hadn't been listening when I told him about them. 'They're my sisters and brother,' I explained.

'Bit of an age gap.' He eyed me thoughtfully. 'Are you sure they're your siblings, and not your illegitimate offspring that your parents are covering up for?'

'Nathaniel!' snapped Woody.

He laughed. 'Oh, come on, it was a joke. Not that it's impossible. One reads of such things all the time. Anyway, what are they doing here?'

'I told you. I wanted to give Eliza a break, so I asked Will if I could spend the day with them here. That's why I've been working extra hours the last couple of days, to make up for not working today.'

His smile faded. 'You mean they're going to be here all day? Seriously?'

I nodded, looking worriedly at Amy, who was listening to our conversation with keen interest. It would be just my luck if she repeated it word for word when she got home later.

'Christ, what are you thinking? And Will's okay with this, I suppose?'

'Absolutely fine.' Will entered the kitchen, wearing a clean shirt and carrying a trio of crash helmets in his arms, with Buttons trotting by his side. 'It will be fun. Here, Amy, I've brought some old riding hats for you to try on. One of them's bound to fit, and then we can go to the stables and find old Frosty. What do you say?'

Amy's eyes lit up, and as she rushed over to Will's side to try them on, Nat got to his feet.

'Where are you going?' I asked.

'Out. I'm not hanging round here playing Mary Poppins all day. I've got things to do.'

'Really?' Will glanced up at him. 'Like what? Riding? Watching television? Browsing Facebook?'

'None of your fucking business,' snapped Nat. 'I'll be back for dinner, Woody. Probably.' He stalked out of the kitchen without a backward glance.

Amy tutted. 'Don't like him,' she told Will. 'Is he really your cousin?'

'He is,' confirmed Will, tapping a helmet onto her head and stepping back to study her. 'He's all right, really. Just gets a bit cross sometimes.'

'If Mikey grows up like that, I'll make him live in a shed, and I won't let him back in 'til he's nice again and says he's sorry,' she told him.

Will raised an eyebrow. 'Good idea,' he mused. 'Might try that one out. Now, I think that hat's the right fit. Shall we go and say hello to Frosty?'

Amy whooped and ran out of the room before he could change his mind.

He glanced over at me and smiled. 'I'll be careful with her, don't worry,' he said. 'When she's done, maybe we could take the twins for a walk around the estate. I'm sure the fresh air will do them good. We could feed the ducks on the lake?'

I nodded. 'Sounds good, Will. Thanks.'

He smiled, then he and Buttons headed out after Amy.

Woody sighed. 'Make a good father himself one day, that man. What do you think, Lexi?'

Funnily enough, I'd just been thinking the same thing.

I swallowed. 'Any angel cake going spare?'

Chapter 12

'I wouldn't let it worry you, Will. It's only riding lessons, and Lexi's no pushover. If Nat tried to force her to do something she didn't want to do, I'm certain she'd make a stand. Maybe she's just decided to face her fears. It's something we all have to do at some point.' Rhiannon sighed and sipped her coffee. 'Sometimes, we simply don't have a choice.'

'Are things no better?' Will watched her, noting the tired eyes and lack of sparkle. Rhiannon was the eternal optimist. He hated seeing her like this.

She shook her head. 'Not really. Derry rarely talks to me. I knew it would come one day. Sir Paul told me years ago that he'd leave him something in his will, but truthfully, I wasn't sure he would, and I didn't know how I was going to explain it away if he did. I just didn't expect it to be so much, or that he'd give a full account of why he was doing so. Most awkward.'

Will didn't know what to say. He'd listened to Rhiannon's story, the night he and Lexi came to The Hare and Moon, with an open mind and a willing heart. She'd assured him that Elisabeth had known all about the little dalliance she'd had with her husband and had approved.

'Things were already over between them. All she wanted to do was get away from him. When I arrived at the Hall, with nowhere else to go after the row with my father, they took me in and were very kind to me. It could have been difficult. After all, I was the cousin of your father's first wife, and Elisabeth could have been very unfriendly towards me, but I think she saw me as an ally, a friend. And I was, Will. I swear to you. I really liked your mother, and we talked a lot. I kept up her spirits when she was low, and there were times when she was very low indeed.

'The trouble was, I could see that Sir Paul was also very low. He was bluff and could be very cold and insensitive, but I could see he was hurting. Before long, he was confiding in me, too. He knew he should never have married Elisabeth. If Jane had survived, he wouldn't have done, of course, because he really loved her. Such a shame Jane couldn't have children, because I truly believe if she had he'd never have sought another wife, and maybe they'd both have been happier. But then, you wouldn't have been born, and the world would have been a far sadder place.'

She'd smiled and squeezed his hand. 'As he talked things over with me, I began to really care about him, and we grew close. Your mother understood. She didn't mind at all. She was just glad he left her alone.

'Our little affair didn't last very long. When I found out Derry was on the way, it gave Elisabeth the ammunition she needed, and he had to agree to a divorce, or she could have dragged him through the courts. Sometimes, I wonder if that's why she encouraged me ... I don't know. But it wasn't that she loved him, and I betrayed her. I promise you that. She was fully aware from the start, and not in the slightest bit hurt. I would never have done anything to hurt her. I adored her.'

Will believed her, though he knew he would never convince Nat. Rhiannon had assured him that she'd asked for nothing from his father. He'd wanted to put her in one of the estate cottages and pay her an allowance, but she'd asked instead if she could take over the tenancy of The Hare and Moon, which had just become vacant. She'd wanted to pay her own way, make her own living in a building she adored, and was fascinated by.

'And I paid full rent the whole time,' she told Will. 'I supported Derry myself, and your father rarely saw him. In fact, I thought he'd quite forgotten he was his son, until I got the visit from

Archie around ten years ago, when he told me I was now the owner of The Hare and Moon.'

'And no else knew?' he asked her, wondering if anyone had guessed.

Rhiannon seemed certain that no one did. 'I went back to my family just after I found out I was pregnant. They were absolutely furious and wanted nothing more to do with me. I didn't tell them who the father was, of course. When I got back here, I insinuated that the child had been conceived in Cornwall. No one questioned it. I did what I thought was best at the time. I kept quiet. Clearly, I made a serious error of judgment.'

Sitting there with her, seeing the sadness that was all too evident in her eyes, Will wished Derry would listen to her side of the story. He could at least give her a chance. It seemed, however, that his half-brother was unwilling, or unable, to stand any more. Will racked his brains, trying to think of something that would bring them back together, but he was out of ideas.

Rhiannon sat up straight suddenly. 'Goodness, listen to me going on about my problems. What's the situation at the Hall? Have you decided what you're going to do next?'

Will brightened. 'I think I have, yes. We have experts from English Heritage coming to examine the place to report back to the tax office. Archie and John are going to be trustees of the Maintenance Fund, and we have to get the place fully open to the public for a minimum number of days every year, so we've got to up our game. Lexi came up with the good idea of hiring a House Manager — someone with experience in opening this sort of building to the public, and who can help in the day-to-day running of the Hall. I want to give it my best shot, and I'm not best qualified to do it.'

'You've done very well so far,' Rhiannon said. 'Especially given the opposition you had to face.'

'Yes, I know, but I want to take this to a much higher level. I feel like I've dabbled for ages, but it's time to take the plunge. The estate does well. The tenancies bring in good rents, the home farm is flourishing, the shops and café and gardens are big draws, but they all have to pay for the house. It's time it started to pay its own way. It has to attract enough people to ensure we can hang onto it and keep it in good condition. It's far too important to be left entirely in my hands.'

'So, have you found someone?'

'No, but Nat's advertised, and we've already had a huge response. He's trawling through the applications, as we speak, drawing up a shortlist for interviews.'

'That's very kind of him,' said Rhiannon suspiciously. 'What's brought about that change of heart?'

'I don't know,' Will confessed. 'I just hope it lasts.'

Rhiannon eyed him, her expression thoughtful. 'Has Nat said anything about how long he intends to stay? He's been here almost a month now. I thought he'd be long gone.'

Will drained his coffee. 'Not really. He's rather vague on the subject, actually. I thought he'd have got bored and left for London ages ago, but then again...'

Rhiannon raised an eyebrow. 'You can't think he's staying for Lexi?'

'Well, I can't think of any other reason, can you?'

She laughed. 'Nat wouldn't hang around for her, or any other woman. He's not in love with her. She's just a distraction, and one that will wear off very soon, I'm sure. He'll get bored and head back to London in the near future, don't you worry about it.'

'Perhaps. Have you made any plans for Samhain?'

'Not really.' She sighed. 'I think I'll mark this one in strict privacy. Derry is barely speaking to me, and the villagers are being distinctly cold towards me. I keep expecting to find them outside with pitchforks in their hands.'

'So, you're not having your usual Hallowe'en party for the village?'

'Not this year. I doubt anyone would turn up. It's been awfully quiet in here lately. If it wasn't for the occasional tourist, the place would be completely empty. Still, on the bright side, I think the other pubs in the village are seeing a huge increase in trade.'

She gave a weak laugh, and Will squeezed her hand. 'It will pass,' he said. 'Everything does. You know what this place is like.

Everyone gossips, but no one means anything by it. If you do have the party, I'll make it known that I'm going to attend. Then they can hardly justify their indignation on my behalf, can they?'

Rhiannon's eyes softened. 'I'm sorry, Will.'

'For what?'

'For everything you're going through — all the financial stress, losing your father, and coping with Nat. And mostly, for not telling you about what happened between Sir Paul and me. I appreciate how weird it must feel, given what happened between us, and I'm sorry you didn't know Derry was your brother. I would have liked the two of you to be closer. You'd have been an excellent role model for him.'

'I don't think he needed me. You were a wonderful mother. He's grown up a fine young man, and I'm proud to call him my brother. We all make mistakes, Rhiannon. We all have things we wish we'd done differently. I don't bear you any grudges.'

'Unlike Nathaniel.'

'Nat's a law unto himself,' Will acknowledged. 'I just wish I knew what Lexi saw in him, as they're so very different. I suppose he is very good looking. Maybe that's enough.'

'Maybe it is. For now.' Rhiannon smiled at him, and he raised an eyebrow.

'What's so funny?'

'Nothing, nothing. I just think that, at the moment, Nat is exactly what Lexi needs.'

'You do?' It wasn't what he wanted her to say, and he couldn't deny it stung a little to hear it.

'Yes, I do. But don't worry about it, because he won't be what she needs forever. Right now, he's her safest option.'

'Safest option? Nat? Are you joking?'

For a moment, he saw a twinkle of amusement in her eyes and she looked like her old self again, then her face clouded, and he turned to see Derry standing in the doorway, wearing an odd expression. In his hand, he carried a piece of paper.

'Is something wrong?' Rhiannon moved towards him, but as was always the case lately, Derry veered away from her outstretched hand.

'I've got something to tell you. You won't like it.'

Will thought Derry's face had probably already told her that. As Rhiannon sat down again, Will cleared his throat. 'Well, I, er, I'll be getting off. Lots to do before our experts arrive.'

'No, don't go. You may as well hear this, *Sir William,*' said Derry.

Will frowned. He really didn't like his tone of voice.

'I just wanted you to know that I got hold of Grandfather's address and wrote to him. I wasn't sure he'd write back, not after all those things you said about him. You know, how he wouldn't want to know me.' Derry raised his hands as his mother began to protest. 'You said he didn't care about us, that he wasn't interested in meeting me. Funny that, 'cos he's just written back, and he's delighted to hear from me. He said he's been longing for the day when I get in touch with him.'

'What?' Rhiannon's voice sounded choked.

Will held his breath. There was no doubt in his mind that Rhiannon's father was playing some sort of game, probably aimed at causing the maximum amount of distress to his daughter. Her father had never taken to her, and had made that quite clear to her, which was why she'd left home and run to the widower of her late cousin, to a village that had resonated with her and made her feel at home and accepted. In all that time, her parents had never once asked to see her, or indeed the new grandson that she'd written to them about. Will couldn't understand an attitude like that. They hadn't even asked for a photograph of him.

Rhiannon had told him she was convinced that her mother would have liked to meet Derry but was too afraid of her husband's disapproval. Then it had grown too late, as she'd died some years ago without ever seeing her daughter again or meeting her grandson. The thought that her father was suddenly making some sort of pretence of caring would be a bitter blow for Rhiannon to take.

'Don't fall for this,' she told her son, her eyes wide with anxiety. 'You don't know what you're getting yourself into. What he's like.'

'You said he wouldn't want to know me,' accused Derry, 'but

here's the proof that you lied. I bet he always wanted to meet me, but you kept us apart to suit yourself.'

'I did no such thing! I never lied to you about him,' she protested.

'And why would I take your word for that? You're a liar, Mum. You've lied to me all my life. You betrayed your best friend. You've slept with just about every married man in the district. You even had sex with my own brother,' he added, sneering at a mortified Will. 'You have no morals whatsoever, yet you insist that it's my grandfather who's the bad one in all this? Unbelievable. I'm glad he's got in touch with me. I'm going to write back, and one day soon, I'll bet you anything you like that he invites me to meet him. Then I'll be gone, and there's nothing you can do to stop me.'

Her brown eyes filled with tears as he left the room, and Will's heart ached for her.

'He doesn't mean it. He's just angry,' he soothed, putting his arms around her.

She shook her head, her dark curls bouncing against his cheek. 'He's right. Every word he said was the truth,' she murmured. 'I never saw myself as a bad person before, but it's true.'

'Of course it isn't! You're just—'

'I thought I was doing the right thing, but I got everything wrong, didn't I? Now I'm losing my son because of it. How can I bear it, Will? He's the person I love most in the world. And, worst of all, it's all my own fault.'

Will held her gently, as her tears made scalding tracks down her face.

Chapter 13

Will was ridiculously nervous as he paced the room, awaiting the arrival of the three shortlisted candidates. Anyone would think he was the one being interviewed for the job. He glanced again at the sheet of paper in his hand. Debra Shaw, Reuben Latimer, and Darcey Hatch. All highly qualified, all experienced, all competent. At least on paper. He hoped he would be able to make the right choice.

He jumped at a hand on his shoulder, and the knot in his stomach tightened to an almost unbearable level as he turned and saw Lexi standing beside him.

'Don't look so worried.' She gave him a reassuring smile. 'You've done the right thing. From now on, you'll have someone to help, to share the burden. We'll get through this, Will, I'm sure of it.'

There she went again, talking about Kearton Hall as if it really mattered to her.

'Would you like to sit in on these interviews?' he asked impulsively.

Her mouth dropped open in surprise. 'Me? Why would you want me to sit in?'

'Yes, why *would* you want her to sit in?'

Will inwardly groaned as Nat appeared, looking formal in a smart, well-cut navy suit, shirt and tie. Will glanced down at his own attire. Perhaps he should have changed, but he hadn't wanted to make the interviewees too nervous. He wanted to keep things as informal and friendly as possible. He imagined that, if he was as anxious as he was, *they* must be terrified.

'I just thought, since she'll be working closely with whoever is chosen, it might be nice for her to have a say in who we pick.'

'Of course,' said Nat. 'How stupid of me. Let's go and round up Bernie, too, and Woody, and the cleaners, and the women who work in the shop, and—'

'Yeah, all right, Nat. I get the drift,' said Lexi, sounding cross. 'I'm just another member of staff. Don't worry.' She bobbed a curtsey to him. 'I know me place, guv. I'll be orf now.'

'You don't have to go,' said Will.

'Don't worry, master. I have a scullery to clean and bedpans to empty. I'll see you later.'

She stormed out of the room, and Will shook his head at Nat.

His cousin raised an eyebrow and shrugged. 'What?'

'You know what! Why do you have to be so rude to her?'

'Lexi knows the score. Look, she's a member of staff, just like the others, as she said. You can't let personal feelings get in the way of business.'

Woody entered the hall. 'The first applicant's here,' she announced. 'I've shown her into the sitting room. Where do you intend to interview?'

'The study,' said Nat firmly.

'Wouldn't the sitting room be friendlier?' said Will.

Nat gave an exasperated sigh. 'We're not trying to be friendly, Will. We're trying to find someone suitable to save your precious home. Remember? The study will be much more appropriate. There's that big desk we can both sit behind for a start. Makes it more official.'

Woody waited, looking steadfastly at Will and ignoring Nat. Will hesitated then nodded. 'Okay, Woody. Show them into the study in five minutes.'

'Very good,' she said, leaving the hall.

Nat looked him up and down. 'You could've dressed a bit smarter,' he said. 'Honestly, Will, don't let sentiment get in the way today. Follow my lead and don't fall for any flattery or sob stories. This is business. Remember?'

Will swallowed, and Nat shook his head.

'Fat chance,' he murmured. 'Tell you what, just leave it to me.'

****

'So, have you reached a decision?' Woody handed Will a cup of tea and settled herself down in the comfy armchair by the range.

Will glanced at Nat. 'They were three good candidates,' he said cautiously, stroking Buttons as the Labrador settled by his side. 'In terms of experience and qualifications, I couldn't fault them.'

Nat sipped his drink, then gave Will a wolfish grin. 'There was one outstanding candidate for me,' he said. 'At least, she had two rather prominent qualities to recommend her.'

'Oh?' Woody sounded curious. 'What were they, then?'

'You don't want to know, Woody,' Will assured her. He gave Nat a determined look. 'I'm not about to give someone a job just because she has — er — just because she's well-endowed in one area.'

'Huh?' Woody paused, her cup midway in the air.

'Stop being so bloody polite' Nat laughed. 'He means the lady in question had a rather large pair of breasts, Woody. Quite spectacular, in fact.'

She banged her cup on the table, spilling a little tea on the cloth, evidently too annoyed to notice. 'Disgusting, you are,' she said. 'Always lowering the tone. Honestly.'

Laughing again, Nat stood up. 'I'm off outside for a breath of fresh air. I'll leave you two to talk things over.'

He left the kitchen, and Will let out a sigh of relief.

'Well, you can't hire that one, that's for sure,' said Woody firmly.

'What? You mean the lady with — er, well … I can't rule her out, Woody, on that basis. That wouldn't be fair.'

'Suppose not. I guess it's not her fault that Nat can't see past her bra size. Still, it would make things a bit awkward. I mean, could you trust him to keep his hands off her? And what would young Lexi have to say, if she saw him lusting after her?'

Will could well imagine. It was irrelevant, anyway. He already knew which candidate he favoured. The trouble was, he didn't think Nat would agree.

Debra Shaw had been the first candidate they'd interviewed. Pretty, blonde, and immaculately made up, with breasts that entered the room before she did, she'd attracted Nat's attention immediately. Debra had a degree in history and experience in administration and was clearly enthusiastic about the Hall. However, in Will's mind, she was rather too optimistic and a bit naïve. She'd seemed awestruck by the house and kept pronouncing everything to be "wonderful" and "awesome", as they'd showed her some of the ground floor rooms. Will was concerned that she wasn't adequately prepared for the demands that would be made on her. The fact that Nat was practically drooling was neither here nor there. She wasn't the right candidate for the job, and that was that.

Reuben Latimer had seemed more practical and sensible. He'd had extensive management experience and was a businessman through and through. However, he had an annoying habit of interrupting Will and talking over him. He was also rather too confident. He'd seemed absolutely certain that he could turn Kearton Hall around and make it a glowing success. He appeared unmoved by the house or its contents, more interested in facts and figures than any historical or aesthetic factors, and Will had felt quite irritated by Reuben's distinct lack of admiration for his home. If Debra was too gushing about the place, Reuben had gone too far the other way.

All right, so he needed someone practical, but Kearton Hall wasn't just another business. It was far more than that, and Will didn't feel Reuben understood that. He also had to admit, if only to himself, that the man had been patronising to him, making him feel too young and too stupid to have his views taken seriously. He had a feeling that working with Mr Latimer would be a nightmare, with a real tug-of-war for control going on. He could imagine Nat punching the man before long, if they hired him. No, he was definitely out of the running.

Which left candidate number three, Darcey Hatch. Will smiled to himself. Like Baby Bear's porridge in the tale of Goldilocks, she was just right. He wondered how he could talk Nat into taking her on.

Woody was chopping carrots and Will was peeling potatoes when Nat walked back into the kitchen. In the corner by the range, Buttons snored gently in his basket.

'What the hell are you doing?' Nat shook his head. 'Honestly, Will. I give up with you. Can you imagine your father peeling spuds for dinner?'

Woody sniffed. 'I can't, and if he'd tried, he'd have got short shrift from me I can tell you. Thank God Will's nothing like him, and that's all I have to say on the matter.'

'Good.' Nat sat down at the table, ignoring her poisonous looks, and eyed Will curiously. 'Well? Have you come to any decisions?'

Will turned back to the potatoes. 'I have. But you're not going to like it.'

'I bloody knew it!' Nat stood and leaned on the draining board, as Will drew the knife across the potato, expertly taking off the peel with one continuous cut. 'You're going for the sob story, aren't you? Honestly, Will, you're so predictable. I mean, this is the best candidate for the job we're talking about here, not some bloody TV talent show contestant.'

'I'm perfectly well aware of that,' said Will, putting down the knife. 'And Darcey Hatch is the best candidate for the job.'

'Bollocks,' snarled Nat.

'Language,' warned Woody, before looking enquiringly at Will. 'Who is this woman? What makes her the right one?'

'Simple,' said Nat, before Will had a chance to say anything. 'She's a timid little mouse with a story to break your heart, and she's just the sort that Will can't resist.'

'Meaning?'

'Meaning if you think someone's had a rough time, you always want to step in and help.'

'Well, that's no bad thing,' said Woody.

'It is when it comes to business.'

'Nat, you've got this all wrong,' said Will. 'I admit, I felt for her when she said she'd lost her mother a few months ago, and that her father had left them years ago. I know how that feels. She's all alone, and I did feel sorry for her, of course I did. But the fact remains, she's sensible, practical, and more than capable of doing this job.' He turned to Woody. 'After college, she did an internship at a stately home in Devon, and then she moved on to work for ECHOES.'

'ECHOES?' Woody screwed up her nose. 'What's that?'

'Enterprise for the Conservation of Historic Old English Sites,' he said. 'They manage Helmston Castle, and many other old buildings in England. Darcey's worked at several, and she's also worked at head office. She's advised many owners over the last few years about making their country homes pay. She has a degree in art history, and qualifications in business studies and accounting, and she's just the right balance of being admiring of this house while, at the same time, recognising the work that has to be done. She understands we've a lot to do to get this right. I think she's perfect.'

'Who's perfect?'

Will turned and found Lexi standing by the table, munching on an apple as she eyed him with obvious curiosity.

'Darcey Hatch,' said Nat, before he could answer.

'So, you've made a decision then?'

Nat put his arm around her. 'It would seem so.'

She pushed him away, evidently still smarting from his earlier refusal to let her sit in on the interviews.

'You're not sulking, are you?' Nat's eyes widened. 'You know I didn't mean anything earlier. Just me being me.'

'Maybe I'm fed up with you being you,' she said, eyeing him in obvious annoyance. 'You shouldn't have spoken to me like that.'

'But it was the truth!' Nat appealed to Will. 'It was just business, wasn't it? Tell her, Will! It wouldn't be fair to Bernie, or Woody, if she'd been allowed to sit in on the interviews, just because she's shagging the boss's cousin, now would it?'

Will shook his head. 'Oh, no. You can leave me out of this one.'

Lexi sighed. 'I suppose you're right. But there are ways of saying things, Nat, and you haven't really mastered the art of tact, have you?'

He kissed her lightly on the cheek. 'Evidently not. Sorry. Still, it's all done and dusted now. We've picked our new House

Manager. At least, Will has, and he has the final say.' He shook his head, patently not convinced by the choice. 'He's quite smitten with her. I just hope he doesn't live to regret it.'

Chapter 14

Darcey Hatch accepted the post, and a starting date of October the first was agreed on.

For some reason, Nat couldn't wait for me to meet her. 'She's perfectly suited to Will,' he said. 'Talk about a match made in heaven.'

'What do you mean?' I asked, but Nat just grinned and told me I'd find out soon enough.

It had been decided that Darcey should have a room in the Hall, at least initially. If she wanted to rent somewhere nearby eventually, that would be up to her.

'If things work out,' mused Will, 'we could see about converting some of the rooms in the upper west wing into a flat for her. Then she could have some independence, while being on site.'

'Hmm. Very convenient,' Nat whispered. 'I'm telling you, Lexi, he's far too keen on her for my liking. Not sure it's a good idea, this. Still, what do I know?'

I felt distinctly uneasy. Nat had told me the woman's sob story — how she'd lost her mother a few months ago and had only a maiden aunt left in all the world — and Will was such a sucker for stuff like that. I'd have to watch him. More importantly, I'd have to watch her.

At last the day dawned, and Will seemed surprisingly nervous as he paced up and down, eyeing the clock, with Buttons trotting by his side.

I failed to quell my irritation as I watched them. 'What's up with you, for God's sake? So, you're getting a new member of staff. Do you pace up and down like this when we get a new gardener?'

'This is different,' he insisted.

'Why? Because she's female and vulnerable?' I snapped, aware that I sounded pathetic.

He looked taken aback. 'Because this is where it all begins, really. This is where we start to pull this place together. And if we fail this time, there's nowhere left to go.'

Sunk by a wave of sympathy and shame, I squeezed his arm. 'We won't fail, Will. You'll see. This house is going to be the biggest draw in North Yorkshire.'

He laughed. 'I sincerely doubt that, but thanks.'

I found myself smiling, my annoyance forgotten. 'Come on. Let's go and wait in the car park for her.'

We headed out through the main entrance, Buttons following behind, and waited at the foot of the steps, casting nervous glances down the drive and then laughing at each other for our cowardice.

Will nodded as a black hatchback drove through the arch under the gatehouse and up the drive. 'She's here.'

We waved her round to the side of the house, to the staff car park, where she pulled up. The car door opened, and she stepped out, carrying a briefcase and a bag.

Immediately, I saw what Nat had been talking about. Close to, she was quite young — maybe only in her early thirties — but someone had apparently convinced her she was at least sixty. She had brown hair pulled back into a tight bun, dark rimmed glasses, and was wearing a very sensible dark brown skirt and jacket, with flat brown brogues on her feet.

'She's like you,' I blurted out. 'She dresses about thirty years older than she actually is. You're a match made in heaven.' I remembered Nat saying those exact words, and for some reason, my laughter died.

'Sir William.' The woman held out her hand in greeting. 'How kind of you to meet me in person.'

Will shook her hand, a wide smile on his face. 'Not at all. Please, call me Will,' he insisted.

She gazed up at him, quite coyly. 'Really, I couldn't. It seems far too disrespectful.'

Bloody hell. She'd annoyed me already and she'd only been here five minutes. This was going to be fun. Not.

Look at her, simpering over him like that! It's disgusting. And she'd totally blanked Buttons, which said it all.

I cleared my throat, and Darcey noticed me at last.

'Hello. And you are?'

I waited, but Will seemed to have forgotten his manners, or lost his voice. I almost growled at her. 'Lexi Bailey. I work here.'

Darcey hesitated for a moment, then said coolly, 'Really. Doing what?'

'Well, mostly admin, at the moment, though I help out in the shop and café when needed. I'm currently researching the history of the family, so that Will and I can produce a booklet on the subject.'

'You're a historian? A writer?'

What was this? Was she interviewing me, or something? Bloody cheek. 'I've nearly finished my degree in Humanities, specialising in History and History of Art.'

'And when we open up the house full-time, I want her to be the main tour guide,' said Will. 'She's a very valuable member of the team.'

Darcey looked me up and down, then at Will. She didn't seem at all impressed, but she merely shrugged and said, 'Shall we go inside? It's rather chilly here.'

Will, of course, was contrite. 'I'm so sorry. Of course, please follow me. I'll get someone to collect your bags later.'

No you won't, Will, I thought. *You'll collect them yourself.*

I felt strangely angry with him. All sorts of warnings and alarms fired off rounds in my head, though I couldn't think why. There was something about the way she watched him, and something about the way she eyed me, too. I didn't trust her.

We led her to the front entrance where she stepped back, taking a good look at the house, surveying it all with a critical eye. I saw Will follow her gaze, and recognised that mixture of pride and love in his expression, one I experienced myself, whenever I took the time to gaze at the beautiful Elizabethan manor that was his home, and the place I was so proud to be a part of.

'So, here I am again,' said Darcey. 'Kearton Hall.'

'What do you think?' I asked, almost daring her to say anything derogatory.

Darcey said nothing for ages, simply staring at the Hall. I wondered what she was thinking.

Beside me, I felt Will quivering with nerves, and grew even more annoyed. I half hoped Darcey would be rude about the place. Maybe then he'd wise up and send her packing.

Eventually, Darcey spoke. 'It's beautiful,' she said.

Will beamed at her.

'Of course, it's not as large as I was expecting,' she continued. 'I was quite surprised on my last visit.'

'Jeez, how big's *your* house?' I demanded.

Darcey tutted. 'I meant in the scheme of things. It's hardly Castle Howard,' she explained, as if to a six-year-old. 'However, it appears to be in good condition, which is a bonus, although obviously, appearances can be deceptive. I'm sure we can knock this place into shape, but there'll be a lot of paring down to do in some areas, and investment in others. It's all about priorities.'

'Yes, well, that's what you're here for. Any advice and ideas you have would be most welcome.' Will smiled at her, and after a second's hesitation, she smiled back at him.

The change that smile made to her face was astounding, and I swallowed when I realised that she looked quite pretty.

'Would you like to step inside, and I'll ask Mrs Woodrow to make us some tea,' Will asked, holding out a hand in invitation.

'Thank you, Sir William. It's been a long journey. A cup of tea would be most appreciated.'

Will led her inside, with me trailing along behind them, feeling like a spare part.

Well, the whole introduction had started well. I was definitely going to have to watch her.

****

Will showed Darcey into the dining room, which was one of his favourite rooms in the Hall. It was in the north-east corner of the house, and in spite of its dark red walls had a light and airy feel, due to its large sash windows, one facing the north lawn with the woodland walk beyond, and one set in the bay, looking out across the east lawns and the ornamental pond. There was a rather lovely, informal feel to the room, despite the landscape portraits on the walls, the bronze statues of several long-dead dogs and horses of his ancestors, and the Chippendale furniture.

Leaving Will alone with the newcomer, Lexi went off, Buttons in tow, to inform Woody that their guest had arrived, and to ask for tea to be served in the dining room, as if it were an everyday occurrence.

Darcey took off her jacket and put her handbag and briefcase on the floor, then wandered around the dining room, examining the paintings with evident interest.

'Marlow?' she asked him, as she paused by a rather lovely landscape of Kearton Hall and lawns, dating from the eighteenth century.

Will nodded.

'Charming,' she said. 'This is a lovely room, Sir William. Is it open to the public?'

'No,' he said. 'It's never been part of the tour.'

'So, you live in this part of the house?'

Will shook his head. 'Not really. We tend to stay in the north side of the house. Our bedrooms, living quarters and kitchen are there. We've got offices and staff rooms in the west wing.'

'So, the south and the east side are open to visitors?'

'Well, some of the rooms. But there are a couple of rooms in the north side that we let them wander around, too. It's all a bit complicated to explain.'

'It sounds it,' she said. 'The first rule of opening your house to the public, in my experience, is to keep it simple. Make sure that your own living quarters are well off the beaten track and devise a simple route through the rooms you want to be seen. I don't suppose you have a floor plan of the house? It would make things so much clearer.'

'Of course. I have a tour map in my office. One moment. Ah, Lexi!' He half stood, then paused as Lexi came back into the room. 'Could you do me a favour? In my father's desk drawer, there's a tour map. Could you fetch it in? Darcey would like to see it.'

'No need,' Lexi said, pulling a folded piece of paper from her jeans pocket. 'I always keep one on me. Here you go.'

She handed the map to Darcey, who sat down and unfolded it, studying it carefully. Will and Lexi exchanged glances as she peered at it closely, shaking her head slightly, and tutting every now and then.

'Well, this won't do,' she said eventually. She looked up, her brow furrowed. 'This is far too complicated and messy. There's no real flow. No, we need to reorganise this straight away.'

Will joined her on the sofa. 'What do you suggest?' he said.

'Well,' she pointed out, 'the tour starts in the Great Hall, but then it shoots off in all sorts of awkward directions, and you've got visitors passing far too many rooms that are off limits to them. And really, if you're going to open the house, you need to give them a bit more value for money than this. A handful of rooms is hardly worth paying for, is it? You need a simple, straightforward walk around the house, which makes them believe they're seeing far more of the place than they really are but gives them more than they're currently being offered. Look, you say you live in the north side of the house, with the west wing used mostly for work purposes?'

Will nodded.

'Well, then, the east wing and south side of the house should be utilised to their full advantage. There should be rooms to visit on every floor but the attics. What condition are the attics in, by the way?'

'Not too good,' he admitted. 'At least, some of them. There's quite a bit of damp up there now.'

'Well, that has to be fixed immediately,' she said. 'No point sorting out the place if it's going to be riddled with mould before the winter's over. Obviously, I'll need to take a full tour of the house and see the rooms currently on display, get a feel for the route myself. However, as a general principle, do you see what we should be aiming for? Keep them well away from the north and west but position the tour so they don't realise they've missed out half the house. I think you said at the interview that you had around fifty staff here?'

'Er yes.' Will blinked. 'About that.'

'And what do they do?'

'Well, obviously, we have cleaners, gardeners, forestry staff, maintenance workers, tour guides, and people who work in the farm shop and the café. Then there's Woody and Bernie.'

'And they are?'

'Woody is our housekeeper and cook, and Bernie is our estate manager. You'll be liaising with the two of them quite a lot. Bernie's in charge of the tenancies and the outdoor staff, and Woody — well, she's in charge of just about everything else. Me included.'

She didn't smile. 'And how many of these people live in?'

Will wondered why it mattered. 'None. They all live in the villages nearby, except for Bernie. He lives in the cottage at the entrance to the lane. You'll have passed it on your way in. I'll take you there later and introduce you to him.'

'Are they all paid?'

'Well, no. We rely rather heavily on our wonderful volunteers. They turn their hand to all sorts, especially the gardens. We have several people who are more than happy to help out with the planting and weeding, and such. Our tour guides are volunteers, and we have a few who help out in the shop and café when needed. Why?'

'I'm just trying to get a picture of how this place works,' she said. 'Nothing to worry about. Standard practice.'

They all glanced up as the door opened and Nat strolled in. He stopped as his gaze landed on Darcey. 'Ah, you've arrived, then!'

She looked him up and down, not altogether politely. 'I'm sorry. I've quite forgotten your name.'

Will sensed trouble ahead. He felt quite relieved, although amazed, when Nat didn't seem offended.

'Nathaniel Boden-Kean,' he said cheerfully. 'Nat to my friends.'

He threw himself down on a chair next to Lexi, reached out a hand and squeezed hers. 'So, what do you think to the place then, Miss, er ...?'

'Hatch,' she said primly. She stared meaningfully at his hand, clasping Lexi's, and raised an eyebrow, but made no comment.

Will felt he should clarify the situation. 'As I think I explained at the interview, Darcey, Nat's my cousin. He and Lexi are...' He broke off, not sure what they were.

'Quite,' she said.

There was a silence for a moment, broken, to Will's relief, by Woody entering the room carrying a tray. She placed it on the occasional table and bobbed a curtsey to Will. 'There you go, Sir William,' she said, a definite gleam of mischief in her eye. 'If Sir requires anything else, please be sure to ring the bell, and I'll be here in two shakes of a lamb's tail.'

'Er, yes, thanks, Mrs Woodrow.' Will tried to hide the laughter in his voice. Curtseying, indeed! He'd be having words with her later.

'Are you going to be mother?' enquired Nat to Lexi.

'Sexist pig,' was her response, pretty much as Will had predicted it would be.

Darcey looked quite disgusted at the exchange, but Will poured the tea and gave her a cup before she could say anything. She didn't take sugar and she didn't take milk. She also refused one of Woody's chocolate brownies. Will could feel the disapproval radiating from Lexi and hoped she'd keep her opinions to herself, at least until Darcey had unpacked.

'So, apart from the tour,' said Darcey, after taking a sip of tea and demonstrating how to hold a cup with a little finger perked up in the air, much to Lexi's apparent — though thankfully silent — amusement, 'what else do you do here to raise funds?'

'Well…' Will leaned back on the sofa and began to relax a little. 'We have the farm shop. That does rather well. We sell produce from our own farm, and from the tenant farms. The organic fruit and vegetables from our gardens and orchard are especially popular. People like the idea of knowing where their food comes from. We supply other shops, as far afield as Whitby and

Helmston, with our produce now. It's really taking off.'

'Hmm. Anything else?'

'Well, as you know, the gardens and woodland are open to the public all year round, and we have a thriving café, which makes a good profit, particularly in the summer.'

'How often is the house actually open to the public?'

Will shifted uncomfortably. 'Well, the thing is, my father wasn't keen on having people in here, so it was all a bit difficult. We had to strike a delicate balance, and it wasn't an easy compromise, I'm afraid.'

'So?'

'We've been opening for one weekend every month, during the summer, from nine in the morning until four in the afternoon. The gardens are open every day.'

'Well, that's not good enough. I presume, now that you're in charge, the house will be opening every day?'

'Every day?'

'Absolutely. I would suggest opening times of eleven until five. That's ample. I wouldn't, however, recommend that you stay open all year round. Kearton Bay is beautiful, I'm sure, but these coastal places tend to be busy in the summer and dead in the winter. I would suggest going along with the season — perhaps opening from the end of March until the end of October. That will fulfil your obligations to the tax office. Besides, the house will need cleaning, and the furniture and paintings need to be covered and stored for the winter.'

'Right,' said Will, feeling as if he were on a runaway train. Whatever else Darcey Hatch was, she certainly had firm ideas and wasn't shy about expressing them.

'Except for Christmas, of course.'

'Christmas?'

'Of course. The Hall should be dressed for the festive season and open to guests. Just the ground floor rooms. And we should organise outdoor events, too. Perhaps a Christmas market and carol singers, a special Christmas menu in the café. That sort of thing. I would suggest opening from the middle of November until a couple of days before Christmas. That would give you around two weeks to decorate the place and get it ready. Obviously, it's too late this year. I'm talking about next Christmas. We have a lot to do before then.'

'Goodness,' murmured Will.

'Well, you seem to know your stuff,' said Nat, watching Darcey through narrowed eyes. 'But let's be honest here. Do you really think it's possible, in this day and age, to make a house this size pay for itself? I mean, wouldn't you, hand on heart, recommend selling it?'

'Selling it?' Darcey peered round at them all. 'Am I to understand there's some doubt about the intention of keeping this place running as a private home? If there's the possibility that it will be going up for sale in the near future, there seems little point in me being here.'

'Not at all,' said Will firmly. 'This house is not going up for sale, whatever Nat says.'

'Shut up causing trouble, Nat,' said Lexi.

'I'm not causing trouble,' he protested. 'I'm being realistic. This house costs a fortune to run, and there's always something needs repairing. I just don't know why you'd want to run yourself ragged trying to keep on top of it all, when you could sell the lot and live a life of luxury and peace of mind.'

'Because it's our home,' said Will wearily. 'And I never want to leave it. I'll never sell it, and that's that.'

Darcey put down her cup. 'You know, I've worked with many owners of houses like this one, Sir William. Would you allow me to speak frankly?'

'Of course,' said Will.

'I have to state, here and now, that not every house can be saved. Of course, ECHOES does sterling work, doing its best to help in any way it can, as do other similar organisations, but they don't have a magic wand. Even the National Trust has to refuse to take on some properties, after all. There are limited finances, and this country is littered with stately homes, castles, abbeys and suchlike. Working with ECHOES, I realised that even they don't have all the answers.'

'What are you saying?' Will looked dazed.

'What I'm saying is that, although I'll do everything I can, there are no guarantees. If you do have other options, it would be wrong of me to try to persuade you not to take them.'

'Options?'

'Yes. This house is in a very picturesque location. It would make a wonderful hotel. I'm sure there are several companies who'd be willing to take it off your hands.'

'Are you serious?'

'I am. I worked for ECHOES for long enough to know that, in this line of work, you have to consider every possibility. The truth is, Sir William, your priority is to preserve this building. You may think that turning it into a hotel won't do that, but I've found, during the course of my career, that these conversions are done extremely sympathetically. As a Grade One listed building, the beautiful features in this house would be kept intact, and there would be money for any repairs needed. You might not live here in the future, but Kearton Hall would be cared for. Isn't that what you really want, most of all?'

Will felt bewildered. He glanced across at Lexi, who was gaping at Darcey. She glanced at him, then seemed to realise her mouth was open and snapped it shut. She looked as shocked as he felt. This wasn't what he'd been hoping for at all.

'I — I can't sell this house,' he managed eventually. 'And I can't let it be turned into a hotel. I just can't. It's out of the question. I won't sell up. Frankly, Darcey, I'm astonished. You appear to be trying to talk yourself out of a job before you've even started.'

'Not at all,' she said. 'I merely think there are far more important things at stake than my career. I can get a job elsewhere. My skills and experience are always in demand. I could even go back to ECHOES, if I wished.'

'Why did you leave in the first place?' Lexi asked, her voice heavy with suspicion.

A shadow flitted across Darcey's face. 'My mother became very ill. I knew I'd have to be there for her, and caring for her interfered with my work. I didn't feel able to give my job the commitment it deserved, so I resigned. Unfortunately, my mother passed away some months later, and after a period of adjustment, I decided it was time for me to make a fresh start. That's why I didn't try to return to my old job. Sometimes, we need to move on, don't you think?'

There was an uncomfortable silence as they all considered her words. Will thought how well Darcey was handling the awful events that had happened to her. There was no trace of self-pity in her voice. He rather admired that. Even so…

'Well, I'm sorry, but I won't be moving on from here. It's out of the question. Perhaps you'd like me to show you to your room?' he said, smiling pleasantly at her in the hope that she wouldn't take offence at his refusal to engage with her ideas.

'Certainly,' she said, standing and collecting her things. 'I would rather like to freshen up. It was a long journey.'

Will led her from the dining room, his heart heavy. However far Darcey had come, he knew that the journey to save Kearton Hall was going to be much longer.

Chapter 15

The dreaded day had arrived. As Nat's car swept up the drive of White Rose Riding School, I felt as if my stomach was trying to crawl out of my mouth. 'You didn't have to come, you know,' I said. 'I could have managed on my own.'

'But I'm dying to see you on a horse,' he insisted. 'And, for God's sake, try to look a bit more cheerful. Anyone would think you were on your way to the Tower. Riding is fun, you know. It's not a method of torture.'

'So you say,' I said, far from convinced.

We pulled up in the car park and I climbed out, feeling shaky and sick. Georgia came to meet us almost instantly, so I guessed she'd been watching out for my arrival.

'How are you feeling?' she asked. 'Nervous?'

'Yeah, you could say that,' I mumbled, hoping she wouldn't see my hands trembling.

'You'll be fine. I'm putting you on Macduff. He's lovely, and kind to beginners. Come on. Let's find you a hat.'

'Nice to see you again, too,' called Nat, as she led me towards the stables.

She looked round. 'Oh, yeah. Hello,' she called over her shoulder, not stopping.

'You could be a bit more polite to him,' I said, as we entered the tack room.

Georgia wandered over to a large cupboard against the far wall, where she kept a selection of hard hats. 'Sorry.' She pulled out a handful and studied them critically. 'I do try, but he's not easy to like, is he? Here, try this one.'

I did as she said, then clenched my fists tightly as, after adjusting the strap, she pronounced me ready to go. 'Come on, let's get Macduff. He's all tacked up and ready.'

'I'm not sure about this,' I said faintly, as she led what looked like a very big, very hairy, grey horse out into the yard.

'About what? Do you want to learn to ride or not, because if you don't—'

'Of course she does.' Nat stood beside us, eyeing the horse critically. 'Is he a Highland?'

'He is, and very reliable. She'll be fine on him.'

'I'm sure she will. Go on, then, Lexi, get up.'

'Give her a chance,' snapped Georgia.

I put my foot in the stirrup, and Nat shook his head, pulling on my shoulder. 'Not like that. You're facing the wrong way.'

'Who's teaching her — me or you?' demanded Georgia. 'Look, let's go over to the mounting block. It will be easier.'

'The mounting block? How feeble,' said Nat.

'If you don't shut up, I'll make you go home,' Georgia said. 'You're putting her off.'

'I'm terribly sorry, headmistress. Are you going to spank me?'

I managed to lead Macduff to the mounting block, but when I looked round for help, they were standing right where I'd left them, still bickering. For God's sake, didn't I have enough to worry about?

'Sorry to interrupt,' I called, 'but can you pay attention to me, please? You're leaving me in charge of a lethal weapon, so the least you can do is supervise.'

'Sorry,' said Georgia. She glared at Nat. 'You go and sit on the fence,' she instructed. 'I need to concentrate on Lexi. I don't need your sarcastic comments distracting us.'

He grinned. 'You're awfully feisty for someone so small,' he said. 'You have a mighty big attitude wrapped up in that pocket-sized body.'

'Yes, well, I'm full of surprises.'

'I reckon you are, too. I heard good things came in small

packages. I've never believed that, myself, and neither have my girlfriends.'

I scowled at him, when he winked at me. 'Will you just shut up and go away? I'm trying to climb on this horse, in case you hadn't noticed.'

'He's a pony,' said Nat.

'Bugger off,' said Georgia, 'or I swear you'll be banned from this establishment.'

'Heaven forbid,' said Nat. 'All right, all right, I'll go and sit on the fence over there. Good luck, Lexi. Break a leg. Not literally, of course.'

That time, we both glared at him, and he sauntered off, leaving us to it. I wished he'd never come with me.

Somehow, more by luck than judgement, I managed to climb onto Macduff's back, and sat trembling as I tried to take in what Georgia was telling me.

Pandora appeared out of one of the looseboxes, and she raised an arm and waved, an encouraging smile on her face.

And so my lesson began.

Twenty minutes later, I had sweat pouring down my face, my legs ached, I had cramp in my hands, and I was getting a headache.

'Sit well down, Lexi. Use your seat, your seat! Don't pull at the reins, you're sawing his mouth. Relax!'

Relax? Fat chance. It was taking every ounce of determination I possessed not to throw my arms around the pony's neck and cling on for dear life. It didn't help that Georgia was being highly critical. I'd seen her with youngsters loads of times, and she'd always been very kind and patient with them. For some reason, she seemed to expect that I'd be able to do what she told me instantly and was displaying uncharacteristic intolerance.

Even Pandora seemed to notice. She leaned on the fence, frowning as Georgia barked instructions at me. 'Blimey, Georgia, give her a break. It's her first time in the saddle, remember? Are you trying to scare her off completely? Get her on a leading rein.'

'She's not six,' snapped Georgia.

Pandora gave her a filthy look and strolled into the paddock.

'You okay, Lexi?' she asked, taking hold of Macduff's reins and slowing me to a halt.

I nodded shakily.

Nat called across to me from his spot on the top bar of the fence. 'What have you stopped for? Don't be pathetic.'

'What's wrong with you two?' demanded Pandora. 'Can't you remember your first riding lesson? What it felt like?'

'Christ, no,' said Nat. 'I was only three. Can't remember a time I didn't ride. What about you, Georgie?'

'*Georgia*,' she snapped. 'I was about six, I think. I just remember being really excited and having the time of my life.'

'You're a natural born rider, like me,' said Nat. 'Some of us have it, some of us don't.'

Georgia walked over to me. 'Sorry, Lexi,' she said, avoiding looking at me. 'I've been a total cow today.'

'Yeah,' said Pandora, watching her curiously. 'You have. What's up with you?'

'I just don't feel very well. Probably a bad idea to teach you any more today. Maybe we should leave it 'til Friday.'

'You're not serious?' Nat strolled up and patted the horse's neck. 'Can't you take over?' he asked Pan.

'Got a riding lesson booked in five minutes,' she said. 'Anyway, I think Lexi's had enough for now. Friday will be fine.'

'Well, I never thought she'd be so useless,' said Nat. He glanced at his watch. 'Twenty minutes! Christ, I hope she's getting a serious discount.'

'Why don't you just shut up?' demanded Georgia. 'Honestly, you never stop, do you? Why are you even here? Haven't you got a life of your own?'

He grinned. 'Maybe I wanted to be here,' he said. 'Are you seriously going to send me away? You can try.'

Pandora turned my horse towards the gate. 'I don't know what's got into you today, Georgia, but I think maybe you should take half an hour and get yourself together. I'll see to Macduff, even though it does mean I'll be late for Roger Wilson.'

'Goodness, you don't want to be late for a roger,' Nat said, laughing.

Pandora gave him a withering look and began to lead me back to the stable yard.

Risking a glance back over my shoulder, I saw Nat and Georgia arguing. Georgia's face was pinched and white. She obviously wasn't well, and Nat was just being his usual obnoxious self, winding her up, which didn't help.

As I sighed, Pandora squinted up at me. 'Don't let it put you off,' she said. 'I don't know what's up with her today, but usually she's good at this. I'll take your next lesson, if you like.'

'It would only make her feel worse,' I said. 'I can do this, Pan. I'll be back on Friday.'

Although it occurred to me that, come Friday, if I had another lesson like this one, I doubted I'd go anywhere near a horse again, and sod what Nat thought.

****

Darcey settled in so quickly it was as if she'd always been there. Before we knew it, she'd completely taken charge. She spent the first few days making sure she was introduced to all members of staff, finding out their names and the exact nature of their work. She went on a full tour of the Hall — and I mean a full tour. No rooms were off limits to Darcey, it seemed, as Will accompanied her to parts of the house that even I'd never seen. She took lots of photographs, demanded to see the current inventory, viewed the archives, and made loads of notes. She seemed to have a clipboard clutched permanently to her chest. Within days, she'd planned a whole new route around the house, and had decided which rooms would be used for what purposes.

Two rooms on the first floor of the east wing, which had originally been part of a guest suite, but had been used as little more than storage space in recent years, would once more be dressed as bedrooms. She'd seen two ancient four-poster beds in the upper north side of the house and wanted them moving to those rooms. One room would be the gentleman's bedroom, dressed in a very masculine fashion. The other, a lighter room, owing to it having a double aspect over both the east and south lawns, would be a lady's bedroom. The two were connected by third room, which would become a dressing room.

She wanted a room dedicated to the Keartons, and another to the Boden-Keans. She and Will talked for hours about what he wanted for the tour. He didn't want 'Keep Off' signs and hushed tones, but a welcoming, homely atmosphere, where visitors could relax and take photos if they wished. Darcey suggested dotting family photographs around the rooms, to give it a more homely feel, and dressing one or two of the rooms, to show that they were very much in use still, and not just show rooms full of museum pieces. She also suggested a room where visitors could sit and catch their breath, perhaps read, or simply admire the paintings on the walls. She thought a room with a sea view would be best for that purpose, so they could also look out of the windows and take in the stunning scenery.

She spent ages talking to Bernie, getting a feel for what went on in the estate as a whole. He seemed quite impressed with her and told Will he'd made a good choice, which just showed what a crap judge of character he was.

It didn't take long before she'd forgotten all about calling him Sir William, and was soon referring to him as Will, just like the rest of us — something that clearly delighted him.

I walked in on them one day, discussing Will's ancestor, James Boden-Kean, Sixth Baronet and apparent smuggler, and she was positively gushing.

'Oh, Will, that's fascinating.' 'That would make such a good feature for the tour, Will.' 'Oh, Will, you're so right! We *must* find out more about him.'

Yuk.

Evidently, Will couldn't see through her phony charms, and they headed out to Kearton Bay together, to visit the old Lifeboat Museum, which housed a whole lot of information about the village's smuggling history. Apparently, there was an awful lot to see, because they were gone the entire day.

When I clapped eyes on her the following morning, I couldn't believe what I was seeing.

'Darcey?'

Was that really her? She looked like a different person. Her hair, which had always been scraped back in a bun, was a shiny reddish-brown colour and cut into a trendy bob. She was wearing makeup — makeup! And her plain brown skirt, flat shoes and shapeless jumper had been replaced with a black pencil skirt, fitted red top, black tights and court shoes. As she picked up her beloved clipboard, I noticed she was sporting long red nails, too.

What the hell had happened to her?

'Do you like it?' she said, smiling. 'We had a lovely morning in Kearton Bay then, after lunch at The Kearton Arms, Will asked if I minded him visiting some friend of his in the village for an hour. I didn't mind, at all, because I'd spotted the hairdresser's and thought I could spend the time getting my hair trimmed. The hairdresser was so kind, and so enthusiastic. She told me I wasn't making the most of myself, and we had a lovely long chat. The upshot was, when Will finally came to collect me, over two hours later, and full of apologies I might add, I had a new colour on my hair, a new cut, and some wonderful new nails. Will thought I deserved a complete makeover, so he drove me to Helmston, and I got some new clothes and some makeup. I must say, I feel like a new woman.'

Bloody Denise! I'd kill her. Why couldn't she just stick to trimming hair? No one was safe when they walked through the door of Klassy Kutz. She'd unleashed a monster.

'Very nice,' I said. 'Which friend was Will visiting?' I asked, though I knew the answer before she'd even given it.

'I don't know, but I believe he said they lived in a pub in the village,' she said, holding out her hand to admire her new claws. 'This all feels very strange. I hope I can type with these.'

If not, I'm sure you can cast a bloody spell on the computer, I thought bitterly.

Nat was right. With all the women gushing round him, Will would be able to start a harem soon at the rate he was going.

Why else would Darcey change her appearance?

And what was he visiting Rhiannon for? As if I couldn't guess. *Comforting* her, no doubt.

Ugh.

'What the fuck's happened to Miss Tweedy?' demanded Nat, as Darcey trotted off down the corridor looking about ten years younger than she had the previous day.

'Your cousin,' I said sulkily.

His eyes widened. 'No! You don't think she's—' He gave a whoop of laughter. 'I wonder if it's reciprocated. My God, do you think they've done the deed? What a laugh. That means Will's slept with two women in his life.'

'Of course they haven't *done the deed*,' I snapped. 'She's quite obviously set her sights on him, though. She positively simpers around him.'

He shook his head. 'Fuck it, let them get on with it,' he said. 'At least she's closer to his own age group than the witch. And I reckon she's still a virgin, so that's got to be an improvement.'

I decided it was probably wiser not to mention Will's visit to The Hare and Moon the previous day. As I headed back to work, I wondered which one of them would win the battle for Will's heart — the witch, or the enchantress. I almost felt sorry for him.

Chapter 16

As I entered twelve Tippet's Yard that evening, I'd never felt so glad to be home. It had been a busy day at work. Although the house was closed, the gardens and woodland walk remained open, and the farm shop and café were fairly busy, thanks to the mild early October weather. People were already placing orders for Christmas, wanting to splash out on organic meat and preserves from the shop, and in the café, Woody's cakes were going down a treat with a mug of hot chocolate to accompany them. Many people had asked when the Hall would be reopening, and I'd told them that, come the spring, the house would be open every day, and they would be able to enjoy a much improved experience, thanks to the hard work that was currently being undertaken by our enthusiastic team.

When I'd headed indoors during my lunch break, it'd been to find chaos in the Great Hall, as Will and Nat argued about the chosen route, and which rooms should be included in the tour, and what paintings should go where. Darcey was telling Nat that the decision had already been made — which didn't go down too well with him — and barking orders at several disgruntled-looking workmen, who appeared heartily sick of being told conflicting things, as Nat immediately contradicted everything she said. There seemed to be a definite bad atmosphere between the two of them. No doubt, Nat had been winding her up, and poor Will had been stuck in the middle of it all.

Frankly, Kearton Hall was currently a stressful place to be, so the cottage had become a sanctuary, and I heaved a sigh of relief as I closed the front door behind me and kicked off my boots. I could smell something cooking in the oven and heard voices in the kitchen. At first, I thought it was the radio, but then I realised it was Dad and Eliza — and they were arguing. So much for sanctuary.

I pushed open the kitchen door and they stopped rowing immediately.

'Good day, Lexi?' Dad put the kettle on and tried for a smile, but his mouth was tight, and Eliza's face was scarlet.

'Okay,' I said, 'drop the act. What's happened?'

'Happened? Nothing's happened. Why?'

'Because I heard you rowing just now, that's why. What's going on?'

'You're imagining things.'

'Don't do that,' I said. 'Don't pretend that everything's fine, when I know damn well it isn't. I'm not deaf, blind, or stupid. I heard you when I came in, and I can see just by looking at you that it's daggers drawn again.'

'Again? What are you talking about?'

'Do you seriously think I haven't picked up on the tension between you both lately? Or the fact that you hardly spend any time together any more? Or how bloody miserable you both look? Stop treating me like a kid.'

They both seemed embarrassed, as well they might.

I suddenly needed some air. 'Forget it. Leave my tea in the oven, will you? I have to go out.'

'But you've just come in,' protested Dad.

'Yeah, well, I've just remembered something I meant to do. I'll be back later.'

I didn't give them chance to argue about it. I left the cottage and began to run, heading out of Tippet's Yard and along King's Row in the darkness, my lungs straining as I sped up the steep hill, refusing to slow down. As I turned into Water's Edge, I stopped and bent over, taking deep breaths.

I didn't know what to do. I didn't want to be at home, and there was no one to talk things over with. All my usual confidantes had become part of the problem. Georgia was being a real pain in the neck, Dad and Eliza were a mess, and as for Will … I shook my head gloomily. Bloody hell, what a situation to be in. Even Rhiannon was out of the question those days. Even if I could get past the fact that she'd slept with Will — and I wasn't sure I could, at least not yet — she had enough worries of her own. Derry was being completely obnoxious towards her, and he wasn't much better with me. He was no fun to be around, so I certainly wasn't going near The Hare and Moon.

I found myself walking along Water's Edge, then headed up Bay Street. I didn't really think about what I was doing. My legs just seemed to carry me forward, as if my body knew where it wanted to be before my mind caught up.

So busy thinking about the mess that my life was in, it was a while before I took any notice of my surroundings and finally realised where I was. Clover Lane. I was heading to Whisperwood Farm, the place where I'd once worked when it'd been owned by Hannah, Eliza's grandmother.

I missed Hannah. She'd been so sensible and practical, full of advice, and always ready with a hug. She would have known what to do. She'd have told me in no uncertain terms. I could almost hear her voice.

Stop being so daft and sort yourself out. Get rid of that jumped-up waste of space and pay attention to the real treasure before it's too late.

Real treasure? Where had that come from?

I frowned as I remembered Rhiannon telling me to seek out the real treasure, and to always keep a clear head. Well, right now my head was far from clear. I felt as if I were knitting fog. Something was nagging away at me, but I didn't want to listen.

Eddie, who kept his donkeys at the farm, had left for the night, and I headed to the paddock behind the barn to visit my old donkey pals, wishing I had Polos. I rubbed Blackberry's nose, as the little donkey came over to see me, and apologised for having nothing to give him.

'What's wrong, Lexi?'

I jumped at Joe's voice right beside me.

He gave me a sympathetic smile and put his arm around me.

'What's happened?'

'Nothing. I just thought I'd come up to see the donkeys.'

'Then why are you crying?'

'I'm not!' But I found I was, and as I lifted a hand to wipe away a tear, I launched myself into the haven of Joe's arms and cried pathetically on his chest.

Well, how humiliating. How could I ever look him in the face again?

Joe let me cry, making soothing noises until I stopped my undignified sobbing and pulled away from him, apologising for my embarrassing behaviour.

'Don't be so daft. Come on. Nice cup of tea's what you need. Let's put the kettle on, shall we?'

It was so much the sort of thing that Hannah would say that I found myself crying again.

Joe sighed. 'Blimey. I can do coffee, if it upsets you that much.' I gave a snort of laughter, and he grinned. 'Best get inside and get you some tissue, an' all. Come on, Charlie will be delighted to see you. He was only saying this morning how we hardly see our little Gingernut these days.'

'Charlie can bugger off,' I said, but I smiled. *Bloody Gingernut.*

Charlie *was* thrilled to see me, but his smile faded when he saw the state of me. 'Aw, what's wrong, darlin'? Come in and tell your Auntie Charlie all about it.'

'I feel stupid,' I moaned, letting myself be led into the living room, where Honoria Glossop, Joe's Yorkshire terrier puppy, was curled up in an armchair, and Charlie's cat, Lady Gaga, lay on the windowsill, luxuriating in the heat from the radiator below.

'What for?' he asked. 'Everyone needs a good cry sometimes. What's happened?'

While Joe made tea, I stroked Honoria Glossop and tried to compose myself. 'Everything's such a mess,' I told Charlie.

'Is it? What, *everything*? Blimey.' Leaning toward the open doorway, Charlie yelled through into the kitchen, 'Best bring that chocolate cake in, Joe. This could be a long night.'

'I'm sorry,' I said. 'I didn't intend to come in. I didn't even mean to come to the farm. I just found myself walking in this direction, and then Joe saw me, and, well, that was that.'

'Good job he was out there, feeding Jeeves and Wooster then,' said Charlie, referring to Joe's beloved micro pigs. 'Look, love, I dunno what's wrong, but don't you ever apologise for coming here. We love to see you. You're family.'

Joe carried in tea and cake. 'Absolutely right. Now, why don't you start at the beginning and tell us what's upset you?'

I shrugged. 'Like I said. Everything.'

'Well, that's pretty bad, I'll give you that,' he acknowledged. 'Best start with the thing that tipped you over, eh?'

So, between mouthfuls of chocolate cake, and gulps of tea, I explained about Dad and Eliza, and their apparent rift.

'They've been snappy with each other for a while. They never go out together any more, and I know that things in the bedroom aren't great, because Eliza told me. They were rowing again tonight, and they wouldn't tell me what it was about, and I'd just had enough. For all I know, they're already planning to separate.'

'Jumping the gun a bit there, love. Every couple goes through bad times,' said Charlie. 'Even me and Joe have been known to bicker.'

'I know that,' I said. 'And I suppose, deep down, I never expected it to last, anyway. It's just the waiting for it to end that's so hard.'

'What do you mean, you never expected it to last?' Joe laughed. 'Your dad and Eliza? Rock solid, those two.'

I shook my head. 'You haven't seen them together lately.'

'Yes I have. I saw them this lunchtime. If it's any help, I think I know why they were rowing.'

'Really? Why?'

'Mrs Lovelace made an offer for the cottage. Twenty grand under the asking price, but she's a cash buyer, and the sale would go through quickly.'

I was appalled. Mrs Lovelace already owned five cottages in Kearton Bay, and they were all used as holiday rentals. A few years ago, she'd turfed Dad and me out of our rented cottage because she knew she could make more from holidaymakers.

Dad despised her, and everything she stood for.

'There's no way Dad would sell to her.'

'Exactly. Thing is, Eliza was all for it.'

'What? But Eliza wouldn't want the cottage turned into a holiday let, surely?'

'Normally, no. But then, it's not normal times, is it? She's extremely emotional at the moment, and then there's the other problem.'

'What problem?'

'Well, she's found a house she wants, but your dad's totally against it, isn't he?'

'What? Where?'

'Don't you know? It's on the Farthingdale border. New build, very grand. All mod cons, loads of space, and twice the price of the cottage.'

'Jeez,' I said, stunned, 'how come I didn't know about this?'

'No idea. She's been going on about it for a few days. That's why she wants a quick sale, in case she loses the house. But your dad thinks it's too expensive. Even with the money from the cottage, it would mean a hefty mortgage, and he's very reluctant to take it on.'

'Well, of course he is!' I shuddered at the memory of the debt my mother had left us in, and how hard he'd worked to clear it off. 'He's already had to sell one house. Do you think he's going to risk that again? He's very careful about money, and no bloody wonder. If you'd lived with my mother, you'd understand. It will remind him of her.'

'Yes, well.' Joe shifted, looking uncomfortable. 'Unfortunately, that's what he said. Practically accused her of turning into Zoe. You can imagine how well that went down.'

'Oh no.' I lowered the plate of cake I was holding and put my head in my hands. Honoria Glossop nudged my face with her wet nose and peered up at me, evidently alarmed at my despair.

'Look, Lexi, I know they're going through a rough time of it at the moment, but it *will* pass. Honestly.'

'How can you say that?' I blinked away the tears momentarily blinding me. Really, I was getting too embarrassing for words.

Nat was quite right: I was becoming totally feeble. 'I can see the way this is heading, and I don't know what to do. Dad's not going to be able to pick up the pieces this time. He must be in bits. How am I going to get him through it all again?'

Charlie and Joe glanced at each other, and then back at me. 'Seems to me you've got yourself in a bit of a tizz,' said Charlie. 'Look, love, I can see that what happened between your mum and dad was really horrible, and obviously it's affected you badly, but Eliza's not your mum, and it's a very different relationship.'

'I used to think that,' I said, sniffing, 'until the twins came along.'

'Well, there you go,' said Joe. 'Babies are tough to cope with, and two are even harder. Eliza's tired, your dad's tired, they need a bigger house, the babies are crying all the time, your dad's got problems at work—'

'Has he?' It was the first I'd heard of it. 'What problems?'

'I dunno. Something about changes in funding and cash flow problems. He wanted to get a locum in so that he could spend more time helping out at home for a bit, but they can't afford it at the moment. It's all a bit stressful, and it's come at the wrong time.'

I felt hot with shame. Why didn't I know what was going on in my own father's life? When had I become so selfish?

Joe smiled at me. 'Don't go blaming yourself. You've got a lot on at work, and you've been doing your best to help. Eliza told me about you taking the kids to Kearton Hall to give her a break. She was really touched. How did it go?'

'It went really well.' I gave Honoria a reassuring pat, and she settled back on my lap with a contented sigh. 'Amy had a ride on Frosty, and the twins were quite good all day, and we all went for a walk in the afternoon and fed the ducks on the lake. Amy loved it.'

'Who's all?'

'Well, me, Will, and the kids,' I said.

They glanced at each other again. 'Nice,' said Charlie. 'What about Nat?'

'He had to go out,' I said, not meeting their eyes.

'What a shame,' said Joe, in a tone of voice that said he thought it was far from a shame. 'So, you and Will babysat the kids all by yourselves, eh? Did you enjoy it?'

'Yeah, it was okay.' I didn't want to talk about it. I took a bite of cake and chewed determinedly.

'I love Will, he's ever so friendly,' said Charlie. 'How's it going with this new woman you've got staying there?'

I nearly choked on my cake as I swallowed. 'Darcey Hatch,' I growled. 'It's going very well. In fact, they're besties. It's all happened very suddenly.'

'Really?' I'm almost sure Joe suppressed a smile. 'He was quite nervous about her, wasn't he? They get on then?'

'Get on? They're inseparable. She fawns over him like a groupie. It's pathetic. And all that guff she gave him about only calling him Sir William — well, that's gone out of the window. Now it's *Will this*, and *Will that*. And she looks like she's just rolled in from Hollywood.'

'Eh?' Charlie seemed puzzled. 'But Will said she was the old-fashioned type.'

'Yeah, that was her cunning disguise,' I said. 'When she got here, she was all buttoned up and proper, but first she caved in and began calling him Will, and then she started laughing and joking with him, and cooing over his ancestors, and telling him how interesting they were, which is an outrageous lie 'cos they're dull as ditch-water, and then she buggered off to Klassy Kutz and came back looking like a page three model. God knows what Denise said to persuade her, but she's dyed, bobbed, and has nails like frigging eagle claws. It's pathetic.' Wasn't it just! The more I thought about it, the angrier I felt. She must have done it for a reason, and I'd put money on what that reason was.

'Really?' Joe sipped his tea thoughtfully. 'When did this happen?'

'A few days ago,' I muttered.

'Strange,' said Joe, 'because I met her this morning when I went to the farm shop. Will introduced me to her. I have to say, I don't recognise her from your description, at all.'

'What do you mean by that?' I said indignantly.

'Well, all this page three model stuff. She's just an ordinary looking girl with a brown bob and a bit of makeup. And eagle claws? Her nails are no longer than yours. If you wore red nail varnish, they'd probably look exactly the same.'

'You must be blind,' I said, astonished that he didn't see Darcey's obvious attempts to dazzle Will with her stunning makeover.

'Well, one of us is, clearly,' said Joe, with a decided smirk on his face.

Charlie watched me with a mischievous gleam in his eyes. 'And what does Will make of this transformation?'

'Huh, he loves it,' I said bitterly. 'Keeps telling me how intelligent she is, how much she understands the problems, what brilliant ideas she's coming up with. I mean, I could have come up with those ideas myself. Opening the house seven days a week, changing the tour route. Big deal.'

'Well, why didn't you say so then?' asked Joe, not entirely unreasonably.

'Because I thought they were *too* obvious,' I lied. 'Thought Will was bound to have already thought of those. Surely, she can do better than that? She's banging on about the stupid Sixth Baronet, too.'

'Who's he when he's at home?'

'Apparently, he was involved in the smuggling round here,' I said. 'In fact, Darcey's convinced he was one of the ringleaders. Says it's been documented somewhere. She's trying to find out more.'

'Ooh, that sounds exciting,' said Charlie.

'She wants to focus on him as a draw for the house,' I said. 'It's stupid. Even if he did turn out to be involved, so what? Round here, everyone was involved. Smuggling is old hat.'

'But you *do* need an interesting ancestor to draw people to the Hall,' said Joe. 'And it may be old hat round here, but many people from further afield are fascinated by smuggling history. It could help to bring a lot more tourists in.'

'That's what *she* said,' I muttered.

'Sounds very sensible to me,' said Charlie.

I decided they either understood nothing, or were going out of their way to annoy me.

'What about Nat?' Joe asked.

'What about him?'

'Well, how are things between you and him? Is it serious?'

'Of course it's not serious. Honestly, I don't know why people always ask that question. Haven't I said, over and over again, that I don't do serious?'

'Well, yes, but I thought maybe you'd made an exception in his case.'

'Why would I?'

'Because it seems to me that you don't have an awful lot in common, and given that you don't socialise together, and he hasn't even been to formally meet your father, or anyone else for that matter, and couldn't even be bothered to hang out with your siblings for a day, I figured that there must be something that keeps you seeing him. Like love, maybe?'

I pulled a face. 'No. I don't love him, and he certainly doesn't love me.'

'Then, why are you seeing him?' Charlie sounded baffled. 'I don't get it. I ain't being funny, Lexi, but he ain't the most likeable chap, is he? I mean, he's all right to look at, if you like that sort of thing, but there doesn't seem to be much else to him.'

'He's a charmer,' said Joe. 'He can make women fall for him and believe anything he tells them.'

I considered Joe's description of Nat for a moment. 'I guess he is,' I said, remembering how easily I'd fallen into bed with him, and how I'd succumbed that night at The Fox and Hounds. 'He knows what to say, and he knows which buttons to press.' I found myself blushing.

'Ah,' said Charlie. 'I get the attraction now.'

'No, it's not just that!' I didn't want them to get the wrong idea.

Charlie frowned. 'So, what is it? I don't get it.'

I shrugged. How to explain? Most of the time I didn't get it, either. Nat was good in bed, there was no doubt about it, but truthfully, he didn't have a lot else going for him. But then, what else did I want?

'I suppose I'd better be going,' I said, standing up and collecting my cup and plate. 'Thank you ever so much for listening. I'm sorry if I interrupted your evening together.'

'Not at all. You come round any time you like,' said Joe. 'I'll be glad of the company, truth to tell. Charlie's heading to London in a few weeks, and he'll be away, on and off, until Christmas.' Charlie was a stand-up comedian, and hugely popular. His tours always sold out, and his chat show was regularly top of the ratings. 'So, it'll be nice to have someone here. Will pops round quite a lot, but he's been busier lately.'

'Will does?' I was surprised. 'He never said. Why does he come here?'

'I think,' said Joe, standing up and following me into the kitchen, 'that he needs an escape. Somewhere to put all his worries aside and just relax and think about something else. Someone to talk to, I suppose.'

That stung. Will was my friend. My best friend — along with Georgia. Why couldn't he talk to me? But then, I hadn't been able to talk to him, either lately. There was something in the way, like things were changing between us, and I hated it. I just didn't see what I could do about it.

'You gonna be all right, Lexi?' asked Charlie.

As I headed into the farmyard with a nod, the darkness wrapped around me, and the air was still and quiet. I knew it wouldn't be much busier in the Old Town, since most of the holidaymakers were gone, and the vast majority of cafés and teashops had closed for the winter. I wondered if the kids were asleep yet. I wondered if the rowing had stopped. Pausing, I took a deep breath. 'Suppose I'd better see what's going on at home.'

'Things will be all right there, you know.' Joe planted a kiss on my forehead. 'Trust me. Your dad and Eliza are for keeps. They'll work their way through this. You'll see.'

I wasn't convinced. I gave a weak smile and bid them goodnight, my spirits sinking as I headed home to Tippet's Yard.

Chapter 17

I'd never been in the upper west wing before. I'd never had reason to. I knew Sir Paul had stored a lot of belongings in the upper rooms, and Archie and Will had spent ages up there recently, with the experts sent by the tax office, as they worked their way through the house, making a detailed inventory of everything in it. I'd occasionally wondered what secrets those rooms contained, and at last I was about to find out.

'Don't get your hopes up, Lexi,' Will warned me, as we crept up the stairs and along the gloomy landing that was heavy with dust. Obviously, Woody didn't go up there much either. Her feather duster would have made short work of all those particles swirling around, tickling my nose. 'There's nothing special or exciting about this place.'

'If that's true,' I said, 'why are you whispering? And why are we creeping along like two cat burglars?'

He stopped suddenly, looking puzzled. 'Gosh, we are, aren't we? I never even noticed.'

He laughed and I nudged him. 'Idiot. There must be something interesting up here, or why are we even bothering?'

Will gave me a look that said I should know all too well why we were bothering. We were under orders from Darcey, and who dared disobey The Mighty One? We had to fill the rooms that were going to be part of the tour with the most interesting artefacts and paintings we could find — and preferably include plenty of stuff that either personally belonged to, or were portraits of, his ancestors.

Lady Darcey herself would be joining us, as soon as she'd finished her tour of the old stables with Bernie. The stables, built in the early nineteenth century, clustered around a courtyard on the opposite side of the lane to the Hall. Will's grandfather had built new stables in the nineteen-thirties, and the old ones had been used recently for storing machinery and tools. Darcey had got it into her head that the whole building could be turned into a complex, consisting of shops and a new improved tearoom. She felt that the current farm shop was too isolated, situated as it was on the lane running alongside the wall at the west of the house. And of course, Will thought she had a point. And Nat thought she had a point. It seemed even Bernie thought she had a bloody point.

Thank God for Woody, who wasn't fooled for a second. Her lip positively curled whenever Darcey walked into the kitchen.

'Women sense things,' she told me sagely, 'but you'll never convince the menfolk. They're all idiots when it comes to a pretty face. No use denying it. We know.'

She reckoned Darcey had a dark side, and she disapproved of the way she fawned over Will. She said you couldn't trust a woman with such thin eyebrows, and personally I think she had a point. However, since Will was — officially at least — in charge, I had no choice but to grit my teeth and go along with her stupid plans.

So, there I was in the west wing, creeping along with Will, hoping to find enough precious possessions to please Her Ladyship.

'Are all these things covered with dustsheets?' I asked.

'Of course. Why do you ask?'

'Just wondering how we're going to find the sort of thing Darcey wants. Do you even know what you're searching for?'

'I have a pretty good idea,' he said. 'When we were up here with the advisers from English Heritage recently, I saw quite a few things that I thought at the time would be interesting to visitors. It's not so much the valuable things we're seeking today — more the things which lend a personal touch to the house. We have to rotate the items on display at various points anyway. We've made a deal that the public must have fair access to them all. Did I tell you the archives are going to be housed in Oddborough Council's records office? There has to be reasonable access to them, you see, and it seemed the fairest way of doing it. They'll be going just after Christmas.'

'I'm sorry, Will,' I said suddenly.

'What on earth for?' He stopped, looking at me with a puzzled expression.

'You're having to jump through hoops because of this tax bill already, opening your home up to the public. To have to send the archives away too … It's such a shame.'

He sighed. 'It *is* a shame. Not for me, but for the estate. Still, I don't mind about the house being opened up to the public. It's far too beautiful to be kept for just one family to enjoy, don't you think? Everyone deserves to see it. And the main thing is, the bullet's been dodged. For now, at least.'

'Except that—' I broke off, not sure whether to voice my opinion.

He raised an eyebrow. 'Except what?'

I hesitated, but there seemed no way out of finishing the sentence. 'Except that, well, what happens when the next inheritance bill comes in?'

He gave a wry smile. 'You mean, when it's my turn to be interred in the family mausoleum?'

I felt a shiver run down my spine. 'Well, I suppose. I mean, I know it won't be your problem, but the Hall will still need repairing and maintaining, and it's only going to need more care as the years go by. God, I don't mean to sound so gloomy, but where does it end? How much will the family have to sacrifice to keep it going?'

He rubbed the back of his head and seemed to be thinking, and I immediately felt mean. I was supposed to be keeping him cheerful, not making him feel worse.

'I'm sorry,' I said miserably.

'Don't be sorry,' he said. 'I love the fact that Kearton Hall matters so much to you, even beyond my lifetime. You're thinking ahead, as I have to. Don't, for one minute, think that I don't already know all this. It weighs on me heavily, this responsibility to the next generation.'

It felt weird, Will talking about the next generation. I realised suddenly that he meant his children. I'd never really thought about Will having children before, until Woody had mentioned that he'd make a good father. Truthfully, I'd never even thought about him getting married, never mind building a family, but when I stopped to consider it, he probably thought about it a lot. After all, handing the Hall on to his children was what he was destined to do, wasn't it? He often said the Hall wasn't his. He was just keeping it safe for the future owners. Future owners — his children. I felt a funny fluttering in my stomach.

He reached out and gently touched my cheek. 'Hey, don't look so down. We'll make it, you'll see.'

I swallowed. 'We will?' I felt strangely breathless.

'Of course.' He gave me a cheerful smile. 'Darcey won't let us down. She's got so many ideas, and she's checking out grants and all sorts of things. It will work out.'

Bloody Darcey! I scowled. 'We'd better get on with it then.'

He nodded, and we headed up more stairs to the second floor. Pushing open a door, he flicked the light switch, then ushered me inside a room that was full of weird and wonderful shapes, as almost everything was draped in dustsheets. There were a few paintings on the walls, and I looked around me and felt a thrill at so many wonderful items to discover. I loved it.

Will must have seen the expression on my face, because he gave a short laugh. 'Don't look so enthusiastic. There's nothing very valuable, as I said. If you're expecting to find another Gainsborough, you'll be disappointed.'

I gave a nonchalant shrug. 'Pah! Who needs another Gainsborough? We've already got two.'

He grinned. 'That's the spirit.'

'I wonder what this room used to be used for?' I said, wandering over to the window and pulling a dusty curtain aside to peer outside. Below were the lane and the courtyard, and I could see Bernie and Darcey chatting to one of the village girls, who worked in the farm shop. I swore, I could see Darcey's painted talons from all the way up here.

'It was the school room, many years ago. My great-grandfather had lessons here. The governess slept next door.'

'Governess? Crikey, it was a different world.'

He sighed. 'It was. In those days, they didn't have to worry about opening the house to visitors, or where to position a farm shop, or designing a logo to go on a pack of Kearton Hall lamb chops.'

He gazed around him, seeming to be absorbing everything, and I wondered what he was thinking. Then he pulled off a dustsheet, revealing a statue of a cherub with a veil over its face, and said, 'Right, let's get to work.'

I pulled a face. 'How about we start with covering that back up? Creepy or what?'

'It's a lovely statue,' he protested.

'Yeah, I'm sure Stephen King has one just like it,' I said. 'Come on, Will, we can do better than that, surely?' I began to wander around, staring up at the portraits. 'Are these all family members?' I asked.

He paused in examining a vase that was standing on a dresser and glanced up toward the portraits. 'Most of them. There are more over there,' he added, nodding towards a bulky shape in the corner of the room, draped in a sheet.

I wandered over and carefully removed the cover, to discover a stack of paintings, propped up on blocks, and separated by acid free boards. I re-covered them, not wanting to disturb them, and returned to admiring the ones on the walls.

'Some of these are lovely. Why did they never go on display? Your father was a strange man.' That was one way of putting it.

'He left things pretty much as his own father had them. He wasn't particularly interested in change, as we both know. He tended to live in the past rather a lot. His glory days.'

I couldn't help myself. 'He needed a good kick up the arse.'

'Lexi!' Will stared at me in astonishment for a moment, then his eyes crinkled and he bit his lip. 'Good job he's not around to hear you say that. You know what would have happened.'

'Public flogging, no doubt,' I muttered.

It still made my blood boil that Sir Paul had been a firm believer in corporal punishment. Will had been well and truly beaten by the old buzzard when he was younger. I knew that, because Woody had gone overboard with the sherry one Christmas Eve and got all emotional about him, in between telling me how much she loved me and hunting for another bottle of Harvey's Bristol Cream.

'Well, I was thinking more that you'd have been fired,' Will said, his eyes twinkling. He had lovely eyes. Deep green and full of kindness. If eyes were the window to the soul, then Will's soul was as pure as an angel's. He nodded towards the door. 'There's a larger room just up the landing,' he said. 'There's more stuff in there.'

'Why didn't your dad just put it in the attic, like normal people?' I asked. 'Oops, silly me. Your family thought attics were for staff, not old paintings and stuff. What was I thinking?'

Will put down the vase, not smiling. 'I was up there last week. Some of the attics aren't in great condition, you know. I think they're getting worse.' A worried expression crossed his face. 'We're going to have to address the damp issue up there, and it's going to have to be soon. That's more money, but it can't be helped. We don't want things to deteriorate, and we certainly don't want English Heritage on our case. Darcey thinks we should get someone in to survey them. She's recommended a firm that does a lot of work with ECHOES. I'm just hoping the situation isn't too bad.'

I looked away, hating the unmistakable anxiety on his face, knowing I couldn't take it away. Instead, I focused on the paintings. When one caught my eye, I moved towards it, suddenly fascinated. 'Will! He looks like you!'

He came to stand beside me, and we stared up at a portrait of a dark-haired man, with a neat pointed beard. He wore a gold satin coat, slashed, as if to reveal more of the crisp white shirt he wore underneath, with a broad white lace collar, and a gold cape draped over one shoulder. One rather graceful hand rested lightly on his chest, as if he was swearing an oath. I couldn't take my eyes off him.

Will gave an embarrassed laugh. 'I hardly think he looks anything like me, Lexi.'

'Oh, but he does! Can't you see it?' I couldn't imagine how he was missing the likeness. Those eyes! They were exactly the same as Will's — deep-set, green, full of kindness and warmth. 'He's lovely. Who is he?'

Will cleared his throat. 'That's William, the Third Earl Kearton. The last of his direct line.'

'His name was William, too? Wasn't he the one that lost the Hall?' I turned to him. 'What happened to him?'

Will seemed surprised by my interest. 'Well, actually, he was killed during the Civil War. He was only twenty-eight.'

'Twenty-eight!' I gazed up at the Earl, then looked at Will again. Will had turned twenty-eight in September. 'So, he never married?'

'Yes, he did marry,' Will said, frowning. 'From what I remember, his wife died three years before him, in sixteen-forty-two. There were complications during childbirth, which killed both her and the baby. When William went off to fight, the Parliamentarians took over the house for a while. Later, it was passed to my direct ancestor, Charles Boden-Kean, who was William's cousin but, unlike him, had fought for Cromwell's army. Charles was a staunch protestant, and was rewarded for his loyalty to Cromwell by being made First Baronet Kearton.'

'I didn't know Cromwell created any baronets,' I said, surprised.

'He did but, during the Restoration, they were declared to be void. Now, one can only speculate what he did to deserve it, but the king bestowed the honour on him again in sixteen-sixty-one.'

I stared up at the portrait again, seeing, what I was certain, was sadness in those green eyes. 'He looks so tired and — I don't know — lost, somehow.'

'Not surprising. This was painted in sixteen-forty-four, the year before he was killed. England was in chaos, he'd lost his wife and child … Not much to be happy about, really.'

I sighed. 'I'd quite forgotten the Keartons were Catholics,' I admitted. 'That must have made things very tricky for them.'

'They were playing a very dangerous game indeed, particularly as they mixed with extremely important people, who were protestant to the core. They lived through some of the most perilous times in history. The Keartons were very diplomatic.'

'Or sneaky,' I said.

He laughed. 'Well, that's another way of putting it.'

I knew a little of the story of Will's ancestors, of course, and I knew how they'd come to own the Hall, but I'd never thought about them too much before. The painting made me think more deeply about the issues they'd faced, for some reason.

Will grinned at me. 'I can show you some of their priest holes, if you like.'

'There are priest holes?' How had I not known this? 'For God's sake, why didn't you tell me? I'd love to see them!'

'Father wasn't exactly keen to publicise them,' he admitted. 'There are at least two that used to be on display. Of course, there may be more. Nicholas Owen was a genius, and we may yet discover another one. When the original Tudor hall was demolished, and this one built during Elizabeth's reign, the First Earl made sure that he'd done his best to safeguard any visiting priests.'

'Nicholas Owen.' I searched my memory banks. 'The man who was responsible for saving so many Catholics, by creating such ingenious hiding places for them, that the Church made him a saint. Poor man, he died a horrific death.'

'He was tortured mercilessly, but he never revealed his secrets. He could create such well-concealed rooms. I'll show you ours later today.'

'Show her what?'

I stiffened, the hairs on the back of my neck standing on end. *She* was with us then.

'Darcey!' Will turned to her, all smiles as usual. It was quite sickening to watch. 'I was just showing Lexi the portrait of the Third Earl — Lord Kearton.'

Darcey gave him a feeble smile. 'How lovely.' She prowled the room, her eyes flicking around, like a big cat searching for prey. 'Interesting. Have you found anything that has special significance to your *direct* ancestors?'

'How about this painting for a start?' I said, annoyed that she was dismissing him, as if his opinions were of no consequence. 'I think this is a fantastic portrait, and the earl's grandfather was Charles Boden-Kean's grandfather, too, so he and Will *are* related. It should definitely be on display.'

She gave a heavy sigh, as if humouring me, then came to stand next to us. We all stared up toward Lord Kearton, who looked back at us benignly.

'Isn't he the double of Will?' I demanded.

She glanced at Will, then back to the portrait. 'Not remotely,' she said.

Will flushed. 'Honestly, Lexi, I don't know what you're seeing, but there's no likeness whatsoever.'

'But there is!' My annoyance started to grow. 'Why can't you see it? Look at his eyes.'

'Who painted this?' Darcey enquired, brushing off my comments as if I had no right to make any.

'It's believed to be by William Dobson,' Will said. 'Do you know of him?'

She nodded. 'English. Replaced Van Dyck as Charles the First's painter. He's known for being the Civil War artist.'

I tutted. I could have told him that, if she'd given me a chance. 'I'm surprised your father didn't sell this,' I said. 'I'm really glad he didn't though.'

'I'm quite sure he'd have got round to it sooner or later,' he replied wryly.

'What about his wife?' I asked. 'Have you a portrait of her?'

Will sighed. 'I'm afraid not. There was one, but it was sold. It was painted by your friend Van Dyck,' he added, nodding at Darcey. 'Father sent it to auction more than ten years ago. It's such a shame.'

'Isn't it?' She hesitated. 'Maybe you're right. Maybe Lord Kearton *should* be part of the tour. After all, this was his home, too. Do you know much about him?'

Will smiled, obviously pleased to have won her approval. How pathetic, I thought, as he relayed what he knew to her. 'He was a devout Catholic, like his father and grandfather before him, and managed to keep that hidden,' he finished. 'At least until the war.' His eyes widened suddenly. 'Perhaps the priest holes could be part of the tour?'

'Priest holes? There are priest holes?' Now she sounded interested. *Too little, too late, you old trout*, I thought. 'How marvellous. Of course they must be part of the tour. Where are they?'

'I'll show them to you later today,' he promised, and I glared at him. I thought he was only going to show me. And I'd been defending Lord Kearton! Charming.

'Is there anything else you can tell me, Will?' she asked. 'Anything remotely interesting that could be brought up in the booklet, and on the tour?'

'Not really,' he said thoughtfully. 'I mean, there's the legend of his hidden treasure, of course, but that's just a story.'

I gaped at him. 'Treasure? Why didn't you mention that before? That's so exciting.'

Darcey gave me a pitying look. 'It's obviously just a story,' she said. 'Having said that, it's something fun to add to his own story. It will no doubt fascinate the visitors, whether it's true or not.'

'So, we'll definitely include this portrait in the tour?' Will asked.

I could have kicked him. What was he asking her for? He should be telling her. Honestly, he was such a drip sometimes.

'I think so,' she said, graciously. 'Now, what else do we have here? I don't suppose there are any possessions of the Sixth Baronet in here?'

The sodding Sixth Baronet again! The woman was obsessed.

I folded my arms in disgust as they moved off, murmuring together as they perused the other paintings.

'Never mind, William,' I whispered. 'I know you're the really important man in this story. Never mind the stupid Sixth Baronet.'

He gazed down at me from his portrait, with green eyes so familiar to me that it hurt to look at them. I blew him a kiss, then blushed at my own weird behaviour. All this history stuff was addling my brain.

Chapter 18

Nat wanted to see the priest holes too.

'I remember one of them,' he admitted. 'When we were kids, I shut Will in it. Do you remember, Will? Bloody Woody came in and heard you screaming and kicking the wall. Got a tanned hide from your father, as I recall.'

'I remember.' Will shuddered slightly, and I thought how horrible it would have been to be shut up in one. I sometimes wondered about Nat. He had a cruel streak, there was no doubt about it.

'So, where are they?' asked Darcey. 'I must say, this is rather exciting. I've wandered around this house so many times, and never noticed anything untoward.'

'Well, you wouldn't,' I said. 'That's the point.'

She gave me a withering look, as Will said, 'Right, shall we start with the closest one? Father's study.'

'The study?' I frowned for a moment, then nodded. 'I can believe that. No wonder it's got such a horrible atmosphere in there. Even Buttons hates it.'

'I reckon a priest suffocated or starved to death in there,' said Nat, his eyes shining with delight.

'You're weird,' I said.

He grinned. 'I know. And don't you just love it?'

Will cleared his throat. 'Right, well, follow me.'

We all traipsed into the study and I felt rather than heard Will inhale deeply. He'd never liked the room, and I knew why. It was the scene of most of his beatings, according to Woody. I took hold of his hand and squeezed it, and he gave me a surprised look, before squeezing my own hand in return.

'This is the one I remember!' Nat laughed, and headed over to the panelling at the side of the fireplace.

Will sighed. 'I thought you would.'

Darcey frowned. 'Is this where he shut you in? In this study?'

'It is.'

I wanted to kick Nat. As if this room wasn't bad enough for Will. I squeezed Will's hand again and he smiled.

'It's all right. It was a long time ago, and I think I'm over it now.'

'Never mind all that mumbo jumbo psychology stuff. Are you interested or not?'

Nat had obviously located some sort of mechanism in the panelling because he stood with a look of triumph by a hole in the wall. Buttons barked in alarm and I stepped forward, wanting to peer through the gap, but reluctant to go too close in case he decided to shut me in too. I wouldn't put anything past him.

Darcey obviously wasn't put off. She had her head stuck through the hole before I had chance to even get near. 'It's tiny!' She withdrew, wrinkling her nose. 'And it smells horrible. It must have been terrifying.'

I peered inside and shivered. It was very small. Any priest hiding in there would have had barely any room to turn around. I reluctantly had to agree with Darcey: it must, indeed, have been terrifying.

'Okay, you can close it up now, Nat,' said Will. 'I'll show you the other one. Be prepared to be surprised!'

'My father told me about the other one,' said Nat. 'I know where it is, but I've never seen it.'

He replaced the panelling, and we left the study, heading out along the passageway and into the Dining Room.

Will opened a door at the end of the room and took us towards the back stairs that led to the upper floors of the north side of the Hall.

'Is it upstairs?' I asked.

Nat grinned. 'Watch.'

Will climbed up a couple of stairs, then bent down, fiddling with something. I watched, astounded, as the step lifted and revealed a hole beneath it.

'I don't believe it!' That staircase was made of solid oak and was centuries old. It creaked most annoyingly whenever anyone walked up it. Nobody could sneak upstairs without being heard.

We all peered down into a room that seemed even smaller than the one in the study, and I shuddered. Those priests must really have had their faith tested. I imagined being shut up in there in darkness, hearing footsteps running up the stairs above me, as people hunted me. I knew panelling had been ripped out, and even walls demolished, in the course of the searches. It was hard to imagine how scared they must have been, knowing the fate that awaited them, if they were ever caught.

'If we rope off the hallway and landing, we could certainly make this priest hole part of the tour,' said Darcey.

'Yeah, people love stuff like this,' added Nat. 'They'd pay good money to see it. Have you been inside it?'

Will nodded. 'Yes, when I was much younger. There's nothing down there now, obviously. If there ever was anything in there, it would have been removed years ago. It's just a dusty old room with rather putrid air. Still, it's certainly a point of interest.'

'Have these priest holes been thoroughly examined?' Darcey asked. 'Only, Nicholas Owen did sometimes make double hides — a second room leading from the first to fool the soldiers.'

'They have,' said Will. 'Neither of these two are double hides.'

'Are there any more in the Hall?' she demanded.

Will shrugged. 'It's possible. I'd imagine there are some still waiting to be found in houses like these all around the country.'

As Darcey turned back to peer into the room below the stairs, a faint flush rose on Will's face. Was he keeping something from her? Catching his eye, I raised an eyebrow, and when he gave me an almost imperceptible shake of the head in return, I felt a thrill of excitement. Will knew something he wasn't telling Darcey!

Was it wrong of me to hope that Nat knew nothing about

whatever it was, too? I wondered why I felt such a glow of delight that Will had let me know he was keeping something back. It felt like the old days, I supposed — before Nat and Darcey arrived, before I knew about him and Rhiannon, even before Sir Paul's stroke — when we'd worked together so closely and told each other everything.

I realised suddenly how much I missed him, and knew I had to do something to restore our friendship. I just wasn't sure what.

****

I couldn't sleep. Nat was snoring his head off, and I was growing increasingly irritated. He'd downed half a bottle of wine before we went to bed, and it always made him snore.

I peered at the alarm clock. Was it still only eleven? It felt as if we'd been in bed for hours.

We'd actually gone upstairs at half-past nine, as Nat was most definitely in a passionate mood. He'd been full of the joys of spring all day, unlike Will, who'd been a nervous wreck as the roofing specialists, recommended by ECHOES and invited by Darcey, had spent the last few days examining the Hall's roofs, chimneys, guttering and attics, and eaten and drank their way through Woody's stores like a plague of locusts.

They'd finally left, promising to be in touch, but Will was worried they seemed concerned. Nat had merely told him to stop being so pessimistic and suggested alcohol as a solution. Will had declined, but Nat had helped himself and then started eyeing me with a most unsavoury expression, which had been quite inconvenient, as there was a programme on television about owls and I'd forgotten to ask Dad to record it for me. I wouldn't have minded so much, but by ten-to ten Nat's passion was spent, and he fell asleep almost immediately.

I wondered what had happened to the man who used to wear me out with his adventurous lovemaking. I used to keep my Fitbit on during the early sessions, just because it was fun to see how many calories I'd burned off, and how much my heart rate soared. Lately, I'd barely worked out enough to deserve a cup of

172

tea, and my heart rate went up more when I was babysitting the twins, so I'd taken to removing it. I didn't need reminding that we were turning into a very dull couple indeed.

The truth was, I was rapidly growing bored with our sex life, and since that was all there was to our so-called relationship, I was growing bored with Nat, full stop. It felt uncomfortably like a repeat of my relationship with Derry, and even my short-lived one with Robbie. They'd all been about sex, too, but when that'd waned, there was nothing left. Yet if I didn't want anything beyond a physical relationship, what did I expect? I didn't know what to think. I was certainly difficult to please, that much was obvious.

Fed up, I climbed out of bed, pulled on my dressing gown and slippers, and wandered downstairs. A cup of hot chocolate would be good. Maybe there were some of Woody's chocolate chip cookies left. I knew I shouldn't really eat so late, but what the hell.

The stairs creaked and groaned most annoyingly, as I headed down them. Remembering the secret room beneath the north back staircase, I shivered. I remembered Will's expression when Darcey had asked him if there were any more in the house. He was definitely hiding something. I should tackle him, find out if he was willing to let me in on the secret.

I nearly screamed as I turned into the corridor and went slap bang into Will. 'Jesus!'

He held a mug of hot chocolate, which he almost spilt over himself and Buttons, who stood beside him, looking up at me as if surprised to see me at that time of night.

'Sorry, Lexi.' He steadied his drink then put a hand on my shoulder. 'I didn't mean to scare you. Couldn't you sleep?'

I shook my head, taking deep breaths. 'No. I was just thinking about that priest hole under the stairs, and then I bumped into you and ...Well, I didn't mean to make you jump. At least you saved your drink.'

He smiled. 'Would you like one? The kettle's just boiled.'

'I was going to make one myself,' I admitted. 'And maybe sneak a choc chip cookie, if there are any left.'

'I'm sure there are,' he said. 'Come on, let's go and find out. I quite fancy one myself now.'

We headed into the kitchen and Will flicked on the light. Immediately, I felt relaxed. The kitchen was a lovely, warm room. It had been modernised by Will's mother, and although it needed updating again, it wasn't anything like the original, gloomy old kitchen, which was actually below ground and like something from a museum.

In fact, that was another room that Darcey considered might be appropriate to include in the tour. She was even thinking about dressing some of the volunteers in Victorian costumes and getting them to pretend to be maids and cooks and footmen. Who was supposed to pay for the costumes, she hadn't said.

'I can make it,' I protested, as Will reached for a mug and the tin of hot chocolate.

'It's no problem. I can make this while mine cools. Why don't you search for those cookies?'

I didn't need asking twice. I went to the cupboard where Woody stashed her baked goods and reached for the biscuit tin. Prising off the lid, I peered inside. 'There are three left.'

'Three?' He shook his head. 'Nat certainly loves those chocolate chip cookies.'

'May have been the roofers.' I took two out and put them on the table, then sat down, smiling when Will handed me my mug of hot chocolate and pulled up a chair beside me. We sipped our drinks quietly for a few minutes, before I decided to be brave. 'Will, the other day, when you were showing us the priest holes…'

He said cautiously, 'What about it?'

'Well, forgive me if I'm wrong, but it looked to me as if you knew something you weren't letting on. Like, maybe another priest hole that you're keeping quiet about?'

He took another sip of hot chocolate and stared straight ahead, not answering me. I wondered if I'd overstepped the mark. After all, it was his house, his history. If he wanted to keep some things to himself, it was none of my business was it?

When he did turn to me, he had a distinct gleam in his eye.

I grinned at him. 'There *is* something! I knew it!'

He put his finger to his lips. 'Shh! No one in this house knows about it, even Nat. And I'd like it to stay that way.'

'How come? How did you find it?'

'Well I didn't to be honest. My father told me about it. He made me swear not to reveal its location to anyone, as his father made him swear, and his father before that.'

'Jeez,' I said, 'why is it such a big secret?'

'It's to do with a rather dubious time in our family history,' he admitted. 'The Sixth Baronet.'

'Oh, not him again,' I muttered, disappointed. 'What's he got to do with it?'

'It would be easier to show you,' he said, considering.

'I thought no one was allowed to know.'

'No one is. But then, Father's not here to do anything about it now, is he? Besides, I already broke my promise and told someone else.'

'Not Darcey?'

'Darcey?' He looked puzzled. 'No. I told you, no else in this house knows about it.'

I felt a stab of jealousy. 'You told Rhiannon, didn't you?'

'No, I didn't. I told Bernie.'

'Right. Of course.' I should have guessed. Bernie had been like a father to Will, and they thought the world of each other. If he was going to tell anyone, it would be him. I felt thrilled that I was going to be allowed to share in the great secret.

'Shall we go now?' I asked, eager to get on with it.

He glanced up at the clock and shook his head. 'Let's finish our drinks and our cookies first. There's no rush. I want to make sure Nat and Darcey are fast asleep before I show you this. It would be awful if someone caught us.'

We sat for another fifteen minutes, and I tried very hard not to get impatient, or hurry him along. Finally, just when I'd given up all hope and thought he must have changed his mind, he stood, took our plates and cups to the sink, then turned to me. 'Okay, let's go.'

I resisted clapping my hands together in delight and nodded

sensibly instead.

We left the kitchen, flicking off the light and closing the door quietly behind us, then headed along the corridor, up the stairs in the north side of the house. We climbed to the second floor, where the bedrooms were located, and crept as quietly as we could, given the creaking floorboards, along the landing to the very end, where Will's room was located.

He opened the door and beckoned me in. I'd never been in Will's room before, and it was rather lovely. The cream walls contrasted nicely with the dark oak panelling that adorned the lower half of the walls. He had a modern bed, thank goodness. His duvet, complete with pale blue cotton cover, had been thrown back, revealing crisp white sheets. I'd had visions of him sleeping in an ancient four-poster, but there was nothing creepy about his room at all. He'd made it contemporary and comfortable, and it was delightful as a result.

'What are you doing?' I whispered, as he crept over to a chest of drawers on the far side of the room and started to pull out some clothing.

'It's just occurred to me that you're not exactly dressed for exploring,' he replied softly.

Well, give the boy a goldfish. He'd finally noticed that I was barely dressed at all. I pulled a face when he handed me a pair of tracksuit bottoms and an old jumper. Lovely. I would look so attractive.

I shook my head at myself. What the hell did it matter how I looked? Quickly, I pulled on the tracksuit bottoms, but hesitated before continuing. 'Er, could you look away, please?'

I didn't have a bra on. The sight of me topless might kill Will off.

Annoyingly, an image of a naked Rhiannon flashed into my mind, and I almost snatched the jumper out of his hand as he turned away, clearly embarrassed. Bet he hadn't turned away when *she* took her top off.

God, what the hell was wrong with me? I was becoming deranged. I threw off my dressing gown, pulled on Will's jumper, and whispered, 'Okay, you can look now.'

'You'll need something on your feet,' he said. 'Those slippers could fall off. They're too dangerous. My shoes will be way too big for you, but you could put a couple of pairs of my socks on. That should keep you warm.'

'Blimey,' I said, 'how big is this room?'

'You'll see,' he whispered.

He rummaged in the drawer, found some socks and handed them to me. I sat on his bed and pulled them on, then stood up.

'Okay. Ready.'

Will nodded, patted the bed, and told Buttons to lie down. Buttons shifted his eyebrows about, looking rather indignant at this unexpected order, but he obeyed as always.

'He can't follow us. I don't want him making a noise or giving anything away.' Will rummaged in his bedside cabinet and drew out a torch. 'Okay, let's go.'

'Where are we going?' I asked, but he shook his head and led the way back into the corridor.

We descended, as quietly as we could possibly manage, down the flight of stairs and arrived on the first-floor landing. My eyes widened as he led me into the gentleman's bedroom that Darcey had earmarked for the tour.

'In here?' I whispered, shivering. As if this room wasn't creepy enough! The electric light helped a bit, but I still thought four walls of full-length panelling was enough to make any room scary, especially at night. Even empty of furniture, as it currently was, it was gloomy and had a strange atmosphere.

I watched, open-mouthed, as Will went over to the corner of the room, bent down, and ran his hand gently but deftly over the panelling and around some intricate carving. As I watched, it swung open to reveal a room behind it.

Excitedly, I crouched down and crawled inside, but had to struggle to contain my disappointment. The priest hole, although deep, and full height once inside, wasn't very wide. It was little more than a cupboard, really. The walls were brick, with thick wooden beams running through them. I touched the cold brick and shivered, wondering at the stamina needed to remain hidden in places like this for hours, or even days at a time.

Withdrawing, I rubbed my arms, suddenly cold. 'It's horrible. Those poor priests. I don't get why this one is such a big secret, though. There's nothing special about it, is there?'

'That's what you think,' he said, grinning.

He ducked down and crawled into the room, beckoning for me to follow him. Feeling a bit nervous suddenly, I went inside again, aware that we'd never been so physically close before.

Will didn't seem to notice, which didn't surprise me. He stood, and seemed to be feeling for something, then he leaned forward, reached towards a thick, blackened beam, and pushed carefully at the top of it. You could have knocked me down with a feather, as the beam swung up, just about missing my head, and revealed a concealed space behind it.

He grinned, while I gaped at him in astonishment. 'Are you up for this?'

'Darcey's double hide!' I felt a fleeting satisfaction as I thought how much she'd love to see it. 'You bet I am,' I whispered.

'Shut the panel door,' he instructed.

I swallowed nervously. 'Are you sure? What if we get stuck in here forever?'

He smiled. 'Don't worry. I've done this lots of times. It can be opened from the inside. Look.'

He was right. There was a large, black metal handle attached to the door on our side. Cautiously, I closed the door, and immediately realised just how tiny the room actually was. Good job I wasn't claustrophobic, especially given that the entrance to the second room wasn't much wider than my body, even turned sideways. It was lucky that both Will and I were so slim, I thought. There must have been some very tiny priests back in the day — that was all I could think. Someone built like Friar Tuck wouldn't have stood a prayer. So to speak.

Will squeezed through the gap where the beam had been, and I followed, somewhat reluctantly. I was up for an adventure but crawling through tiny spaces was scary stuff.

I took a deep breath and gazed around me, while Will swung the torch around what was little more than a passageway. Not even that. It was more of a landing.

As soon as the thought struck me, I realised the light was shining on a stone staircase.

It wasn't just a room. It was a secret passage. A ripple of delight ran through me, all my fears rolling away on its tide.

Will took my hand, smiling at my obvious excitement. 'Ready?'

I nodded. 'Ready.'

We edged forward and began a slow descent down the spiral staircase. The stone was cold beneath my feet, even with two pairs of socks on, and it was hard going. The steps twisted and were very narrow. There was no handrail to hold onto, just the bare brick walls, and I was petrified I'd slip and fall onto Will, sending us both tumbling into the darkness.

He had one hand in mine, and the other carried the torch. I hoped the batteries were full. God help us if they ran out down here.

Eventually, we came to another landing. Feeling creaking wooden boards beneath me, I stumbled forwards, clutching Will's hand in mine tightly. Ahead of us appeared another flight of stairs.

'Where are we?' I murmured.

'We're in a gap inside the interior walls,' he whispered back. 'We've just reached the ground floor. We should be somewhere near the Chinese room. Probably just behind it.'

I screwed up my face, concentrating as I tried to picture where the landing might be in relation to what lay behind the walls. I knew the walls of the house were thick, but this was unbelievable. Eventually I nodded. 'So, do we come out in that room?'

He shook his head. 'You'll see.'

We began to descend a second staircase, and I suddenly thought what a pain it was going to be to climb back up them again. 'Bloody hell,' I murmured, 'whoever built this put some hard graft into it.'

He nodded. 'You're not wrong there.'

'So, we're now below ground?'

'We are, and we're almost done.'

Finally, I thought with relief, as the stairs ended, and we stepped forward into a passageway.

Will squeezed my hand. 'Okay?'

'I think so. Where are we?'

'This,' he said, 'is a tunnel that used to run all the way to the coast.'

'Used to?' I said. 'What do you mean, used to?'

We edged forward, the floor uneven and rough on my feet. 'Ouch!' I exclaimed, standing on a lump of stone. I hopped forward, grimacing in pain, but as Will put his arms around me and steadied me, I experienced a fleeting moment of pleasure. I felt safe and secure with him holding me.

Evidently, the tunnel had unnerved me more than I'd realised.

'Sorry,' said Will. 'I should have let you get some shoes. Stupid of me.'

'It's okay,' I breathed, feeling a brief pang as he let me go. 'I'll live.'

We walked for a while, and Will flashed the torch around, showing me the brick walls of the tunnel. As we rounded a corner, he stopped, shining his torch in front of us. Ahead, I could see a wall of stones. It completely blocked the way forward.

'Where do we go from here?' I said.

'This is as far as we can go,' he admitted. 'The tunnel used to come out at Hob's Cave. Originally, it was probably used to help any visiting priest make his escape, should soldiers come searching. However — and this is our dirty family secret — my dastardly ancestor, the Sixth Baronet, used it in his smuggling adventures. His son, who was a great deal more decent than his father, decided that, since quite a few of his gang knew of its existence, and had used it to bring smuggled goods to safety, it would be prudent to block it up and make sure that no one untoward had access to the Hall. There are several blockades along the route, so it's highly unlikely that anyone would get through. Nowadays, I sincerely doubt that anyone even knows of its whereabouts. The Seventh Baronet told only his son and made him swear that it would only ever be passed on to the heir to the Hall.'

'I'm very honoured that you showed it to me,' I said.

'The thing is, should I show it to Darcey?'

'Darcey!' My eyes widened. 'Why would you show it to *her*?'

'She seems quite certain that the smuggling history would be a huge draw. This would be a real feature and could attract so many more visitors. Have I got the right to keep it a secret, when the Hall needs as many paying visitors as it can get?'

'But it's a family secret,' I said, conveniently forgetting that he'd already told both me and Bernie.

'Yes, but when it's the very survival of Kearton Hall that's at stake, isn't it worth it?'

'You're not serious?'

He rubbed the back of his head, the way he always did when he was confused, or thinking deeply about something. 'I don't know. Maybe. I just don't know.'

I shivered. 'Come on,' I said. 'We need to get back before Nat wakes up and comes searching for me.'

He nodded, and we made our way back along the passageway, stopping at the steps. 'You go first,' he said. 'Here, you can hold the torch.'

I was deeply grateful. The thought of being last down there wasn't a cheery thought. I took the torch, shone it up the spiral stone staircase, and took a deep breath.

Well, I'd certainly had my work out for the night, I thought. Trust me to have left my Fitbit on Nat's bedside table.

Chapter 19

Macduff was lame when I went back to the riding school. 'Nothing serious,' said Georgia. 'He'll be back in action in a couple of days. Meanwhile, I've got Macbeth ready for you.'

'Macbeth? You're kidding, right?' Portent of doom, if ever I heard one. I should have known, taken it as a warning. Instead, aware of Nat's watchful eyes as he sat on the fence and waited, I mounted the chestnut gelding and pretended I wasn't in the slightest bit worried.

Georgia smiled up at me. 'That's the spirit. Well done.'

I hadn't done anything yet. What was with the endless praise? It was like she'd had a personality transplant lately. First she'd been all moody and horrible to me, then she'd done a complete U-turn and become my biggest champion. Maybe she felt she had to compensate for Nat's sneering remarks as I trotted breathlessly around the paddock, praying I wouldn't fall off, and worrying as my boobs bounced up and down so hard I thought they were going to fly up and knock my hat off. I didn't like it, either way. It felt patronising, and I wished I could just have my normal mate back, rather than this weird version of her.

I peered down at her, suddenly aware that she was wearing makeup. A slick of lip gloss and a coat of mascara. Subtle, but noticeable. Maybe she was having a mid-life crisis? Though at twenty-seven, it didn't seem likely.

I managed to halt Macbeth and Georgia stood for a moment, giving me a brief overview of what she intended for me to achieve today. I glanced across at Nat. He'd obviously got bored already, as he was busy texting on his mobile phone. As I tried to concentrate on Georgia, Macbeth quivered beneath me. He danced slightly, not as steady as Macduff, and I tensed, unsure.

'Just relax,' said Georgia, obviously sensing my discomfort. 'You'll be fine.'

A suspicious tone came from Nat's phone. Was he playing bloody poker again? I glared at him, but he was too busy tapping away to notice.

Macbeth was practically jogging on the spot. Icy cold fingers crept down my spine, and I gathered the reins. He tensed and I felt his muscles ripple.

'What's wrong with him?'

Georgia tutted. 'Nothing's wrong with him. It's your tension, he can feel it. You're communicating your fear. You mustn't do that. He'll think there's something to be afraid of and it will spook him.'

Well, that didn't reassure me. I sat there, trying to be calm, but all I could think of was that I was conveying my terror to an animal who couldn't cope with it. He'd bolt or buck me off. God, what if he reared and went over on top of me? I could feel beads of sweat on my forehead, and my hands felt slippery on the reins. I bunched them in one hand and wiped the other on my jeans, then repeated the process with the other hand.

Macbeth tossed his head, snorted, snatched at the bit.

'Okay,' I said. 'I really don't feel comfortable on this horse. Isn't there another?'

'Macbeth's a sweetie,' she said. 'Just calm down.'

'What's going on?' Nat called. 'Are you just going to sit there all day?'

I tried to listen to Georgia's instructions. I moved him forward, trying to focus on my seat and my hands. *Think about the job. Forget what could happen.* What could happen? *I could be crushed beneath this ton of horseflesh, that's what could happen.*

'What are you doing?' Georgia sounded exasperated. 'Where the hell are you going?'

'I'm not doing it!' I wailed, as Macbeth carted me off to the fence and began to rub his hind quarters along the rails. 'What's he doing?'

'He's trying to scare you,' said Georgia. 'He does this sometimes when people don't concentrate. Take control.'

'He's going to break my leg!' I squealed in terror.

Macbeth snorted again. He pulled at the reins, almost snatching them out of my hand. He squeezed against the fence, trapping my leg between the rail and his body.

Nat jumped off the fence. 'Behave your bloody self,' he told the horse, taking hold of the reins, and slapping him on the neck. 'Go on.'

Macbeth moved away, and I heaved a sigh of relief.

'For God's sake,' said Nat. 'What are you doing? Show him who's boss.'

'I think he knows who the boss is,' I muttered.

Nat rolled his eyes at me and climbed back on the fence. 'Sod it, I've timed out now.'

Charming. I could see how concerned he was for my safety. I glared at him, wondering how he'd feel if I'd been crushed to death by the sodding horse. Would he feel any remorse, or would it just annoy him that his game of poker had been interrupted?

I was so distracted by the thought, that when Nat's phone suddenly rang, I wasn't prepared when Macbeth shied away. No time to think about it, or take any action. One moment I was sitting in the saddle glaring at Nat, the next I was on the ground and the world was spinning.

From somewhere far away, I heard Georgia calling, 'Are you okay?' and then the sound of laughter.

Laughter!

Nat loomed over me. 'Serves you right for not concentrating. Come on, jump up. Go and catch the bugger and get back on.'

I clambered to my feet, hurt at his lack of concern. 'I could have been killed,' I pointed out.

'Don't be stupid. It was a tiny tumble. It takes seven falls to make a rider,' he said calmly. 'Go on, get him, or he'll think he's won.'

Macbeth stood just a few feet away, grazing.

Georgia had her hands in her pockets. She obviously wasn't going to help. 'Get back on,' she said. 'Go on.'

I reached for the reins, my hands shaking. Macbeth's head shot up, and he snorted, showing me his teeth, which appeared suddenly like something from a poster of *Jaws*.

'There's a good boy,' I soothed, thinking he was a devil and I hated him.

He backed away, and as I pulled on the reins, he revealed his teeth again. He was definitely warning me off.

Georgia strolled over. She took the reins and rubbed Macbeth's nose, making soothing noises as if he were the one suffering, while I just stood there, wondering what to do next.

'Go on, get back in the saddle,' she instructed. 'I'll hold him steady.'

I looked at Macbeth, and he looked back at me, all big brown eyes and whiskers. He seemed totally benign. I swore, if Georgia had glanced away, he'd have given me an evil look again. He knew what he was doing, that horse.

I shook my head.

'What's wrong? Get back up there, for God's sake,' Nat said.

I backed away. 'I can't.'

'What do you mean, you can't? You have to. You'll lose your nerve if you don't.'

'Nat's right, Lexi.' Georgia sounded apologetic. 'If you don't do it now, it will just get harder and harder to get back on a horse. Go for it. We're here. We won't let anything happen to you.'

They'd both been there when the demon horse had thrown me off. Fat lot of good it had done. I shook my head again. 'Sorry. I can't.'

'Well, of all the—' Nat looked stunned. 'You're completely feeble. I'm embarrassed for you.'

'Not helping, Nat,' said Georgia. They stared at each other a moment, and she shrugged. 'If she doesn't want to do it ... Not everyone's cut out for this. Sorry, but that's the truth. I'm not forcing her.'

'For fuck's sake.' Nat looked at me, then back to Georgia, then back to me again. 'Well, if you're really not going to get back on the bloody nag, I'm off. I've wasted enough time around here. I'll see you later. Maybe.'

He turned and left the paddock, leaving me standing there, feeling like a complete and utter failure.

Georgia squeezed my arm. 'Don't worry about it. You're not the first it's happened to. Unless ... Unless you'd like to try again now that he's gone?'

I turned to Macbeth, who was standing there like butter wouldn't melt in his enormous, toothy mouth. I looked at the saddle, which suddenly seemed so high up.

I shook my head. 'No, it's okay. I think I'll pass.'

She nodded. 'Okay, Lexi. I'm just going to see to this fella. Why don't you go indoors and make us both a nice cup of tea, eh? Let's forget all about horses for the next half hour.'

It sounded like a good plan to me, and I was grateful that she was being kind after my pathetic display. Somehow, I doubted that I'd get off so lightly with Nat.

****

Frosty was pleased to see me, although she seemed a bit put out that I didn't have Polos with me.

'Sorry, old girl. I wasn't planning a visit, or I'd have come prepared. Shame on me, eh?'

She nudged my hand with her nose, and I stroked her, wishing I could have had riding lessons on her. Somehow, I didn't think it would seem so scary, sitting on horseback when my feet were still on the ground. I thought about Amy, and how much she'd enjoyed riding Frosty. I wished I wasn't such a wimp. I couldn't understand why I was so scared. I mean, I loved horses. I really did. I just didn't love sitting on them, apparently. Pathetic. No wonder Nat had been so scornful.

'Lexi?'

I turned at my name and felt a surge of joy as Will walked towards me. He was in jeans and wellies and had obviously been up a while, mucking out, feeding and watering the horses. I wasn't sure why he always made me feel better, but he did. It was like, when he was around, I always had someone on my side.

'What are you doing here so early? Oh...'

'No,' I said, shaking my head, 'I haven't stayed the night. I couldn't sleep, that's all.'

'Is something worrying you?'

He stood beside me and rummaged in his jacket pocket. Frosty abandoned me and reached for him with indecent haste when he held out a Polo. Trust Will.

'Do you ever get scared, Will?'

He looked at me curiously. 'All the time. What are you scared of?'

'That.' I nodded at Frosty, and he smiled.

'Horses in general? Or do you mean Frosty, in particular? She can be quite fierce, I must admit.'

I shook my head. 'I fell off yesterday.'

His smile vanished. 'I'm sorry. Were you hurt?'

'Not really. More shocked. I'm not cut out for this riding lark. They scare me to death.'

'Well...' He shrugged. 'If you don't want to ride, it's your decision. Not everyone's the same, after all.'

'But I have to be able to ride,' I protested. 'It's what Nat lives for. And Georgia's my best mate — well, best female mate. It would be so much easier if we could go for a ride out sometimes. I feel like a prize idiot, especially now that Amy's developed this massive desire to ride too. What's wrong with me?'

'Nothing's wrong with you,' he assured me. 'Perhaps you're trying too hard — taking it too fast?'

'I wouldn't get back in the saddle,' I admitted, my face scarlet. 'I was too scared. They said I had to, or I'd lose my nerve forever, but I just couldn't make myself do it. They thought I was completely feeble.'

'I'm sure they didn't.'

'They did. Nat actually said, *you're completely feeble*, so I think that kind of gives it away.'

'Ah.' Will rubbed Frosty's nose and sighed. 'Nat can be a bit … tactless. I'm sure he didn't mean to hurt you.'

'You think?' I wasn't so sure. I'd seen the look of contempt he'd given me, and even Georgia had rolled her eyes when she thought I wasn't looking.

Will's kind eyes focused on me. 'I'm certain. Maybe you should go to another riding school. It's awkward, sometimes, being taught by a friend. And having Nat there can't be easy. You could have lessons in secret with someone they don't know. There's a riding school over near Moreton Cross. I could call them for you?'

'Will?'

'Yes?'

I stared at him as he peeled back the paper on his tube of mints and took out another Polo for Frosty. 'Would you teach me?'

He was quiet for a moment, watching the pony crunching her sweet, as if he hadn't heard me.

'Will?'

'I — I don't know that's such a good idea.'

'But why? You're so patient. The way you were with Amy — I just know I'd feel safer with you.'

'And what about Nat? How do you think he'd take that?'

'He needn't know. He's never out of bed before eleven, and we could do it early in the morning. Would you? Please?'

His eyes met mine, and I could see the doubt in them and wondered why. Then he sighed. 'All right. If that's what you want.'

'Thank you!'

I threw my arms around him and hugged him. He was a total star.

We smiled at each other, then he shrugged. 'So, what about now?'

'Now?' A chill of fear rippled through me, and my smile died instantly.

'Yes. As you say, Nat won't surface until eleven. Come and say good morning to Captain.'

'Captain?' I paled. 'He's enormous!'

'But he's the gentlest horse you'll ever meet. Come on, before I turn them all out for the day.'

He led the way to Captain's loosebox, and I gulped as I looked up at the Cleveland Bay's wide head. It seemed very high up. 'I'm not sure about this, Will.'

He unbolted the door and we walked inside. Will handed me the Polos. 'Give him one of those, while I get his head-collar,' he said.

Captain took the mint from my outstretched palm, and I stood, my legs shaking, while Will went to fetch the tack.

'No saddle or bridle?' I asked, my anxiety growing ever greater, as Will slipped the head-collar over Captain's ears.

'Not today. We're not going far. Just out into the stable yard.'

He led the enormous horse outside and stood rubbing Captain's nose, as he watched me, his eyes warm with compassion.

'It's all right, Lexi. Get on the mounting block and climb on. It's only going to be for a couple of minutes. Just to get used to sitting on his back and seeing how gentle he is.'

'But he's so big!'

'I know, but I won't let anything happen to you. He won't do anything to hurt you, I promise. Trust me.'

I looked at him uncertainly, but he was so calm, so kind, I knew I did trust him. I gulped and climbed onto the mounting block, heaving myself onto Captain's back. He stood like a rock, totally still and not in the slightest bit put out that this sack of potatoes had suddenly landed on him.

Will rubbed his ears and told him what a good lad he was, while I sat there shaking. 'There. You're back on a horse. Well done, Lexi!'

Was he taking the mickey? But no, I knew he meant it. He seemed genuinely proud of me for overcoming my fear.

I smiled. I was pretty proud of me, too.

We stayed still for a couple of minutes, and I tentatively reached out and patted Captain's neck. He was incredibly good.

'Lovely, isn't he?' said Will with obvious pride. 'Solid and reliable and totally trustworthy. He'll never let you down. I know he's not as glamorous as Masquerade, but then, I'd never risk putting you up on *him*. Not for a long time. He's beautiful, but a bit unpredictable I'm afraid. Captain will always take care of you, that's the difference.'

I had a sudden thought that, really, the horses were perfectly suited to their riders. Will smiled up at me, and I thought that, sometimes, the solid and reliable was infinitely preferable to the beautiful but unpredictable.

'That's enough for now,' he said, and I blinked, realising that I'd been daydreaming.

Jeez, I really had been relaxed. It was so different to yesterday I could hardly believe it. 'Really? Already?'

He grinned. 'Told you it's not so bad. We won't push it. You did a very brave thing just now, Lexi. It was a big step, but we won't go too fast. Tomorrow, I'll tack him up, and we'll go into the paddock and have a walk round. It's just a case of getting you to trust him and building up your confidence first. That's the main thing.'

I nodded. 'Thank you, Will.'

I managed to climb off, and jumped down from the mounting block, to stand shakily by his side.

He took my hand. 'Seriously, that was very brave of you. I'm so proud of you.'

His green eyes looked deep into mine, and I felt a sudden tremor go through me. He was smiling gently at me, his expression so kind, and as I smiled back, I saw the look in his eyes change. The softness disappeared, and an intensity moved into his gaze.

I caught my breath, unable to turn away. Not wanting to turn away.

'Good morning!'

I blinked, dazed, and Will turned, leading Captain back into his loosebox.

'Good morning, Darcey. How are you?' he said.

She gave me a suspicious look. 'Fine, thank you, Will. Have you been out for a ride?'

'No, just checking Captain's hooves. All well. Have you had breakfast?'

'Just a coffee.'

'Well, we must put that right,' he said, removing the horse's head-collar. 'I'm sure Woody will be starting to cook mine about now. Would you both like to join me?'

'Goodness, I couldn't possibly manage a full English.' She laughed, patting her flat stomach with her clawed hand. 'I usually have half a grapefruit. I will join you for a coffee, though.'

'Lexi?' He glanced across at me.

I shook my head. 'I'm going to pop home, help Eliza with the twins. I'll see you at nine.'

'Are you sure?'

He sounded disappointed, but I was already walking away. I had no idea what just happened, but I had to get my head straight. Too much adrenaline — that was it. A couple of dirty nappies and a demanding seven-year-old would soon bring me down to earth.

Chapter 20

It seemed like an awfully long time since we'd had cause to celebrate, but twelve Tippet's Yard was the scene of much frivolity when I got home one Friday evening in mid-October.

Eliza was beaming from ear to ear as I opened the kitchen door, and the fact that Dad had his arm around her was reassuring. It was great to see them both looking so happy.

'O-kay,' I said slowly, 'what have I missed? Who's won the lottery?'

'Better than that,' said Dad, who looked, suddenly, as if he'd shed ten years. 'We've accepted an offer on the cottage.'

'Really?' I felt a sudden pang. We were leaving the place we'd been happiest. 'Not to Mrs Lovelace?' I said anxiously. I knew they were desperate to move, but surely Dad wouldn't have caved on that important point?

'Of course not! To a lovely young couple,' said Eliza. 'The ones I told you about, remember? They viewed it last week. Well, they rang me this morning and asked if they could come for another viewing, then I got a call this afternoon. They put a good offer in, and we've accepted. They're really excited. They only work in Whitby, so not far for them to commute, and they absolutely love this village. Isn't it wonderful?'

'Hmm,' I said. 'So, does this mean we're moving to that new-build in Farthingdale, after all?'

They exchanged glances, and I noticed Dad hug Eliza a little tighter.

'No,' she said. 'I was being stupid. We don't need a house like that, and we certainly don't need the pressure of a huge mortgage. I think my emotions must have got the better of me.'

'You're not kidding,' I said. 'Still, I expect you're awash with hormones, so I'll forgive you. Does this mean we have to find a house really quickly?'

'Not at all. Joe and Charlie have offered to let us stay at Whisperwood. There's plenty of room, now the renovations are completed.'

'And is that what we're doing?' I asked. It would be the perfect solution, and great fun to be back at the farm and in the company of two such funny, lovely men.

'We'll definitely think about it,' said Dad. 'If we can't find anywhere soon, we may take them up on their offer. I don't want to buy something we're not really sure about, just to get out of here quickly.'

'So, good news all round,' said Eliza.

'And about time too,' Dad said. He reached over and planted a long, and rather too lingering, kiss on her lips.

I groaned and tutted, but inside my heart was leaping. They were going to be all right. The crisis had surely passed.

****

'So, remind me. What are we doing here?' I peered out of the window as Will manoeuvred his ancient Land Rover through the bustling streets of Scarborough. It was a mild day, and the sight of blue skies always ensured flocks of eager visitors to the North Yorkshire coast. Kearton Bay had been pretty busy, but Scarborough was in a different league. I suspected the seafront would be heaving.

Will had collared me as soon I'd arrived at work that morning, not even giving me the chance to take off my coat.

'Where are we going?' I'd asked as he led me over to the car park, jingling his car keys as he walked.

'Have to go to Scarborough,' he'd informed me, not even glancing round. 'I thought you could come with me. I could use some company.'

It wasn't like Will, and I'd been quite intrigued. We'd driven for half an hour and he still hadn't told me why he needed to be in Scarborough.

'I needed to get out of the house,' he said now, as the car began to climb up a steep road. 'I'm going stir crazy in there, and there was something I thought you'd like to see.'

'Okay. So where are we going?' I looked around me, and a sudden thought struck me. 'Are we going to the castle?'

He glanced at me. 'We are. Is that all right?'

'More than all right,' I confirmed, folding my arms and settling back in my seat. 'You know I'm always up for a walk round an old building.'

'That's what I thought,' he said, smiling. We headed up Castle Road, and Will pulled over near St Mary's church. Fumbling in the glove compartment, he pulled out his parking disc and set the time of arrival, before placing it on the dashboard. 'I've been thinking about coming here for a while,' he admitted, as we unclipped our seatbelts. 'I'm glad you don't mind.'

I clambered out onto the road and slammed the door behind me. Stretching, I smiled across at him. 'Why would I mind? I'm supposed to be at work, and here I am, getting a trip around Scarborough Castle with my boss. I'm not likely to complain, am I?'

He leaned against the Land Rover for a moment, his face turned up to the sky. 'It's so good to be breathing the sea air again. I hardly seem to get down to the village these days, and just the thought of a few hours away from the house … I'm so looking forward to it.'

'Good,' I said, walking round to join him on the pavement. I hooked my arm through his and smiled up at him. It was great to see him looking so relaxed for once.

We walked up the steep — though mercifully short — road to the castle, and when we entered the gift shop, he insisted on paying my entrance fee, ignoring my protests. He also bought a guidebook, then arm in arm we took our tickets and trudged up the cobbled path towards the ruins. Immediately, I felt the usual mixture of joy and awe that such ancient buildings always stirred in me.

Steeped in history, Scarborough Castle had always fascinated me, and I was soon absorbed in reading the information boards, learning about the turbulent times the place had been through. We wandered through the grounds, exclaiming at the fabulous views to be had from this headland.

Inside the Master Gunner's house, we climbed the stairs to view the exhibits, and I felt quite sick, examining the display of cannon balls that had bombarded the castle. Some were huge, and I could only imagine what it must have felt like to have them hurtling through the air towards you.

'A cup of tea?' Will enquired, as we made our way downstairs. I nodded, and we headed into the tearoom, ordering two drinks and two slices of cake. We carried them across the hallway into the little room opposite and found a table by the window. It was lovely to have my friend all to myself again.

'So, what's this really about?' I said, as he sipped his tea. 'Don't get me wrong, I'm enjoying myself, but it seems weird coming here for no reason.'

'Do we need a reason?' he asked, putting down his cup. 'Can't we just have a few hours off, and spend some time together, away from the Hall? We never seem to have any time these days.'

'Apart from the riding lessons,' I reminded him.

He smiled, his eyes twinkling. 'I think Captain takes most of our attention. We don't really get the chance to talk, do we? And that's a shame. I mean, we used to talk a lot, didn't we? Before…'

I broke off a piece of cake and tried to stop my hands from shaking. There was something about the way he was watching me that made me feel quite peculiar. 'Before Nat,' I said.

He shrugged. 'Maybe even before that. Life's become so busy, don't you think? Sometimes, we just need to step away from it all.'

I chewed the cake, which was tasty, but I no longer felt hungry. I'd quite lost my appetite and pushed the plate away.

Will stared into his cup. 'There *is* another reason I brought you here, Lexi. When you're ready, I'll show you.'

'I'm ready now,' I assured him, suddenly desperate to get back outside into the fresh air. I was feeling quite hot all of a sudden.

'You're sure? Okay, well shall we have a look in the keep?' Will watched me, his expression suddenly serious. 'I think we'll get a real sense of history in there.'

'Of course.'

We headed to the keep, climbing the worn, stone steps, and then the short flight of newer, wooden ones. Finally, we stood in the ruins of the tower. The view from up there was amazing, but boy, was it draughty. There was a hell of a sea breeze blowing in, and I thought what it must have been like, actually having to live there all the time. It must have been freezing, even when all the walls were intact.

I clambered up into an alcove set in one wall, and gazed up at the ceiling, wondering what the space had been used for. There was a window in the far wall, and I stared out at the sea and shivered as I got that horrible feeling that someone had just walked over my grave. I turned away, searching for Will. He was standing by what was left of a fireplace. I jumped down from the alcove and wandered over to stand beside him, peering up into the chimney. I imagined a roaring fire burning there and wondered if the flames had managed to warm the castle's occupants and bring them some comfort.

'It must have been awful for them,' I said, thinking aloud.

He glanced across at me and nodded. 'It was here, Lexi.'

'What was?' I said puzzled.

'The Siege of Scarborough Castle, sixteen forty-five. That's why I wanted to bring you here. This is where William Kearton died.'

I stared at him, shocked, then looked back at the fireplace. I imagined William standing in front of it, holding out his hands to stave off the cold. My hand reached out and touched the stone, and I shivered, remembering his sad and rather lost expression in the Dobson painting. Just a year later, he would be dead. He couldn't possibly have known, as he sat for that portrait, what lay ahead of him. He'd already suffered so much, yet he'd had to endure so much more.

Will's eyes were soft with understanding. 'You feel it, too?'

I nodded. 'It means so much more now. Knowing, I mean. What must it have been like for him? For all of them?'

The Siege of Scarborough Castle had gone on for months, with soldiers killed in battle, or starved into submission. So much suffering. A country torn. Families destroyed. All that pain and bloodshed. I shivered, and Will put his arm around me, drawing me near.

'Thank you for bringing me,' I murmured, and he shook his head.

'Not at all. I wanted to tell you while we were here. You seem so fascinated by him, and I thought it would mean a lot to you, actually standing where he stood.'

He gazed around him, his imagination clearly working overtime, and I thought how amazing it was that he understood me so perfectly, and that he felt the same way. I didn't have to explain things to Will. He just *knew*.

He turned and saw me staring at him. For a moment I couldn't breathe as his eyes locked on mine, and I got that same strange feeling that I'd experienced outside Captain's loosebox. What was happening to me?

'Come on,' he said, his voice finally breaking the spell. 'I suppose we'd better get back before Darcey and Nat start a civil war of their own.'

Reluctantly, we made our way out of the castle grounds and back towards the car.

'Would you like a moment at Anne Bronte's grave?' he asked, as we reached the church. 'It's only behind that wall.'

There he went again. How did he *know*?

'Would you mind?' I asked.

'Of course not. I'd like to see it myself,' he replied.

We headed through the gate, into the little graveyard where Anne Bronte had been laid to rest. Her gravestone was so worn and chipped I could barely read it, but the Bronte Society had laid a stone in front of it, which had the original inscription on it. Someone had left some flowers on her grave. I wished I'd thought to bring some.

'We should have brought flowers,' said Will.

I felt my skin prickle. Okay, this was getting spooky. 'Come on,' I said. 'Let's go before you get a parking ticket.'

'It feels quite sad,' Will said, fastening his seat belt, as I climbed into the passenger seat moments later. 'I mean, her being here all alone, while her family are in Haworth.'

'But she loved it here,' I said. 'When she got ill, it was Scarborough she wanted to visit. Although,' I admitted, 'I think she hoped the sea air would improve her health.'

'I just think it's a shame,' he said. 'I know it's lovely here, but when my time comes, if I had the choice, I'd want to be with the people who loved me. She was so lucky to have all those siblings. People matter more than places.'

I heard the longing in his voice. There was no mistaking the loneliness behind the words. I could hear it in every sentence. 'But it's only her body that lies here,' I reminded him. 'I'm sure she's reunited with her family somewhere. Bet they're having a great time, making up new stories together.'

He started the car. 'Let's hope so.'

We pulled away, heading back towards Kearton Bay and home. Our time out of time was over. But the feeling I'd had at the castle persisted. Something between Will and I had changed — but what it was, or why it had changed, I couldn't say.

****

I suppose we could have put the young couple off a while, but Eliza and Dad were determined to let them have the cottage as soon as the sale completed, and since it completed rapidly, we found ourselves packing up our belongings six weeks after we'd accepted their offer, ready to move to Whisperwood Farm. The new owners didn't have a home to sell, having previously rented a flat in Whitby, so there was nothing to stop us all going ahead with our new lives.

I stood crying as I gazed around my little attic room for the last time and said goodbye. At the sound of footsteps on the stairs I wiped away my tears, just as Dad opened the door. I spun round, giving him a bright smile.

Shaking his head, he stood beside me, and put his arm around my shoulders. 'You don't have to pretend with me,' he said softly. 'I feel just the same.'

'I don't know what's wrong with me,' I admitted. 'It's just a house, after all.'

'It's home,' he said, 'and we both know how long we waited, and how much we went through, to get one of those.'

Nodding, I wandered over to the window and stared down over Tippet's Yard. It would be weird to be Up Top, away from the hustle and bustle of Old Town, the screeching of the seagulls, the salty tang of the sea in the air. Clover Lane was a different world. Up there was space, and wide open fields, and no tourists. It was hard to imagine waking up in such tranquillity.

'Do you ever think of her?'

Frowning, I whirled back to face him.

Dad stood with his hands in his pockets, watching me with a sad expression on his face, and I didn't have to ask who he meant.

I wanted to tell him that, of course I never thought of her. I didn't want him to worry or feel guilty. But I couldn't lie. Not about that. 'Sometimes,' I said. 'I wonder if she's all right. If she's safe, happy. Alive.'

He nodded and sighed. 'I know. Me too.'

'You do?'

'Of course I do.' He seemed startled that I could even doubt it. 'Your mother may have been a difficult person to be married to, but I wouldn't wish her any harm. I would have given anything to stop her leaving with that man. You know that, surely?'

Hugh Appleton, my mother's lover. Rich and successful, he'd beaten my mother black and blue, got her to blame Dad, and then bought her silence with money, possessions, and the promise of a new life in France.

Sophie was of the firm opinion that Mum had got everything she deserved. Hadn't she practically forced Dad into bankruptcy? Hadn't she had him arrested and thrown in a cell? Hadn't she lied and cheated, had affairs, spent all his money, made fools of us both? If she was so selfish and greedy that she was willing to put up with her lover's vicious temper, for the sake of a platinum credit card and an apartment in Paris, that was her look out.

Dad — who had, after all, been the biggest victim of her bad behaviour — didn't agree. He'd begged her to stay and give up Appleton, but she'd been blinded by her love of the finer things in life. She'd walked away and left us, so in a way, I understood where Sophie was coming from. It didn't stop me from feeling a chill of dread every time I allowed myself to think about her, though. Sadly, for all I knew, she could be buried in a graveyard somewhere in France.

'I want her to be okay,' I said. 'Even so, I wouldn't want her to come back and ruin things, Dad. And she *would* ruin things, wouldn't she?' Truthfully, I couldn't bear to think about my mother's fate. I wanted her to be safe and happy, but at the same time, I was glad she'd gone. She'd caused enough pain.

He joined me by the window, and we looked out over the red roofs of Kearton Bay.

'God, I love this place,' he murmured. 'Not just this cottage, but this whole village. How could anyone want anything more than this?'

'Better than Paris, any day,' I said, in a feeble attempt at a joke.

He hugged me, his turquoise eyes suspiciously bright. 'We'll be all right, Lexi, you know that, don't you? Wherever we are, it will be home. We've got each other, we've got Eliza, we've got Amy and the twins.'

'And Joe and Charlie,' I reminded him. 'Don't forget those two.'

He laughed. 'Of course. It'll be fine.'

'And you and Eliza?' I asked, nervously. 'Will you two be fine?'

He stepped back and frowned down at me. 'Are you seriously asking me that?'

'You've been under so much stress lately,' I mumbled. 'I don't want you to go through all that stuff again.'

'All what stuff?' He appeared baffled for a moment, then his expression changed, and he pulled me to him. 'Listen to me, sweetheart. Couples argue and bicker. It's normal. It doesn't mean that we love each other any less. It doesn't mean we're going to split up. For God's sake, you have to believe me on that.

I love Eliza with every fibre of my being, and I know she feels the same about me. It's just exhaustion and stress, but it will pass. Trust me on this. Do you trust me?'

I trusted my dad one hundred per cent. He'd never let me down. If he said it was okay, it was okay. I nodded, and he kissed the top of my head.

'Come on, the removal van's already on its way to the storage unit in Helmston. Let's help Eliza get the kids in the car, then we're off to Whisperwood and the start of a new chapter. Yes?'

I smiled. 'Yes.'

We headed downstairs, out along the passageway to King's Row, where Dad's people carrier was parked. The back of the car was piled high, with what looked like the entire contents of a baby goods catalogue, and Eliza was busy strapping Hannah into her car seat. Mikey was already fast asleep in his, one chubby fist pushed into his mouth. Every few moments, he would suck contentedly on his knuckles. Amy was cantering up and down the path, telling Twinkle to giddy up.

Dad and I glanced at each other and grinned. Family.

'There you both are.' Eliza straightened and gave us a stern look. 'I wondered what had happened to you. Thanks very much for your help.'

'Sorry,' I said. 'It was my fault.'

She smiled. 'Don't worry, I'm only teasing. That's everything. Amy are you coming with us, or are you going in Lexi's car?'

'I'm going with Lexi,' she said immediately.

'Okay, we'd better set off then,' I said, taking hold of her hand.

'Do you want to say one last goodbye?' said Dad, taking the house keys out of his pocket and nodding at the cottage.

Eliza squeezed my arm, her eyes full of understanding. 'We'll wait, if you need a few moments,' she said.

I hesitated a moment, then shook my head. 'It's okay. I've said all I needed to say. I'm good.'

They nodded, and Eliza climbed into the car while Dad went to lock up one final time.

'Come on, Lexi,' said Amy, pulling at my hand.

As we turned to head up Bay Street, I took one last glance over my shoulder at the cottage.

'Thank you,' I murmured, feeling a lump in my throat.

Within seconds, we neared The Hare and Moon, and twelve Tippet's Yard was lost to my sight.

Chapter 21

Will gave Captain one final pat and rubbed his nose affectionately. 'Good lad. You're really taking care of her, aren't you? Do you have any idea of the difference you've made to her?'

Captain blew gently through his nostrils and nudged Will, as if to say, *That's all very well. But kind words aren't half as good a reward as mints.*

Will grinned and fished in his pocket. 'Go on. Just one, mind. And only because you're working miracles and I'm very grateful to you.'

Captain crunched the mint, and Will leaned against the loosebox wall, watching him fondly. It was true, Captain really had worked miracles. Lexi was still a beginner, but she was doing well, and most importantly, she was actually enjoying herself. She'd always been adamant that she didn't want to ride, and he'd been furious on her behalf when Nat had insisted she learn.

That first morning, when he'd found her feeling so low, he'd doubted that he could help her regain her confidence, but he'd known that, if there was one horse who could make it happen, it was Captain. Sure enough, the big, gentle Cleveland Bay had worked his magic. As solid and reliable as Masquerade was flighty and unpredictable, Captain had stood placidly and never done anything to worry or alarm Lexi, no matter how many mistakes she made, or how clumsily she sat on his broad back.

Nat still didn't have a clue. They'd been very careful to only do the lessons in the paddock beyond the woods, and early enough that they were pretty certain Nat would still be fast asleep. The day was coming, Will realised, when Lexi would feel confident enough to tell Nat what she'd been doing. He hoped his cousin would be encouraging and give her plenty of praise, not make fun, or belittle her. Maybe he would surprise him. Maybe they'd go riding together and discover something they had in common, other than their undoubted passion in the bedroom.

He tried his best to push all thoughts of Lexi and Nat together away. It didn't do any good to dwell, but sometimes they were stubborn, refusing to leave him in peace. He'd worked so hard to bury his feelings for Lexi, and sometimes he thought he'd almost managed to succeed. Then she would do something funny, or something kind, or she'd look at him with that warm, affectionate expression in those beautiful turquoise eyes, and he'd melt. At those times, he had to walk away. He couldn't let her see how she affected him, and he wasn't convinced that he could hide his emotions. They were so strong that, sometimes, they overwhelmed him.

Occasionally, when he wasn't busy, he'd start brooding about her, and despair would overwhelm him. Panic rose up, convincing him that he was facing a lost cause. Lexi would never be his, and he needed to let go of her, once and for all. But he couldn't do it. He wondered if he'd ever be free of the hold she had over him. But then, without her, what did he have? Yes, he'd built his life around his home, but it couldn't be everything to him.

He shivered and stepped out of the loosebox into the cold, crisp November air. Bolting the door behind him, he stood for a moment, wondering what to do next. He didn't want to go indoors. Lexi had gone home to change, and he wasn't hungry, so he didn't want Woody nagging him to eat something.

As he stood, contemplating his next course of action, a sound came to him from nearby. He frowned, wondering what it was he'd heard. Then he heard it again. Was that...?

Puzzled, he peered round, realising that it was coming from the tack room further down the block. He froze for a moment, wondering if it could be Lexi. Was she in there with Nat? But she couldn't be. He'd seen her heading off to the car park, and she'd have had to pass him to get to the tack room. A different sound came to him, a low groan, and Will squared his shoulders. Only one way to find out. He marched over to the tack room and opened the door.

Whatever he'd been expecting, it wasn't that. He gaped in astonishment at the sight of Nat in the throes of passion with a woman who most definitely wasn't Lexi. They were leaning against the tack room wall, and both were in a state of undress. Nat held the woman's arms above her head, pinning her against the brickwork, and she had her head turned away, so all Will could see was a mane of fine blonde hair. Judging by her groans, she was clearly enjoying herself, and Nat had an expression of triumph on his face as he pushed himself into her, Lexi apparently the last thing on his mind.

Will felt outraged on Lexi's behalf. 'What the hell do you think you're doing?'

The words were out before he could stop them, and the woman turned her head, a gasp of horror escaping her lips.

His eyes widened in shock. 'Georgia!'

Of all the people Nat could have betrayed Lexi with, she was the worst he could have chosen.

'Shit! Will, I'm so sorry. Please...' She managed to shove Nat away from her, then reached down, scrabbling on the floor for her clothes. As she shrugged her shirt on over her unfastened bra, she stared at him with pleading eyes. 'Please, don't say anything. It won't happen again. It was a mistake. A one-off.'

'Well, that's nice,' Nat drawled, fastening his jeans with an apparent lack of concern. 'I've never been called a mistake before.'

'Nat, don't. Think of Lexi,' Georgia begged him.

'Think of Lexi!' Will couldn't believe it. 'It's a bit late to think of Lexi, isn't it? How could you? I mean, you—' He glared at Nat. 'I expect it of you! But you, Georgia? How could you do this to her? She's your best friend, for God's sake.'

'I know that. I'm so sorry.' She bit her lip, her eyes full of shame. 'I tried to stop it, really I did.'

'What, by coming all the way up here and meeting up with him in our stables? Tried really hard, didn't you?'

She shook her head. 'It wasn't like that. I was coming to tell him to stop texting me, to stop flirting with me behind her back. I wanted him to end it, not this.'

'Well, you didn't succeed, did you?'

She shook her head, tears rolling down her cheeks.

Nat tutted. 'For God's sake. We had an itch, Will, and we needed to scratch it. Simple as that. No harm done.'

Georgia's head shot up. 'An itch? Is that all I am? After all that stuff you said?'

In spite of himself, Will couldn't help but pity her. She sounded stricken. Evidently, Nat had promised her a whole lot more than a quick bunk up in the tack room.

Nat had the grace to look ashamed, but only for a moment. 'Okay, Will, I hold my hands up. I shouldn't have done it, but the deed's done now. Let's forget it ever happened, shall we?'

Georgia gave a strangled sob and pushed past him, running out of the tack room so fast she nearly knocked Will over.

'Georgia, wait!' Will felt suddenly desperately sorry for her. Whatever she said about it being a mistake, she was doubtless smitten with Nat. Another heart broken. He turned back to look at his cousin.

Nat had his back to him, fastening his shirt, so Will couldn't see his expression. No doubt he was smirking. Nothing much mattered to his cousin, especially the feelings of other people.

'Well, that was a different start to the day,' Nat said, turning to face him. 'Beats Woody's porridge anyway. What do you say? Shake hands and forget about it?'

'Forget about it?' Will could barely get the words out. 'You're disgusting. Can't you see how upset Georgia was? She feels used, and she's thrown away her friendship with Lexi, for what? A quick fumble with a man who couldn't give a damn about her.'

'It wouldn't have been a quick fumble, if you hadn't interrupted,' said Nat cheerfully.

'You bastard!'

Nat blinked, shocked. 'I never thought I'd hear language like that pass your lips, Will. Shame on you.' He sauntered past his cousin, into the stable yard.

'You don't care about anyone, do you?' Will felt a lump in his throat and swallowed hard, desperate to tell him what he thought of him at last. 'No one's feelings matter to you. As long as you're all right, forget everyone else. You're a hateful, selfish, sorry excuse for a man.'

Nat stopped and turned slowly to look at him. 'Please. If anyone's a pathetic excuse for a man, it's you.'

Will glared at him. 'I'd never treat a woman the way you just have. Poor Georgia, she was mortified. And what about Lexi? You'll break her heart. How could you do that to someone who loves you?'

He couldn't believe it when Nat let out a shout of laughter. 'You know, Will, you're priceless. Honestly, you're funnier than Charlie Hope. Well done.'

'What's so funny?'

'What's so funny? You have to ask? Jesus Christ.' The smile dropped from Nat's face, and he sneered at Will. 'You, thinking Lexi's heart will be broken. Don't you know anything about her, yet? That cold bitch doesn't have a heart.'

'Don't talk about her like that.'

'Why not? Why shouldn't I? You think she loves me? What a joke. She's not capable of loving anyone. Not me, and certainly not you. And isn't that just the way you like it?'

Will felt the colour drain from his face. 'What are you talking about? What do you mean, the way I like it?'

Nat curled up his hands, pretending to rub tears from his face while wailing in a childish voice, 'Nobody loves me. My mummy left me, and she didn't come back. And I'm so screwed up about it that I've fallen for a girl who's just as cold-hearted as she was.'

'What the hell is wrong with you?' Will glared at him. 'Stop it.'

'Stop what?' Nat straightened, giving Will a look of contempt. 'Stop telling you the truth? Why should I? Someone needs to. Your mother walked out on you, Will, and you still haven't dealt with it. Now you're desperately recreating your childhood, by falling for a woman who's incapable of love, who keeps everyone at arm's length, and who'll never be able to give you the thing you crave most. She'll never love you. She'll never want to be with you. She'll walk away from you, just like your mother did, and inside that oh-so-controlled shell of yours, there's a little boy nodding and crying inside, who knows that what I'm saying is the truth. Honestly, it's so pathetic. Anyone with even a passing knowledge of psychology could work it out. You've chosen your mother all over again, which is fine, if it makes you happy to spend the rest of your life alone in this mausoleum. But don't you dare condemn the rest of us because we happen to need someone who can actually feel something, who can actually care.'

'Like Georgia?'

'Who knows? I'll tell you one thing, Will, whoever it is, she can't be more damaged than your precious Lexi. You're both locked in your little boxes, keeping the world at arm's length. Carry on, both of you. But don't dare to look down at the rest of us mere mortals for wanting a real, grownup relationship.'

Will's body trembled, but his voice was strong. 'A real, grownup relationship? You wouldn't know what one was. You only care about sex. You're disgusting.'

'Well, in that case, you should find Lexi disgusting, too. Because that little tart jumped into bed with me the first night we met, and she's the one who wants a no-strings relationship. You know — no feelings involved. Just pure, wanton sex. In the stables. In the bedroom. Behind the farm shop. Even on the beach, tut-tut. There's no stopping her. Hmm, I wonder if your little brother had her on the sands, too? I reckon—'

He never got the chance to say what he reckoned, because Will's fist smashed into his face, sending him flying onto the ground and winding him momentarily.

He lay there, gasping, whether with shock or pain, or a combination of both, Will wasn't sure. He only knew he couldn't stick around to hear any more of Nat's vile thoughts.

He turned and marched back into the Hall, slamming the door shut behind him.

****

'Jeez! What on earth happened to you?' I stopped dead, staring at Nat in astonishment. Surprising enough that he was even up at that time of morning, but there was no mistaking the bruise growing along his cheekbone and into the inner corner of his eye.

He gave me a filthy look, as if it were all my fault.

'Had a fall, if you must know,' he snapped. 'Bloody Masquerade, playing up.'

I was astonished. I hadn't thought that even a moody horse like Masquerade could unseat Nat. 'Does it hurt?' I asked.

He glared at me. 'Well, what do you bloody think? *Does it hurt*! For God's sake.'

'Sorry,' I said, my sympathy draining away as he rummaged around in the kitchen, slamming doors and banging drawers shut.

Woody came rushing in, her face red with annoyance. 'What are you doing? What's with all that noise?' She gave him a look that showed, unlike me, she had no sympathy to drain away.

'What happened to you?' she demanded, much as I'd done just minutes before.

'What the hell's it got to do with you?' he said. 'Where do you keep the paracetamol? My head's pounding.'

'Well, banging and clattering like that won't help. They're in the drawer in the dresser,' she said, irritably. 'And I'd thank you to keep a civil tongue in your head.'

Nat growled at her, grabbed the tablets from the drawer, snatched up a glass of water, and stormed out of the kitchen.

Woody and I stared at each other.

'Can't believe he fell off his horse,' I said.

She shook her head. 'Is that what he said? Hmm.'

'What do you mean? What's going on?'

'I'm not sure,' she admitted, 'but I'll tell you this. Will's in a very odd mood. Never seen him like this before. If I didn't know better, I'd say he was in a temper.'

'A temper? Will?' I considered that possibility for a moment. In all the years I'd known him, I'd never seen him really lose his temper. I wasn't sure he could. If he had, then something very bad must have happened. And where did Nat fit into the picture?

'Cup of tea, love?' Woody picked up the kettle and filled it with water.

I shook my head. 'No thanks. I'm starting at the shop in a minute. I only popped in to say good morning. I'll be across later though.'

She smiled. I'll make sure you have a cup of tea ready and waiting at eleven then.'

I left the Hall and walked slowly out through the west gate and into the lane, distracted by the possibility that Will could really be in a bad mood. I wondered what he looked like in a temper. I had to admit, I was a bit intrigued.

'Lexi!'

I glanced up, startled to see Georgia walking towards me. 'Hello! What are you doing here?' My smile died as I took in the expression on her face.

Her skin was blotchy, her eyelids were red and swollen. She seemed desolate, if I had to put a label on it. She swallowed, and I realised she was anxious, too.

'God, you look awful.'

'Thanks.' She pushed a strand of hair behind her ear and wrapped her arms around herself. 'Have you got a minute?'

'I was just about to open the shop,' I said. 'Come with me, if you like? There'll be no one else there.'

She nodded, and we walked together in silence. My mind raced as I wondered what the hell had happened to her. Something bad, obviously, because I'd never seen her looking so shaken.

I unlocked the shop door and ushered her in, then dropped the latch behind us. I pulled out the stool that was kept behind the till and motioned to her to sit down.

She practically fell onto it, and I put out my arms to steady her. 'Hey, what's wrong? You've got me really worried now,' I said.

'Lexi, I'm so sorry.' Her voice was little more than a whisper, and at first I wasn't sure I'd heard her right.

'Sorry? Sorry for what?' Even as I asked, I felt a cold chill suddenly. 'Is it Pandora? Has there been an accident?'

She shook her head, placing her hand on my arm. 'Nothing like that. Don't worry. It's me. I've let you down so badly. I've done something unforgivable.'

'You have?' I frowned. 'Like what?'

She stared up at me, and suddenly tears spilled out of her eyes and rolled down her cheeks — enough so it scared me.

What was going on? First Nat with a black eye, then Will in a temper, and on top of those, Georgia crying and telling me she was sorry.

I straightened suddenly as light began to dawn. Were all those things connected, somehow? Without warning, images flashed into my mind. Georgia and Nat, muttering to each other by the fence as I struggled to control Macbeth. Georgia's uncharacteristic behaviour towards me, veering between rudeness and cruelty to over-the-top kindness. Her sudden habit of wearing makeup when I had riding lessons.

I shook my head, denying my own thoughts. She wouldn't do that. Not Georgia.

But Nat could be very persuasive, as I knew all too well.

'It's you and Nat, isn't it?' I said, my voice flat.

She gasped and struggled to her feet. 'I'm so sorry, Lexi. It was just the once, and even then, the deed wasn't really done. I mean, I can't deny that if Will hadn't walked in—'

'Will knows?'

She wiped her eyes. 'He caught us this morning, but honestly, Lexi, I swear to you, it was the only time. I came up here to tell Nat to leave me alone. He's been flirting, sending me texts, and then I got these flowers, and I thought enough was enough.'

'Flowers?' Bloody hell. Nat had never bought me flowers. 'So, you came up here to tell him to leave you alone, and ended up having sex with him?'

'It just happened. One minute we were arguing, and the next ... Then Will opened the tack room door and saw us.'

'The tack room door?' I gave a snort of laughter. 'Classy.'

'Are you okay?'

'Well, what do you think? You're supposed to be my best friend.'

'And I am! That's why I tried to stop it.'

'Yeah well, good job there, mate.' There was no way I wanted her to know how devastated I felt. Never in a million years would I have believed Georgia would betray me. We'd been friends ever since I'd moved back to the village and had taken my cousins to the riding school one day, when Sophie couldn't make it. We'd got talking and bonded almost instantly. I loved her. How could she sleep with Nat behind my back? And why hadn't I realised sooner?

I remembered, suddenly, the first words she'd ever spoken about him. *Who's that bit of all right?* The reason for her animosity towards him was suddenly so obvious. When I'd accused her that day at the riding school of being jealous, I'd been more right than I could ever have guessed. She'd wanted him from the start.

Trembling, I said, 'Do me a favour and just go. I don't want to talk about this any more.'

'But, Lexi, we need to sort this. I don't want to fall out with you.'

Was she for real? Fighting the urge to drag her outside by her hair, I walked haughtily to the door and opened it. 'Just go, Georgia. I've got nothing to say to you.'

She stared at me beseechingly, but obviously realised that I wasn't in any mood for negotiations. She got slowly to her feet then headed past me, out into the cold air. She opened her mouth as if to say something but was almost knocked to the ground as Nat rushed up, skidding to a halt at the door.

He looked at her, then at me, then back at her. 'Shit,' was all he managed.

'Exactly,' I said.

'She's told you then?'

'Is that all you've got to say?' I demanded. 'Yes, she's told me. The point is, why didn't *you* tell me? And how did you really get that black eye?'

Georgia lifted a hand to touch the bruise, then dropped it to her side again as if she'd thought better of it.

'If you must know, Saint William came to your rescue.' Nat practically spat the words at me. 'You know Will, always the chivalrous one.'

'*Will* did that?'

Georgia and I stared at each other. She looked as stunned as I was at the revelation.

I admit, I felt a quiver of delight at the thought. I wouldn't have believed he had it in him. 'Well, good for him.'

'Yes. Good for him. Because, obviously, I've broken your heart,' Nat said, sarcasm dripping from every word.

'Hardly,' I said. 'I think I'm a bit tougher than that.'

'You don't have to tell me,' he said. 'I was trying to explain to Will that you wouldn't give a damn who I was shagging, because you haven't *got* a heart, and you're not capable of emotions, but he wouldn't believe me.'

The shock of his words hit me like a slap across the face. 'What do you mean by that? I do have a heart. I just refuse to let it be broken by someone like you. We both know you were never up for a long-term relationship.'

'Exactly,' he said. 'Which is why you chose me in the first place. I wasn't a boyfriend. I was protection.'

'Protection? I don't need protection, thanks very much.'

'Oh, I think you do.' He actually laughed. What a shit he was. 'It's quite amusing, how similar you and Will are. Both with abandonment issues, both with absent mothers who didn't care about you. Both putting up brick walls to keep the nasty world out.'

'Who told you about my mother?' I demanded, aware that I'd never breathed a word about her to him.

Georgia's face turned scarlet.

'You?' I could hardly believe it. 'You told him about my mum?'

'She did. How you don't trust relationships. How you never want to give your heart to any man. How you keep all men at arm's length, happy to use them for sex, but God forbid they ever want anything more. You really are Will's perfect woman.'

'Leave Will out of this,' I snapped. 'He's got nothing to do with it.'

'If you really believe that you're even more stupid than you look,' he said.

'It wasn't how it sounds,' Georgia said, eyes wide with sadness.

'Honestly, Lexi. I wasn't telling him for the fun of it. He wasn't being very kind about you. I was trying to make him understand why you behave the way you do.'

'Thanks,' I said. 'I'm so glad I've got you to watch my back.'

'You're wasting your time, Georgia,' Nat said, putting his arm around her. 'Come on, let's leave her to it.'

She shrugged him away from her, never taking her eyes off me. 'Lexi, can we talk about this properly? Please?'

I shook my head and pushed past them. 'You can mind the shop today, Nat. I'm going home.'

I refused to stick around another moment. Especially as Nat's words kept running through my mind.

You haven't got a heart. You're not capable of emotions. You keep all men at arm's length, happy to use them for sex.

I ran my hand over my face, realising it was wet with tears. What I was crying for, I couldn't imagine. After all, he hadn't told me anything I didn't already know.

****

Joe and Charlie were, to my immense satisfaction, deeply sympathetic and completely outraged by Nat's behaviour.

'What a tosspot,' Charlie said, as we leaned on the paddock fence, watching the donkeys graze. 'He was never good enough for you, my little Gingernut. I knew that from the first day I saw him. I thought to myself, *that one's a proper twat.* I've been waiting for you to realise that.'

'I'm surprised at Georgia,' mused Joe, where he sat on the top bar of the fence, clutching a mug of hot chocolate. It was the end of November, and we were all well wrapped up, wearing thick jumpers, jackets, gloves and scarves. The afternoon had turned bitterly cold. It seemed winter was really on its way. 'I wouldn't have thought she'd ever hurt you like that.'

'No, well, you and me both,' I muttered. 'Just shows you. You can't trust anyone, can you?'

Charlie frowned. 'I hope you ain't including me and Joe in that statement. Anyway, seems to me that Nat has a way with him.

214

He could charm the birds off the trees.'

'And the pants off any woman, evidently,' said Joe. 'I'll bet she's feeling awful about it. Are you going to go and see her?'

'Why the hell would I want to do that?' I leaned over and pinched his mug of hot chocolate, taking a large swig of the liquid that was now a bit too cool for my taste. 'Me and Georgia are finished.'

They glanced at each other. 'Are you sure?' Joe asked, turning back to me. 'It seems a terrible shame to let your friendship be ruined by one mistake with that idiot.'

'It was a very big mistake,' I said. 'She really let me down. I can never trust her again.'

'Crikey.' Charlie sighed. 'Well, I'll say one thing for you, you've taken it well. I mean, you hardly seem heartbroken, which is good. I take it we won't hear you sobbing into your pillow tonight?'

'Hardly,' I said quietly. 'I don't have a heart to be broken, apparently.'

'Who the hell said that?' Joe demanded. 'Was that Nat? Ignore him. He's just trying to make you feel bad because he got caught out. You don't want to take any notice of him.'

When I didn't reply, Charlie put his arm around me. 'You don't believe him, do you, Lexi?'

Joe jumped down from the fence and lifted my chin, giving me no choice but to face him. 'You don't believe that, surely?'

'Well, maybe he's right. Maybe I'm the cold, heartless bitch he says I am.'

'Is that what he said? I'll slap the little shit,' said Charlie indignantly.

I laughed. The thought of Charlie taking on Nat was too funny, even in my miserable mood. 'Don't worry about it,' I said. 'Will beat you to it.'

Their eyes widened in shock. 'Will? Will slapped Nat?' Charlie shook his head. 'I can't believe it.'

'He did more than slap him.' I felt a sudden warm, bubbling thrill run through me. 'He punched him. You should see Nat's face. He's got a proper shiner. Not that I condone violence, of course.'

Joe couldn't have smiled any wider if he'd tried. 'Of course, but ... Oh, good old Will,' he said. 'I'm so proud.'

'Aw, Joe,' said Charlie, 'the boy's all grown up.'

'You two are crackers,' I told them. 'Anyway, can we change the subject now please? I've had enough thinking about Nat and Georgia.'

'But what about Will?' Charlie said.

'What about him?'

'Well, what did he say to you about it all?' They were looking at each other in a very peculiar way.

I frowned. 'He didn't say anything. I haven't seen him since early this morning, before all this happened.'

'What? You mean you haven't been to thank him for decking that scumbag for you?'

I shook my head, suddenly guilty. Put like that, I suppose I should have done really. 'I just wanted to get away. I was supposed to be working at the shop today, but I told Nat he'd have to do it. I hope he has, otherwise I've really dropped Will in it. God, I'm a horrible person.'

'Don't be daft. You're not a horrible person at all, and don't you ever let them tell you that you're heartless. You're a kind, generous, loving girl, and anyone who says different will have me to answer to.'

'And me,' said Charlie.

I smiled at them both. 'Thank you. I don't know what I'd do without you. I love you both so much.'

'Well of course you do,' said Charlie. 'You're only human.'

'And that proves you've got a heart,' said Joe. 'So, let's put all that talk behind us, eh? Nat's out of the picture, and I reckon he'll be gone by the time you get back.'

'Gone? From the Hall, you mean?' I said. 'But he's Will's cousin.'

'Yeah, who's well and truly outstayed his welcome,' said Joe. 'He turned up, out of the blue, and then just didn't leave. He's contributed nothing to Will's life, and now he's upset him so much that he's acted completely out of character and punched

him. I can't see Will wanting him around any longer, can you? I'll
bet Nat's packing his stuff, even as we speak.'
 'You really think so?' I said.
 'Definitely. Is that okay with you?'
 I nodded. 'More than okay. I never want to see that nasty piece
of work again.'

Chapter 22

Will wanted to punch something. It was an unfamiliar feeling, but he'd had a pig of a day. As if things weren't bad enough, the quotation from Clarke's had arrived, and things were much, much worse than he'd feared. The entire roof needed replacing, and there was no way on earth he could imagine raising the kind of money he'd need for that much work.

He knew Clarke's came highly recommended by ECHOES, so he had no cause to question their recommendations, but it had been a bitter blow. It would have to wait for now, though, until he had the time to investigate ways of raising funds. That, plus his argument with Nat, was bad enough, but then he'd discovered that Lexi had found out what had gone on. Woody had run into Georgia, and Georgia had confessed everything to her, and told her tearfully that Lexi had gone home, leaving Nat to run the shop.

Since Nat couldn't be trusted to run anything, Will had stormed over and sent him packing, telling him to go back to the Hall, get his things together and leave. He'd then phoned one of the girls who worked in the shop and asked her if she'd like some overtime — which had delighted her, luckily, as she was saving up to go to Magaluf with her mates. Once she'd arrived, Will had headed back to the Hall, carefully avoiding Nat, and helped the workmen haul furniture around until he was absolutely shattered, but at least he hadn't had time to think much.

Darcey had seemed startled to see him there, and sounded a bit awkward ordering him around and telling him where to shift things, but he'd merely nodded when she asked if everything was okay, and she'd apparently understood he was only interested in working, not talking, and treated him just like the other men, which had suited him fine.

The tour was shaping up wonderfully. As Will glanced around him at what they'd named The Earl's Bedroom, he felt a sense of satisfaction. The seventeenth-century four-poster bed was surprisingly short. He couldn't imagine it had been very comfortable. His own feet would have been dangling over the edge if he'd had to sleep in that thing. Maybe the earl had slept propped up on pillows. Or maybe he'd been a short man. Although, if so, he must have needed a box to stand on to climb into bed, as it was so high.

He shuddered at the thought of sleeping in that room, especially knowing the secret that lay behind the panelling. With all that dark wood, heavy curtains at the windows, and the thick drapes around the bed, it must have been so dark and gloomy, it would have driven him mad.

'What do you think?' Darcey's voice broke into his thoughts, and he turned, managing a smile on seeing the excitement in her eyes. 'It's looking great, isn't it?'

'Really good. I don't like this room much, though. I think The Countess's Room is much nicer.'

'Well, that's as it should be,' she teased. 'The lady of the house deserves the best.'

He nodded. 'I suppose you're right.'

'Do you think they really had separate rooms?' she mused. 'William and Elinor, I mean?'

He shrugged. 'I've no idea. Why do you ask? Was it those two you particularly had in mind when you named these rooms?'

'Well, of course.' She seemed surprised at the question. 'Who else?'

'There were two other earls and countesses before them,' he reminded her. 'I thought you'd just plucked the titles out of thin air.'

'Not at all.' She walked over to the bed, straightening a nonexistent wrinkle in the silk coverlet. 'I suppose Lexi's put them in my mind. She seems quite taken with that Dobson portrait of him, doesn't she?'

'Hmm.' In truth, he found the whole subject of the portrait embarrassing. Lexi was so insistent that Lord Kearton resembled Will, and no one else could see any likeness. Of course they couldn't. William had been a handsome, heroic sort of chap. Will knew all too well that he didn't share his ancestor's features. He couldn't imagine what Lexi was seeing, but it was humiliating, seeing the expression of disbelief on everyone else's faces when she demanded to know if they could see the similarity between them. He wished she'd drop the subject.

'Have you told her about the second portrait of him we found covered over?' she asked. 'The Cornelius Johnson. I thought maybe we could put it in here? What do you think?'

'I suppose.'

'Maybe we should ask Lexi. After all, Lord Kearton is her pet project, isn't he?'

'I guess so.'

She came to stand beside him, watching him with evident concern. 'Will, are you sure you're all right?'

'Why shouldn't I be?'

'Well, you've been extremely quiet today. Not your usual friendly self at all.'

'Sorry,' he mumbled. 'I've had some bad news. Clarke's got back to me, and it's worse than I thought. They say we need a complete new roof, and it's going to cost a fortune. I simply don't have that kind of money.'

'May I see?'

He fumbled in his back pocket, pulling out the letter. She scanned it quickly and took a deep breath. 'I'm so sorry, Will.'

'Me, too.'

'Clarke's are the best in the business. If they say it's this bad ... What are you going to do?'

'I have no idea,' he admitted. 'We have so many other things to pay for out of the Maintenance Fund, and it will take ages to raise this much cash.'

'Will…' She seemed to hesitate a moment, then ploughed on. 'I'm sorry, I really am, but maybe this is one step too far? Have you really ruled out selling the Hall? I happen to know that Grant's Hotels are seeking to expand, and this is very much the sort of house they'd snap up. It would solve all your problems and save the building at the same time. You could be free of the burden, and I'm sure it's a very heavy one to bear at times.'

She wasn't wrong, thought Will. He felt he was suffocating under the pressure lately, and the latest blow had sent him reeling.

'I can't talk about it now,' he managed. 'I just can't think straight. I'm sorry.'

'You don't have to apologise. I'm just worried about you, with all these money troubles. And then there's Nat.' She hesitated. 'I see he has a black eye, and he seems very depressed.'

'Is he still here then?'

She raised an eyebrow. 'Still here? Why, is he leaving?'

'He'd better be,' Will muttered.

'Goodness. I appear to have missed something huge.'

'Where is he?'

'Last time I saw him, he was in the Reading Room.'

'Huh! Ironic. Since when did Nat ever read?'

'I don't know. Will, is there anything I can do to help? You seem really upset about something.'

He looked down into her hazel eyes, which clearly expressed concern. 'I'm sorry, Darcey. I've been very rude today and I apologise. Nat and I have had words, and I need to finish this. Will you excuse me?'

'Of course.'

She stepped aside, and he left the room and headed upstairs to the second floor. Entering through the Long Gallery, where two elderly female volunteers were carefully dusting the display cabinets, he walked into the Reading Room, which was a smallish room set in one of the bays off the Gallery. Closing the door behind him, he faltered, seeing Nat slumped on the curved window seat, set under the large bay window that overlooked the south lawns and the sea. Nat had one elbow resting on the sill and seemed lost in thought. He didn't appear to have heard Will's arrival.

Will took in the room, thinking how different it appeared since Darcey had worked her magic on it. It was the first room to be completed for the new tour. She'd taken a room mainly used for storage and decorated it in a coastal theme, adding some paintings of the area — images of Kearton Bay and Farthingdale in years gone by, a painting of Helmston on market day, a lovely landscape of the majestic sweep of the bay at Scarborough, crowned with the proud ruin of the castle, and a wonderful water colour of Whitby Abbey — all painted by local artists. The room was intended to give their visitors a chance to rest for a while. They could admire the paintings, or sit and take in the view over the Yorkshire coast. It was up to them. Will wanted them to relax in the house, and he felt it was one of the best rooms on the tour from that point of view.

He, on the other hand, felt far from relaxed as he surveyed Nat. 'I thought you'd be gone by now.'

Nat jumped. 'No, sorry. Still here.'

'Well, have you at least packed?'

Nat shook his head. 'I started to, then I thought no, I don't think I'll leave after all. Thought I'd give you a chance to calm down, and then we can talk about this properly, like rational human beings.'

Will's heart thudded. Was Nat determined to start another fight? 'There's nothing to talk about. I think you said everything you wanted to say earlier.'

'Still defending the lady's honour then?' Nat shook his head. 'Honestly, Will. You're wasting your time there. Trust me.'

'I wouldn't trust you with anything,' Will said, trying to keep his voice steady. 'Now, can you please pack your things and go home. We're done.'

He turned to leave, but Nat's voice stopped him. 'Will, please. Can you — can you just give me another chance?'

Will could hardly believe it. Was that Nat sounding so *desperate?* He turned around, staring at his cousin in surprise. 'Another chance?'

Nat heaved a big sigh and stood. He held up his hands in a gesture of defeat. 'I admit it, I behaved badly. I should never have said those things to you, and I should never have done the dirty on Lexi. It wasn't honourable behaviour. My father would have been furious with me.'

'No doubt,' said Will.

'The thing is, Will...' He stuck his hands in his pockets and hung his head, as though thinking for a moment. When he looked up, a pleading expression had taken over his face. 'The thing is, I don't want to leave. I don't want to go home. Hell, I don't really have a home. Not any more.'

'What are you talking about?' Will sank into one of the sofas, fleetingly registering how comfortable it was. 'You have a rather grand house in London, from what I've heard.'

'My mother does.' Nat shook his head. 'Since Father died, she's been having the time of her life. You know they never really got on. She found him tedious, and to be honest, I can't say I blame her. He was obsessed with this house. He was convinced he'd been robbed of it, and it made him a nightmare to live with.'

'Robbed of it? I don't understand.'

'When Grandfather died, your father was in line for the baronetcy. There was no disputing that. But Kearton Hall wasn't entailed. It could have been left to anyone. Your father wasn't interested in saving this place. He never was. Father said that, when they were younger, he was the one who worried about ways to earn money for it, and he was full of ideas and plans. Your father only wanted to ride, shoot game, and chase women.'

He gave a rueful grin. 'I guess I've got more of Uncle Paul's genes in me than I realised. Anyway, he hoped, prayed that Grandfather would leave the Hall to him, but he didn't. It went to Uncle, who pretty much ignored all the problems, and my father just worried his life away, resenting the fact that he could have done so much to bring it into the twenty-first century, but wasn't given the chance. I kind of understand him more, being around you, Will. You and he were very alike. I think we got the wrong fathers, to be honest.' He laughed, but Will didn't find it amusing.

'What's your point?' he asked.

Nat appeared a bit perplexed. Evidently, he'd expected Will to be more sympathetic. 'I'm just trying to paint a picture of what life was like with him. He was bitter, and he got more bad-tempered and mean the older he got. So when he died, well, I think Mother went a bit mad. She sold Park House, which was only ever a very poor substitute for the Hall, and bought the house in London, where she's been splashing out on every manner of luxury ever since. I can't blame her, I suppose. Father was a tight git, no denying it, but I do think she's gone over the top. Way over the top. And since she inherited everything, and Rebecca and I got nothing, it leaves us both in a bit of a pickle, as you can imagine.'

'Are you saying you're broke?'

Nat seemed nervous suddenly. 'I'm being honest with you here, Will. The truth is, by the time the old woman pops her clogs, there'll probably be nothing left except the house. That's if she hasn't sold it before she shuffles off the mortal coil. There's not much in the trust fund from Uncle Paul to look forward to. And what I've realised lately — rather late in the day, admittedly — is that I'm not best equipped to deal with the outside world, in terms of finances.'

'So, you're saying you're broke.'

'Well, the thing is, we had a bit of a ding dong. Me and the old woman. When I went back to London, after I'd stayed in Helmston, before the funeral, I had to face her wrath over my latest credit card bill. She said I was overspending. I told her that was a bit rich, considering she'd spent the last few years spending mine and Rebecca's inheritance, and that she was, to all intents and purposes, stealing from us. She took exception to that. Actually, she was livid. Upshot of it is, she cut up my credit card and told me to get out and make my own living. It's all a bit awkward. Hence my returning to Kearton Hall.'

'So, you're broke.'

Nat had evidently run out of ways to deny it. He ran his hand through his blond hair and shrugged. 'I guess I am. Yes. So, there you have it. I know it's not good, but I'm being honest with you here, Will. Doesn't that count for something?'

There was quiet for a moment, while Will digested this news. Nat watched him, clearly anxious. 'Are you going to say something?' he asked.

'How old are you, Nat?'

Nat blinked, surprised by the question. 'A year younger than you, as you very well know.'

'So, you're twenty-seven, and the only income you had was a credit card, supplied and paid for by your mother?'

Nat dropped down onto the window seat. 'There's no need to say it like that,' he muttered. 'You make me sound pathetic.'

'That's because it *is* pathetic,' said Will. 'Why haven't you got a job?'

'Well, that's bloody rich coming from you,' snapped Nat. 'You've never had a job or worked a day in your life!'

'Really? I've been training to run this place ever since I can remember. I've had to learn about the estate, about our tenants, about our finances. I've helped Bernie organise the shoots, gone with him to check on the farms, helped out on our own farm. I've dug and weeded and planted and planned with our head gardener. I've organised teams of volunteers. I've hired and trained people to work in the house and shop. I've *worked* in the shop. I've *set up* the bloody shop. I've taken admissions to the house and gardens. I've painted walls and shifted furniture. I've had endless meetings with staff, the accountant, the tenants, the solicitor. I've trawled through archives, trying to come up with a family history that would be of any interest to anyone. I've learned to do accounts. I've driven tractors, delivered lambs, fed pigs. I've even been known to clean the public toilets. I've unblocked sinks. I've served in the café. I've cleaned out the pond, stocked the lake, helped dredge the lake. I've cleared paths in the woods, chopped trees, planted trees, mucked out horses, mended fences, and generally been a dogsbody since the day I left school. And I've never had the luxury of a willing parent supplying me with a credit card so I could go out and treat myself to whatever I fancied. Perhaps you'd like to rethink your statement.'

The silence hung heavy between them. Will shook his head, leaned back on the sofa and closed his eyes. He had a headache coming on.

'We used to hide in here, do you remember?'

Will's eyes snapped open.

Nat was staring out of the window again, his chin propped on his arm, which rested on the windowsill. He thought back to when they were children. Whenever they'd done something naughty, Nat's first thought had always been to hide. Will hadn't really seen the point. He'd learned pretty quickly that his father would always get hold of them eventually, and they were only delaying the inevitable. He'd gone along with it, though. Nat had been able to talk him into almost anything. This room had always been great for hiding in, because there was so much old furniture crammed into it back then, there was always a cupboard to sneak into. And, for some reason, no one ever seemed to think of searching in there. It had been pretty much forgotten about, an afterthought to the impressive Long Gallery.

He remembered them holding their breath, hoping no one had seen them come up the second flight of stairs. He remembered Nat's smothered laughter, and his own pounding heartbeat. Nat often got away with being yelled at. Will had never been that lucky. At least he'd had company, though. And Nat had been fun, even if he was a bad influence.

Will wondered how much lonelier and duller his childhood would have been if it hadn't been for his cousin's regular visits. 'I remember,' he said.

'I got you into a lot of bother, didn't I? I'm sorry, Will.'

Will felt the tension seeping out of him. He remembered a small, fair-haired boy, with laughter in his blue eyes and dimples in his cheeks. He remembered the endless games of cowboys and Indians in the woods. The times they'd pinched old Stan the gardener's wheelbarrow, giving each other rides in it 'til the wheel dropped off. The time they'd bought cheap fishing nets from the shop in the village, then been soundly whipped for standing in the ornamental pond, trying to catch the expensive koi carp in their nets. The day they'd almost given Woody a heart attack when she'd found them sliding down the bannister of the ancient oak stairs.

He smiled suddenly. 'I was a willing accomplice, for the most part.'

Nat turned to look at him, and he smiled too.

'The thing with Lexi.' Will hesitated, not sure how to finish what he wanted to say.

Nat shook his head. 'I'm sorry. I really am. I'll apologise to her, of course.'

'If I let you stay, you'll have to work. I mean it. No dossing around or spending your days riding and watching television. You'll have to pull your weight. We have a lot to do to get this place in a good financial position. Everyone has to muck in.'

'Absolutely. I'd like to do it. Honestly.'

'Hmm.' Will doubted it.

Nat leaned forward. 'Really, Will, I'm starting to get it. Being here as an adult, you see things differently. I've accepted that you won't sell the place. I admit it, I probably wouldn't have come back for the funeral if the old woman hadn't thrown a wobbly, and I can't deny that, initially, I was counting on you getting rid of the estate and giving me a share of any profits, but I can see now that this place is more than just an old house to you. It's probably your entire life.' He paused. 'What I said about Lexi was unforgivably rude. And what I said about you and your mother — well, that was just plain cruel. I'm truly sorry, Will.'

Will stood up. He didn't want to discuss it. 'You'll have to put things right with her. Lexi, I mean. She works here, and I don't want her to feel awkward or hurt. You'll apologise, and you'll be pleasant to her. Understand?'

'Understood.'

'And you really don't think she'll be heartbroken?' He wondered why he'd asked. Why did he have to turn the screws?

'She won't be heartbroken, Will. Truly. She doesn't love me. She never did. I didn't mince my words, and I should have been more polite, but the fact is, what I said has more than a grain of truth to it. She *is* damaged. She doesn't want to love any man, and I don't think she ever will. I'm so sorry.'

'Why are you saying sorry to me?'

'Oh, Will. Really?' Nat shook his head, and Will swallowed.

'I'm going downstairs to finish off The Earl's Bedroom. If you want to make yourself useful, speak to Darcey. No doubt, she can find you something to do until dinner.'

'Okay, and Will...'

Will turned, to see his cousin standing again, seeming smaller somehow, less sure of himself. 'Yes?'

'Thank you.'

****

Woody broke the news to me. I was just about to sink my teeth into a gorgeous homemade flapjack, but that stopped me in my tracks. 'You're kidding. I don't believe it.'

'I couldn't believe it either. Thought the young devil was having me on, but then Will confirmed it. Nat's staying. And that's not all. Will's given him a job.'

'A job?' I put the flapjack back on my plate, unable to even think about eating it any more, which just shows you how shocked I was. 'Will wouldn't do that. Not after what Nat's done.'

'I'm sorry, love. He said Nat's family, can you believe? So, that's that. How that man manages to con his way round Will every time, I have no idea, but he's done it again. Reckon Will's been taken for a ride, and not for the first time. Don't suppose there's much we can do about it.'

'Really? Well, we'll see about that.' I stood up, pushing my chair away with such violence it almost fell over. 'Do you know where Will is?'

'Last I heard he was in the library with Darcey.'

'Well, I think it's time I had a word with him, don't you?'

'Just be careful, love,' she said. 'I know you and Will are good friends, but Nat has a hold over him. Always has had. Don't go falling out over this.'

I shook my head. 'We won't. Will just needs someone to put him straight.'

And I was just the person to do it, I decided. Honestly, he was

228

far too soft. Nat had behaved abominably, and he couldn't get away with it. Will would see that it would be impossible for me to work alongside him, surely? And, anyway, what job had he given Nat? Nat couldn't do anything. He was useless, and Will wasn't running a charity, for God's sake. Time to send Nat home and let him earn his own living.

The Long Gallery was on the second floor and covered the entire length of the house, running along the south side of the Hall, with views over the east lawns and ornamental pond at one end, and the stables and lane at the other. The Library and Reading Rooms were set in bays off each end of the Gallery, and the Library was the first one I came to. I threw open the door and marched in. Will and Darcey were leaning over the large table that took up a corner of the room. Will wore cotton gloves and was carefully examining some ancient tome, while Darcey stood beside him, watching him intently, a clipboard and pen clutched to her chest.

They looked up in surprise at my entrance.

'What on earth's the matter?' Darcey said, telling me my face must have given away the anger I felt inside.

'Can I have a word, Will?' I said, ignoring her. 'In private.'

They glanced at each other, then he turned the page in the book with exaggerated care and peered closely at it. I couldn't believe it. Was he winding me up or something?

'Will?' I repeated.

He didn't look at me. 'I can guess what this is about. Would you mind leaving us alone for a moment, Darcey?'

'Sure.' She left the room, giving me a curious look as she passed.

The door had barely closed before I rounded on him. 'Is this true? You're letting Nat stay? After everything he's done!'

He didn't reply and he didn't look at me. No bloody wonder. He should've been ashamed of himself.

Well, there was no way I was letting him get away with that. 'Are you listening to me?'

'I'm listening,' he said, then he gently closed the book, took a deep breath, and lifted his eyes to mine. His face was pale, and he seemed tense. I hoped Nat wasn't bullying him or making unreasonable demands. 'Now *you* listen to *me*, please. I understand that Nat has upset you—'

'Upset me! That's one way of putting it! He's made a complete fool of me!'

'Well, perhaps you could look it at it like that.'

'*Perhaps?*' What the hell was wrong with him?

'Nevertheless, Nat's my cousin. Family. Kearton Hall is as much a part of his heritage as it is mine, and he wants to help me safeguard its future.'

'Since when? Last I heard, he wanted to sell the whole lot and let them turn it into a hotel!'

'Things have changed since then. He's recognised how much this house means to me, and he's realised it means just as much to him. He wants to start afresh, and he's determined to make a go of this.'

'So, you've given him a job?'

'I have. He's going to be our new events manager.'

'Events manager? Since when did we need an events manager?'

'Since Darcey and I were discussing other ways of making this place pay.'

'And when was this?'

'Last night.'

Last night? So, they'd been having a cosy little meeting, had they? When had it suddenly become all about them, and where did I fit in now? Will used to tell me everything, run everything past me. Why was Darcey now his sounding board? And why was he taking Nat's side over mine?

'We think we should host major events. We'd like to involve the local area, get them to come to parties and shows here. We have lots of ideas.'

'So, why include Nat in it?'

'Because if anyone knows what makes a good social event, it's Nat. Frankly, I wouldn't have a clue, but he's been to more sporting events, shows, parties and dinners than I could count.'

'I can believe that.' I felt empty inside, as if I'd been hollowed out.

Will was looking at me, but it was as if he were no longer seeing me. And watching him, I realised that the Will I knew wasn't really there, either. This strange, cold man was standing in front of me, saying words I didn't understand. His eyes were expressionless, as if he'd been hollowed out, too.

'So, the fact that he cheated on me with my best friend means nothing?'

'Well…' He gazed down at the book, his gloved fingers softly stroking the cover. 'I accept that it must have been embarrassing. But it's not as if you were in love with him, is it?' He glanced up at me, and I saw something in his expression that I simply couldn't fathom. All I knew was, he wasn't my Will any longer.

'You know,' I said, heading towards the door, 'they're quite right about that portrait.'

'I'm sorry?'

'Lord Kearton. He doesn't look anything like you. I can't imagine what I was thinking.'

I saw him flinch, then I slammed the door behind me. Darcey was waiting in the Long Gallery, clipboard clutched to her chest. Great. No doubt she'd heard every word.

'Are you all right, Lexi?' she asked.

I was about to make some sarcastic comment, but as I looked at her, I realised she actually seemed concerned. Surprised, I muttered, 'Not really. As I'm sure you gathered from that conversation.'

She hesitated a moment then put her hand on my arm. I glanced down, taken aback to find her hand wrapped around my flesh. Her nail varnish was chipped. I hadn't noticed that before. 'Nat's been cheating on you with your friend? You're sure?'

'Of course I'm sure. Will caught them at it — hence Nat's black eye. And she confessed to me. I suppose guilt got the better of her. Too little, too late.'

She bit her lip. 'I can't believe it.'

'Can't you? Really? I should have known he'd do the dirty on me. He's the type, and deep down, I always knew it. It's Georgia. I mean—' My voice distinctly wobbled, and I swallowed down the pain as best I could. '—she's my best friend. *Was* my best friend. How could she do that? And now Will's taken Nat's side against me, too. What have I done to deserve all this?'

Compassion filled her eyes, completely bewildering me. 'I think Will's being a fool,' she whispered. 'I'm worried, Lexi.'

I couldn't have been more astonished if she'd told me she was really Woody's secret love child. 'Worried? What about?'

She looked around, rather dramatically, and whispered, 'I don't trust Nat. I don't believe for an instant that he's had this sudden amazing turnaround. Do you?'

'Not for a moment,' I said, with feeling. 'Nat doesn't care about Kearton Hall. All he wants is money.'

'Exactly,' she said. 'So, why is he suddenly pretending that he's going to help Will make this place work? I suspect sabotage, Lexi. Will's a nice man, but he's rather naive, don't you think?'

'You can say that again,' I said. 'Have you told Will how you feel?'

'How can I?' she said. 'I only work here. He's not going to take my opinions about his family seriously.'

'Well, he certainly isn't listening to me.' I felt nauseated as I thought how easily he'd dismissed my concerns.

'Nat's very good at this,' she said. 'I sussed him out pretty quickly. He's a liar and a schemer, and I really don't think he likes Will much.'

I couldn't believe it. She was quite right. When I thought about it, I realised Nat had been causing trouble for Will from the first. I thought again about Woody's suspicions that day of the funeral. Had Nat spiked Will's drink just to make him look a fool? Was he capable of that? I thought he probably was.

'What can we do about it, though?'

'Nothing, as yet,' she admitted. 'But I think Will needs someone to watch out for him. He's a sweet boy, but far too trusting. I think you and I are going to have to protect him, Lexi. We can't let Nat ruin our chances of saving Kearton Hall, can we?'

It took me a moment to catch up with what she'd said. My mind was temporarily frozen on *he's a sweet boy*. That certainly didn't sound like someone who fancied him. Had I been completely wrong about Darcey, after all? As her words sank in, I realised she was right. Will had been fooled by Nat, and I couldn't blame him. He'd fooled me, and he'd probably fooled Georgia, too. He was exceptionally good at the games he played. Darcey and I had to work together, if we were going to stop him sabotaging Will's chances of making a go of the Hall. I nodded and said the words I never in a million years thought I'd be saying.

'Okay, Darcey. I'm with you on this.'

Chapter 23

November gave way to December, and life at the farm had settled into a sort of routine. Charlie had gone back to London, staying in his flat there for a few weeks, as he was doing a series of gigs in the southeast, and filming the Christmas episode of his chat show. Joe and Eliza got to work decorating the farmhouse for Christmas and choosing the tree — something they'd apparently done together every year since she was a little girl.

Dad and Eliza seemed more settled too. Dad whistled whenever he set off to work, which was always a good sign, and Eliza seemed happier, having other people around her for company again. I guessed being stuck in the cottage with two babies, while Dad and I were at work and Amy was at school, must have been making her more depressed than I'd realised. She was talking excitedly about going back to work as soon as they found a house.

They'd viewed several properties, mostly in Whitby and Farthingdale, but hadn't fallen in love with any of them. Dad had been a bit panicky at first, not wanting to outstay our welcome, but Joe and Charlie were so reassuring that we could stay as long as we wanted, he'd started to finally believe them and had decided that he and Eliza would take their time and find something they truly wanted. After all, more houses were put on the market in the spring, and we could wait until then. There was no rush.

Amy loved being on the farm, and Twinkle had been left in his stable more and more, as she cadged rides on the donkeys and helped Eddie groom them every morning. It felt like old times, spending so much time at Whisperwood, having Eddie to talk to again, feeding the hens, cleaning the henhouse, and collecting eggs. Things would have been perfect if my home life was all I had to think about.

Unfortunately, I also spent a lot of time at Kearton Hall, and that was no longer my refuge. In fact, it had become increasingly difficult to be there. Nat had apologised to me with all the sincerity of a politician caught fiddling his expenses, and I'd told him to just stay out of my way. I couldn't, in all honesty, say I missed being with him, and any passion I'd had for him had died instantly. Seeing him lately, I couldn't imagine what I'd ever seen in him. What I couldn't forgive him for was sleeping with my best friend and ruining our friendship. I really did miss Georgia, but I couldn't face seeing her, and she'd made no attempt to contact me since that day, so I felt even lonelier.

By far the worst thing, though, was the change in Will. He seemed to go out of his way to avoid me, and when we did meet up, he was polite, civil, and completely detached. It was as if all our years of friendship had been erased from his memory. I couldn't understand it. It was almost as though he was punishing *me* for what had happened with Nat. It made no sense at all, and I felt completely bereft, having lost my two best friends at the same time.

Funnily enough, Darcey had proved to be the opposite of what I'd imagined. She seemed to feel real sympathy, and was kindness itself to me. If anything was discussed about the Hall, she made sure I was informed. It was really good of her, though it broke my heart that Will hadn't told me himself. I'd tried to convince Woody that we'd misjudged Darcey, but she wasn't sure.

'I'll reserve my opinion for the moment,' was the most I could get from her, though she did relent and offer to make Darcey a healthy salad one lunchtime, rather than trying to force her into eating a hearty meal, as she usually did. Darcey seemed surprisingly touched and grateful, which had so startled Woody, she went so far as to make her a fresh fruit salad for pudding.

One morning, I decided to walk up to the Hall, rather than drive, and approached the house through the main entrance, rather than along the little lane that ran parallel to the west side of the house. The main entrance was through an archway under the gatehouse. I walked up the long, gravel drive, which cut through the south topiary lawns, and felt a lump in my throat as I faced the house in all its majestic glory. I rarely saw it from that angle, as I usually entered by the side gate on the west, but seeing the Hall standing at the end of the drive, I felt it was as a first-time visitor might see it, and experienced a rush of pride and love for the place. Its beautiful symmetry, its fourteen blocks of tall chimneys, its mixture of sash and mullioned windows, its red brick walls and stone quoins, filled me with a delight I could hardly put into words. The Hall wasn't mine, but somehow, it felt as if it was part of me, and I was part of it. I belonged there. I'd felt that way since I'd first visited the house, as a paying guest, long before I ever started working there.

Heading towards the stone steps, I glanced around me at the lawns, which even at this time of year were lush and green, and thought I was the luckiest person on earth to have the job I did, in spite of the problems I was currently having. The people may all be behaving like idiots, but the house had never let me down. I wouldn't let it down either. If Nat was up to something, I'd stop him. No one was going to turn the place into a hotel.

The entrance door was set in the side of one of the projecting bays. I headed through there, and pushed open the door to the Outer Hall, then walked through the archway to the Great Hall.

Immediately, a sense of calm washed over me. All around me portraits of Will's ancestors stared down at me, and for the first time I saw them as allies, not judgmental bullies. They would be on my side, I was sure of it. They would be able to see Nat for what he was, and they would want me to stop him.

I smiled up at them, silently promising them that I wouldn't let them down.

I stood for a few moments, breathing in the atmosphere that's only present in an ancient house like Kearton Hall, before reluctantly turning back for the Outer Hall, heading through the door into the west wing.

I was startled when I almost bumped into Nat, Will and Darcey, all standing in the corridor outside one of the empty rooms. My legs turned to jelly, and a weird churning began in my stomach as I wondered what reaction I could expect from Will today.

He and Nat exchanged glances, then Darcey gave me a bright smile and said, 'Good morning, Lexi. Isn't it freezing? Very much a hot tomato soup and buttered toast sort of a day.'

Really? I would have thought every day for Darcey was a rice cake and beetroot juice sort of day, but what did I know? Clearly, I was an appalling judge of character.

'We were just choosing an office for Nat,' she continued. 'As events manager, he feels he needs his own space.'

'Of course he does.' As a blush heated my cheeks, I felt furious with myself. I shouldn't let them see that it got to me, but it was tough. I felt like an outsider, like I was being bullied and ostracised, and I had no idea why.

I began to walk away, thinking I'd head to the kitchen to share a few minutes with Woody, have a cup of tea, and gather my strength before I started work.

Nat mumbled something behind me, before Darcey called, 'Lexi!'

Reluctantly, I stopped and turned to face her, keeping my eyes well averted from Will. 'What?'

'I think you'll be pleased to know that I've discovered there's a rather fabulous portrait of Lady Kearton at Burton Sipling Hall. It was her family home, so I'm heading over to East Yorkshire today to view it and try to find out more about her. I think we should make more of a feature of the two of them, as you suggested.'

She was trying to be kind, I knew that, and I was grateful to her for trying. The fact was though, that just the thought of the Third Earl and Countess was enough to increase my depression. Despite what I'd said to Will, I couldn't disentangle him from his namesake, and I didn't want to think about him at all. Will had hurt me far more than Nat could ever have managed. So, in spite of Darcey's attempts to include me in the conversation, I merely shrugged, muttered, 'Fine,' and walked away.

Finding Woody loading the washing machine, I went to help her, much to her surprise.

'You feeling all right, love? Since when did you have any truck with the washing machine?' She grinned at me, but the twinkle in her eyes died when she saw my face, as if my depression was clear to see. 'Lexi, what's wrong? You look as if you're going to burst into tears any minute.'

She ushered me over to the chair by the fire and pushed me down into it. I remembered doing the same to Will, the day I'd visited him after Sir Paul's death. I thought how close we'd been then, and I stared at her, stricken.

Woody put her arms around me. 'Aw, petal. What's happened? Tell me what I can do to help.'

I shook my head, wiping my eyes and sniffing. 'Nothing. Sorry, Woody, I don't know what came over me.'

She peered closely at me for a moment, then straightened, hands on her hips. 'Is it that Nat? Is he giving you a hard time?'

I swallowed. 'I can cope with Nat. I don't care what he says or doesn't say. He's irrelevant.'

'Darcey then? I thought it was too good to be true, her being nice. What did she say? I'll throttle the little madam.'

'She hasn't said anything. She's been really kind, actually. Lovely. I feel awful when I think what I used to say about her. It's not Darcey, or Nat. It's Will.'

Her eyes widened. 'Will? How has Will upset you?'

'You wouldn't believe me,' I said, because I suddenly realised that I wouldn't have believed it either. Will had never behaved like that towards me before. It was as if I'd ceased to exist to him. 'He's fallen out with me, and I don't know why.'

'Will, fallen out with you!' She started to laugh, which was pretty annoying. 'Never in a million years. He thinks the world of you. I reckon you're being a bit oversensitive, what with Nat and Georgia doing the dirty on you like that.'

'You're wrong,' I said. 'I'm telling you, he's—'

I shut up quickly when the kitchen door opened and Will stood there, looking uncomfortable.

Woody stared at me, then at him. 'Cup of tea, Will?' she said. 'I'm just about to make one for me and Lexi.'

He shook his head. 'Sorry, Woody. I'm too busy. I just wanted to tell you not to make Bernie any lunch today. Darcey's car won't start, so he's driving her down to East Yorkshire and they'll be gone most of the day.'

'Right. Fair enough.' She eyed him, evidently waiting. I ventured a quick glance at him, but he wasn't looking in my direction.

He cleared his throat and said, 'Right, well, that's all.' The door closed behind him and Woody gaped at it for a moment.

'Well,' she said.

'You see?' I said, dully. 'I'm not imagining it, am I?'

She sank into the chair opposite me, looking stunned. 'I never would have believed it. What can have happened? Are you sure you didn't say anything to upset him?'

'Only that I thought he should send Nat home. He wasn't having it, of course. Nat is family, after all, and I appear to be just the hired help.' I heard a distinct wobble in my voice and swallowed hard. 'I thought we were friends,' I said. 'I thought he cared about me. Obviously, I was wrong about that. I don't know, Woody, I love it here, but I think, if it carries on like this much longer, I'll be searching for another job.'

'You don't mean that.'

'I do. I don't feel welcome here any more. I'll give it a month or so, but then, if things are no better, I'm out of here.'

Woody squeezed my hand. 'It won't come to that, petal, I'm sure. I don't know what's going on in that lad's mind, but things will sort themselves out. He's far too decent to behave like this for long, and besides he—' she broke off, shaking her head.

'He what?' I said.

'He's very fond of you,' she said firmly, standing up and heading back to the washing machine. 'It will all come out in the wash,' she said, reaching for the fabric conditioner. 'You just wait and see.'

****

Darcey and Bernie were gone for most of the day, as Will had said they would be. I was about to leave for the night when I heard the side door close and Darcey's heels clicking along the passageway. I came out of the cloakroom, pulling the strap of my bag over my head, and almost collided with her.

'You're back, then,' I said. 'Good day?'

'Most productive,' she said. 'Where's Will?'

'I've no idea. Haven't seen him for hours. I'm about to leave, anyway, so I'll see you tomorrow.'

'Tomorrow? But aren't you interested in what I found out about the Earl and Countess?' she asked. 'I thought you'd be dying to hear all about it.'

I bit my lip. At one time, I would have been. Right now, though, I just wanted to go home before either Will or Nat made an appearance.

Darcey seemed to sense what I was thinking. She sighed then, to my astonishment, she hugged me. 'I'm sorry things are so bad for you at the moment, Lexi, I really am. Please don't let Nat win. If you show him he's upset you, you've given him what he wants. Men like that thrive on it.' She tutted in disgust. 'Believe me, I know.'

'You do?' I peered at her with interest. 'Well, the thing is, it's not Nat that's bothering me. It's Will. He's a different person these days, and not one I like.'

'So I've noticed,' she said, with some feeling. 'But don't you see? That just shows how under Nat's influence he really is. We have to stand by him and protect him, because I'm sure Nat has ulterior motives for being here, and we have to do everything we can to scupper his plans, whatever they are.'

'I suppose you're right,' I said, half-heartedly.

'Then, come with me to find Will, because I have some exciting news for him.'

'All right,' I muttered, thinking that, really, I was a glutton for punishment and deserved everything I got.

Unfortunately, when we found Will, he was with Nat. Of course he was. They were practically glued to each other these days.

They were in the new office that Nat had bagged for himself, just a few doors down from the cloakroom, and we found them easily enough because we heard them laughing, as if they were best friends or something. Honestly, it was enough to make me want to poke them both in the eye with a sharp stick, and I speak as a vegetarian pacifist.

Of course, the laughter died when we walked into the room. Will was sitting on the edge of Nat's desk, and he rose to his feet immediately and dug his hands in his pockets, his face taking on a cool expression. Who did he think he was trying to impress? Because if it was Darcey, he was out of luck.

I'd finally realised that she didn't see Will that way. Although she couldn't have been more than five or six years older than him, she definitely saw him as a young man who needed protecting, rather than a prospective lover. Tough luck, Will.

'You're back,' he said, giving her a faint smile. 'How did it go?'

I seethed. It was if I were invisible. What the hell was going on with him?

'As I was just telling Lexi here,' said Darcey, touching my arm pointedly, 'Bernie and I had a rather productive day. I have some interesting news for you. Shall we head into the sitting room?'

'Go ahead,' said Will. 'We'll follow you in a moment. We just have a few things to tie up first.' He glanced at his watch. 'Shouldn't you have gone home, Lexi? It's gone half-past five you know.'

I wanted to give him a flippant answer, but I couldn't. I felt as if he'd just punched me in the guts. He stared at me for a moment, then turned away and looked out of the window at something that was evidently far more interesting.

To my astonishment, Nat said, quite gently, 'I think Lexi probably wants to hear all about Darcey's trip. I vote we leave what we were discussing until later, Will. Let's all go to the sitting room, have a drink, unwind, and find out what Darcey's discovered.'

He sounded almost kind, and I found myself in the unlikely position of feeling grateful to him. I didn't know which way was up any longer. The world had gone crazy.

I turned and left the room, realising that Darcey was just behind me. She caught up with me and whispered, 'Well done for not giving in. Chin up.'

Yep, the world had gone crazy all right. When Darcey was the one I could trust, Nat was being kind, and Will was being positively vile to me, something had gone seriously wrong with reality. I wondered briefly if I'd actually been injured when I fell off Macbeth, and was lying in a coma in the hospital, having weird hallucinatory dreams. Anything seemed possible lately.

As we all sat down, Nat headed over to the bar and poured us all drinks. I realised my hands were trembling and took a large gulp of the wine he'd handed me to steady my nerves. I didn't even like wine much.

Keeping my head down, I peered up at Will and found him staring into his glass, looking pretty downcast. Good. I hoped he felt bloody miserable and thoroughly guilty about his behaviour. Somehow, though, I doubted it.

'So,' said Nat, sitting down and facing Darcey, 'what's the good news?'

'Well, Burton Sipling Hall is still in private hands, as I said, and the owners were at home and rather lovely. They're not descended from the original family. In fact, they only bought the house around ten years ago, but they do have a lot of the original furniture and possessions there. They showed me the portrait of the Countess, and when I explained the reason for my interest, they offered to loan it to us indefinitely. It was recently valued at eighty-eight thousand pounds, but that, apparently, is chicken feed to these people. He's American and terribly wealthy, and she's a hopeless romantic. They loved the idea of reuniting the married couple in what was once their marital home. Of course, it's only on loan, and there will have to be an official agreement drawn up, but the upshot is, the Countess is returning to Kearton Hall. That's if you want her of course, Will?'

I watched Will's face. He swilled his wine around in the glass for a moment, took a large gulp of the liquid, then nodded. 'Of course. That's really generous of them.'

'I suppose it's good to complete the set,' said Nat. 'Did you find

242

out anything else?'

'Yes. Did you know that Elinor's father died just before her engagement?'

Nat shook his head. 'I didn't, no. Did you, Will?'

Will looked satisfyingly surprised by that piece of news. 'No. What a shame.'

'I have to say, the Siplings didn't seem to have any more luck than the Keartons. He was thrown from his horse and killed.'

'Must have been a horse like Macbeth,' I muttered. For a moment, I thought Will's lips twitched with amusement, and felt a flare of hope.

Nat swigged the last of his whisky and went over to refresh his glass. 'So, who inherited the house and the dosh?' He opened the bottle and held it out, silently asking if any of us wanted to join him. We all shook our heads, and he poured himself another tot and screwed the cap back on.

'Elinor's brother. He became her guardian, and within months, she was engaged to William.'

Nat laughed. 'Didn't waste much time, did he? Palmed her off as quickly as he could and reaped the financial rewards of being connected to the Keartons, no doubt.'

'Don't be so cynical,' I said, forgetting for a moment that I was sulking and not interested in the story. 'I'll bet William and Elinor married for love, and love alone.'

'I very much doubt that.' Nat laughed and plonked himself back in his chair. 'It was all about money and connections in those days. Bet the poor cow didn't have any say at all.'

Darcey seemed uncomfortable. 'There is some evidence that an engagement was about to be announced between herself and a local landowner, but after her father's death, that never happened. It could be that her father was going to allow her to marry the man she wanted — by all accounts he absolutely doted on his daughter — but her brother thought an earl would be a more profitable match. Still, that's speculation, and anyway, it doesn't mean that she didn't come to care for William after their marriage.'

'I doubt she had time,' said Nat, 'since she snuffed it pretty quickly. How do you know all this, anyway?'

'As I said, the owners of the house aren't connected to the original family, but they kept on some of the staff, and one of them has been there for simply ages.'

'What, since the seventeenth century?' Nat cackled with amusement. Whisky obviously made him hilariously funny — in his own mind, at least.

'Of course not, but his family were in the employment of the Siplings and their descendants for centuries. He's very loyal to them, and to their memory. He knows loads about the history, and he couldn't wait to tell me all about it. It seems Elinor left East Yorkshire to move to Kearton Hall after her marriage, and never returned. She was dead within eighteen months. She was just twenty-five when she died.'

We were all quiet as we digested that information. Even Nat seemed to sober up instantly.

'Pretty awful story,' said Will eventually. 'Such a shame.'

Nat tutted. 'Well, anyway, never mind all that now. Did you find anything out about the treasure?'

'Oh, Nat, that's just a story,' said Will with a sigh.

'So you say. It's a pretty exciting one, though, you must admit,' said Nat. 'Besides, if there *is* treasure somewhere in Kearton Hall, it could really help us out financially. It could be worth a fortune in today's money.'

'Actually, the man I spoke to *did* mention it. He remembers his grandfather telling him about a letter that William Kearton apparently wrote to Elinor's brother, before he went off to fight, assuring him that he'd taken steps to ensure his treasure was kept safe.'

'I knew it!' Nat shook his head and swallowed another mouthful of whisky. 'Mark my words, we're sitting on a gold mine here.'

'Do you believe that?' I asked Darcey. If anyone was going to give me a sensible and reasonable opinion, it was her.

She considered for a moment. 'It would be lovely to think so. But do bear in mind that, after William's departure, this house was taken over by the Parliamentarians, who no doubt helped themselves to all sorts of things. Really, it's amazing you have anything left from that period of history at all, so it would be a miracle if you came across a hoard of gold any time soon.'

I didn't really want to talk too much, with Will being the way he was, and Nat being so sarcastic, but I couldn't contain my curiosity. 'What sort of treasure are we talking about?'

Since Will didn't answer, Nat jumped in. 'Well, as it was hidden just before he went off to fight in the war, when he probably knew Cromwell's men were likely to get hold of this place, he no doubt hid the most valuable stuff in the house. He also likely stashed away all the money he could get his hands on, so that he'd have something to come back to. Of course, he never came back, so all that gold is just sitting there somewhere, being wasted. God!' He sighed deeply. 'The things we could do with that money, eh, Will?'

'Like a flashy new car?' I snapped. 'Holidays abroad? Posh clothes? Designer watch?'

'Actually,' he said, giving me a filthy look, 'I was thinking of all the things we could do to this place. We could go ahead with the stables conversion, for a start. And get that roof fixed. Speaking of which, I was thinking I might get someone else to come up here and check out the roof. See what they think.'

Darcey bristled. 'What on earth for?'

'It never hurts to get a second opinion,' said Nat calmly.

'Of course not,' she said, 'but ECHOES only recommends the best. We've worked with that company for years, and they really know what they're talking about. I don't see the point of wasting yet more money, getting someone else to tell us what we already know.'

'Yeah, but as I'd started to tell Will, before you so rudely interrupted us, I've been doing a bit of research, too. In fact, I called ECHOES. You know about their heritage grants, I take it?'

She stared at him. 'Of course I do. What about them?'

'Well, it seems that fixing roofs are one of the things they're able to help with. We could apply for a grant, and then it wouldn't cost us a penny. I'm surprised you didn't think of that yourself, Darcey.'

She tutted. 'Well, of course I thought of it. The problem with ECHOES is that they have a limit for each grant, and I wanted to find out if we needed more than they would allow. That's why I got Clarke's in to give us an estimate. As soon as I knew what the work would cost, I realised that a grant was out of the question.'

'Which is why I think we need a second opinion. Who's to say that Clarke's is right? Besides, I can call in a favour,' said Nat. 'This firm that I'm talking about has done work for Pa. They understand the problems with houses like this, and if Pa trusted them, then I'm sure I can, too. They have plenty of experience with listed buildings. What do you think, Will?'

'Well, I suppose it can't do any harm,' Will said, sounding a bit surprised.

'That's settled, then,' said Nat.

Darcey looked as if she could strangle him. He smirked back at her. There was definitely something going on, and I had a very uneasy feeling indeed. Nat was up to something, and it seemed Will was completely oblivious to the fact. What would it take to make him see what was going on right under his nose? Nat seemed to have cast a spell on his cousin, and right now, I couldn't think of a way to break it.

Chapter 24

'You can't possibly agree to that!'

Standing in Will's new office in the west wing, I glared at him. Yep, they all had offices. It was no longer a case of carrying a laptop into the sitting room, or the library, or even the kitchen. Everything was business-like and official, these days. Nat, Darcey, Will, and even Bernie, had their own office. I was amazed Woody didn't have a bloody office.

Did I have one? Of course not. I was just a minion, at the beck and call of everyone else, and ready to cover wherever, whenever needed. Lately, I seemed to spend most of my time working in the shop, which was all very well, but hardly what I'd imagined when I'd started work at the Hall. I *was* studying for a degree, after all. Shop assistant wasn't what I'd envisioned as a career. I mean, if I wanted to work in a shop, I could have started at Mallow Magic.

I was beginning to feel pretty resentful, and Nat's latest idea had pushed me to my limit, so much so that I'd swallowed my pride and marched off to confront Will — an act that necessitated my actually speaking to him, which was unfortunate, as I didn't do speaking to Will very much these days.

He was sitting at his desk, writing Christmas cards. How lovely for him that he had the time. He glanced up, obviously startled by my sudden appearance at his door, and judging by the pensive look on his face, recognising my anger.

Nat had caught up with me, and I had to force myself not to

lose my temper as he said, 'Sorry, Will. I tried to stop her disturbing you, but you know what she's like.'

'Who the hell do you think you are?' I spun round, wondering what on earth I'd ever seen in him. What had I been thinking? He was the spawn of Satan.

'What's this about?' Will demanded. He sounded bad tempered and snappy, and I quailed for a moment, wishing I'd done what I always did lately and avoided him.

Then I remembered why I was there and lifted my chin defiantly. 'You can't let the hunt meet here on Boxing Day. You just can't.'

'I think you'll find he can do what he likes,' said Nat. 'It's his house, after all.'

'Congratulations,' I said. 'You've finally remembered that have you? About bloody time. Why would Will want the hunt on Kearton Hall land? He doesn't even hunt, do you, Will? And it's barbaric. We can't be seen to be encouraging such a vile activity.'

'Get over yourself,' snapped Nat. 'The hunt is a fine tradition. It's part of our heritage. I don't know why you're getting so worked up, anyway. Fox hunting's illegal now, remember? It's a drag hunt, that's all. The hounds follow a scent. *No foxes will be harmed in the making of this day's entertainment.* Sadly.'

'You evil prat,' I said. 'You'd happily chase a fox all over the countryside, wouldn't you? Go on, admit it.'

'I freely admit it,' he said, with no trace of shame whatsoever. 'Foxes are vermin. If you'd seen the damage they cause for yourself, you might not see them as innocent victims. This isn't a Disney film, you know. This is real life.'

'They have to eat,' I protested. 'That's nature.'

'Bollocks. They kill for the fun of it, half the time,' he snapped. 'Besides, like I said, there's no fox involved in the hunt now. It's just following a trail, and how can you object to that?'

'I don't believe it, that's how,' I said. 'I know these hunts break the law. They're devious, cunning and sly.'

'Like foxes then,' he said. 'And I'll have you know that the Farthingdale Hunt is a very old, very respectable hunt. The Master was a friend of my father's and wouldn't dream of breaking the law. That's slander.'

'Sue me,' I said.

'You're ridiculous,' he said. 'You'll be moaning about the shoot next. You and your stupid vegetarian ideals.'

'What bloody shoot?' I demanded. I knew there'd used to be a game shoot held at the Hall each year, but it had stopped before I started working there. Surely to God they weren't starting up again? Bewildered, I clutched the desk for support, staring at Will appealingly. 'You're not having a shoot here? You wouldn't. What the hell's happened to you?'

'It's called developing a business brain,' said Nat. 'Something you clearly haven't managed. While you're tripping around in your pretty little bubble, dreaming about the Third Earl, and selling jars of chutney, we have to come up with ways of actually making this place pay, and we've decided that the shoot could be a pretty effective business.'

'Oh, have *we*? *You* have, you mean. This is just a giant playground to you, isn't it? It's not about saving Kearton Hall. You don't care about that. You just want to impress all your poncy pals and invite them up to hunt and shoot, as if you're some sort of country gent. You're supposed to be an events manager. Why don't you start organising some events?'

'And what do you think a shoot and a hunt meet are?'

'You don't want to know what I think they are,' I assured him. 'My language would make even you blush.'

'*For God's sake!*'

Nat and I both jumped as Will banged his fist on the desk. To be honest, I think we'd both forgotten he was there for a moment. I folded my arms, confident that he was about to tell Nat to bugger off, and there was no way on earth he was having a meet or a shoot on his land. He knew how I felt about blood sports. Nat would have to find other ways of satisfying his blood lust, and hopefully, he could go somewhere else to do it.

Will looked from one to the other of us, his face paler than usual. He seemed tired, I thought suddenly, feeling a pang of guilt. He wasn't sleeping much, according to Woody. Worrying about the state of the roof was affecting him badly, and she was quite anxious about him, fretting that he seemed to have the weight of the world on his shoulders. Since I'd mostly avoided him lately, I hadn't noticed, but seeing it in him now, I felt quite alarmed, too. He'd even lost a bit of weight, and God knows, Will could hardly afford to do that. He needed a good meal inside him. A few good meals, to be fair. Some of Eliza's Yorkshire puddings were better than medicine. If only things had been right between us, I could have invited him round to the farm for dinner.

As it was, I merely stared at him, feeling sad and guilty and concerned, and trying not to show it.

'The shoot is a good idea, and definitely worth investigating further,' he said, not looking at me, and I was so shocked I couldn't speak. He seemed to suddenly feel the need to shuffle the Christmas cards on his desk. 'Lots of very wealthy people like to shoot, and it used to be very popular when Father ran one. I've consulted Bernie about this, and he agrees with Nat that it could make money. We're looking into the details.'

'Why didn't you tell me?' I could barely get the words out.

He finally met my gaze, and I saw a faint look of pleading in his eyes. 'I knew you wouldn't approve and saw no reason to upset you.'

'And it's got nothing to do with you,' said Nat triumphantly.

Will turned to him. 'I've been thinking over what you said about the Boxing Day meet. The answer's no. I don't want the hunt here.'

'What?' Nat sounded appalled, and it was my turn to give *him* a smug look. 'Why on earth not?'

'I don't see that it will make any contribution to our main aim, which is to save the Hall. And, frankly, it's not worth the bother. Too many people around here don't approve of hunting — drag hunting or not. I don't see the point in stirring up locals for something that, to be honest, I don't care for. I want people on our side, not against us. The hunt has plenty of other places to meet, so no, it can't meet here, and that's the end of the matter.'

'But—'

'That's my final word,' said Will. 'Now, if you'll excuse me, I have work to do.'

'Writing Christmas cards!' Nat sounded scornful. 'Big deal.'

'These are going to people on Darcey's list,' said Will. 'People who she thinks could be useful contacts. They're a sort of business card. Like just about everything else I do lately, this is for financial purposes, not fun.'

He sounded so depressed, I forgot I was angry with him about the shoot and longed to give him a hug. But I couldn't. Those days were over. And I couldn't see them ever returning.

****

Arriving at work few days later, I was met in the Outer Hall by an excited sounding Darcey. 'Lexi! You must come and look!'

'What's happened now?' I asked, but didn't even have time to take my coat off, as she beckoned me to follow her through the Great Hall and into the Parlour, where Nat and Will stood by a large, framed painting.

'She's here? The Countess?' I rushed forward, forgetting that I wasn't talking to either man, and gazed eagerly at the portrait of the woman who'd won William Kearton's heart. I felt a twinge of disappointment as I took it in, though.

The trouble was, like so many portraits of the time, the painting was a stylised version of the woman. I supposed I'd hoped for something a little more personal, more revealing, but the portrait was very formal, making it hard to get the essence of the real person. Labelled *The Hon Elinor Sipling, Cornelius Johnson, 1639*, the painting revealed little more than that Elinor had been a brunette, with blue eyes and pale skin. Other than that, it was hard to tell. It seemed to me there was a great deal more detail in the clothes she was wearing — a green satin dress, with an embroidered bodice. Typical of Cornelius Johnson, who was renowned for his meticulous recording of his subjects' attire. I peered closely at a brooch pinned to her bodice, admiring its unusual shape. It was star-shaped, with a large central emerald surrounded by smaller emeralds, and seed pearls at each point. I'd never seen anything quite like it.

'That's gorgeous,' I said, pointing at the brooch. I'd never been much of a one for jewellery, and brooches definitely weren't my thing, but there was something about that one that had caught my eye. 'Absolutely beautiful, and so unusual. I love it. But what a shame her personality doesn't come through.'

'What were you expecting?' said Nat. 'That she'd be wearing a T-shirt proclaiming *I heart Will*?'

'Oh, shut up,' I said. 'Why do you always have to shove your oar in, anyway?'

'Why do you have to be such a drip? For someone who doesn't believe in true love, you're pretty obsessed with these two. Maybe you should try a bit of romance in real life, instead of living vicariously through a couple that's been dead for nearly four centuries.'

'*Why don't you both just shut up?*'

We both stopped arguing and turned, shocked, toward Will, who gave us both despairing looks then left the room, banging the door behind him.

'What's got into him?' I said.

'He had some bad news this morning,' said Nat, sounding guilty. 'I'll go after him.'

As he closed the door on us, I turned to Darcey. 'What's going on?' I felt deeply hurt, and not a little jealous, that I was the last to know what had happened to Will. At one time, I'd have been the first.

She sat down. 'He had a letter this morning from his mother. I don't know the details, but I don't think it was particularly pleasant.'

His mother! Elisabeth had finally got in touch? Evidently, she hadn't said anything to make him feel any better about their relationship.

Ignoring Darcey's calls of, 'Wait, Lexi. Leave them to it,' I hurried out of the Parlour toward the west wing. As I neared Will's office, though, my steps slowed. The door was open, and I could hear voices.

Should I walk away and forget it? It was private, after all.

Except, the truth was, I wanted to know what Elisabeth had

said to upset Will, and hell, I freely admit I'm no saint. I edged closer, holding my breath as I listened in.

'You're not going to give her anything?'

'What do you think?'

'I wouldn't be surprised, knowing you, Will. You're far too nice for your own good.'

'Not in this case. I have made her an offer, though.'

'Christ, what have you said?'

'Just that, if she's really as destitute as she claims, she can always come back here, and I'll provide her with a home.'

'You really want her living with you?'

'I was thinking of the Gatehouse. I know it needs some work, as it hasn't been lived in for some years, but it could be a decent home, and it's big enough.'

'Huh. And you really think she'll take you up on it?'

'Not at all. Her letter made it quite clear that she adores living in New York and has no desire to return to England, not even to — how did she put it — oh, yes, to *offer comfort and deepest sympathies* to me. What a way to phrase it. You'd never know she was my mother, would you?'

'She's not really, though, is she, Will? I mean, she gave birth to you, and that's about it. But look, it's her loss, and I'm proud of you for not sending her the money she asked for. Let her pay her own way, for once in her life. It's not as if you're leaving her to starve. You've offered her a way out, if she really needs it. As you say, I very much doubt she'll need, or want, to take it.'

'I suppose you're right. Wish I knew why I felt so miserable about the whole thing, though. It's not as if I expected anything else, is it?'

'It's her loss, Will. Not yours.'

'Really? So, why do I feel as if I've just lost her all over again?'

I put my hand to my mouth, feeling his sadness. This was no place for me. I had no right to be listening. Besides, I honestly didn't think I could bear to listen to any more of Will's pain.

I turned and crept away.

Chapter 25

Will had turned into a shadowy figure that I rarely saw. He spent a lot of time out and about the estate with Bernie.

Darcey also seemed to be busy all the time. She'd finalised a design for a new tour map of the Hall, which had gone to the printers, and had made her selections of artefacts, ornaments and paintings that were to go in each room, having studied the inventory and wandered the house with a clipboard, pen, and camera. She'd placed advertisements for more volunteers and was busy making lists of where they were needed and what jobs they'd be doing. She'd also been badgering me about the booklet, wanting to know how it was coming along.

I hadn't done too badly, given the circumstances. I'd included the story of how the house had come to be built on land once owned by Farthingdale Priory, having given a very brief history of the dissolution of the monasteries. I'd explained about the Kearton family's popularity at court, and how amazing it was they'd managed to keep their Catholicism a secret. I'd mentioned the priest hole under the stairs and given teasing hints that there might well be more, just waiting to be discovered. In just a page, I'd managed to convey how the earldom had been created and lost in the space of three generations, and then detailed a very brief history of each of the baronets — or, at least, as much as I'd managed to find out.

In my opinion, the only Boden-Kean ancestor who was of any real interest was James, Sixth Baronet, who — much as I hated to admit it — was the only one worth drawing attention to. Darcey was very keen that I concentrate my investigations on him, and browsing through the family archives, as well as the books in the library, it became quite clear to me that he not only took part in the smuggling activities in Kearton Bay, but that he was a ringleader, just as Darcey had suspected. Given the secret tunnel that ran from under the hall to Hob's Cave, there was no wonder that he'd managed to get away with it. I wondered how much of the family fortune came from his ill-gotten gains.

It had also occurred to me — because he was never far from my thoughts — that if William *had* hidden treasure in the house, then James Boden-Kean was the man most likely to have found it. After all, he would probably have searched every nook and cranny, seeking escape routes and hiding places. If he'd come across it, no doubt he'd have spent it and kept very quiet about the fact. He didn't strike me as a man with many morals, nor as a man who had much respect for his family's history or good name.

Darcey made lots of visits to the village, and to Whitby and the surrounding area, hunting for information and artefacts to do with the smuggling history. I, meanwhile, having written what I could about the Boden-Keans, and how each successive generation had added to or changed the house and estate, had decided to spend a little more time studying the Keartons.

I trawled through *A History of the Kearton Earls*, a dry and dusty tome that had been written with the kind of deferential respect used in the nineteenth century, when discussing landed gentry. I wasn't sure how much of the book could be trusted, as it was apparent the author held the family up to be saintly, and I highly doubted that they were as noble and perfect as he made out. Still, it did reveal that William had a sister, and she, too, had a tragic ending.

I told Darcey all about it one afternoon, as we huddled in the kitchen, drinking coffee and discussing where we were at with our plans, while Woody rolled pastry and listened keenly.

'A younger sister? That explains it,' Darcey said, sipping her drink, and watching me over the rim of her coffee cup with a curious expression in her hazel eyes. 'Was her name Margaret by any chance?'

I gaped at her. 'It was. How did you know that?'

She shook her head. 'I'll tell you in a minute. What did you find out about her?'

'Mainly that she had a short life, just like her brother,' I said, reaching over and helping myself to a shortbread biscuit. I figured there was no point wasting them. Darcey wouldn't touch them, that was for sure.

'What happened?'

'Smallpox,' I explained. 'It carried her off when she was just eighteen, and then it took her mother, weeks later. Two years after that, William himself was killed.'

'Bless them,' said Woody. 'Poor things. What a life, eh? We don't know we're born these days.'

'I know. It's really sad, isn't it? Margaret was apparently very pretty, and rather gifted artistically. She loved painting and sang beautifully, too. At least,' I added, 'that's what the author of that grovelling book about the Keartons says. I suppose she might actually have looked like a troll and howled like a dog with its tail caught in the door, but the fact is, she still died far too young.'

Darcey sighed. 'As did so many. It's quite a coincidence that you read about her today, because I've just come across a rather lovely painting of the two of them.'

'A painting? Is that how you knew about her?'

'Yes. I suspected she must have been a sibling we knew nothing about. The painting is simply catalogued as *Summer at Kearton Hall, English School circa 1630*, but someone has pencilled in, William and Margaret. It was in storage in the upper west wing. Would you like to see it?'

'Of course.'

'I've sent the original to London to be cleaned, along with some others that are going to be part of the tour, but I've got this photograph.'

She picked up her clipboard and shuffled through the attached papers, before handing me a photo. As Woody and I leaned in to examine it, she said, 'I think the author was right about

Margaret being pretty, actually. What do you think?'

The painting was of two children. The boy, William, was perhaps around fourteen at the time and had an unruly mop of dark hair, and those gentle, green eyes. I felt a lump in my throat as I gazed at him. He was so like Will, and I just couldn't imagine how other people didn't see that. Beside him, to his left, was a girl of around six. She had fair curls and a round face with rosy cheeks, and big blue eyes, and looked quite cherubic. So, that was Margaret? Poor little thing.

'William must have gone through hell. He lost his father when he was only nineteen. Then to lose his sister, mother, then wife and child within the space of a year…' Darcey shook her head. 'Include the story in the booklet,' she said, taking the photo back and returning it to its folder. 'I'll get an information card printed to go next to the painting, and we'll hang it on the first landing of the main staircase. I was searching for something similar to replace the portrait of Oliver Cromwell. I think he can go somewhere a little less prominent. Vile man.'

I looked at her with amusement. 'Guess you wouldn't have been on the side of the Roundheads, then.'

'Look what they cost this family,' she said. 'Look what happened to your beloved William because of him, for a start. No, I'm no fan of Oliver Cromwell. I'm tempted to hang his picture in the public toilets.'

I couldn't help laughing at Darcey's outraged expression and, eventually, she also started to laugh. Even Woody had a smile on her face. It seemed she was coming round to Darcey at last.

'Did Will tell you about the ball?' Darcey asked, as I drained the last of my coffee and stood, ready to get back to work.

I went cold. 'What ball?'

She sighed. 'I thought not. Really, this situation is getting ridiculous. I can't think what's going on with Will. He's a different person lately.'

'You're not kidding,' I said, trying not to show how hurt I was. 'So, what ball is this?'

'We were thinking of events to open the season with, and Nat suggested a grand ball. He's managed to book a marquee, and tickets will go on sale very soon. Hopefully, it will raise a lot of money. Will's hoping to launch a friendship scheme at the event, so that people can sign up to be Friends of Kearton Hall.'

'What would that involve?' I asked.

'Basically, they'd pay an annual sum of money by card, or direct debit, and it would entitle them to as many visits to the Hall during the year as they wish, plus they'd get a newsletter and invitations to membership only events. Not sure what those events are yet, but I'm sure Nat's working on it, even as we speak.'

'Is he really?' I muttered. 'What a devoted member of the team he is.'

'Isn't he just?' She shook her head. 'This place has gone topsy-turvy lately. Anyway, I must get on. How are those Christmas hampers selling?'

'Flying off the shelves,' I said. 'Really, the shop's packed out.'

'Told you.' She smiled. 'Place could be a goldmine. We just need to improve it and expand it. I'll work on Will — he'd be a fool not to listen. I'll see you later. Thanks for the coffee, Woody.'

Woody nodded. 'You're welcome.'

As Darcey left the kitchen, she put down her rolling pin and tutted. 'So, go on. Spill.'

'What about?'

'You and Will. I saw the expression on your face. Is he still not talking to you?'

I was about to brush it off, but to my horror, I found I was in tears again. 'Sorry,' I managed. 'I don't know what's wrong with me lately. I've turned into a first-class wimp.'

'Hmm.' She picked up her pastry cutter and attacked the pastry with alarming savagery. 'Reckon someone needs to have a word with that lad. And I know just the man for the job.'

****

Will looked up, as Bernie closed the office door behind him. He raised an eyebrow as his estate manager held up two bottles of beer.

'Thought we could use these, after a long day at work.' Bernie grinned at him, placed the bottles on the desk, and pulled up a chair. 'It *is* Christmas Eve, after all.'

'I suppose it is.' Will smiled, picked up a bottle, and raised it in a toast. 'Merry Christmas, Bernie.'

'Merry Christmas, Will.' They both took a long swig of beer and returned the bottles to the table. Bernie leaned back in his chair, surveying Will thoughtfully. 'You seem worried, lad. What's on your mind?'

Will wasn't quite sure how to say it. 'Something puzzling's happened. I really don't know what to make of it.'

'Well, why don't you run it past me? Maybe I can help.'

Will considered for a moment. He didn't want to stir up trouble, and he knew how Bernie felt about Nat, but he was baffled. 'It's this new quote from the firm of builders Nat brought in.'

'Oh, aye? Let me guess. They want double what the other firm want.' Bernie shook his head. 'Cowboys.'

'But that's just it, Bernie. It's the opposite.'

'Eh?' Bernie narrowed his eyes. 'What are you on about?'

Will sighed and handed Bernie the sheets of paper that the builder from Marcus Leigh and Sons had handed him that evening. 'According to Mr Leigh, they can bring the work in at just under three hundred thousand pounds.'

'And how much did the builders that ECHOES recommended quote?'

Will stared at him for a moment, before responding, 'Over three million.'

'What?' Bernie gaped at him, then started to laugh. 'Well, someone's got their wires crossed. What's this Leigh bloke replacing the roof with? Cereal boxes and Sellotape?'

'That's what I don't understand. The company that ECHOES work with said we would need a whole new roof — that all the lead and tiles would need replacing, and the chimneys needed attending to. Leigh and Sons say it's a case of dealing with some lead flashing and replacing tiles on the west wing. Other than that, the roof is absolutely fine. I don't know what to think.'

'This company that ECHOES work with — I mean, if they

recommend them, surely they know what they're talking about? Darcey knows what she's doing, an' all.'

'But Marcus Leigh and Sons are a very well-respected company. They do an enormous amount of work on listed buildings and have a very impressive portfolio of work done on houses just like this one. I checked. Their website is excellent.'

'Anyone can fake a website, Will,' began Bernie.

'Of course they can,' Will cut in. 'That's why I checked up on them. I rang round, spoke to several people who know of them and of the work they do. I also emailed Rebecca.'

'Rebecca?'

'My cousin. Nat's sister. She remembers them working on Park House, and she says her father swore by them. He was no fool, and he would only accept the best. I'm completely baffled.'

'Maybe ECHOES need to rethink recommending this company then,' said Bernie. 'What are you going to do?'

'I've talked it over with Nat. He says that if we get two more quotes, each in a similar ballpark to this one, we can go ahead and apply for a grant from ECHOES. He thinks we stand a really good chance of getting all the work paid for.'

'So, what's your problem? You've got references, you've spoken to your own cousin, what more do you need?'

'A crystal ball?' Will shook his head. 'Listen to me, you'd think this was bad news. I mean, it's good news, right?'

'It's very good news, lad. Maybe this Clarke bloke just wants to make a fast buck out of people he perceives to be well off. Reckon someone should tip ECHOES off. It needs to investigate.'

'You're right. I'll have a word with Darcey. You know, it would be such a weight off my mind.'

'Hmm. So maybe now you'll be more like your old self again.'

Will looked at him in surprise. 'Meaning what?'

'You tell me, lad. You tell me.'

'I don't know what you mean.' Will took another sip of beer.

'Nat,' said Bernie. 'Let's start there, shall we?'

Will sighed. 'What about Nat?'

'What hold's he got over you?'

'Hold? He hasn't got any hold over me. What a strange thing to say.'

'Well, you see, if he hasn't got any hold over you, then the only conclusion I can come to is that you've lost your marbles somewhere along the way, because why else would you be letting him swan around here as if he's in charge? And why would you trust him to work here, when he made it very clear that he wanted you to sell up to some bloody hotel chain?'

Will shook his head. 'It's not like that. He's changed.'

'Sure he has. Come on, Will, you're not a stupid man. You must know that he'll never change. If he's helping here, it's because he has an ulterior motive.'

'When he first came here, he wanted me to get rid of the Hall. He was hoping for a share of the profits. He's admitted that to me.'

'The cheeky bugger!'

Will held up his hand. 'It's different now. He's had time to think things through. He sees now why his own father loved this place so much. He's happy living and working here. Nat never had much purpose before, but now that he's made up his mind about keeping the Hall in the family, he's really doing his best to help.'

'I can't believe you've fallen for that,' said Bernie.

'I know Nat,' began Will, but Bernie leaned forward, his expression serious.

'Aye, and I know Nat, too. I've seen him around here since he was a bairn, and I saw how he bullied and manipulated you, even then.'

'But there's another side to him,' persisted Will. 'I've seen that side. You haven't. You'll have to trust me on this, Bernie.'

Bernie swilled the beer around in his bottle thoughtfully. 'Well, even if you insist he's on your side now, it doesn't explain the other matter.'

'What other matter?'

'Why you've taken *his* side over Lexi's.'

Will swallowed. 'What do you mean?'

'You know full well what I mean. Have you forgotten that it was *him* who did the dirty on *her*?'

'Of course I haven't forgotten.'

'Then, perhaps you'd be so good as to tell me why it's Lexi you're punishing, and not him?'

Will stared at him, shocked. 'Punishing her? What on earth are you talking about?'

'If you're not punishing her, you're doing a bloody good impression of it. Ignoring her, cutting her out of your plans, not inviting her to meetings. Lexi was your right-hand girl a few weeks ago. Now, it's as if she means nothing to you. Do you know how much you've hurt her?'

'I'm sure she's not hurt, Bernie,' Will said quietly. 'I doubt she's even noticed.'

'Well, shows how much you know her then.'

'Has she said something to you?'

'Not to me, but she's been pouring her heart out to Woody. What the hell are you playing at? It's not like you to be cruel, Will.'

Will tried to quell the churning in his stomach. He picked up a pen, tapping it repeatedly on the desk as he struggled to put into words what he wanted to say.

Eventually, Bernie reached over and took the pen from him. 'For God's sake! Getting on my wick. You need to explain, Will. Woody says you've had that lass in tears, more than once. Do you think that's fair?'

'In tears?' Will's eyes widened. 'Are you serious?'

'Of course I'm serious. You've really upset her. Is that what you wanted? To punish her for going out with Nat?'

'Of course not! I'd never do that. I didn't think … I mean, I didn't realise. I'd never hurt her on purpose, Bernie, you know that. Poor Lexi.'

'So if you weren't trying to hurt her on purpose, what were you doing?'

Will couldn't look at him. 'I was just trying to save myself,' he mumbled.

'Save yourself? From what?'

'From the bitter truth.' Finally, Will met his friend's eyes and shrugged. 'Hard though it was to listen, I had to accept that Nat was right.'

'Oh, him again! What's he been saying now? Bloody trouble causer.'

'No, no. He wasn't trying to cause trouble. He was just explaining things. He had no idea how I felt...'

Bernie gazed at him with sudden sympathy. 'What did he say, lad? What's made you act this way? It's so out of character. I'm worried about you.'

'Nat and I were arguing about him hurting Lexi. He pointed out that he couldn't hurt her because she didn't love him. He said—' He took a deep breath. 'He said she wasn't capable of loving any man.'

'And you believe that?'

Will bit his lip. 'I didn't want to. But you know what, Bernie? I think he was right. The more I thought about it, the more I realised he knew her better than I did. I mean, how many years have I been trailing around after her like some lost puppy? Did she ever give me any hint that she felt more for me than friendship? No. Not once. And she's made it so clear, during that time, that she doesn't want to commit to anyone. She's never lied about it. So, why did I always kid myself that she'd change?'

'Because she will. Give her time.'

'No, Bernie. No more time. Look at the facts. She had relationships with Derry, Robbie and Nat, three extremely good-looking men — exceptionally so, in Derry's case. If none of those could make her change her mind, what the hell chance would I have?'

'They weren't the right ones for her,' said Bernie. 'You, on the other hand—'

'Bernie, don't. Don't.' Will lowered his head and covered his eyes with his hands for a moment. 'This is tearing me apart as it is.' After a moment, he raised his head and gave Bernie an impassioned look. 'The fact is, Lexi and I will only ever be friends. I've accepted that. It's the way it's got to be.'

Bernie seemed as if he were about to say something, but instead he took another sip of beer. After a moment, he said quietly, 'Well, if you're friends, you've got to start being kind to her again.

No more ignoring her, leaving her out of things. You hear me? It's not fair on the lass.'

'It was just protection. I had to put some distance between us. But you're right, it's not fair. I'll try harder, I promise.'

'What will you do now? Can you carry on working with her?'

'I can't sack her. She loves this place. Besides, she's done nothing wrong. This is my problem, and one I'll have to deal with.'

'And how will you do that?'

Will hesitated. He'd done nothing but ponder that question for weeks. Eventually, he said, 'By concentrating on the future. I have work to do, and I intend to throw myself into it.'

'There's more to life than work, lad. You're young. You need some fun in your life. And you're looking tired, too. Are you still not sleeping?'

'Not much,' Will admitted. 'But things will get better. Now that I know where I stand, I can start to look to the future. Who knows,' he said, trying to sound optimistic, 'maybe one day I'll meet someone who'll actually want to be with me. Stranger things have happened.'

Bernie swallowed. 'You will, lad. You're a good, kind man, and any woman would be lucky to have you. Don't you forget that.'

'I won't,' said Will. He drained the bottle and stood up. 'I enjoyed that. Would you like to stay for dinner? Perhaps we could open a bottle of whisky afterwards. As you say, it's Christmas Eve.'

Bernie paused, then nodded. 'Aye, go on, then. And I'll even try to be polite to Nat, it being the season of goodwill, an' all.'

As Will locked the office door behind him, he felt utterly wretched. He had to make it up with Lexi. He felt sick with shame that he'd hurt her. Maybe the gift he'd got for her would show her that he cared about her and go some way to making things up to her.

Whatever he'd said to Bernie about finding someone else, he knew it would never happen. Lexi was the only woman he'd ever wanted. He just had to accept that he'd always be alone. It was time to find a different dream.

Chapter 26

Christmas Day arrived, and the farm was a complete madhouse. Amy was up at half past four, and nothing anyone could say or do would make her go back to bed. She wanted to see what Father Christmas had brought her, so Dad and Eliza, being the suckers they were, gave in and came downstairs to let her open her presents.

Hearing the muttering and excited squeals on the landing had woken me up too, so I pulled my dressing gown over my pyjamas and followed them into the living room. Within minutes, Joe and Charlie had joined us. Joe was practically sleepwalking, but refused to go back to bed, as he wanted to see Amy opening her gifts. Charlie, on the other hand, was more excited than Amy, and was shrieking with delight at the number of parcels there were, telling Amy that they both must have been exceptionally good that year, because look how many presents Father Christmas had given them.

'If you must shriek,' said Eliza, 'can you shriek a little quieter? If the twins wake up, I'll throttle you.'

'Aw,' said Charlie, 'you can't blame her for getting all excited.'

'I was talking to you,' Eliza said pointedly.

Charlie reddened. 'Oops. I see what you mean. Sorry. Where's Joe gone?'

'I'm in here,' Joe called from the kitchen. 'Just putting the kettle on. Does anyone want toast?'

'Are you mad? Who can eat toast on Christmas morning? I'm saving meself for me selection box,' said Charlie.

So the madness commenced, with Amy ripping off the wrapping paper on her gifts as if she were under starter's orders.

'Slow down,' said Joe. 'It's not a race, you know.'

It was pointless even trying to get Amy to slow down. She was a girl on a mission, and within ten minutes, we couldn't see the floor in the living room for wrapping paper and a mountain of toys, books, clothes and sweets. She was delighted with everything, as well she should have been, given the amount of money that had been spent on her, but her eyes lit up when she opened her last gift.

Tearing off the wrapping paper, she opened a large box, to reveal a pair of jodhpurs, a crash hat, and a trio of pony books, especially aimed at girls around her age.

Amy let out an ecstatic squeal and immediately put the hat on, flicking eagerly through the books.

'What a lovely thoughtful present,' said Eliza. 'Who got her those?'

'They're from Will,' said Charlie.

My stomach somersaulted. 'Will? When did he drop them off?'

'He came by yesterday afternoon, while you were working. Brought me and Charlie the Christmas hamper we ordered and wouldn't take payment for it. Said it was a gift to us all from him. Then he gave us Amy's present to hide.'

'That's so kind of him,' said Dad.

While they all nodded and smiled, and agreed how wonderful Will was, I could barely stand up. My legs had suddenly turned to jelly, which was a bit weird, and bloody inconvenient. I was just about to sit down when Charlie added, 'He asked us to give this to you, Lexi.'

'Me?' I wasn't expecting anything from Will for Christmas. Knowing my luck, it was my notice. Nothing would surprise me any more. Or so I thought.

I peeled the paper from the small, carefully wrapped package with shaking hands. As I opened the small box inside, I almost dropped it. What had I been saying about surprise?

My legs finally gave way, and I found myself sitting on the floor, staring in astonishment at a beautiful gold and emerald brooch.

Dad and Eliza peered into the box, and Dad whistled. 'Whew! That's lovely. Although, you're not really the brooch type, are you? Still, it's a lovely thought.'

'It looks expensive,' said Eliza. 'You'd better be careful with it. You know what you're like for losing or damaging jewellery.'

'Yeah. Like that watch Sophie and Archie bought you,' said Dad, laughing. 'Didn't take you long to break it, did it? What a panic that was, getting it fixed before they noticed. Remember?'

Vaguely, I nodded, my thoughts far too preoccupied to really pay attention. Because it wasn't just any old brooch. It was, I was almost sure, an exact replica of the one the Countess wore in her portrait. The star shape, the tiny emeralds surrounding one large central emerald, and the little seed pearls on each point ... It was just the same. Will must have had it made especially for me. But why? Why would he go to all that trouble, when clearly he didn't even want to talk to me?

'Well, somebody loves you,' said Charlie, nodding at the brooch and raising his eyebrows in a meaningful way.

I tried desperately to think of something casual and offhand to reply with, but I couldn't think of anything. I couldn't get my head around it all. What was going on? Why was Will ignoring me at work, yet secretly having this beautiful, and oh-so-meaningful gift made for me? Nothing made sense any more. I closed the box and stood up. 'It's not real. It's paste. A replica.'

'Well, obviously. It would be worth thousands otherwise,' said Dad.

'Still a lovely thought though,' said Joe.

'I think I'll get a shower.'

'Don't you want to open your other presents?' asked Eliza.

'I'll do that later. I need to wake myself up properly first,' I said, trying to sound flippant. 'Not even five o'clock! We must be mad.'

They laughed and went back to opening their presents, and I headed upstairs, clutching the little box in my hand, not understanding, not sure what to think anymore.

No doubt about it, the entire world had gone topsy-turvy.

****

I didn't have to work Christmas Day or Boxing Day, so I didn't see Will. I'd toyed with the idea of calling him, to thank him for the gift, but I couldn't bring myself to do it. I was too nervous. It was a weird thing to acknowledge. I'd never been nervous of Will before. I couldn't work out what was happening, and I had a feeling that if I rang him, I'd go all tongue-tied and make a complete pig's ear of the whole thing.

I could have gone up there to see him, I supposed, but Nat would be there, which put me off. Besides, I wasn't sure Will would thank me for interrupting his Christmas. Who knew what was going on up at the Hall? Darcey wasn't there, as she'd gone to visit her aunt for a couple of days, and God alone knows what Nat and Will would be up to in the house.

I wondered if Will had visited Rhiannon over Christmas, then hated myself for thinking about it. It was none of my business what they did after all. I hoped Derry was okay though. On Boxing Day night, I popped into The Hare and Moon to find out for myself.

The pub was quite busy, and it seemed most of the villagers had forgotten all about their shock at the revelations over Derry's parentage. It was as Will had said, nothing lasts forever. Everything passes, even the worst of times. I hoped that the gift of the beautiful brooch meant that the worst of times between him and me was also over.

Derry ushered me upstairs into the kitchen and made me a coffee. He told me that his relationship with Lucie, the girl from Moreton Cross, was over.

'I'm so sorry,' I said, feeling genuinely sympathetic. The last thing he needed was to be rejected by his girlfriend, after having such a traumatic few months. Especially over Christmas.

'Don't be,' he said. 'It was me who finished with her.'

'But I thought you really liked her?'

'I did. At least, I thought I did. But what was the point, anyway?'

268

'What do you mean?' I thought how different he sounded, how cold he'd become, and felt a sudden sadness at the change in him.

'It would have finished sooner or later. And one of us would have been hurt, so better to end it now, before we got in too deep.'

'What the hell are you talking about? That's the most ridiculous thing I've ever heard. You said you really liked Lucie, that she was a lovely girl.'

'I did. She is. But it wouldn't have lasted. Nothing does. Who needs the grief? Anyway, I've got more important things to think about.' He grinned, waving an envelope in my face.

'What's that?' I asked, still feeling dazed that he'd finished with Lucie so casually.

'A letter from Grandfather. He sent me a Christmas card and a cheque for five hundred quid. What do you think of that?'

'Well, that's all very well,' I said, 'but you hardly need the money, do you? I mean, you've got the trust fund from your father, and I'll bet that's worth more than five hundred pounds.'

'Don't call him that,' snapped Derry. 'I haven't touched that money, and I don't want to. He can stick it where the sun doesn't shine. Anyway, the main thing is, my grandfather wants me to visit him. He thinks it's high time we met, and he's talking about me going to Fernley Court, maybe around Easter time.'

'Fernley Court?'

'Yeah, that's the ancestral home.' He gave an embarrassed laugh.

I pulled a face. 'Get you. Nobility on both sides of the family.'

'Lexi,' he said in a warning tone.

'Sorry. So it's true, then? Rhiannon is from a titled family?'

'Yeah.' He seemed a bit uncomfortable about it. 'She's from an even grander family than Will's. Of course, she was the black sheep. I mean, can you imagine her fitting in with a family like that?'

I really felt weird listening to him. Derry wasn't like this. He sounded so bitter and so angry. He'd always been tolerant of his mother's *quirks*, as he always referred to them. I didn't like the new version of him — a version who seemed to enjoy getting one over on his own mother, and who'd dumped his girlfriend just because something was bound to go wrong between them in the future.

'Will's been coming over,' he said suddenly.

I steeled myself, waiting for the next revelation. 'Oh?' I didn't want to let him think I'd been aware of the situation. He'd probably demand to know why I hadn't tipped him off. The question was, how much did he know? How far had things gone between Will and Rhiannon this time? I didn't think I wanted to hear any more.

'Yeah, he's been coming to see me, trying to *bond*. You know, us being brothers, and all.'

He'd been going to see *Derry*? I wondered why I hadn't thought of that. Of course he would attempt to befriend his new brother. He would want to put things right for him, get to know him better. That was Will all over. Why had I been so quick to believe the worst?

'So, what are your thoughts on that?'

He shrugged. 'Will's okay. It's not his fault, any more than it's mine, I suppose.' He sat down, giving me a rueful look. 'He wants me to go up to the Hall. He says it's my home, as much as his and Nat's.'

'Well, so it is, I guess,' I said.

'Not really. I can't reconcile myself to being a Boden-Kean. I know he means well, and I can't dislike him. I shouldn't think anyone could dislike Will, to be honest. He's always so bloody nice. God knows, I wanted to hate him for shagging my mother, but no doubt it was all her doing anyway.'

'Derry, you've got to give your mum a break,' I said. I didn't know why, but I felt my resentment towards Rhiannon blowing away, like leaves in an autumn breeze. I felt suddenly lighter, and much more like my old self. 'She's a good person. She's always been so kind and understanding. Stop making her out to be some sort of evil, lying trollop. She's not that person, and you know it.'

'Huh, tell that to all the wives around here whose husbands she's screwed. Look, I don't want to row with you, but let's not talk about her any more, okay? I'm sick of the whole subject. So, how was your Christmas? Get anything good?'

I found myself unable to mention the brooch, so I merely told him about the other presents I'd got — the new clothes, the iPad, the perfume and books. He nodded and listened, and before long we were embroiled in a conversation about Amy, and her excitement at Christmas, and her passion for horses, and just about anything rather than Rhiannon or Will, as I wondered, yet again, how it had come to this, and how the hell I was going to face Will the next morning.

'Have you made it up with Georgia, yet?' he asked, as we curled up on the sofa a little later and helped ourselves from a tin of Quality Street.

I screwed up my nose. 'No. And I thought uncomfortable subjects were out of bounds?'

He rummaged around in the chocolates. 'Bloody hell! Why are there never any purple ones left?'

I grinned and waved the empty wrapper in his face.

'Might have known,' he said. 'Well, in that case, I bags the last strawberry cream.'

'Pig,' I said.

He laughed and stuffed the chocolate in his mouth. 'It's been great having you here, Lexi. I really needed a mate. Thanks.'

'No problem. I've enjoyed myself.'

'But, seriously, what about Georgia?'

I opened an orange cream, even though I felt as sick as a seaside donkey and didn't think I could manage another thing. 'What about her?'

'She's been your best friend for years. Why are you letting that prick come between you and her?'

'She did the damage, Derry. Not me. She betrayed me. How am I supposed to get over that?'

'Come on. You said yourself how persuasive Nat can be. She's not still seeing him, you know.'

'And how would you know that?' I demanded.

'Pan and Fuchsia came in for a drink this afternoon. Pan said Georgia's been really down these last few weeks, and she's been asking about you loads. She hasn't seen Nat since that day. He's texted her loads of times, but she's ignored him. She just wants to make things right.'

'Well, she can lump it,' I said. 'And Pan can tell her that from me.'

He looked at me curiously. 'Do you really mean that?'

'Yes,' I said.

'Really?'

I sighed and threw the orange cream wrapper at him. 'Okay, I miss her, I admit it. Maybe I have been a bit harsh. I just felt so let down and stupid. But you're right. Ignoring Georgia is letting Nat win. Maybe it's time I made it up with her.'

'Thank God for that,' he said. 'Although, it will have to wait a couple of days. She's gone home to spend Christmas with her parents.'

'Jeez, there's a turn up for the books,' I said. 'She hasn't prised herself away from those horses in years.'

'I know, but Pan says she really needed to get some space between her and the village. She needed time to think and felt it was about time she got a break.'

'To be fair, she's right. She hasn't had a holiday in yonks,' I admitted. 'So, Pan's been landed with the horses? Bet Fuchsia's thrilled about that.'

'Well, it won't take her long. They've roped Tally in to help.'

'Of course they have,' I said. 'Poor Tally gets roped into helping everyone.'

'Sophie's perfect child,' said Derry, laughing. 'After Oliver's antics in Bristol — which she's desperately trying to keep quiet, little suspecting that he plasters them all over Facebook — and Pandora chucking in university to work at a riding school, I'll bet she's pinning all her hopes on Tallulah. Poor sod.'

'Tally's lovely,' I mused. 'I just hope she learns to stand up for herself and doesn't let Sophie and everyone else try to force her into being something she doesn't want to be.'

'Does she know what she wants to be?'

'Haven't a clue,' I said, suddenly aware that I hadn't really spoken properly to my youngest cousin for ages. Tally was just there — kind, thoughtful, obliging. I supposed I took her for granted, a bit like everyone else. I decided there and then to pay more attention to her in the future.

'So, when Georgia comes back, you'll try to make things up with her?'

'Sure I will,' I said, slyly. 'Just as you'll make it up with your mum?'

He sighed and shook his head. 'I dunno, Lexi. I'm not sure I can get past what she did. I mean, that horrible old bloke! How would you feel if he turned out to be your dad? And she's humiliated me in front of the entire village. It's hard to forgive and forget.'

'I know,' I said gently. 'But it's over and done with, Derry. Don't let the past ruin your future. You've always had such a good relationship with Rhiannon. Don't throw that away. Believe me, you're so lucky to have a mother like her.'

He pulled a sympathetic face. 'Sorry. I guess you must miss yours even more at Christmas.'

I didn't want to dwell on my own mother. 'I was thinking about Will, actually. Look how Elisabeth treated him.'

'Because of my mother.'

'You don't know that. And even if she did leave because of the affair, and Rhiannon swears she didn't, she didn't have to cut Will out of her life, did she? There was no excuse for that.'

'Suppose not.' He picked up the remote and began to flick through the television channels. 'I don't know. Bloody mothers, eh? Hey, do you fancy watching a film?'

I glanced at my watch and let out a squeal of horror. 'Can't Derry, sorry. *Charlie Hope's Christmas Cracker* is on in forty minutes, and I promised Charlie faithfully that I'd be home to watch it. I'll have to go.'

'Fair enough.' He grinned. 'Wouldn't want to upset Charlie, eh? Thanks for coming, Lexi. I really appreciate it.'

'Don't be daft.' I leaned forward and planted a kiss on his cheek. 'Merry Christmas, Derry.'

'Merry Christmas, and Gawd bless us — every one,' he said.

'Silly sod,' I said, laughing.

As I made my way downstairs towards the back door, Rhiannon

was just coming out of the bar. She stopped and looked at me, an unmistakable sadness in her eyes. I felt overwhelmed with guilt. I'd been so distant and offhand with her lately. What the hell had I been thinking?

Impulsively, I planted a kiss on her cheek too. 'Merry Christmas, Rhiannon,' I said. 'And a very happy new year.'

As I watched the dimpled smile spread across her pretty face, I felt lighter than I had in weeks. I left The Hare and Moon and headed up Bay Street towards home, the steepness of the hill suddenly seeming no effort at all.

Chapter 27

I felt stupidly nervous, arriving at Kearton Hall the next morning. My stomach was churning and my palms sweating. I parked the car and headed down the lane, through the side gate.

Bernie was just coming out of the door as I approached the west wing, and he gave me a hug. 'Good to see you back. Did you have a nice time?'

'Smashing, thanks. You?'

'Aye. Can't complain. Had Eddie round for Christmas dinner, and spent Boxing Day with Robbie and Chrissie, and Chrissie's mum and dad, so it was a pleasant break.'

'Good, good.' I swallowed, not daring to mention Will's name. 'Have you seen Darcey? Is she back?' *You wimp, Lexi*, I thought. *Why are you avoiding the issue?*

'Aye, she got back late last night. You know Darcey, she's already back at work, and she's been cracking the whip this morning, telling Nat that, if he's organising this spring ball, he'd better get a bloody shifty on and get the tickets printed and advertising sorted.'

'Good. Someone ought to tell him,' I said.

There was an awkward silence for a moment. I thought Bernie was about to say something, but if so, he must have changed his mind as he merely patted my arm. 'Well, I'd better get on. See you later, love.'

'See you, Bernie.' I took a deep breath and entered the house, heading for the kitchen.

Woody was baking, and I'd never been so glad to see anyone in my life. She glanced up as I walked in and gave me a megawatt smile. 'Lexi! Did you have a good Christmas, petal?'

'I did. Did you?'

'Oh, you know. Quiet, like. My Bobby's back was giving him gip again, but we managed. We'll be eating turkey until Easter, though,' she added. 'Would you like a jam tart? I've made far too many.'

'What's new?' I plonked myself down on the chair and sighed contentedly. In spite of my fears, in spite of everything that had happened recently, it was good to be back. I loved this house so much.

Woody handed me a jam tart and switched the kettle on. 'Nice cup of tea's what we need now. Reckon I've earned a ten-minute break, and you could use a drink before you start work.'

'How's everything here?' I asked, trying to sound casual.

She smiled. 'It's been very quiet, really. I came up here to check on the boys, even though Will told me not to. I wanted to make sure they were all right.'

'And — and were they?'

'Seemed to be. Will said they had a peaceful, relaxing break. Well, with Darcey away, things were bound to be quieter. Nat's been a bit subdued — don't know what's gone on there. Tell you what, though...' She leaned forward, casting a shifty look around, as if someone might be hiding under the table or something. 'Darcey's got egg on her face today.'

'Why?'

'Seems that company that ECHOES work with are rip-off merchants. They told Will loads of work was needed, and that it would cost millions to do, but on Christmas Eve, the company Nat brought in said only a small section of the roof needs sorting, and it will cost a fraction of the price. Will's going to get two more quotes and, if they agree, apply for a grant to cover the costs. He's that relieved, I can't tell you.'

'Huh. Well, I'm no fan of Nat's, but if he's saved Will all that money...'

'Made Darcey look a fool, though, and she's not happy about it.' She gave a little chuckle, and I shook my head.

'I thought you were coming round to Darcey, Woody?'

'Huh. Well, maybe she's not as bad as I thought, but there's still something … Any road, it won't do her any harm to be taken down a peg, or two. Not that Bernie would agree, I'm sure.'

I grinned. 'So, you've noticed it too?'

'Can't miss it, can you? I dunno. No fool like an old fool.'

We drank our mugs of tea, then I stood up, deciding I'd hidden away for long enough and it was time to find out what mood Will was in. I was just about to tell Woody that I'd see her later, when the door opened and the man himself walked in.

It was most peculiar. My legs seemed to turn to water, and I felt strangely nauseated. It wasn't like me to be so gutless, and I felt quite furious with myself, but I couldn't help it. I gaped at him, unable to speak, dreading his response to finding me there.

I went weak with relief when he smiled suddenly and said, 'You're back. It's great to see you. Did you have a good Christmas?'

I tried to answer him, but my throat appeared to have dried up. I swallowed hard, aware that both he and Woody were watching me expectantly. 'Er, yes, thanks. Did you?'

'I did. It was nice having Nat around. And, of course, Woody did us an excellent dinner, even though I told her to stay home and let us fend for ourselves.'

'As if I'd let you down,' said Woody indignantly. She eyed us curiously, and I was sure I was blushing.

'Thank you, Will, for the lovely present,' I said awkwardly. 'I couldn't believe it when I opened it.'

He lowered his eyes, as if embarrassed. 'That's all right. I hoped you'd like it.'

'Like it? I love it. And it looks so realistic. Honestly, you'd think they were real emeralds, the way they gleam. Thank you so much.'

A faint flush spread across his cheeks. 'Yes, well, I thought the green would suit your hair. Well, I must get on. Lots to do.'

'Of course. See you later.' I sat down again, needing a moment to recover from the encounter, but Will stopped suddenly, as he turned to leave.

'I wonder — I mean, no doubt you've already made plans, but

I was wondering — if you're not doing anything else, of course — if you'd like to stay over on New Year's Eve?'

I gulped. 'Stay over?'

'Yes. I mean, we've worked hard, and we've got a lot more work ahead of us, and I thought it would be good for us to have an evening together just to socialise. You know, a few drinks, some supper, bring in the New Year together.'

I felt quite dazed. 'Er, yeah. That would be great.'

'Lovely. Darcey will be glad. I don't think she fancied being the only woman with two men.'

'Sorry?'

'I mean, it will be good for her to have a woman to talk to. Bernie can't come, unfortunately, as he and Robbie have been invited round to Meggie and Ben's, and Woody and Bobby are going to have a quiet night at home. Isn't that right, Woody?'

'It is. Don't think Bobby's back will let him come all the way up here, and I'm not going to leave him on his own on New Year's Eve.'

'Quite right. So, that's settled. Just the four of us. It will be nice to spend some time together without talking shop, won't it?'

'Oh, yeah, 'course.' I felt foolish. Why would I think Will would want to spend the evening with just me? Idiot. 'Yes, that will be great. Looking forward to it.'

He nodded and flashed me a brief smile, then left the kitchen.

Woody beamed. 'Well, that's nice. Seems things are back to normal. He's quite his old self with you, isn't he?'

'I suppose so.' I wasn't so sure. He was friendly, polite and had invited me round for the New Year, so why did I still feel there was a sheet of invisible glass between us? It was all very odd.

I gave Will chance to get well away from the kitchen, then headed out to meet Darcey. We were finalising the booklet that day, getting it ready to send to the printers in January, and I went down the corridor hoping she'd be in her office. She wasn't, but when I rounded the corner, I could hear angry rumblings coming from Nat's office. As I approached, I distinctly heard Darcey's raised voice.

'You're a bloody idiot. You ought to make up your mind exactly what it is you want, because you're making a complete fool of me!'

'Believe me, Darcey, I know exactly what it is I want,' came the reply. 'Now, drop the wounded innocent act, or pack your bags and leave. I think you've more than outstayed your welcome anyway.'

'I'm going nowhere. I love it here, and I've found something worth hanging around for. You wouldn't understand that in a million years.'

'I don't see what the point is. Why would you want to stay? Because as far as I can tell, you've already failed in every way possible, so you may as well sling your hook and go home.'

I pushed open the door and stared at the two of them in bewilderment. 'What the hell's going on?' I demanded.

Darcey looked at me, anxiety in her eyes. 'Oh, Lexi. I'm so glad you're back.'

'For God's sake.' Nat shook his head then stormed past me, showing no sign that he shared her sentiment.

'What was that about?' I asked.

'Nat being Nat. It doesn't matter.'

'It does matter. Was he threatening you?'

She rubbed her forehead and sank into her chair. 'I think he may have been. Yes.'

'But, why? Is this about the building company?'

She bit her lip and nodded. 'He thinks I was trying to pull some sort of scam. I swear, Lexi, I wasn't. ECHOES uses that firm all the time. I've fired off an email to head office, telling them what's happened and recommending that they investigate further. It could well be that Clarke's have been doing work that didn't need doing, but if so, it's a recent development. How could I possibly know that? I'd never do anything to hurt Will. As I said to Nat, I came here to help. He was the one who came here to persuade Will to sell up, so why is he now acting as if he's the one on Will's side, and the rest of us are against him?'

'I'm worried, too,' I said, 'but don't let Nat get to you. He's a bully, and bullies thrive on making their victims feel small. You're a professional, and you have more integrity in your little finger than he has in his whole body. Ignore him. Leave it to ECHOES now.'

She nodded. 'I will. Thanks, Lexi.'

'No problem.'

I hugged her, and she smiled. 'Did you have a good Christmas?'

'You know what?' I said. 'I'm sick of hearing about Christmas. Let's just get back to work, shall we?'

'Thank God,' she said, her eyes bright with relief. 'I couldn't agree more!'

****

'Well, this should be fun.' Nat picked up his glass of whisky and raised it in a toast. 'To the four of us — and a very happy New Year to us all, I'm sure.'

'You could at least wait for Will,' said Darcey disapprovingly. She took a sip of whisky and pulled a face. 'Ugh. How can anyone drink this stuff? It's vile.'

'Perhaps you're more used to wine,' said Nat. 'Dry, bitter, vinegary old wine.'

'Oh shut up, Nat,' I said. 'For God's sake, can't you just behave for one bloody night? It's New Year's Eve, and Will wants us to have a nice evening together. No arguments, no shop talk. Don't you think he at least deserves that, after everything he's been through this year?'

'Huh.' Nat plonked himself on the sofa and stared moodily into his whisky.

'What's wrong with him now?' whispered Darcey.

'God knows. I think he's just naturally belligerent,' I muttered.

Will entered the room, all smiles. 'You're all here. Wonderful.'

'Whisky, Will?' Nat put down his glass and headed over to the drinks cabinet in the corner of the sitting room. The room was in the north side of the house, well away from the tour route, and was very much a well-used family room, with lots of family photographs, modern books and comfortable furniture. It was cosier and smaller than the state rooms, but it still had an enormously high ceiling and a huge fireplace. In one corner of the room stood the Christmas tree, cut from the estate forest. It was about twelve feet tall, but still didn't reach the ceiling.

Will shook his head. 'I think I'll just have a beer,' he said.

'Come on. It's New Year's Eve. Push the boat out,' Nat insisted. He poured Will a whisky and handed it to him. Will hesitated, then took a sip. Smiling, he glanced around at us all.

'Well, this is lovely, isn't it? So, how was your Christmas?'

Darcey and I looked at each other and tried to suppress our smiles. The trouble with Christmas was, you had to recount it to everyone you met for days afterwards, and by January you were sick to death of hearing about it.

Still, I supposed Will was trying to be friendly, for which I was grateful. 'Mine was chaotic and noisy,' I said. 'Lots of squeals and shrieks and laughter and excitement, and too much chocolate eating, and someone throwing up before we even got to Christmas dinner.'

Nat pulled a face. 'Bloody, pukey kids.'

'Actually,' I said, 'that was Charlie. He'd eaten an entire selection box, two mince pies, and a piece of yule log by eleven. He had to lie down for an hour to recover.'

Even Nat laughed at that, and I remembered how nice he was when he wasn't being sulky and obnoxious, and what a shame he couldn't always be like that.

'And you, Darcey? How did you spend Christmas?'

She gave a slight shrug of the shoulders. 'Quietly. I had to go back home to pack the rest of my belongings, as the house has been sold now. The furniture went into storage after Mum died, but there were some personal bits and pieces that I wanted to save. I didn't want them to end up in a skip somewhere. Then I went to my aunt's for Christmas lunch and stayed there until Boxing Day. Very boring, I'm afraid.'

Will seemed a bit dumbfounded. 'You should have said. You could have stayed here, you know. You didn't have to go home.'

'No, it's fine,' she assured him, smiling. 'As I said, I had things to do. Everything's final now. No going back.'

Nat watched her through narrowed eyes. 'Are you sure? You must miss London. It's such a vibrant place compared with

Kearton Bay, after all.'

'Not at all.' She tilted her chin, meeting his stare with defiant eyes. 'I could say the same to you. What's here for you in this little village?'

'It's different for me,' he said. 'I have family. Who have you got?'

Honestly, he was a pain in the arse. Just when I thought he could have a nicer side to him, he had to spoil it again. 'She's got us,' I said. 'Her friends. And we're very glad that she decided to move up to Yorkshire, aren't we, Will?'

'We certainly are.' Will gave her a warm smile, then turned his gaze on me, his eyes sending me a message of pleasure and gratitude. I felt ridiculously pleased to have won his approval. Anyone would have thought I was a seven-year-old getting a merit badge from the teacher. Pathetic.

'Jesus.' Nat scowled into his whisky, then fumbled in his pocket as his mobile phone beeped. He tapped on the screen, sat up straight, and for a few seconds his eyes scanned it before he stood. 'Be back in a minute.'

As he left the room, we all visibly relaxed. Nat had a way of filling everyone with tension, and it was a relief to see the back of him. I wished he'd bugger off for the night.

'Woody's made you up a bed in one of the guest rooms,' said Will, looking across at me. 'It's just two doors down from Darcey. You should be comfortable in there.'

'It hasn't got one of those creepy four-posters, has it?' I asked, shivering.

He laughed. 'No. I promise you. Just a divan.'

'Thank God for that,' I said.

'You don't know what you're missing,' said Darcey, smiling at me. 'I absolutely adore my room. It's so ancient and atmospheric. All that panelling, and that lovely old four-poster bed. I'll bet it could tell a few tales. If only these walls could talk, eh?'

'I have to say, I'm rather glad they can't,' said Will. 'With my ancestors, I'm sure they'd be doing a lot of complaining. Still, I know what you mean. It's a privilege to live somewhere like this, and I'm well aware of the fact. Now, help yourselves to drinks. I want you both to relax and make yourselves at home. I'm going to collect the food in a moment. I don't know about you, but I'm starving.'

'I'll help you fetch it, if you like,' I offered.

Darcey giggled. 'Let's all help. We can go to the kitchen now and grab the goodies before Nat gets back. Come on.'

By the time Nat returned, we'd not only brought all the food, but had started eating it too. To my astonishment, he didn't moan about it, but seemed decidedly cheerful.

'Everything all right?' asked Will.

'Absolutely wonderful,' he said, beaming at his cousin in a most suspicious fashion. 'So, what have we got to eat then? I could eat my own leg, I'm so hungry. Ooh, looks like Woody's done us proud.'

We all exchanged surprised glances. Whatever that text message was about, it had certainly brought about a change in Nat. Well, at least we didn't have to put up with his sarcastic comments and miserable whingeing that night. Maybe we could all actually get along for once.

It turned out to be a lovely evening. We tried to keep off the subject of the Hall, which we'd all agreed had to be out of bounds, since that was work, and the get-together was strictly about enjoying the New Year's celebrations. Darcey made us try her favourite tipple — vodka and cranberry juice. I wasn't too keen, but Will liked it. I was on the Malibu and Coke, which Nat seemed to find highly amusing, for some reason. He — thank goodness — had switched from whisky to beer and seemed remarkably cheerful. I wondered what had brought about the change in him and hoped he wasn't planning anything bad. It was hard to give him the benefit of the doubt.

We played several games of Forehead Detective, which I turned out to be useless at. Then again, I was hardly likely to know who Harvey Smith was. Funnily enough, I wasn't a huge follower of Nineteen-Seventies equestrian stars. Trust Nat to pick that one. I got my revenge, though. He failed miserably at guessing he was the Dalai Lama. My sense of irony served its purpose, all right.

As the evening wore on, and we got more and more tipsy, we played the gargling game. We had to sing a song while gargling with our drinks, which resulted in shrieks of laughter and quite a lot of mess. By the time we got around to charades, we were so drunk that the entire thing descended into chaos, and we all gave up and collapsed on the sofas.

Just before midnight, Will switched on the television, and we all waited for the chimes of Big Ben to sound the death knell of the old year and welcome the new one in. I really wasn't used to drinking, and I felt distinctly lightheaded and more than ready for sleep. It was a struggle to keep my eyes open as we waited for the countdown to begin.

Will was curled up on the sofa beside Darcey, and they mumbled to each other and laughed, a sight that gave me a weird pang of regret, which I immediately berated myself for. They'd both had an awful year. It was nice to see them enjoying themselves.

Nat came staggering over to me and threw his arm around my shoulder. 'I bet you hate me, don't you?'

I shuddered as the beery fumes from his breath hit me square in the face. I'd already drunk far too many Malibus. I didn't need to inhale any more alcohol, thank you very much.

'You do, don't you? You hate me.'

'I don't hate you, Nat,' I assured him. 'I don't like you much, and I wouldn't trust you as far as I could throw you, but I don't hate you.'

He let out a whoop of laughter. 'Always honest. I like that about you, Lex. No games. Always tell the truth as you see it. S'good. No games. I like no games.' He sighed. 'You wouldn't do bad things just to get a shag, would you?'

'If that's a proposition, forget it,' I said, trying to move away from him while I was still conscious.

He pulled me tighter and whispered in my ear, 'But then you get bitten in the arse. I mean, who's the bad one, really? And what can one do, eh? What do you do? You're stuck, aren't you? The worm has turned.'

'What are you talking about?' I said puzzled.

He stared at me for a moment, trying to uncross his eyes, then he shook his head. 'Bloody women. But not you, Lex. You don't play games. I'm sorry. I shouldn't have been so horrible to you. You didn't deserve it. But I didn't expect — I mean, it wasn't supposed to happen. Hit me like a ton of bricks. What can you do?'

'Hmm, whatever.'

'You need to give it a try, you know. It changes everything. I feel so sad for you. For both of you.' His eyes filled with tears and he let out a strangled sob. 'Why can't you just go for it, eh, Lex? Why can't you? Tell me. Tell me why.'

I had no idea what he was muttering about, and I wasn't sure he did, either. He was drunk and rambling, and I couldn't be bothered with it. 'Sit down before you fall down, Nat,' I said, pushing him none-too-gently into an armchair, where his head drooped. Within seconds, he began to snore.

Darcey giggled. 'He sounds like a truffle pig.' She hiccupped. 'I seem to have drunk a teensy bit more than I thought,' she said. 'How embarrassing.'

'It's New Year,' I said. 'We're allowed to get tipsy.'

'I think,' she said, in a dramatic stage whisper, 'we may be more than tipsy.' Giggling, she headed over to the drinks cabinet and poured two more vodka and cranberries.

I thought, on balance, she was probably right. Will's eyes had begun closing. Considering how little sleep he'd had for the last few months, I didn't really want to wake him.

I sighed. How was I going to get them all upstairs? I could barely walk a straight line myself. Bollocks to it. They'd all have to sleep downstairs.

Will's and Nat's heads shot up when Big Ben began to chime.

'It's New Year!' said Will, as he gazed around. Rather confused, he mumbled, '*Is* it New Year?'

'It is,' Darcey confirmed, handing him a glass. 'Happy New Year, Will.' She leaned over and gave him a light kiss on the cheek. 'You're so lovely.' She looked up, beaming at me. 'Isn't he lovely, Lexi? Nat, don't you think Will's lovely?'

'Of course I do,' slurred Nat. 'Now shut the fuck up, Darcey.'

I glared at him — or at least, I hoped I glared at him. It was hard to tell with my slightly blurry vision.

Darcey, however, seemed immune to Nat's insults. 'I wish I'd known,' she said with a sigh. 'I didn't expect you to be so nice. It's not what I thought, at all. Oh, I do love it here. Everyone's so lovely!' She leaned over and stroked Will's cheek. 'Happy New Year.'

She'd already said that, hadn't she? Will smiled and murmured something, and I saw him move slightly, but before I could see if he was going to kiss her back, Nat had grabbed me and spun me round.

Planting a huge kiss on my lips, he said, 'Happy New Year, Lexi.'

'Er, happy New Year, Nat,' I said, trying desperately to turn my head to see what Will and Darcey were up to.

'It *will* be a happy new year, won't it?' said Nat, sounding suddenly anxious.

'Of course it will. We'll make sure of it,' I said distractedly.

'I want us to be friends, Lexi,' he said. He seemed intent on having a conversation with me.

I sighed, giving up on my mission to observe the other two, and gave him my full attention.

'What?' I said. 'Sorry, I didn't hear you.'

'I said, I want us to be friends. We have to be. It's really, really important. Say you forgive me.'

I shrugged. 'There's nothing to forgive.'

'But there is. So many things.' He seemed really downcast. 'I'm not a bad person, but I know I do bad things. New year, new start. What do you say?'

'Yeah, yeah. Fine. As long as you're on Will's side, I'm on yours,' I assured him.

'Thank you for that, Lexi. That's lovely of you to say that,' said Will. Appearing beside me, he looked a bit wobbly, and I grabbed his arm as he swayed. 'Happy New Year, Lexi,' he said. 'And a happy New Year, Nat.'

'And you, cuz. And you. And it could be, you know. You see? You see what I mean? Why don't you just forget the past and do what I say? It's worth it, you know. It really is.'

Will and I exchanged glances. 'Er, what's worth it?' I said.

'Eh? How the bugger should I know?' Nat dropped back onto the armchair, evidently completely spent.

I noticed that Darcey's eyes were closed, and she appeared to have fallen asleep.

'Happy New Year, Will,' I said quietly, suddenly feeling a lot more sober.

He put his arms around me and pulled me to him. 'I want to believe that. I really do. But I can't any more.'

'What do you mean?' I asked. 'Everything will be okay, Will. I promise you.'

He stepped back, peering at me with slightly unfocused eyes. 'Don't make promises you can't keep. And you can't keep that one. Really, you can't. But it's all right, it doesn't matter, because time moves on, and everything passes. Haven't I always said that? Everything passes. Even the worst of times. And it will, won't it? This will pass?'

'Er, I suppose so.' It would have been helpful if he'd explained what he was talking about, but never mind. It was lovely to have him so close. I'd missed him so much.

He swayed again, and I put my arms around him to steady him. He suddenly squeezed me so tightly I could hardly breathe. I could smell his aftershave, feel the silky softness of that unruly hair against my cheek, the pressure of his chest against mine.

Impulsively, I turned my head and kissed him softly on the lips. They were warm and welcoming, and I felt my heart thud as he gave a small sigh. Then his eyes opened, and he seemed to stare right through me, his gaze penetrating the innermost layers of me, peeling away all my pretence and peering into my soul.

I shivered. My mouth parted. My heart thumped loudly. I couldn't think of anything but those green eyes locked onto mine.

'He's going to fall over in a minute,' Nat observed.

I blinked, and the room came back into focus. A man in a kilt was singing some jolly Scottish song on the television, and Darcey rolled off the sofa, landing with a thud on the carpet.

Nat whooped with laughter, while I steered Will over to the sofa, then helped Darcey up. I felt drained and bewildered and knew I had to get to bed. I needed to sleep off the alcohol and try to make sense of what was happening to me.

Will had closed his eyes again, his head drooping.

'I'm going up,' I said. 'Are you lot coming to bed, too?'

Nat yawned. 'In a minute.'

'What about Will?' I said.

'I'll help him up when I go. Don't worry.'

'Darcey?'

She shook her head. 'I don't want this night to end. I haven't had this much fun in ages.' She lifted her empty glass and waved it around. 'I think I'll have a nightcap. Join me, boys?'

'Don't think I could face it,' admitted Nat.

'Will?'

'I don't think so,' he mumbled.

Nat slapped his thigh and sat up straight. 'Bloody hell, we're such lightweights. Come on, Darcey, get those drinks poured. It's New Year's Eve, for God's sake.'

'Well, I'm going to bed,' I said. 'Night all.'

'Night, Lexi,' said Darcey.

'G'night,' slurred Nat.

Will said nothing, but I felt his gaze following me as I left the room. I headed upstairs, thinking that was the weirdest New Year party I'd ever been to.

****

I fell asleep as soon as my head touched the pillow, worn out and, quite honestly, a bit pissed. I wasn't sure what woke me up. Something in my subconscious stirred me to open my eyes, and I lay there for a few moments, trying to remember where I was and what had happened.

As memories of that evening pushed their way into my fuddled mind, I sat up, frowning in the darkness, as I tried to make sense of what had occurred between Will and myself. What was wrong with me lately? Why was he having such a weird effect on me? And why, more to the point, had he been behaving so strangely in return?

I glanced at my phone. Half-past two. I wondered if they'd made it up to bed, or if they were all snoring their heads off downstairs. I yawned and lay down again, then tutted in annoyance when I realised I needed the loo.

Reluctantly, I climbed out of bed and reached for my dressing gown. It was cold upstairs, and I thought how dark and creepy this room was, even with its more modern furniture. I crept over to the door and flicked on the light switch, sighing with relief when light flooded the room, making it seem quite ordinary and non-threatening. I spotted the lamp on the bedside table and tutted again. Idiot. Why hadn't I just switched that on? My thinking was clearly still confused. Alcohol had a lot to answer for.

I opened the bedroom door and padded along the landing, trying hard to be quiet. It wasn't easy though. Despite my best efforts, the floorboards creaked and groaned annoyingly.

Once I'd finished in the bathroom, I crept back towards my room, hoping the flushing of the toilet hadn't disturbed anyone. Mind you, I thought, judging by how far gone everyone had been earlier, they'd probably sleep 'til midday.

I hesitated outside my bedroom door, gazing thoughtfully down the long corridor, towards Will's room. I remembered when he'd shared the secret of the hidden room with me. I'd felt so close to him that day, as if we were best friends forever. What had gone wrong? And were things really on the road to recovery, or was this just a blip, brought about by the festivities and too much alcohol?

I needed to know. I wanted to be sure that we were really okay again, because if tonight was just a temporary truce, I didn't think I could stand it.

Squaring my shoulders, trying to suppress the trembling in my limbs, I walked down the corridor towards his room while hoping he was still conscious, or at least, not so drunk he wouldn't hear me as I tapped gently on the bedroom door.

'Will?'

There was no sound. I tapped again, but still nothing. Was he asleep downstairs? Had they left him? Because, if so, I'd have to go and rescue him. He'd be frozen when he woke up, otherwise.

I pushed the door open gently and peered inside.

He was fast asleep, one arm hanging over the bed, completely out for the count. Beside him, Darcey murmured something in her sleep, then turned over, pulling the duvet tight around her neck, shifting it off Will a little, and revealing his bare chest.

I realised I wasn't breathing. Heart hammering, I backed away and closed the door on the two of them. I headed back to my room, my mind whirling.

As I threw myself on the bed and reached for the pillow to hug, I kept asking myself one question. *How could he do this to me?*

It was a while before I realised that it was none of my business who Will slept with. He wasn't mine, after all. And that was when the tears came.

Chapter 28

I left the Hall at half past four in the morning, and walked in darkness back to Whisperwood Farm, as I was fairly certain I would still be over the limit. I knew Dad would be furious if he knew, but I had a key and let myself in quietly, then sneaked up to my room, determined to sleep until midday.

Even so, I was quite surprised to find that it was, indeed, gone twelve when I finally woke up. Heading downstairs, I found everyone sitting around the table, eating lunch. They all looked up and exchanged knowing glances, as I staggered into the kitchen, still wearing pyjamas and feeling like death warmed up.

'So, there you are,' said Dad. 'And what time did you get home?'

'Early,' I said vaguely. 'I told you I was staying out.'

'Indeed you did,' he said. 'So, what I'd like to know is why you're here? Have you any idea, the panic you caused?'

'Panic? What panic?'

Eliza spooned some food into Mikey's mouth and gave me an accusing look. 'Well, at the Hall for starters. They went searching for you, wondering if you'd been taken ill or something, since your car was still in the car park. Then they realised your overnight bag wasn't in your room and rang here. Of course, as far as we were aware, you were there, so we started panicking too, until I found you fast asleep in bed. It was very thoughtless of you, Lexi.'

'Hmm. Sorry.'

'And what time did you come home?' demanded Dad. 'Darcey

said you didn't go to bed until gone midnight, so it must have been well after that. You walked home in the darkness, all alone! What the hell were you thinking? Anything could have happened to you.'

'Yeah, all right, Dad,' I muttered. 'I get it. I'm sorry, okay?'

He ran a hand over his eyes and took a deep breath. 'Okay. Just — just don't do it again. Promise?'

'Promise. And don't worry. I won't be staying over at the Hall again, anyway.'

I saw them all glance at each other. Charlie opened his mouth, but Joe gripped his arm and he shut it again. Good job. I definitely wasn't up to an interrogation.

As I headed over to the sink to fill the kettle, Joe sidled up to me. 'You okay, love?' he asked softly.

I shook my head, too overwhelmed with misery to reply.

'If you want to talk, you know where I am,' he murmured, patting my hand, then turned to everyone else and asked, rather too brightly, 'Who's for another cuppa?'

I was quiet all day, but if anyone noticed they had the good sense not to comment. They were all busy making plans for January. Eliza and Dad were determined to start house-hunting in earnest, even though Joe and Charlie assured them there was no rush.

'Maybe not,' said Dad, 'and I have to say, being here has done us the world of good. But we need our own place, and maybe now Christmas is over, more houses will go on the market.'

Joe was psyching himself up to say goodbye to Charlie, who would be leaving in a few days to start touring the country with his new *Hope Springs* stand-up show. He was planning a new book to take his mind off missing his partner. 'You've inspired me,' he told me, grinning. 'Think I'm going to set my next murder mystery in a stately home.'

'Good idea,' I said. 'They're the ideal setting for tales of treachery, deceit and stabbing people in the back.'

He raised an eyebrow. 'You sure you don't want to talk, love? I'm a good listener.'

'I know you are.' I heaved a heavy sigh. 'Maybe soon. I'm still trying to come to terms with things in my own head. I need to sort it out myself first, okay?'

'Of course.' He ruffled my hair. 'You're a bright girl, Lexi. Whatever the problem is, I'm sure you can deal with it.'

I wished I could share his faith. My stomach churned at the thought of going back to work the next day, but I knew I couldn't put it off forever. Even if I called in sick, I would still have to face them the next day, or the day after. I may as well get it over with.

When I arrived at the Hall the following day, I headed straight to the kitchen, relieved to find Woody and Bernie in there, eating fried egg sandwiches. After wishing them a muttered happy New Year, I sank into the chair and stared gloomily at the range, shaking my head when Bernie offered me half of his sandwich.

'Another one down in the dumps,' said Woody. 'I dunno. You youngsters don't half have a miserable time of it. Whatever's the matter now?'

'Whatever it is, I'll bet it has something to do with Nat,' said Bernie bitterly.

'Nat? No, actually, it hasn't. Why do you say that?' I tutted in exasperation. 'Don't tell me he's been misbehaving again.'

'Huh. You could say that.'

'You sure you should say anything, Bernie?' said Woody. 'I mean, it's private, like. Not sure you should tell anyone else.'

'It's Lexi!' said Bernie, as if that answered *that* dilemma. 'Thing is, I've had Darcey in tears this morning, and I tell you, I'd like to throttle that little bugger.'

'Who — Darcey?'

'No. Nat. Do you know what he did? I mean, you won't believe it, because even I can't believe he'd stoop this low. Only got Darcey and Will drunk, and put her in Will's bed. Can you believe that?'

'What?' I sat up straight, staring at him in astonishment. 'Are you sure about that?'

'Of course. Darcey was mortified. Said she couldn't believe it when she woke up on New Year's Day and found Will beside her, and her in his bed and no idea how she'd got there.'

'But how do you know Nat was responsible?'

He stared at me. 'Who else? He flatly denied it at first, of course, and Will kept making excuses for him, same as always. But then, this morning, Darcey said she was going to hand in her notice, and Will got all angry with Nat and demanded to know the truth, so Nat confessed.'

'Not that it came as any surprise to us, eh, Bernie?' said Woody. 'I mean, who's got form for spiking drinks, eh? Remember the state of Will at his father's funeral? I tell you, that lad should have been reined in when he was a nipper. Too late now.'

'What did Will say?'

'Well, it all kicked off. There was loads of yelling in the sitting room, wasn't there, Woody? And then the next thing we know, Will comes in here and tells us that he's locked them both in there and we're not to let them out until he says so.'

'As if we would.' Woody sniffed. 'They can stay up there forever, for all I care.'

'It's not Darcey's fault,' Bernie said. 'It's all that Nat's doing. Anyway, Will's determined they're going to sort things out and make it up. Reckon he's pretty miffed with Nat. I mean, he stuck up for him, didn't he? And he must have been so embarrassed when he woke up yesterday morning. He can't remember a thing about New Year's Eve.'

'Oh,' I said, disappointed. 'Can't he?'

Bernie shook his head. 'Well, not getting to bed, any road. Said the last thing he recalls is wishing you a happy New Year. It's a blank after that.'

My heart leapt. He remembered that bit. And he hadn't slept with Darcey. I jumped up, hugged Bernie tightly, then threw my arms around a startled Woody.

'What on earth's that about?' she asked, laughing.

'Just wanted to say, happy New Year,' I told her, unable to wipe the grin from my face. 'Now, can I have an egg sandwich please?'

****

It was an hour or so later when I saw Darcey. Evidently, Will had released her and Nat from their prison. She was outside the old stables, talking to Bernie, as I headed up the path towards the farm shop. She seemed quite chipper, to my surprise, and waved to me as I passed. I made a detour and went to see if she was okay.

'Good morning, Lexi,' she said, quite cheerfully. 'How's your hangover?'

I watched her, puzzled. 'Fine thanks,' I said. 'Well, it is now. I felt pretty wretched yesterday.'

'Why on earth did you go home so late?' she said. 'We were worried sick when we saw you were missing. I can't tell you what I was imagining.'

I frowned. It wasn't what I'd been expecting from her at all, especially after Bernie's assertion that she was in pieces.

'I woke up feeling really sick,' I lied. 'I thought the walk would do me good. If I'd been sober, I probably wouldn't have done it. It was a stupid thing to do, but then, we all do stupid things when we're drunk, don't we?'

I gave her a very pointed look, and she laughed. 'You've heard, then? Yes, it *was* all rather stupid, but I suppose we can put it behind us now.'

I glanced at Bernie, and he shrugged. 'Seems it's all sorted,' he said.

'Really? So, what happened?' I was half afraid to ask, but my need to know the truth forced the question out.

She rolled her eyes. 'What do you think happened? Nat. He thought it would be hilarious to put me in bed with Will.'

'I can't believe he admitted it,' I said.

She nodded. 'He denied it at first, but then came clean when Will wouldn't let it drop. Nat confessed that he'd been drunk and foolish, and thought it was a good idea at the time. He's apologised, though, so that's the end of it.'

'The end of it? Are you serious?'

Bernie scowled. 'Seems they've made up.'

'What?' Had the world gone mad? Nat and Darcey had made up?

Darcey folded her arms and shrugged, kicking gently at a stone on the path. 'It was a stupid thing for him to do, and he knows that. It wasn't done maliciously. Will forced us to talk, to sort out our differences.'

'And it worked?' I could hardly believe what I was hearing.

Darcey sighed. 'Eventually. Nat and I had some issues. I think that was fairly obvious to everyone. I suppose we can't get along instantly with everyone we meet. He shouldn't have done what he did, but — well — he wasn't doing it to embarrass either of us and he certainly didn't mean things to get as unpleasant as they did. He genuinely seems sorry. Actually, he was rather nice to me this morning. It was quite strange. We agreed to call a truce and work together. There are more important things than our silly feuding, and Will needs us to all pull together. He's been through enough, don't you agree?'

She smiled at me, and I gaped back, unable to process what I'd just heard. I looked at Bernie again and realised he was as bewildered as I was about the unexpected turn of events.

Eventually, I closed my mouth and shook my head slightly. 'Right. Well, if that's the way it is, fair enough. Not much else I can say, is there? I just hope you know what you're doing.'

'I do, Lexi, I promise you. Now, Bernie, back to business.' She gazed up at him, and I saw him visibly melt. Just another weird thing to get my head around.

Chapter 29

January flew by, which was odd because, usually, January was about twice as long as every other month, in my experience. Things at the Hall were ticking along nicely. Paintings were sent off for cleaning, while others were returned and carefully hung in their new positions. The cleaning ladies worked hard, carefully dusting and brushing and sweeping. Carpets were gently vacuumed under a layer of protective mesh. Curtains and drapes were cleared of dust, chandeliers cleaned, and ceilings brushed, with the aid of some portable scaffolding on wheels, which was pushed from room to room. Furniture received its annual polish, dust covers were removed, and ornaments, statues, and valuable pieces of porcelain were taken to their new settings. The booklet was finished and sent to the printers, the new maps arrived, and Darcey interviewed volunteers, allocating them various roles.

The shop was quieter in January, as were the café and gardens, but there were still plenty of visitors eager to see the carpet of snowdrops that adorned the woods throughout late January and February. They all seemed delighted that they were soon going to be allowed to look around the inside of the Hall, and all assured us that they would be coming back when it finally opened.

The tickets for the ball sold out fast. Nat had hired a firm of caterers for the occasion, which Woody was quite put out about, but I pacified her by handing her a complimentary ticket to the ball for herself and her Bobby. She was quite chuffed to be a guest, for once, and didn't mind about the caterers after that. It was to be a fancy-dress ball, and the villagers were buzzing with ideas for costumes.

To my delight, Derry confided that Will had asked him and his band to perform at the ball, and, after much debating, and a great deal of pressure from his bandmates, he'd agreed. There was also going to be a string quartet, who would play classical music, as there would be a mixture of contemporary and ballroom dances. The event was really taking shape. I just had to sort out my costume.

I'd given it a lot of thought. The theme for the ball was historical figures from the seventeenth century onwards, to coincide roughly with the age of the present Hall. That in mind, there was no contest. I wanted to go as Elinor Kearton, but finding a costume locally was proving impossible. It was Eliza who'd suggested Dad's receptionist, and Chrissie's mum, Meggie. I'd quite forgotten that she was a dab hand with the sewing machine and made all her own clothes. Eliza thought that, if I provided a snapshot of the portrait of the countess, Meggie would be able to create something in time for the ball. I duly did exactly that. After examining it thoroughly, Meggie said that, with a bit of help from the internet, she should be able to come up with a suitable pattern.

'Mind,' she added, 'it's going to cost a fair bit. All that green satin, and all them layers of petticoats, and the like. Plus, there's shoes to find. It'll set you back a bit, Lexi. Are you sure it's worth the time and trouble?'

To me, it was. Since moving in to Whisperwood, I'd had nothing to spend my money on, anyway, since Joe and Charlie refused point blank to take a penny from any of us, and it wasn't as if I had any kind of a social life. Apart from the occasional visit to The Hare and Moon, to have a drink with Derry, I rarely went out anywhere, except to work. I decided it would be worth every penny, and I couldn't wait to see Will's face when he saw me arrive in costume, my lovely replica of the countess's own brooch pinned to its bodice.

The quotes came in from the other builders and all were around the same figure as Marcus Leigh and Son's. Darcey had warned ECHOES about Clarke's, and she assured us they'd launched a full investigation, and Nat had applied to them for the grant for the roof. It would be a long and nerve-wracking wait, as Darcey warned it could take up to six months before they made their decision.

Thankfully, things between Will and me had become much better, in the sense that he no longer ignored me. On the other hand, he was treating me just the same as Darcey or Nat, and I found, to my discomfort, that I wanted more. He was so busy, working himself into the ground to get things ready for the opening in early April, but I would catch glimpses of him around the gardens, or bump into him in a corridor, or find him coming out of the stables, sleeves rolled up, wellies on, pushing a wheelbarrow of dirty straw to the muck heap. I wanted to ask him for another riding lesson but didn't dare. I genuinely wanted to continue learning to ride, as I had, to my astonishment, really started to enjoy it, and I was quite attached to Captain, who was lovely.

I had to admit, though, that I also wanted the excuse to be with Will. Just him and me, and no Darcey or Nat. No interruptions. An hour with his full attention on me. I knew he was busy, and I wasn't sure he'd have the time or the inclination, so I didn't mention it. I hoped, maybe when the Hall was open and things had settled down, I could approach him then and ask if we could resume the lessons. If I could wait that long.

One morning, I gazed out of the window of Darcey's office and saw him standing in front of the stables, deep in conversation with Bernie. I watched him as he stood, arms folded, nodding now and then as Bernie made some point or other. He was tall — probably around six-foot-three — and quite lean, but not skinny. He wore old jeans, wellies, and a checked shirt with the sleeves rolled up. His brown hair was thick and silky, and his green eyes narrowed as he listened to whatever Bernie was telling him. Suddenly, they crinkled in the corners as he burst out laughing, and my heart jumped for joy at the sight of him, while my insides seemed to fizz with excitement.

I gulped. How had I not noticed before how beautiful Will was? I mean, I'd always thought he was lovely, but I'd never realised just how lovely. Until lately. Lately, I couldn't stop seeing it. Everything about him was wonderful, but those eyes — those beautiful, kind eyes, full of gentleness and understanding — were exceptional. I could gaze forever into those eyes.

As I stared across at him, I was consumed by a longing to be physically close to him. I'd never felt that way before. With Derry and Nat, although I'd thoroughly enjoyed going to bed with them, I hadn't had an overwhelming compulsion to be near them, to touch them. Yet, I couldn't stop imagining what it would be like to be held by Will, to be kissed by him, to be made love to by him. Thinking about it now, I felt quite hot and bothered, and took a deep breath as my imagination took flight and I was no longer in Darcey's office, but rolling around in Will's bed, having the time of my life.

'Sweet Jesus,' I murmured.

'Sorry?'

I jumped, my face burning with embarrassment. I hadn't heard Darcey come in. I hoped I hadn't been making any inappropriate noises or pulling any strange faces while I'd been daydreaming.

She raised an eyebrow. 'What are you looking at?' She peered over my shoulder and smiled. 'Bless them. They seem to be having a good laugh together, don't they?'

'What? Who? Oh, you mean Will and Bernie. I wasn't looking at them,' I lied.

She raised an eyebrow. 'Really? What *were* you looking at then?'

'Just the stables,' I said. 'I was thinking about the other stable block, and your plans for conversion. I think we're going to need to do it sooner or later. You're right about that.'

She sat down at her desk, nodding. 'I know. I wish Will would consider ... Well, we'll keep plodding on.'

I moved away from the window, for the sake of my hormones and my sanity, and sat down opposite her. 'We need to find the earl's treasure,' I told her, grinning. 'That would solve all our problems.'

She laughed. 'Well, quite. So, now all we have to do is find it.'

'Hmm,' I said, 'where to start?'

'If only we knew,' she said.

'Why do I get the feeling you're humouring me? Don't you believe it? There must be some basis for it.'

'I'm sure there is,' she said. 'And I would love to be able to find it and solve all Will's problems at a stroke, but don't you think that, after all these years, it would have been discovered by now? I doubt very much there's anything left to find in this house.'

'I suppose you're right,' I said. Then I remembered the secret passageway and shivered with delight.

Not everything had been discovered. If only Will, Bernie and myself knew about that place's existence, what other secrets might the Hall still be keeping? There could be other priest holes, other hiding places. I wasn't going to give up just yet. Treasure could be the answer to all Will's problems, and if it was somewhere in Kearton Hall, I was suddenly determined to find it.

****

The end of January presented me with a dilemma. It was Georgia's birthday. I thought about ignoring it, but I knew, deep down, that I couldn't. She was my friend, and even though she'd let me down badly, I couldn't carry on punishing her. Besides, I missed her, and I had an awful lot to tell her. So, swallowing my pride, I made my way to Cherry Tree Lane that evening, carrying a bunch of flowers, a box of chocolates, a bottle of her favourite wine, and a card.

I stood on the doorstep, took a steadying breath, and rang the bell.

She took ages to answer. I had to ring three times, and just when I was about to give up and go home, the door opened and there she was. She seemed stunned to see me, and her face flooded with colour. 'Lexi! You're the last person I expected to see.'

I shrugged and gave her a bashful smile. 'Happy birthday!'

She stared at me for a moment, then smiled back. 'Sorry, you've just completely surprised me. Come in.'

She stepped aside, and I walked into the hallway, carrying the goodies with trembling hands. I felt ridiculously nervous. She was my friend, after all, and had been for years. It was crazy to feel so uncomfortable with her.

She led me into the living room, and I looked around at all the birthday cards that adorned every surface.

'You're popular,' I said, nodding at them.

'What? Oh, mostly from pupils,' she said. 'Sit down. Would you like a drink?'

'In a minute maybe. Here, happy birthday.' I handed the presents and card over to her, and she looked at them, then gazed up at me, her eyes full of unshed tears.

'Thank you, Lexi. I wasn't expecting … It's so good to see you.'

We stared at each other for a moment, then both burst out, 'I'm sorry.'

She shook her head, put the presents on the floor and reached for my hands, which she grasped in her own. 'You've got nothing to apologise for, honestly. It was all my fault. I'm so sorry, Lexi.'

'It wasn't all your fault,' I said. 'I know how persuasive Nat can be. He's more at fault than you.'

'That's not true,' she said quietly. 'It takes two to tango.'

'Yeah, well.' I decided not to pursue the subject any further. 'Let's just put it all behind us, shall we? So, what's new?'

We both sat, and she glanced around the room, shrugging casually. 'Nothing much. Same old, same old. What about you?'

I felt my cheeks flush with embarrassment and excitement. It would be so good to finally confess my newfound attraction to Will to someone. 'You'll never believe this,' I began, then stopped. 'What was that?'

'What?' She seemed twitchy, nervous.

'That noise.'

'I didn't hear anything,' she said. 'Go on, what were you saying?'

I studied her. She was blushing, and her voice was distinctly tremulous. Georgia never was good at lying. I narrowed my eyes. 'Have you got someone here?'

She swallowed and glanced down at her lap. I felt my hackles rising.

'Bloody hell. He's here, isn't he? Nat!'

'Lexi, please.'

'So, it's been going on, all this time?' I could hardly believe it. All those weeks I'd been worrying about our friendship, feeling guilty for not making it up with her, and all the time she'd been too busy shagging that swine to care.

'It hasn't been going on all this time,' she pleaded. 'Honestly. I hadn't seen him since that day at the Hall. I ignored his texts and calls. I wanted to put it right with you. I kept hoping you'd forgive me, come round, but you didn't. And Nat was so persistent ... I was at my parents' house, and I felt so lonely, and I thought, well, why not text him? You weren't speaking to me anyway, and — and the truth is, I missed him.'

'Missed him? Nat? Are you mad?'

'Just because you don't like him, it doesn't mean I have to feel the same way, does it? He may not have been right for you, but he's right for me. I — I think I love him, Lexi.'

I shook my head, dazed at her stupidity. 'You're a fool. He's bad news. He's just using you, the way he used me.'

'It's not true,' she said. 'I'm sorry, but I know he likes me. Really likes me. We get on so well, and he's such good company, and so sweet. You don't know him the way I do.' She had the grace to look ashamed. 'Please, Lexi, I just want you to give us a chance. It's really important to me that we're all friends. I told Nat that it would only work if we could all get on.'

Something stirred in my memory. 'When did you tell him that?'

'I texted him on New Year's Eve, and he rang me back. We were talking for ages. He told me he was serious, that he wasn't going to mess me around, that he was sorry for what had happened. I told him then, we had to make it up with you. Both of us, I mean. Not just me. I don't want to lose you, Lexi. You're my best friend.'

So that explained Nat's drunken apology to me that night, and his pleading for us to be friends. I was such an idiot. I stood up.

'Where are you going?'

'Home,' I said. 'I don't want to interrupt your romantic date, do I? Sorry for bothering you.'

'You haven't bothered me,' she insisted. She stood and reached for my hand. 'I'm so glad you came. Stay. Have a drink with us.'

'You've got to be kidding me,' I said. 'I see enough of that twat at work, thanks very much. Honestly, Georgia, I knew you wanted a bloke, but you're scraping the barrel with this one. I'm serious. He's bad news. He's up to something, and you can tell him from me that I'm well aware of the fact, even if he has managed to fool Will, and even Darcey. If you want my advice, you'll steer well clear of him.'

She dropped my hand and gave me a resigned look. 'Well, I'm sorry you feel like that. I don't see him that way, and I don't believe he's bad news. He's lovely to me. We're having fun. I've not been this happy in a long time. If you'd just give him a chance, you'd see...' Her voice trailed off as I pulled a face. 'Clearly, you're not going to give him that chance. I'm sorry.'

'So am I,' I said, walking towards the front door. 'I'm sorry for *you*, Georgia. You're going to be hurt. Nat's going to break your heart, and when he does, don't say I didn't warn you.'

Chapter 30

The twins were one year old. I could hardly believe it. It seemed only weeks ago that Eliza had been plodding around, barely able to fit through the front door of the cottage. A year later, and Hannah and Michael were chubby-cheeked, fair-haired little munchkins, with sixteen teeth between them and an impressive new ability to walk. Well, to take a few steps anyway, although the way Dad and Eliza shrieked with delight as they waddled towards them, anyone would have thought they'd completed the London Marathon.

To celebrate their first birthday, Joe had insisted on throwing them a party. Eliza and Dad weren't so sure, given that the twins had no idea what a birthday was and were more likely to rub cake into each other's hair than actually eat it, but he was insistent.

Eliza told me she thought he was using it as an excuse to entice Charlie home for the day. Their birthday coincided with a tour gig that he was doing in Leeds, so Joe had suggested the party be held the day after, on the Sunday, which would mean Charlie could make it home, enjoy the party, spend the night at Whisperwood, and then head off the next day to Newcastle, which was where his next gig was.

I couldn't blame him for grasping the opportunity. I knew he was missing him, although he spent long hours locked in his study, tapping away at his computer as he worked on his next murder mystery masterpiece.

Initially, it was only supposed to be Dad, Eliza, Joe, Charlie,

Amy, me and the twins, but it kept snowballing, 'til in the end, Joe said he wished he'd never bothered, and did he have time to build an extension?

Luckily, not everyone accepted the invitation. Oliver, as expected, was too busy to attend. Cerise was away, staying with a friend. Darcey and Bernie couldn't come either. Apparently, they'd already made plans to visit Cressingdon Manor, a large stately home in Norfolk, as Darcey wanted to take a look around for inspiration, and Bernie knew the estate manager and wanted to go over plans for the shoot with him, so they'd be away all weekend.

Rhiannon accepted, so Derry declined, citing a gig at a pub in Oddborough as an excuse. It was a crap excuse, given that the party was going to be held in the afternoon, and the gig didn't start 'til eight, but I didn't push him. Other than that, everyone else said they would be delighted to attend, and I felt a rush of excitement, knowing that Will and I would be together away from the Hall.

Could I make a move on him? Did I dare? How would he react? It felt strange even thinking about it. He'd been my friend for so long, but it was as if the scales had fallen from my eyes, and I couldn't fight my attraction for him much longer. I really wanted to get physical with him and, to be honest, it was beginning to get on my nerves, dealing with my surging hormones whenever I saw him. It wasn't very convenient when I had to work with someone every day, talking about where to place a Chippendale table and which room was best suited to show off an expensive, eighteenth century vase, when all I really wanted to say was, *You're bloody gorgeous. Fancy testing that four poster bed out with me?*

When I thought about putting my feelings into words, though, I felt sick with nerves. What if he didn't feel the same? What if he recoiled in horror at the very idea of bumping bits with me, and told me in, no uncertain terms, that I was his employee and would never be anything more. It would ruin our friendship. I wasn't sure it was worth the risk, but I was finding it harder and harder to hide what I was feeling.

I wished I could talk things over with Georgia. I missed having someone to confide in, but she'd chosen Nat, and there was no way I could risk letting him find out how I felt about his cousin. My life wouldn't be worth living.

The farmhouse was a mass of balloons and banners on the day of the party. The table groaned with food, the worktop was loaded with bottles of drink, and the twins were looking like little cherubs in their new birthday outfits. Amy was a bit put out that she wasn't the star of the show for once, and kept reminding everyone that her birthday was in April, when she would be eight, which, apparently, was a very special age to be and worthy of an even bigger party than this one.

Meggie spent most of the afternoon dodging Sophie, who still harboured hopes that, one day, Meggie would stick to the Lightweights diet and win the Slimmer of the Year award, which would mean that, as group leader, Sophie would get a big share of the limelight, including a free trip to London. Meggie, on the other hand, was adamant that the Lightweights diet was torture, and she only went to the meetings for the company, and if Sophie thought she was going to starve herself just so that she could grab all the glory, she could think again. She kept sending Ben into the kitchen with her empty plate, getting him to bring back all her favourite, forbidden snacks.

Sophie — in between checking that Meggie was nowhere near the table, monitoring Rose's alcohol intake, and muttering about the bare-faced cheek of Rhiannon, turning up to a party after everything she'd done — was being equally sneaky about her own food intake, since she couldn't resist Eliza's baking and, as group leader, felt she had an image to maintain. Gran, who liked nothing better than to wind her up, had a fabulous time spying on her and pouncing every time she reached for something not included on the Lightweights diet sheet. Poor Sophie, but she did ask for it sometimes.

Grandad, Flynn and Dad were discussing work, which thoroughly annoyed Eliza and Rose, who conveniently forgot their grievances when they ended up huddled in a corner with Chrissie, chatting about how things were going at Mallow Magic. I heard them commiserating with her that her wedding plans were still on hold, as she and Robbie couldn't find anywhere to rent in the village.

Fuchsia, Pandora and Tally were playing with the twins and Violet, which I thought was very noble of them, but they assured me they were having a lovely time. Rhiannon, Meggie, Ben and Joe were being thoroughly entertained by Charlie, as he recounted his latest adventures on tour, and Eddie, Robbie and Archie were having a serious conversation about house prices in the area, the intolerable situation with second homers, and the fact that, at the rate things were going, the only way Robbie and Chrissie would ever be able to get married was if they moved in with Meggie and Ben, a solution that Robbie seemed less than keen on. I couldn't blame him. Meggie and Ben were lovely, but it was hardly ideal, was it? Starting life with your in-laws, and in such a small house.

I left them to their discussion, took a deep breath, grabbed two bottles of beer, and headed into the living room, where I'd last seen Will. I would engage him in conversation, flirt with him a little — very subtly, of course. I didn't want to scare him off, after all. Maybe the beer would ease the path. I tutted in dismay when I saw him talking to Amy. She was telling him about Twinkle's latest antics and asking him if she could go back to the Hall one day and have another ride on Frosty. I leaned against the doorframe, listening to their conversation with amusement.

'I don't see why not,' he said. 'You're always welcome, Amy. Any time Lexi wants to bring you, it's fine by me.'

'Thanks, Will,' she said, then suddenly launched herself onto his knee and wrapped her arms around his neck. 'I really like you. You're ever so nice. Do you think Woody will make me some of her flapjacks?'

He grinned. 'I'm sure she would.'

'Does Nat still live there?' she asked, screwing up her nose in disapproval. 'I don't like him. I got told off for saying a bad word about him.'

'Did you indeed?' said Will, shaking his head in mock disapproval. 'I won't ask what it was.'

She leaned over, whispering into his ear. His eyes widened, and she giggled as he said, 'Well, I've never heard him called that before. Better not say that again, Amy. Father Christmas might not be so generous next year, if you keep using language like that.'

She tutted. 'Father Christmas isn't real, Will. Everyone knows that.' She hesitated a moment, then added, 'Well, everyone but Charlie. You won't tell him, will you? I don't want to spoil it for him.'

Will bit his lip. 'I promise,' he said.

I strolled casually over to them, ignoring the palpitations in my chest, and handed him a bottle of beer. He smiled up at me, surprised. 'Thank you. I was just going to get myself a drink.'

'Would you like something to eat?' I asked.

He shook his head. 'Not really. If I eat, I might well fall asleep. I'm so tired.'

'You can have a sleep here, if you want,' offered Amy. 'Why don't you go to bed for a bit? He can sleep in your bed, can't he, Lexi?'

I almost dropped my bottle. The most alarming thoughts suddenly ran through my mind, and I was glad Amy couldn't see what I was thinking. I'd have been locked up. Talk about X-rated. 'Er, well...'

'I don't think that would be very polite,' Will told her. 'I'm a guest here, after all.' He yawned and apologised.

I peered at him. Thinking about it, he looked bloody awful, in a gorgeous sort of way. 'Oh, Will, are you still not sleeping properly?'

He seemed a bit downcast. 'Not really. Too many thoughts running through my head. Can't seem to switch off.' He gave a half laugh. 'Anyway, I'm sure it will sort itself out, eventually.'

It hardly seemed the right time to launch my flirting campaign. Besides, being so close to him, I did feel a bit worried. Fatigue was etched in his face. I hoped he wasn't going to be ill.

'Time for birthday cake!' called Eliza, and Amy leapt up, abandoning Will in favour of the massive iced sponge that Eliza had baked.

I held out my hand to Will, and he took it, hauling himself with obvious effort from the sofa. He seemed quite breathless, and I was so alarmed that I quite forgot to be turned on by his hand in mine.

'Are you sure you're all right?' I asked.

He nodded. 'Fine. Honestly, don't worry.'

'Well, I do worry. Do you want me to take you home?'

'No, no. It's lovely being away from the Hall for a bit, to be honest. I'm enjoying myself, seeing all these familiar faces and not thinking about business for a while. It's good to be here. I'm so glad we're friends again, Lexi. I'm sorry things got so difficult after all that business with Nat. I'd hate to lose our friendship.' He smiled and squeezed my hand. 'Come on, let's see how long it takes the twins to extinguish the flames, eh?'

Talking of extinguishing flames, I sighed as I realised there was no way my plan to seduce him was going to be put into action right now — not after he'd made it clear that we were just friends. It simply wasn't worth the risk. I couldn't bear it if it all went wrong and things became difficult between us again. Perhaps it was best if I forgot all about it and ignored my raging libido.

In the event, the twins weren't remotely interested in the cake or the candles, but Amy stepped in, not surprisingly. She even made a wish on their behalf, though how grateful they'd be for a pony was anyone's guess. As everyone clapped and cheered, I felt pressure on my arm. I turned, concerned to see Rhiannon standing beside Will, who looked quite drained.

'I think I'll have to go home,' he whispered. 'Will you thank your father and Eliza for me? I really don't wish to be rude, but I just can't ... Sorry.'

'Don't be silly,' I whispered back. 'You go. Do you want me to give you a lift? I don't think you should be walking home alone, if you feel so bad.'

'Don't worry, Lexi,' said Rhiannon. 'I'm walking him home and I'll stay a while. He'll be fine.'

I tried not to feel jealous, but I simply wasn't that noble.

Will must have seen the expression on my face and misinterpreted it. 'Honestly, I'll be okay. Don't worry,' he said.

'I'll see you tomorrow.'

As they left the house, I frowned, wondering what on earth was wrong with him.

The party continued as Eliza cut the cake and everyone pounced on it, even Sophie. Gran looked at her pointedly, but Sophie said defiantly, 'Birthday cake is exempt from Lightweights units today.'

'Thank God for that,' said Meggie immediately and grabbed a huge slice with eager hands, much to Sophie's annoyance.

I wandered back into the living room, where Dad and Flynn were feeding trifle to Violet and Hannah.

Dad glanced up and smiled. 'Having a good time? Amy seems to be enjoying herself, anyway. Anyone would think it was her birthday.'

'Hmm.' I nodded and sat down, wondering if I should say anything about Will. I was worried, and I wanted their opinion. 'Dad, did you see Will today?'

'Briefly,' he said. 'He didn't say much, to be honest. Looked a bit tired.'

'He seemed rather pale to me,' said Flynn. 'I think he's working too hard.'

I thought about it for a moment, then shook my head. 'I think it's more than that. There's something wrong with him. He's barely slept since Sir Paul's death, and today, just now…'

'What?' said Dad.

'Well, he seemed a bit breathless. Do you think he's ill?'

'He could have a virus,' said Dad, reaching over and wiping Hannah's chin with some tissue. 'Or he could just be rundown. He's been through a lot lately, don't forget.'

'He could even be depressed,' added Flynn thoughtfully. 'God knows, I wouldn't be surprised. He's probably still grieving for his father, for a start.'

I pulled a face, and Flynn grinned.

'You may not think much to Sir Paul, but he was still Will's parent, and no doubt Will loved him, regardless of his behaviour.'

'Then there was the fact that his mother didn't come home to support him,' added Dad. 'I'll bet you a pound to a penny that he secretly hoped she would. That must have been a bitter blow.'

'Yeah, especially after that pathetic begging letter she sent him. Big deal.' I scowled, remembering the pained expression on Will's face as he'd finally showed it to me. It would have been better if she'd sent nothing at all. 'So, you think he could be suffering from depression?'

'He's had a lot of stress lately,' said Flynn. 'All the worry of trying to hang onto Kearton Hall, burying his father, becoming the new Baronet Kearton. It would be extraordinary if he wasn't feeling the pressure. He probably just needs time to adjust, and he could do to rest more. I think sometimes we forget how young he is. He's only in his twenties, after all.'

'Or, as I said, it could be a virus,' said Dad. 'If he's worried, tell him to come to the surgery. We can do blood tests, see if there's anything physically wrong with him.'

'I will,' I said. 'Thanks.'

Dad smiled. 'Don't worry, Lexi. He'll be all right, you'll see. Hmm, who's this?' He reached in his pocket as his mobile beeped and frowned at the screen. 'Don't know that number,' he said, tapping on the phone to open his message.

'Joe's going to throttle us,' said Flynn ruefully. 'We've got more trifle on the floor than in the girls' mouths.'

'You have made a bit of a mess,' I said, laughing. 'Still, Honoria Glossop will make short work of that.'

Dad put his phone back in his pocket. He looked suddenly tense.

'Are you all right, Dad?' I asked.

'What? Yes, yes fine.'

'Who was it?'

He stared at me for a moment, as if trying to take in what I'd said. 'Er, just a message about accident insurance. Sick of receiving them to be honest.'

'You and me both,' said Flynn. 'Do you think they've had enough trifle?' Dad's expression was blank, and Flynn frowned. 'Gabriel?'

'Right. Yes, enough trifle.' He stood up, collecting the bowl from Flynn's hand. 'I'll take these to the sink. Won't be a minute.'

He wandered into the kitchen, and Flynn looked at me, seemingly as confused as I was. Something had evidently rattled Dad, and it wasn't something he was prepared to share. So now I had two men to worry about. Great.

Chapter 31

Eliza went back to work part-time the following week. Joe had offered to take care of the twins while she was at the shop, and she couldn't bring herself to refuse. She'd missed Mallow Magic, and she was more than ready to enter the real world again.

'I love the babies,' she told me, 'but I need more than that. I miss making the marshmallows. I miss serving in the shop. I miss chatting to customers and catching up on the gossip when locals drop in. I think I'll feel more like my old self now I'm back.'

She certainly seemed happier, which was a weight off my mind. Unfortunately, worrying about Eliza had been replaced by worrying about Dad. *He* was definitely not himself. He seemed cagey and evasive, and more than once, he snapped at one or other of us, for something so trivial, he wouldn't normally have even noticed.

I got home from work one night to find Eliza enthusiastically reading aloud from an estate agent's brochure. 'Four bedrooms, one with en suite, family bathroom, kitchen diner, study, sitting room, downstairs cloakroom and utility room. Sounds perfect, doesn't it? It's got a good-sized garden, so the kids would have lots of space to run around and play. And the location couldn't be better, could it?'

'What's this?' I said, peering over her shoulder. 'Wychwood. Where's that? Oh!'

'Exactly,' she said excitedly. 'Daisyfield Walk, off Clover Lane

— not five minutes away from the farm. It's perfect, isn't it?'

Joe nodded, smiling. 'Sounds it. Are you going to book a viewing?'

'Already have.' She reached over and squeezed Dad's hand. 'We're going to see it tomorrow night after work. Okay?'

'It will have to be,' he said, 'since you've already arranged it. But thanks for running it past me first.'

She leaned back, hurt by his attitude. 'What's wrong? Don't you think it's exactly what we're searching for?'

'I haven't seen it,' he pointed out. 'I'll reserve judgment until then.'

We all looked at each other in surprise. Eliza's face was flushed, and I tried to defuse the situation. 'It's not a bad price, either. Much cheaper than that one in Farthingdale.'

'Well, it couldn't have been any bloody more, could it?' said Dad. He took the brochure from Eliza's hand and gave it a cursory glance. 'Still pretty expensive, if you ask me. I'm going to get a shower.'

We all stared after him, as he left the kitchen and headed upstairs.

'Well,' said Joe, shaking his head in bewilderment, 'what the hell's got into him?'

'I don't know.' Eliza was close to tears, and I felt so sorry for her. She'd been so excited about the house, and no wonder. It was ideal for us. What was Dad thinking, spoiling it for her, when she'd waited so long to find a suitable home? She pushed back her chair and stood up, clearly trying not to seem rattled. 'I expect he's tired. It's very busy at the surgery in the winter months — all those coughs and colds and other ailments. Anyone would get grumpy. A hot shower and some of my beef casserole will put him in a better mood.'

When he came back from the bathroom, she fussed round him, giving him a huge plate of casserole, a cup of tea, and a kiss on the forehead. I thought that was pretty big of her. I'd have been more inclined to give him *a clout round the ear*, as Hannah used to say.

He was quiet for a few moments, then he put down his fork

and walked over to her, as she stood spooning food into the twins' plastic bowls. He wrapped his arms around her and kissed her. 'Sorry,' he said. 'I was horrible to you, and you didn't deserve it. Forgive me?'

She smiled. 'Of course I forgive you. Is there anything on your mind that I can help you with?'

He shook his head. 'Nothing. It's just been a long day. No excuse for being so rude.' He kissed her again. 'The house sounds lovely. Looking forward to seeing it.'

'Really?' She beamed at him and he nodded.

'Really.'

I was quite glad that she'd returned to sorting the twins' teas. She didn't get to see the dark shadow that passed over his face as he turned away from her — but I did.

As if the situation at home wasn't bad enough, at work I was watching Will with increasing worry. He was so lethargic that even Darcey started to comment on it, asking him if he'd taken to staying up late, watching old movies, or something.

Nat made a joke of it, of course, telling her that Will's secret porn habit was finally starting to catch up with him. 'If he will take his laptop to bed and watch *Horny Honeys* until the early hours, what can you expect?'

Darcey tutted. 'Now, now, Nat. Don't judge Will by your standards.'

He grinned and winked at her.

I couldn't believe it. It was as if Nat had completely won Darcey over. How had he cast his spell over someone as sensible and rational as her? Will was understandable in a way — they were related, after all, and had been close childhood friends. But Darcey? Was I the only one who could see through him? I wished he'd just clear off back to London and leave us all alone.

'Are you worried about Will?' I asked her, after Nat had strolled out of the room, whistling cheerily to himself.

She looked at me, surprised. 'Why? Are you?'

'Well, as you say, he's been so tired lately. And I've noticed he seems a bit breathless sometimes. He always walks out of the room when he gets like that. Haven't you seen him do it?'

She sighed. 'It's probably just because he's not sleeping. I think he's depressed and grieving. Having been through it myself, I recognise the signs.'

'How do we help him through it?' I asked. 'Do you think he should see a doctor? My dad offered to do some blood tests on him if he felt he needed it. Or perhaps he could do with some anti-depressants? Just to help him through.'

She shook her head. 'Blood tests don't cure depression, and anti-depressants are just a sticking plaster on a burst artery. Time is the only cure, Lexi. Time, and having friends around him to be there for him. Will's got those, hasn't he? We're all here — you, me, Nat, Bernie and Woody.'

'About Nat,' I said. 'Are you really sure you can trust him? I mean, after everything he's done...'

'He's been an idiot, no doubt about it. But we all make mistakes, don't we? The thing is how we move on from them. Sometimes, mistakes lead you to something even more wonderful, so it's not always a bad thing.'

I stared at her, wondering what the hell she was talking about. She'd been full of the joys of spring lately, come to think of it. Even so, I couldn't imagine how she'd been so taken in by someone she'd seemed to loathe just a few weeks ago. There was no point in pressing her, however, so I merely shrugged. 'Okay. If you say so.'

'Honestly, stop worrying. We need to pull together and concentrate on making this house pay its way.'

'And on finding the treasure,' I said.

She raised an eyebrow. 'Seriously?'

'Absolutely. It has to be here, somewhere, and I intend to find it. I'd do anything to help Will save this house.'

She hesitated. 'I will admit, I had the same thought. It would be perfect if we could find it — supposing it really exists, of course. I've actually examined the priest holes again. I wanted to be absolutely certain they weren't double hides. A secondary chamber would have been the ideal spot for Lord Kearton to hide his treasure. Unfortunately, they appear to be single rooms, and I can't think where else to search. I've been studying

Nicholas Owen's work in detail, reading all I can about it, for any clues. But I simply can't find any evidence of another priest hole. It's quite frustrating.'

I hesitated. It would've been the ideal time to tell her about the secret passage, but I couldn't. I'd sworn to Will that I'd say nothing. Besides, I'd been down there, and there was no other room. The walls were bare brick.

It occurred to me suddenly that the treasure could have been hidden farther down the tunnel, where it was blocked off behind a mountain of rubble. That wasn't a cheering thought, so I pushed it away. If one double hide existed in this place, there could well be another. Or even another single room somewhere.

'Well, all we can do is keep searching,' I said finally. 'I'll see you later.'

****

By the end of February, the rooms that were to be opened to the public were fully dressed, and we were all treated to an unofficial tour. Darcey led us — all of the staff and volunteers — around the rooms, and I had to admit the route was a huge improvement.

The other staff members, with the exception of Bernie, got very excited about the priest hole in the stairs, having had no idea it was even there. There were lots of *oohs*, and *aahs*, and *fancy thats*.

I wondered what they'd say if they knew about the secret that lay in The Earl's Bedroom. I smiled to myself as we all gathered in there, admiring the second portrait of William Kearton, looking formal in black silk and wide lace collar, that Darcey had uncovered. Beside it hung information cards, detailing his marriage, and his demise during the Civil War. There was even mention of the legendary hidden treasure.

Moving on through the adjoining dressing room, visitors reached The Countess's Bedroom, a larger and altogether more pleasant room, with an impressive Jacobean ceiling, and two large windows, which compensated for the wooden panelling on the walls. We'd included information about her family home in

318

East Yorkshire, and her early, tragic death.

Up on the second floor was the Long Gallery, the Library and the Reading Room. The portraits of all six of the earls and countesses hung in the Long Gallery, including my beloved portrait of William by Dobson. The Keartons were together, just as the Boden-Keans were together in the Great Hall.

I couldn't believe how easily the whole thing flowed, and how, if you didn't know better, you'd swear you'd been round the entire house. Darcey had done a wonderful job, and I told her so.

'Thank you, Lexi. I'm so glad you approve,' she said, with a warm smile. 'It wasn't down to me though. Everyone's chipped in and worked so hard. I'm delighted with the result.'

'If this doesn't work, nothing will,' I said confidently.

Her smile faded a little. 'Lexi, you do know there are no guarantees? I still think that Will needs to be more realistic.'

'Turn it into a hotel?' I said. 'After all this hard work?'

'No, not that,' she said. 'But the charitable trust idea — it's a safety net, Lexi. This house is beautiful, and I think the tour has vastly improved its chances, but I can't promise you it will be enough. I'm sorry.'

I shivered, knowing that it had to be enough. There was nothing else for it.

****

'They've accepted our offer!' Eliza put down the phone and turned to us, her face bright with excitement.

'That's fabulous!' I laughed, as she threw her arms around me while hopping up and down like a demented kangaroo. 'All right, calm down. You'll do yourself a mischief.'

'I thought this day would never come.' She turned to Joe and enveloped him in a huge hug. 'Thank you for putting up with us for so long. I'll never forget it. We've loved being here, but I'll bet you'll be glad to get your house back.'

He shook his head. 'You must be joking. I've loved having you all here. Be sorry to see you go. Still, at least you're only five minutes away from here. I'll be popping by every day, so don't think you'll be getting rid of me.'

'And Amy will want to see the donkeys every day,' I pointed out. 'You may have trouble persuading her to move out.'

'That's true.' Eliza's face lit up as Dad, who'd been outside mending the paddock fence, strolled into the kitchen. 'You're freezing,' she said, touching his face sympathetically. 'Let me warm you up some soup. I have big news to tell you! Guess what?'

Dad looked tired, and hardly in the mood for guessing games. 'What?'

She gave a whoop of excitement. 'They've accepted our offer! Isn't it fabulous?'

He nodded and smiled. 'Great. That's that sorted, at least.'

Her smile dropped, and she stared at him, disappointed. 'Is that all you can say?'

'What do you want me to say? Hooray, we have a new house. All's well with the world.'

Eliza shrugged, clearly hurt. 'Oh, well. Anyway, I'll warm up that soup.'

'Don't bother,' he said, rubbing his face wearily. 'I have to go out.'

'Go out? Go out where?'

'To the surgery.'

Joe laughed. 'Er, I think someone's forgotten to mention to you that it's Saturday, Gabriel. Surgery's closed.'

'Yes, well, I have a lot of paperwork to catch up on,' he mumbled.

'Can't you do it here?' Eliza said.

'What, with all this noise and chaos going on? I don't think so.'

As if on cue, the twins started squealing, and Joe said, 'It's okay. I'll go.'

'What's wrong with you?' demanded Eliza, as Joe headed upstairs.

'Nothing's wrong with me,' Dad snapped. 'I told you, I have work to do.'

'Can't it wait until Monday?' I said. 'You both work hard all week. You should at least have your weekends together.'

'In an ideal world, Lexi,' said Dad. 'But this isn't an ideal world, is it? I'll see you later.'

He left the house, closing the door none-too-quietly behind him.

I stared at Eliza, dismayed to see her so hurt. 'Don't get upset,' I said. 'He's just got a lot on at work. Things will get better.'

'I know that,' she said, forcing a smile that didn't fool me for a moment. 'Of course they will. We just need a bit of time.'

I swallowed hard. Even a new house wasn't making him happy, and he was behaving completely out of character. How much time would it take?

****

I spent the afternoon trying to keep Amy occupied to give Eliza a break. She was very excited about the new house, and insisted we make a shopping list for her new bedroom. Needless to say, it included a lot of horsy decorations. I wondered how long it would be before she plastered her walls with posters of some boy band. Ugh. She'd be eight next month, and before we knew it, her hormones would be kicking in, heralding the start of a whole new era. I wondered how Dad and Eliza would cope with all that teenage angst. I couldn't help asking myself the question: would they still be together by then?

As Amy scrolled down the pages of eBay, desperately searching for a picture of a pony that resembled Twinkle, I found myself musing over the possibility that they could actually separate.

I'd thought, for a while, that things were better — that their relationship was back on an even keel. Lately, though, I wondered if it was just that living with Joe and Charlie had helped to mask the problems. Things seemed to have improved while we lived at Whisperwood, but the thought of moving out, back to a home of their own, seemed to have had a negative effect on Dad's mood.

Were the children just too much for him to cope with? Had my own recent selfish behaviour driven him to breaking point? Or

— I felt sick with fear as I contemplated the impossible — had Dad fallen out of love with Eliza?

At some point, Amy and I both fell asleep on my bed, and I only woke because I was lying at a funny angle and had cramp in my neck. I yawned and headed downstairs, leaving Amy sleeping soundly.

I found Eliza in the kitchen with Joe. Dad wasn't back.

'He's still at work?' I frowned. 'After four hours?'

'I'm sure he'll be home soon,' Eliza said, her voice brittle. 'Anyway, I'll start dinner.'

'I'm just nipping to Henderson's,' I announced.

'Henderson's? What for?' She sounded puzzled, but Joe gave me a knowing look. No doubt he'd guessed where I was really going.

'Just fancy some chocolate. Won't be long.'

'But dinner won't take long.'

'I'll be back before you know it.'

She sighed, but didn't argue. Joe narrowed his eyes at me, but I merely gave him a weak smile and left. I needed to see Dad. I needed to know why he was avoiding Eliza, and what was really going on with him. He couldn't just give up on his marriage like that. He had to do something — anything — to put things right. He had a duty of care to his children, and to their mother, and whatever the problem was, he was going to have to find a way to resolve it without hurting anyone.

The surgery was in darkness as I drove up Station Lane, and as I pulled up outside, I caught my breath. The shutters were down. There was no way Dad could be inside that building.

I turned into the car park behind the surgery, but sure enough, Dad's car wasn't there. He definitely wasn't at work, and he wasn't at Rose and Flynn's next door, either, as his car wasn't parked outside. I sat there, nibbling at my thumbnail, wondering what to do next.

Slowly I turned back down Station Lane, crawling past The Old Vicarage, where Sophie and Archie lived. His car wasn't in their drive, and I didn't hang around, not wanting to be seen by one of the family and have to field awkward questions.

Reaching the end of Station Lane, I turned back onto Whitby Road and pulled over. I would have to go to Henderson's for some chocolate, but I had something to do first. Taking out my mobile I rang Dad's number.

It took a few rings, but eventually he answered. 'Hello?' His voice sounded shaky.

I gripped the phone tightly and tried to keep my voice light. 'Hi, Dad. It's me. Just wondering if you're going to be long. Eliza's cooking dinner as we speak, and trust me, you don't want to miss out on it. Smells fabulous.'

I closed my eyes as, after a moment's hesitation, his reply cut through my heart like a scalpel. 'Er, yes, tell her I won't be long. I'm just photocopying some forms and then I'll come home.'

I took a steadying breath. 'Great. See you soon.'

I ended the call and sat staring at the road ahead, my mind a blur of confusion, fear, anger and dread. Where was he? What was he doing? And — oh, God — who was he doing it with?

Chapter 32

Will hadn't slept much that night, although that was nothing new. As the first light crept through the window, he realised he'd been lying in his bed, awake for hours, just staring at the ceiling. He'd been too tired to get up, so had spent most of the night running over things in his mind. Fat lot of good it had done him.

Things were getting worse and he knew it. As if worrying about the Hall's future wasn't bad enough, he had his health to concern him too. And Lexi, of course. There was always Lexi. He tried not to think about the situation, but it was impossible.

Darcey had been most odd the last few weeks, dropping hints that maybe Lexi had a secret crush on someone. He'd wondered at first if she'd meant Nat, but Nat seemed to be — weirdly — closer to Darcey than Lexi. That was a turn of events he hadn't foreseen when he'd locked them in the sitting room and made them sort out their differences. Still, he was glad that their relationship seemed to have been sorted at last. It made working life, at least, a lot easier.

Except, if not Nat, then who?

The answer had been given to him when he'd visited a heaving Hare and Moon the previous evening. He'd hoped to catch Derry, but as he'd walked through the door marked private, he'd bumped into the chef, Jack, who informed him that Derry was out, rehearsing with the band. Rhiannon, who was working behind the bar, called him over and handed him a watch.

'Can you give this back to Lexi?' she'd asked. 'She left it on the bathroom windowsill yesterday.'

'The bathroom windowsill?' He'd swallowed, a feeling of nausea sweeping over him without warning. 'She's been staying here?'

Rhiannon frowned as a customer banged on the counter, demanding attention. 'What? Er, yes, she stayed over for the night. Sorry, Will, will you excuse me? We're terribly busy, and Kerry's been off sick this week. I'll see you later.'

Will had shoved the watch in his pocket and gone home, his head spinning with the realisation that Lexi's secret crush was Derry. So, they were back together again. Well, what did it matter? It wasn't as if he'd ever had a chance, was it? He knew that. Of course he did. And he'd thought he'd accepted the situation, but clearly he'd been lying to himself.

He glanced at the clock, realising he should have been up and about ages ago. He sat up and was immediately gripped with panic. It was happening again. He couldn't breathe.

He clutched the duvet in his hands, trying to steady himself. He couldn't deny it any longer. There was something seriously wrong with him. Was he having a heart attack?

Pulling on his dressing gown, he headed to the top of the stairs. He couldn't die alone in his bedroom. He had to get help. It seemed to take forever before he reached the ground floor, and the kitchen seemed a mile away. He leaned against the wall, his heart thudding. He could feel the sweat on his upper lip and forehead, and the world was starting to spin. He tried to take a deep breath but couldn't manage it. His lungs weren't working properly. He was dying.

'Will? What the hell are you doing?' Bernie's voice sounded muffled and distant.

He couldn't answer. He didn't have enough air to make the effort.

'What is it? What's happening?' Darcey had come out of her office, looking most concerned.

'There's summat wrong with him,' said Bernie. His voice was suspiciously gruff, which worried him even more. 'Darcey, call the doctor.'

She nodded and hurried back into her office, as Bernie rushed to him and half carried him to the kitchen. As he lowered him into the chair, Woody gave a cry of alarm, and Will thought for a moment he was going to pass out.

Suddenly Lexi was beside him. She pushed a paper bag onto his face and told him to breathe into it. 'Deep breaths, Will, nice and steady.'

'I — I can't.' He stared up at her with panicked eyes. 'No air.'

'You can do it,' she told him, putting the bag over his nose and mouth. 'Just breathe into it, Will. It will help. Trust me.'

As he absorbed the calm reassurance in her eyes, some of the fear began to ebb away. She rubbed his back, soothingly. He took deep breaths, finding it was becoming easier and the dizziness was passing.

'Doctor's on his way,' said Darcey. 'Luckily, he hasn't started surgery yet.'

Will lowered the paper bag and closed his eyes, leaning back against the sofa. 'Do you think it's my heart?'

Lexi squeezed his hand. 'Of course not. There's nothing wrong with your heart.'

She was wrong about that, though. It was well and truly broken.

****

We were all huddled around the range — me, Woody, Bernie, Nat and Darcey — sipping tea and waiting for Dad to finish examining Will. Buttons sat beside us, looking just as anxious as we were.

'It's all the worry that's brought this on,' said Bernie, shaking his head.

'And grief,' added Darcey.

'You really think so?'

She nodded. 'Grief's a terrible thing. It would knock anyone for six. Believe me, it nearly finished me off at one point. When someone you love is terminally ill, you just go into auto pilot. You have to be there for them, you see, with no time to worry about yourself. But when the end comes...' She closed her eyes briefly. 'It's as if you hit a brick wall. All that time you were running on adrenaline, and suddenly you crash. I honestly thought I was going to die after my mother's funeral. It was a dreadful time.'

Nat's eyes softened. 'I'm really sorry, Darcey.'

She smiled at him. 'Thank you, Nat.'

'Really. I really am. I mean—' He glanced round at us all and shook his head. 'I mean, it must have been awful for you. I wouldn't wish it on anyone.'

She hesitated a moment, then shrugged. 'Time heals everything. Grief, pain, loss, even anger. Will can recover with our help. And we all want to help him, don't we? I mean, we're all here for him.'

Dad entered the kitchen, and we all looked at him expectantly.

'What was it?' I demanded. 'And don't say anything about confidentiality, because we're all desperate here.'

'It's okay. Will's given me permission to fill you all in, anyway. From my examination, and what Will's told me about what's been happening to him lately, it sounds to me as if he's suffered a panic attack. And not for the first time. He's been getting them pretty regularly lately, apparently.'

'Poor Will!' I put my hand to my mouth. 'Why didn't he tell us?'

'He thought it was his heart,' said Dad. 'I've been able to reassure him that it sounds extremely unlikely, but he's going to pop into the surgery tomorrow for some tests, just to put all our minds at rest.'

'What would cause panic attacks?' asked Woody, her eyes full of tears.

'They can come on for no reason, at all,' he said. 'In Will's case, though, I suspect his recent bereavement, combined with the worry about keeping this place going is what's brought it on. There may even be other factors that we don't know about. To be honest, bereavement is enough to start them, even without all the added stress he's faced.'

'Can you do anything for him?' Nat asked.

Dad smiled. 'Lexi did the right thing, giving him that paper bag to breathe into. If it happens again, that's what he must do. However, as I say, he's coming into the surgery tomorrow, and we'll discuss coping strategies and other options then.'

We all looked round when the door opened, and Will walked in, clearly embarrassed.

'Sorry to worry you all,' he said sheepishly. 'I feel a fool. I shouldn't have caused such a fuss.'

We all quickly reassured him that he'd done no such thing, and Dad told him that panic attacks, although not dangerous, were truly terrifying, and that we'd done the right thing calling him out. He glanced at his watch. 'I have to go. Surgery starts in ten minutes.'

'Thanks for coming, Dr Bailey,' said Woody.

'Yes, thank you so much,' said Will. 'I'll show you out.'

Dad glanced across at me. Since I knew Will wasn't in any danger, my feelings of animosity towards my father came back with a vengeance. It seemed he sensed there was something wrong. 'Will you be coming home tonight, or are you staying at The Hare and Moon again?'

Everyone stared at me, and I shook my head. 'I'll be home tonight.'

Nat was watching me through narrowed eyes, and I tutted impatiently. 'Rhiannon was short staffed. Kerry's on sick, so I helped out behind the bar after work for a couple of nights.'

'And stayed over?' demanded Nat.

I glared at him. What the hell did it have to do with him, anyway? There was no way that I wanted to tell them all that I was so upset with my own father that staying at the pub — even with my mixed feelings about Rhiannon — had seemed like a blessing.

'It was late when I finished,' I snapped, 'and Derry's been staying at his mate's, so it seemed logical to stay in his room. He's back now, and covering Kerry's shift tonight, so they don't need me,' I added, turning back to Dad. 'So, yes, I'll be home.'

Will made a funny noise, and we all turned to him immediately.

'Are you all right?' I asked anxiously.

He was watching me, a most peculiar expression on his face. To my relief, he suddenly smiled and said, 'Yes, yes I'm absolutely fine. Please, let me show you out, Dr Bailey. I've wasted enough of your time.'

They left the kitchen together, and we all looked at each other, heaving a collective sigh of relief.

'Well, that was a lot of fuss about nothing,' said Nat. 'Glad it wasn't serious. Back to business.'

'But it *is* serious,' I protested. 'Panic attacks are no fun you know, and it's surely a symptom that Will's struggling.'

'Don't be so dramatic,' he said. 'Now he knows it's not his heart, he'll stop worrying and get back to normal. You'll see. And if it does happen again, we'll just shove a paper bag at him.'

'I don't want to see the lad go through something like that again,' said Woody with a shudder. 'He's taken too much on, and it's got to stop. There's no fun in his life. It's all work and worry.'

'Maybe you've got a point, Darcey,' said Bernie suddenly. 'What you said to me the other day, I mean. I know I said it were a daft idea, but now I'm not so sure.'

'What point?' demanded Nat, sounding more like his old, belligerent self.

'About handing the Hall over to a charitable trust.' Bernie shrugged, evidently too upset to take umbrage at Nat's aggressive tone.

Woody and I exchanged incredulous glances.

'You're not serious?' I asked.

He sighed, rubbing the back of his head thoughtfully. I thought of Will doing the same action and felt a lump in my throat. 'It would help take the pressure off,' Bernie said. 'To be honest, that's my main concern now. This is taking a toll on his health, anyone can see that. I'd rather hand the whole bloody shebang to a charitable trust and see Will okay, than watch him struggle on, ruining his health. Wouldn't you?'

'But it would break his heart,' I said.

'Better than breaking his body,' said Bernie.

I picked up my cup of tea from the table, feeling its warmth flood through my hands while the rest of me turned to ice. Could it really come to this? Will would be devastated to be the one to hand the Hall over. It was too much to ask of him. But if we let him carry on as he was, exhausted and drained, working himself into the ground to preserve what was, when all was said and done, a pile of bricks, could we live with ourselves? If he became seriously ill, how could we bear it? He had no time to himself, and he seemed to have no leisure time at all. No one could live like that forever. I didn't know what to think any more.

'Maybe,' I said hesitantly, 'you're right.'

Everyone stared at me like it was the last thing they'd expected to hear me say.

'You're kidding, right?' Nat's tone was scathing. 'As if Will would ever be so pathetic as to give up now, after all we've done.'

'It wouldn't be giving up,' I said. 'It would just be asking for help.'

'The Hall wouldn't belong to the family any more,' he pointed out.

Darcey murmured, 'It's a technicality really. The charitable trust would own it, but Will could still live here, still run it. It's not as if he'd be turfed out of his home is it?'

'Will would rather die than do that,' snapped Nat.

'And you're willing to risk it, are you?' I yelled.

'Well, I never thought you'd be so bloody feeble,' he said, shaking his head.

'Whereas I totally expected you to be this selfish,' I replied. 'So predictable. Never mind poor Will's health. As long as you get to keep this place in your family, that's all that matters, isn't it? You've changed your bloody tune. It wasn't so long ago that you were trying to persuade him to sell the place to a hotel chain, remember?'

'Things are different now,' he said, his face flushed with anger.

'All right, Nat, calm down,' said Darcey.

'Yeah, put a sock in it,' said Bernie. 'Seems you're in a minority here, anyway.'

Nat turned toward him, his eyes flashing with fury. 'What the hell does that matter? None of you are his family anyway. It's up to me and Will what happens to this place, and none of your opinions count.'

My hackles rose. 'Actually, it's up to Will, and Will alone. It's not your house, however much you try to pretend that it is. And don't give me all that guff about you being his family. You have no idea what being part of a family means.'

'And you do, I suppose?' His jaw pulsed with anger, but I wasn't scared of him. He'd pushed me too far, and I was too wound up to back down.

'I know a damn sight more about it than you do,' I said. 'Your idea of family is having a meal ticket — someone you can sponge off for the rest of your life, so you don't have to actually work for a living. You don't care about Will. You only care about having a roof over your head, money in your pocket, and horses to ride. If Will lost the Hall tomorrow, he wouldn't see you for dust. You'd clear off back to Mummy and leave him to it. You haven't a clue about real love, or about loyalty.'

'Okay, maybe we should calm things down here,' said Darcey, holding up her hands.

Neither of us took any notice. We were too wrapped up in our bitter argument to listen. Weeks of simmering resentment on both sides was finally coming to the boil.

'Whereas the Bailey family are experts,' Nat sneered.

'Compared to you, we wrote the bloody book,' I said.

'Really? So, if your family is so loving and so loyal, perhaps you could clarify something for me? Perhaps you can tell me why it is that I spotted your father in Whitby the other day, with his arm around a woman, who most definitely wasn't your stepmother?'

I felt the blood drain from my face. 'You're lying,' I said.

'It's probably a mistake,' said Darcey comfortingly. 'I'm sure your father would never do such a thing.'

'Shut up, Nat,' said Bernie. 'Always causing trouble. Why do you have to turn everything into a battle?'

'He can't help himself,' said Woody. 'He was born evil, if you ask me.'

Nat stared at us all for a moment, then he thumped the table and stormed out of the kitchen.

We all sat in silence, and I tried to gather my thoughts, make sense of what he'd said. Then I jumped up and headed for the door.

'Lexi, wait. Leave him alone!'

I heard Darcey calling, but I ignored her. I had to know if he was telling the truth, and if so, exactly what he'd seen.

It took me almost an hour to find him. That's the disadvantage of such a large house. You can never find anyone when you want them.

In the end, I came across him in the Reading Room. He was sitting on the window seat, staring out towards the ocean — not that anyone could see it very well. It was a dull, cold day, and the sky and sea had merged into one cloudy grey smudge on the horizon.

He didn't look round as I entered, but he must have known it was me.

'You're wrong, you know,' he said quietly. 'I wouldn't run out on Will. I know what you think, but he was my friend when I was a kid. He was probably my best friend. And I admit, I wanted him to get rid of this place at first, but you can't be here and around him for long without recognising how much it means to him. Working here alongside him, learning about our ancestors — well, I started to realise that maybe it means quite a lot to me, too.'

Finally, he turned his head, and his eyes met mine. 'I've made some stupid mistakes, made a real mess of everything, but I wouldn't do anything to hurt him. Not now. I wish to God...' He broke off, shaking his head slightly, then he shrugged. 'You can call me a liar if you want. I can't make you believe me. But I'm telling you now, handing the Hall over to a trust may be the sensible option, but if Will wants to go down fighting, I'll go down fighting, too. Right by his side.'

I blinked, astonished. If I hadn't known better, I'd have sworn he was telling the truth. But this was Nat talking, and I wasn't that gullible. Besides, I had other things to worry about. 'Did you mean it?' I demanded.

'I just said so, didn't I?'

'I mean about my father and another woman. Did you mean it?'

He sighed. 'I'm sorry. I shouldn't have told you.'

'So, it's true? You're saying you saw him, really? You're not making it up?'

'I'm sure it was nothing. There's bound to have been a perfectly logical explanation,' he said, sounding guilty.

'Did you recognise her? What did she look like?'

He held up his hands. 'Honestly, I don't know. It was hard to see. They were sheltering in a shop doorway. It was pissing down with rain. I only noticed because I was standing in a doorway opposite.'

'Then you must have seen her quite clearly? Can you describe her?' If my dad was seeing another woman, I wanted to know who the hell she was.

'As I said, it was raining heavily. Hard to see anything, and she was wearing a coat with the hood pulled up, so her face was in shadow. She was quite small, though, and slim. They were huddled together, talking. Looked quite intense. Sorry.'

I felt sick. No wonder Dad had gone off Eliza. He was obviously seeing some other woman. Who was she? How could he be so cruel?

I turned and left the room before Nat could see the tears spilling down my cheeks. No way in hell was I going to let him know what he'd just done. My world was in pieces, and before very long, Eliza's world would be, too.

Chapter 33

The atmosphere at Whisperwood Farm was strained, and that was putting it mildly. Even Amy noticed and remarked on everyone's bad mood. The twins seemed to have picked up on it too, as they grizzled and whinged constantly.

Joe tried his best to keep everyone's spirits up, and I was grateful for his efforts. I didn't have the energy to try any more. I felt exhausted, which was ironic, as Will had picked up again and had been almost his old self the following day.

He'd handed me my watch, which I'd apparently left at the pub. He said Rhiannon had given it to him, and I'd had to force myself not to think about what he was doing with Rhiannon. I knew Derry had band practice that evening, so he couldn't have gone to see him, could he? I couldn't worry about that then, though, as I was consumed by my new fears about Dad.

I'd intended to tackle him about the mysterious woman in Whitby, but I hadn't been able to make myself do it. I was afraid. I thought if I brought the matter out into the open, he would panic and take flight. If I kept quiet, maybe the relationship would burn itself out, and he'd tire of the woman and realise what a good thing he had with his wife. It was a pathetic plan, really, but it was all I had. I was beginning to feel like I was going mad.

Dad suddenly, weirdly, started being really loving towards Eliza. He kept hugging her whenever she went past him, and out of the blue, he'd grab her hand and squeeze it, smiling up at her as she squeezed his in return. It was sickening. I mean, I'd have been over the moon, if it wasn't for the fact that he'd been out twice on the flimsiest of excuses. Clearly, he was still seeing that woman, so I could only assume his new behaviour was borne of guilt.

One night, he said he was going to visit Gran and Grandad.

I narrowed my eyes, thinking, *Oh, yeah, another convenient trip to Whitby?* Out loud, I said, 'Great idea, Dad. I'll come with you.'

He was definitely rattled. 'Er, not tonight. I'm going to talk to them about something private.'

'Private?' I laughed. 'From your own daughter? I don't think so.'

He swallowed, a definite flush of scarlet creeping up his neck. *Busted!* 'Honestly, Lexi. We can visit together another time, okay?'

'Come on, Dad, don't be so cagey,' I said, not willing to give up that easily.

Eliza nudged me, laughing. 'You do know it's your birthday in a couple of months? I think maybe there are plans afoot.'

Honestly, I could have throttled her. There I was, desperately trying to save her marriage, and she had to go and give him an excuse.

'That would be telling,' he said, taking his chance in record time, while smiling treacherously. 'Suffice it to say, your grandparents wouldn't be impressed if I turned up with you in tow.'

He kissed Eliza, ruffled my hair, and left.

'Aren't you bothered that he's going out again?' I demanded, as she started clearing away the plates from dinner.

She blinked at me. 'Of course not. Why should I be? He's had a lot on his mind, and it's good to see him smiling again.'

'Isn't it,' I muttered, wondering how she could be so blind, and thinking it was no wonder her nemesis, Melody Bird, had managed to lure Amy's dad into her web. God, life was crap.

At work, the marquee for the ball arrived, and it took two days for the company Nat had hired to erect it on the south lawn. A whole team of people worked on it, and there was obviously lots more to it than I'd realised. I'd nipped into the Great Hall to take a sneaky peek from the window at what was going on, only to see a load of metal poles lying on the ground and some heated discussion happening, but not much else.

A few hours later, and the metal frame was in place. Soon it was topped with a canvas roof, then white "walls" were attached, complete with arched windows.

When I arrived at the Hall the day after Dad's sneaky trip to Whitby, the company had packed up and gone home, leaving behind a quite breath-taking structure. I couldn't resist mooching over to take a peek.

Walking under the grand entrance canopy and into the main marquee, I found Darcey wandering around the interior, clutching her obligatory clipboard and ticking things off a list.

She looked up and gave me a bright smile. 'Looks good, doesn't it?'

'It's beautiful!' I couldn't believe how grand it looked. Soft, white drapes from floor to ceiling, sparkling chandeliers, dozens of tables draped in elegant black linen and white lace, each chair around them similarly dressed. There was a thick carpet on the floor beneath the tables, and over at the other end of the marquee, a hard dance floor, complete with small stage, where Derry's band and the string quartet would be performing. There was even a bar in one corner. It was huge — far bigger than I'd expected, and so much prettier.

I thought about my costume, hanging in the wardrobe in "my" bedroom at the Hall, and felt a thrill of delight. Meggie had done an outstanding job, and the dress was worth every penny it had cost me in materials. I'd sent Meggie a huge bouquet and a mega box of chocolates to say thank you, as she'd refused payment for making it. I just hoped she wouldn't tell Sophie about the chocolates.

The ball was going to be a magnificent event.

I wondered if Will would be all right on the day. What if he got ill again? And would Dad and Eliza still be together? It was only three days away, but would they make it?

A shadow fell across the proceedings, not lightened when Darcey heaved a sigh and sat down, resting her chin in one hand.

'What's up with you?' I said, unused to seeing her looking so down.

She clutched the clipboard tighter to her chest, not quite meeting my gaze. 'I suppose I may as well tell you. You're going to find out soon enough. I've resigned, Lexi.'

'What? But you can't!' I plopped down into the chair next to hers, dismayed. 'Why would you do that? I thought you liked it here.'

'I do. Well, I did.' She gave a little shake of her head and put the clipboard on the table. 'There are several reasons. Individually, I may have been able to overlook them. Put together — well, I think it's just too much. Time for me to move on.'

'But I don't get it.' I really didn't. She'd done a fabulous job. What would make her give up on us after all her hard work? 'Okay,' I said, trying to stay calm, 'you said there were several reasons. What are they? Maybe we can work through them together.'

She smiled. 'I doubt it. Besides, my mind's made up. I need a change, something else to get my teeth into. Perhaps I'll go back to ECHOES, or maybe I'll find another house that needs saving. Maybe,' she added, 'I'll do something completely different. Who knows?'

'Is it Nat?' I asked suspiciously. 'Because if he's been giving you grief again...'

'Nat and I…' She shrugged. 'It's not Nat. Can we just drop it?'

'But you can't go, not now! We all love you, and we want you here.'

She rubbed her forehead. 'We don't always get what we want, Lexi. I learned that in London. I was hoping here, things would be different, and for a little while I thought they would be. I was so happy.' Tears welled in her eyes. 'I really was. Why do things never work out the way we want?'

'I'm the last person you should ask about that,' I said bitterly.

'But it's all within your reach,' she said. 'You only have to be brave and grasp the nettle. I've been watching you these last few weeks. I've seen the way you look at Will when you think no one's watching. I'm right, aren't I?'

My face started to burn. 'Please tell me Nat doesn't know about this.'

'About your secret passion for Will?' She hesitated. 'I think he may have an idea. Don't look at me like that. You know, sometimes you make me so angry. What are you waiting for? You don't realise how lucky you are.'

'It's not that simple,' I protested.

'Why does everyone say that?' She shook her head. 'Why can't people just stop playing games? Why can't everyone just tell the truth?' She gave a bitter laugh. 'Maybe I've got what I deserve. I can't deny it hurts like hell though.'

'What does?' I said. 'Why can't you tell me what's wrong?'

'Because it doesn't just affect me, and I've been sworn to secrecy, on both bloody counts.' She took a deep breath. 'It's okay. It's done now. Sorry, Lexi, I shouldn't have taken it out on you. About Will — no, don't look like that! I'm not trying to tell you what to do about your relationship, or non-relationship. I just want you to promise to keep an eye on him. I'm worried about him, about his health.'

I frowned. 'But you said it was just grief.'

'I said it was grief,' she pointed out, 'not *just* grief. There's nothing trivial about it, believe me.' She bit her lip. 'It can almost destroy you. Seriously, Will is carrying too much of a burden, and he needs to let it go. I can't make him see sense about handing the Hall over and, frankly, I don't want to watch him work himself into an early grave.'

'Are you serious?' I asked.

'I like Will. He wasn't at all what I was expecting, and I really wish … I wish things could have been different. I wish… Oh, well, this year seems to be my year for regrets.' She patted my hand. 'So, you see, it's time I went. I feel ready for a new challenge. I honestly believe I've done my best here, and I think I'm leaving you in good shape — as good as it can be, at any rate. You have a long journey ahead of you, and a hard battle to fight. I wish you luck, honestly I do.'

'Will you at least stay for the ball?' I asked.

She nodded. 'Of course. I'll be here for that, then I'll leave the next morning. I don't want to miss seeing you in your costume, do I? Can't wait. Lady Kearton lives again.'

That reminded me. I rummaged in my pocket and took out the box containing the brooch. 'I've brought this here so I don't forget it on the day,' I told her. 'It's to wear on Saturday night.'

'What is it?' She leaned forward, her eyes opening wide as I revealed what lay inside. 'Where on earth did you get that?'

'Will gave it to me for Christmas,' I said. 'Wasn't that kind of him? He went to all that trouble to get a replica made for me, and it's very realistic isn't it?'

To my surprise, she put her arms around me and hugged me. 'Yes, Lexi, it is. It's quite lovely. Just like the countess's.'

'I thought I'd wear it on my dress,' I said. 'Like she did in the portrait.'

She released me and smiled, in spite of the tears glistening in her eyes. 'That's a lovely idea. You'll look beautiful, especially with that red hair. Well, I suppose we'd both better get back to work.'

'I suppose we had,' I agreed. I stood up and impulsively reached for her hand. 'I really will miss you,' I said. 'Things won't be the same around here without you.'

She blinked away the tears. 'Thank you, Lexi. I can't tell you how much I appreciate that.'

I walked away, thinking that was yet another thing that had gone wrong. How much worse could things get?

Chapter 34

At least Will seemed livelier and had sworn to me he'd had no more panic attacks. He also reported in that the tests he'd had done at the surgery were all clear, which was a huge relief. When I found him in his office, though, studying spreadsheets on his laptop, I still felt quite angry.

'You promised me you'd ease off on work until at least after the ball,' I reminded him. 'What are you doing?'

He tutted. 'I'm fine. I have so much to do. Did you hear about Darcey?'

'I did,' I said. 'It's a bloody shame.'

'It's a catastrophe,' he said, a hint of panic in his voice.

'I wouldn't go that far,' I said, keen to reassure him. 'I mean, she's done a great job, but life will go on.'

'Are you saying you won't miss her?' He sounded surprised.

'Of course I'm not saying that. I'll miss her loads, but more as a friend. It's been great having another woman to talk to. Especially now.'

'Why now, particularly?' He closed the laptop and stroked Buttons' silky head. 'You mean because of Georgia?'

I sat on the opposite chair and stared into those green eyes from across the desk. God, he was lovely. Even then, with all the worry of Darcey leaving, and his recent health scare, he was concerned about me and ready to listen. I wanted to reach out and stroke his face. I wanted to lean over the desk and feel his lips on mine. I wanted to—

'Lexi? Are you okay?'

'What? Sorry. Yeah, Georgia.' I leaned back in the chair and tried to concentrate on the matter in hand. 'Well, Georgia and a whole load of other things.'

'What other things?'

'Trust me, you don't want to know.' I heard the dangerous wobble in my voice and gulped. Uh-oh. I could feel tears coming on. That was the last thing Will needed. 'Sorry,' I managed, and then the tears started to flow.

He was beside me in an instant. He crouched by my chair and took my hand in his. 'Lexi, what is it? What's wrong?'

He seemed so full of concern I nearly lost it. Somehow, I managed to whisper, 'Just a lot of stuff going on, Will. Nothing for you to worry about.'

'I'll be the judge of that.' He stared up at me for what felt like forever, until I wondered what he was thinking. Then he bowed his head and kissed the back of my hand. 'I'm so sorry, Lexi. I've let you down badly.'

Whatever I'd been expecting him to say, it certainly wasn't that. 'Of course you haven't. Don't be daft.'

'But I have.' He stood up, shoved his hands in his pockets and began to pace the room. 'I've pushed you away. It's like I said at Scarborough Castle — how we used to talk. How we used to have our little chats most days, put the world to rights. Remember?'

I nodded tearfully. 'Of course I remember.'

'Then Father had his stroke, and things got more complicated. I got so obsessed with this place, with not letting everyone down. Then, when he died … I don't know. And then, of course, Nat arrived, and we hired Darcey, and it was full steam ahead with our plans. Somehow, you and I — our friendship, I mean — it got lost along the way. I haven't asked you anything about what's going on in your own life. I've been completely selfish.'

'You haven't been selfish, Will,' I insisted. 'You've been grieving. It's normal. Look how ill it's made you.'

'I'm not ill, though,' he said. 'And it wasn't as if I was laid up for weeks, was it? It was just these stupid panic attacks, and not being able to sleep. I should have made more of an effort for you. Can you forgive me?'

'Forgive you for what?' I half laughed, then blushed when I realised I'd snorted and what felt like half a gallon of snot had just shot out of my nose. I reached into my jeans pocket and pulled out a tissue, wiping furiously. Great. How attractive. Buttons surveyed me, and I swear he wrinkled his nose in disgust.

To my relief, Will didn't even seem to have noticed. He'd stopped pacing and was staring out of the window at the stables. 'Bernie thinks I should hand Kearton Hall over to a charitable trust,' he said flatly.

'I know.'

He turned to face me. 'What do you think?'

I took a deep breath. 'Honestly? If you'd asked me that even a couple of weeks ago, I'd have said no chance. But a lot's happened since then. To be truthful, Will, that day we had to call Dad out, you scared me to death. I thought then that if this is what the responsibility of this place does to you, you'd be better off without it.'

'You really think that? You, of all people?' He rubbed the back of his head, and my heart melted. 'I never thought I'd hear you say that.' He gave a rueful laugh. 'I was counting on you to tell me Bernie's wrong.'

'I'm sorry,' I said.

'No, no. You have a right to your opinion. It's just — well — I thought you really cared about this place.'

I gasped. 'I do! Of course I do.'

'Then...?'

'Because I care about you more!' There, I'd said it. It was out there, hanging between us.

For a moment, his eyes widened, and he stared at me in evident astonishment. Then he sank back into his chair. 'Well, that's nice of you to say so. You're a good friend.'

'Yeah,' I said dully. 'A friend.'

We sat there in dumb silence for a moment until he suddenly slapped the desk with his hand. 'Hell! I've done it again, haven't

I?'

'Done what?'

'Brought the conversation round to myself and to the house again. I keep doing it. You see what I mean about being selfish? You were telling me about your problems.'

'No, I wasn't,' I said, managing to smile. 'Nice try, though.'

'Oh, come on. Indulge me, eh? Have you made it up with Georgia yet?'

'Not really,' I said. 'I mean, I tried, but — well — she had company.'

'Nat?' His voice was sympathetic.

'You knew about them?'

'I guessed. He's been full of the joys of spring lately, and he's almost like a different person. He's even being nice to Darcey, and they were working really well together. I walked in on them just yesterday, and they were poring over a floor plan of the Hall, heads together, deep in conversation.' He shook his head. 'That's another reason I don't understand her sudden resignation. She and Nat are finally friends, and then she announces she's leaving. I wish I could work it out.'

I felt my heart thud a little. 'Yeah. You're right. It is odd.'

And Darcey had been full of the joys of spring lately, too. Was that a coincidence? They *had* been weirdly close recently, and given their previous mutual loathing, it was very suspicious. What had Darcey said about people lying, playing games? And that her secret affected other people, too? Did she mean Georgia? Was it possible that Darcey and Nat were having an affair, after the way they'd behaved towards each other all those weeks?

I had a sudden vision of Will locking them in the sitting room that day to sort out their differences. Had their frenzied arguing turned into a passionate encounter? I'd seen that sort of thing in films and had always thought it highly unlikely, but maybe…

'Georgia could be exactly what he needed. I know it was wrong, the way it started, but they do have a lot in common.'

'What?' I blinked, realising Will was talking to me. 'Yes. Do you think he can be trusted, though? Honestly?'

'What he did to you was unforgivable, but there's another side to Nat,' he said.

'I know that,' I admitted. 'When we were together, he could be lovely. But he's also a devious, trouble-causing prat, and I just … Don't you think it odd the way he and Darcey are suddenly so friendly?'

'Not really. They're both adults, and they've talked it out, the way adults do.'

'Yeah.' I sighed, thinking he was being naïve. In my experience, things were never that straightforward.

'So, what else?'

'Huh?'

He leaned forward, resting his head in his hands and fixing me with a stern look. 'You said it was Georgia, among other things. So, what other things?'

'Just stuff at home,' I said. 'Nothing for you to worry your pretty little head about.' He flushed and I laughed. 'You can't take a compliment, can you?'

He sat up straight, shaking his head and trying to look busy, adjusting things on his desk. 'Don't be silly.'

'It's true. Look how you react whenever I say how much you resemble William Kearton. You get all bashful about it, and start denying it straight away.'

'That's because it's not true,' he said.

'But it is true! You have the same eyes. Kind, green, understanding eyes.' I realised I was practically sprawled over the desk towards him, and he stared back at me with alarm in those eyes. 'Sorry.' Then I thought about what I'd said, and something inside just snapped. 'No, you know what? I'm not sorry. You're a bloody good-looking bloke, and I'm sick of you acting as if you look like Quasimodo, or something. It's time you started seeing yourself as others see you.'

'Wh — what are you talking about?'

'Will Boden-Kean, you're bloody gorgeous. Deal with it.'

His face was so red I could have got a suntan from sitting too close. I almost felt sorry for him, but sod it, he needed to start believing in himself. He had to know that, even if Darcey was about to abandon him, the rest of us weren't going anywhere.

'Nat says, if you go down fighting, he'll go down fighting with you. Well, he's not the only one. We're in this together, and whatever you want to do, I'll support you.'

'Really?'

'Absolutely.' My voice cracked as I took in his stunned expression. 'God, Will, I was so bloody worried about you. When you had that panic attack...'

'What about it?' He almost whispered the words, and I reached for his hand.

I had a feeling that it was now or never. No turning back. 'I know I was acting all calm, but I was scared. If anything happened to you, life just wouldn't be worth living. Right now, you're the only thing keeping me going. You're the one I want to see every day. You're the one who makes me want to get out of bed in the morning and get through it all. You're — you're so much more to me than a friend, Will.'

I wondered, for one awful moment, if he was going to have a real heart attack. He just sat there, frozen. I wasn't sure he was even breathing.

'I don't want this to ruin our friendship,' I continued. 'That's why I haven't said anything before now. I don't know why I'm even telling you this. I mean, I could ruin everything, and then where will I be? But I just can't keep this to myself any longer. I don't know. Maybe it's because everything else seems to be going to hell in a handcart, and I'm just thinking, well, so what? What have I got left to lose? All I know is, I had to tell you while I still have the nerve to do it. God, Will, don't sit there staring at me like that. You're really freaking me out. Have I blown it?' I put my head in my hands and groaned. 'I've blown it, haven't I?'

'Lexi…' His voice sounded really odd, and I held my breath, wondering what he was going to say. 'What exactly are you telling me?'

'Haven't I said it?' I thought I'd made it crystal clear. Something made me hesitate, though. Spilling my feelings could be the start of something really exciting, something completely fabulous. On the other hand, it could be the end of a beautiful relationship. I had a feeling, though, that it was too late to back out. I decided to take Darcey's advice and grasp the nettle.

I stood and rounded to his side of the desk. He pushed his chair back a little, making room for my legs, as I sat on the desk in front of him. 'Let me explain it in simple terms,' I said, then I leaned forward and brushed his lips with mine.

That felt good. Reluctant to move away, I cupped his face with my hands. Before I knew it, we were kissing properly. I wasn't imagining it. He was responding.

My heartbeat quickened with excitement as he stood, his lips still locked on mine, and wrapped me in his arms. As I pressed against him, he held me tight, kissing me with a hunger I'd only dreamed of.

Was this really Will? Was this really my sweet, gentle friend? Well, it was a side of him I'd never dared hope existed. He could kiss. I mean, he could *really* kiss.

Sparks flew left right and centre, my heart jumped around in my chest, my stomach flipped about as if it had learned to jive, and my whole body burned with intense longing. It seemed to occur to both of us at the same time that, regrettably, we needed to breathe, and we pulled away from each other with obvious reluctance.

A second later, we were kissing again.

I think we might have stayed there forever, but I wanted more. Breathlessly I pushed him away a little, and before he could start to worry that he'd done the wrong thing — because I absolutely knew he would — I took his hand and pulled him out of the office, Buttons bounding along behind us.

'What are you doing?' he gasped, obviously still reeling from the unexpected development.

'What I've wanted to do for bloody weeks,' I said. 'I'm taking you to bed.'

****

'Your place or mine?' I grinned at him as we reached the second-floor landing of the north side of the house, where Will's bedroom, and the bedroom I'd more or less commandeered, were situated.

'Whichever's closest.' His eyes burned with an intensity that had me hot with desire. Seriously, I could feel the heat rising from both of us. It was a wonder the smoke alarms didn't go off.

I opened my bedroom door and pulled him inside, closing an indignant Buttons out on the other side. Some things, man's best friend just shouldn't witness.

I tutted on realising there wasn't any bedding on the divan, apart from a neatly folded duvet, minus a cover, sitting at the end of the bed. 'Do you want—'

I didn't get the chance to ask him if he'd prefer to go to his room, because he pulled me close and his lips met mine, and I quite forgot about the lack of bedding. His hand traced the line of my breast and I felt his tremor of excitement against me. I waited for him to go further, but he seemed hesitant. Knowing Will, he was far too worried that I'd object. Firmly, I took his hand and guided it under my t-shirt and inside my bra. For a moment, he seemed to still, then gently he began to caress me.

At the change in the pattern of his breathing my excitement mounted. I was disintegrating fast. If I didn't move things on soon, I'd be vapour. I tugged at his belt, but it was so frustratingly difficult to unfasten I had to stop kissing Will and concentrate on the task in hand.

He put his hand on mine, stopping me for a moment.

'What's wrong?' I asked. Had I gone too fast? Scared him off?

His eyes searched mine for reassurance. 'Are you sure about this, Lexi? Is this really what you want? If you want to change your mind...' He sounded breathless, and I didn't think it was due to another panic attack.

I could practically feel my hormones sloshing around impatiently as I answered, 'Change my mind? You've got to be kidding me!'

My words must have reassured him, because after giving me a look that almost vaporised me on the spot, he unbuckled his belt. Not wanting to give him any more opportunities to hesitate, or change his mind, I pulled his jeans down, then, as he tugged his jumper over his head, I began to hurriedly take off my own clothes.

Dropping his jumper on the ground, he skimmed his gaze over me, his eyes widening in evident surprise to find I was already down to my underwear.

For a moment, I worried he might think me a bit forward. After all, Will was a gentleman. Then I thought about Rhiannon and decided nothing I did could ever be as wanton as the things she must have done. God, why had I thought about Rhiannon? That was a passion killer, right there. How could I ever compete with her?

Except then, Will sort of gasped, and his expression told me that, whatever I thought about Rhiannon, his attention was all there with me, and right now, nobody else mattered to him.

We were on the bed in seconds, and somehow my bra was flying through the air, and I couldn't get close enough to Will to satisfy me. He kissed every inch of me and did things with his hands that no gentleman should know about.

Well, Sir William, I thought, *aren't you just full of surprises?*

My own hands were pretty busy, too, and I knew neither of us could wait much longer. Finally, finally, it was going to happen. All those weeks of longing and imagining and dreaming were at last coming to fruition. Teetering on the brink, my desperation for Will to take that final step kicked in.

Frustratingly, he seemed in no hurry to do so. As I practically offered myself to him on a plate, he kissed me again, murmuring that there was no rush, and that he wanted it to be special.

'It will be special,' I gasped. 'It's with you!'

'Oh, Lexi,' he murmured, 'I love you so much. I've always loved you. You know that, don't you?'

You know, when I was a kid, my mum took me to visit her parents once, in their grubby little backstreet terraced house. I remembered hearing the howling of two dogs outside and wondering what they were doing to cause so much noise. I remembered my gran, cigarette dangling from her mouth as she opened the front door and threw a bucket of ice-cold water over them both, muttering, 'That'll put a stop to their flaming antics.'

In that moment, I knew exactly how those dogs had felt. I lay there, frozen and shocked, as a sickening dread replaced the passion.

Will stopped kissing my neck. 'What is it?'

'What did you say?' I whispered.

He smiled softly. 'I said, I love you. I've loved you for years, and I've waited for you for so long. I'd almost given up hope, Lexi. But now...' He shook his head slightly, gazing at me with those green eyes, and in that moment I saw it. I saw it all so clearly.

Will loved me.

But if he'd really loved me all that time … God, and I'd been with Nat, in his own house. How had he stood it? How much had loving me cost him? I suddenly realised, with almost unbearable pain, why he'd pulled away from me. Why he'd withdrawn from our friendship. He'd been protecting himself, and after recent events I, devastatingly, understood that only too well.

The expression of tenderness and wonder in his eyes moved aside for something else — anxiety. He shifted back, giving me room to sit up. I felt exposed, naked, vulnerable. I wanted something to hide myself under.

Somehow, he seemed to sense it. He grabbed the duvet we'd knocked onto the floor and placed it over me. 'You've changed your mind.'

There was so much pain in that sentence that, for a moment, I was almost tempted to deny it. How could I bear to hurt him any more than I already had?

'I didn't know.' Realising my voice was hoarse, I cleared my throat and tried again. 'How you felt, I mean. I didn't realise.'

'Oh.' He sat up, too, and covered himself over.

I felt a fleeting pang of regret, but knew it was too late. I'd never see him naked again.

'I thought that's what this was all about. I thought...'

'I'm sorry.' I didn't know what else to say.

'There's nothing to be sorry for. It was my mistake. Obviously, you don't feel the same way about me.' He stared at the duvet, his fingers plucking at it nervously.

I'd never hated myself more. 'I — I just can't, Will,' I said, desperate to explain. 'It's not you. I just—'

'Just don't want a relationship with anyone,' he finished. 'I know. You've said.'

I had said, over and over again. But all of a sudden, the words sounded hollow, and I was consumed with misery and shame.

'Then, what was this all about?' He turned to me, suddenly bewildered. 'If you were feeling amorous, I'm sure there were plenty of people you could have chosen. Why me? Why now?'

God, was that all he thought this was? Me, feeling horny? Jeez. There was so much more to it than that. Why him? Well, because he was beautiful — inside and out. Because he had kind green eyes. Because he had a gorgeous mouth. Because he was tall and sexy. Because he was generous, gentle, funny and understanding, hard-working, loyal, passionate and sensitive, and ... Because I loved him.

I literally gasped as realisation hit me. I loved Will. But when, how?

I don't know. I just don't know.

It seemed as if it had always been there, thinking about it now, and somewhere deep inside, I'd known it. But look how much I'd already hurt him — him, of all people. I couldn't give Will what he wanted, but I'd let my selfishness get in the way, ruined everything, and Will would pay the price.

I hated myself.

'Where are you going?' Frantically blinking away my tears, I watched him struggling back into his clothes. 'Will?'

He turned, giving me a smile that didn't reach his eyes. Will's smiles always reached his eyes. What had I done to him?

'It's okay, Lexi. Don't worry about it. I'd better get back to work.'

He left the room, closing the door quietly behind him.

I rolled over in bed and hugged the pillow to my face. I remembered the last time I'd clutched that pillow to me, when I'd thought Will was in a relationship with Darcey. I'd felt rejected and sick to my stomach. How much worse must Will be feeling than I had then?

The pain was so bad, I wondered suddenly why I wasn't crying, and unbidden, a line of poetry I'd learned in school nudged its way into my mind. *Thoughts that do often lie too deep for tears.* At the time, I wasn't sure what the poem had been about, and I wasn't even certain who'd written it — maybe Wordsworth — but whoever had written it had nailed it.

Some wounds make you ache, and tears are a release. But some wounds are so big they become you. Like, your entire body and soul get trapped inside the pain, with no release on offer. Even tears can't escape. Nothing can escape. There's just you and a gut-wrenching agony, and nowhere to run to be free from it.

Putting the pillow down, I got out of bed. I needed to talk to someone. I needed help. And for some weird reason, I knew there was only one person I could turn to.

Chapter 35

'You've resigned?' Rhiannon's hands flew to her mouth. 'But why? You love your job!' She studied me thoughtfully, before reaching over the counter and patting my arm. 'Come on. Upstairs. We need to talk.'

I followed her through the door to her private quarters, wondering all the time what I was doing there. Why had I flown to The Hare and Moon? Why had I felt a sudden, desperate need to unburden myself to Rhiannon, of all people? I couldn't explain it. I just knew she'd understand. If anyone could help me make sense of it all, it was Rhiannon.

She made me a coffee: strong, no sugar, just the way I liked it. We sat at the table, and she folded her arms and waited.

I took a sip of the drink, wincing at how hot it was.

I should have waited. *Yeah, story of my life.*

'Where's Derry?' I asked. I didn't want him, of all people, to interrupt our conversation. It was going to be tricky enough as it was.

A shadow crossed her face. 'Now that Kerry's back, he's decided he can justify staying at a friend's house for a few days — again. I'm not sure when he'll be back. Don't worry, he's promised to turn up for the ball.'

Someone else who was suffering. I felt desperately sorry for both of them, for everything they were going through. Their relationship had taken a terrible beating, and I wondered if they could come through it.

Derry wasn't in a forgiving mood, though. I wondered if he'd told Rhiannon of his plans to stay with her father at his home in Cornwall. 'Maybe I shouldn't have come,' I said. 'You've got enough problems of your own. You don't need mine on top of everything else.'

She twisted her bracelet. 'Don't be silly. It will do me good to think about someone else for a change. I'm quite tired of thinking about my own issues, to be honest. Besides...' Her voice trailed off and she shook her head slightly, her dark curls bobbing on her shoulders.

'Besides what?' I said.

'It's good to see you again. You so rarely come here these days, and things appear to have been a little strained between us. It was so good of you to offer to help out behind the bar the other night, but I admit I was quite astonished. You're clearly angry with me. I realise my relationship with Sir Paul came as a shock to you, and of course, I understand that you sympathise with Derry. I'm very glad he's had you to talk to, Lexi, please don't misunderstand me, but it's a relief that you're talking to me, after all this time.'

'You think I was angry with you because of Sir Paul? God, do you really think I'm that judgmental?'

She frowned. 'Are you saying you weren't angry about all that?'

'Of course not. I mean, it was a bolt from the blue, but it's none of my business. Besides, it was years ago. Honestly, Rhiannon, I'm not taking sides between you and Derry. I was just trying to be a friend to him, but that didn't mean I couldn't feel sympathy for you.'

'Then, I don't understand. If not Sir Paul, what caused our sudden rift? Because there *was* a rift, wasn't there? I didn't imagine that.'

I swallowed. 'No, you didn't imagine it. It was me, being pathetically jealous. I'm really sorry.'

'Sorry for what?' She leaned back in her chair, and her gaze penetrated through me, until it felt like she was X-raying my mind. Then she smiled suddenly, sitting up straight, her eyes eager. 'This is about Will, isn't it?'

People in the village always said she was a witch. I knew she was a practising Wiccan, but I felt there was more to it than that, sometimes. Rhiannon had an unnerving way of seeing the truth, no matter how much you tried to hide it. There was no point denying it, and, anyway, wasn't that why I'd come here? To tell the truth, to try to make sense of it all? No point in covering it up. If I needed help, I had to be honest. I nodded miserably, too embarrassed and ashamed to look at her.

She clapped her hands and I glanced up, startled to see the look of obvious delight in her face. 'That's wonderful!'

I frowned. 'Is it? Why?'

'Because you care! I knew you'd realise it eventually. I told him, just be patient, it will happen. The universe unfolds exactly as it should.'

'What? You told who? What are you on about?'

'Will.' She sighed. 'That poor darling has loved you for so, so long.'

'Why did he never tell me?' I felt choked, wondering how he'd managed to keep it a secret all those years. He obviously had more self-control than I had, that was for sure.

'Because he knew you weren't ready,' she said. 'He didn't want to be another Derry, another Nat. When it was time for you and him to be together, he said it had to be forever. He was prepared to wait. I can't tell you how happy I am that you've finally recognised how you feel about him.'

'Oh, Rhiannon,' I said, 'this is such a mess.'

'Obviously,' she said. 'You've resigned, so evidently things haven't gone according to plan. Let's see what we can do to nudge them back in the right direction, shall we? Why don't you start at the beginning?'

Feeling the tears begin to well, I reached into my coat pocket for a tissue and started when my hands closed around the little box containing my brooch. I'd quite forgotten to leave it in the bedroom. Not that it mattered. I'd probably never wear it anyway.

I pulled out the box, staring at a blurry vision of the beautiful gold and emerald star.

Rhiannon leaned forward. 'It's exquisite, isn't it?'

My head shot up. 'You've seen it?'

'Well…' She shrugged. 'He showed it to me before Christmas. He was a bit worried it would be too much, that you'd object.'

'Why would I object?' I said. 'It was such a lovely, thoughtful thing to do. It's an exact replica, you know.'

'I'm sorry?' She sounded confused.

'The brooch. It's an exact replica of the one worn by Lady Kearton in the portrait we have of her. I checked. I don't know how he managed it.'

'Dear me.' Rhiannon watched me, her eyes soft with compassion. 'You really don't know, do you?'

'Know what?'

'My darling girl, it's not a replica. That *is* the brooch that once belonged to Elinor Kearton.'

My mouth dropped open. 'You must be mistaken,' I managed after a few moments. 'It can't be. I'd have seen it in the Hall before, and anyway, Will can't just give away one of the items in the collection. Not without permission from the tax people. It was in the agreement.'

'But it wasn't part of the Kearton Hall collection,' she explained. 'It was part of the Burton Sipling Hall collection. Darcey told Will all about it. She'd seen it while she was there, and he saw how much you liked it when you set eyes on the portrait, so he went off to East Yorkshire and threw himself at the mercy of the American couple who owned it. Fortunately, they have a very romantic outlook on life, and agreed to sell it to him.'

'But it must have cost thousands!'

'Yes. He paid for it out of his trust fund money.'

'Money that he should have spent on the Hall,' I said, horrified.

'Lexi, Will has put almost everything he has into the Maintenance Fund for the Hall. I think he's entitled to keep a little for himself, don't you?'

'For himself, yes! For me, no!'

'You're worth every penny, as far as Will's concerned.'

'But I'm not. I'm so not.'

'Why don't you tell me what's going on? Perhaps things will

seem brighter when you've shared it all with me.'

I gulped down a mouthful of coffee, even though it was still a bit too hot, took a deep breath, and began. I told her everything — glad beyond words to pour it all out and rid myself of the heavy burden I'd been carrying. I told her about the bad atmosphere at work, about my growing attraction to Will, and my unfounded jealousy of her and Darcey. I told her about missing Georgia, and being suspicious of the new warmth between Darcey and Nat.

I hesitated when it came to revealing what had been going on at home, but I knew she was discretion itself, so I told her it all — even about the woman in Whitby. Miserably, I ended my tale of woe with what had happened earlier that day, leading me to leave a letter of resignation on Will's desk.

When I'd finished, I picked up the mug and gulped down the rest of the coffee, pulling a face as I did so. It was cold.

She exhaled slowly and sat quietly for a moment, evidently digesting everything I'd said.

'Well,' she said at last, 'and they say Kearton Bay is a quiet little village.'

'What do I do?' I asked.

Finally, the tears started to fall. I felt overwhelmed by everything. I'd lost my two best friends, my Dad's marriage was on the point of collapse, and I'd hurt the man I loved. The man who loved me. Who'd loved me for years with total unselfishness and complete understanding. A man I had never, and could never, deserve.

'Well, two things occur to me. Firstly, you must stop imagining the worst of everyone and everything,' she said. 'You're picturing the worst-case scenario in each situation. What would happen if you started seeing the best outcome instead?'

'I don't know what you mean,' I said, confused.

'Well, let's start with Nat and Georgia. What if Nat isn't playing games? Imagine for one moment that he's actually in love with Georgia, that he's finally found someone who understands him.'

I thought about it, remembering how hard Nat had tried to make it up with me after Georgia had telephoned him, in spite of our animosity. All for her sake. Was it possible that Nat actually, truly loved Georgia?

'You see? It's an entirely different picture, isn't it? It's all about perspective.'

'But Nat can't be trusted,' I said. 'And why are he and Darcey suddenly so friendly? They hated each other at first, but now they're really close. You know she's resigned?'

'Oh, no, that's such a shame. Will was so impressed with the work she was doing at the Hall, and he really felt that she was part of the team.'

'I'll tell you one thing, Bernie will be devastated,' I mused.

She raised an eyebrow. 'What's Bernie got to do with it?'

Another secret I was betraying. I was shameless. 'Poor bloke's got a massive crush on her,' I said. 'You should see the way he acts around her.'

'Bernie! I don't believe it. He would never reveal his feelings like that,' she said. 'Unless… I wonder…' She fell quiet again, tapping on the table thoughtfully. 'Still,' she continued at last, 'that proves nothing, as far as Nat's concerned. Darcey's had a miserable year, and no doubt she's had a lot of adjustments to make recently. There could be any number of reasons why she feels the need to move on. As for Nat, maybe Will's right. Maybe there truly is another side to him. I know it's hard to imagine, but Will knows him better than anyone, and he's prepared to give him the benefit of the doubt. He's even forgiven him for spiking his drink at the funeral.'

'I knew it!' My eyes widened. 'Why the hell would Nat do something like that?'

'I guessed straightaway, and I tackled him about it at the funeral, after Will's little outburst. Nat said he wanted to loosen him up. I pointed out that his father's funeral was hardly the time for that.'

'I knew something had to have happened,' I said. 'Will behaved so oddly that day. Not like him at all.'

'Nat had just informed him that you and he had slept together after the wedding,' she said gently. 'I rather think that was the cause of his odd behaviour.'

I swallowed, remembering. More pain I'd heaped on Will.

'I suppose,' I said slowly, 'that I just find it hard to forgive Nat, after the way he cheated on me.'

'Did he really cheat on you?' she asked.

'Well, of course he did. Will caught him and Georgia at it in the tack room!'

She took hold of my hand. 'Please don't take this the wrong way, Lexi. Do you remember when you were dating Robbie?'

I nodded. 'Of course. Why?'

'Do you remember how that ended?'

'Well, it kind of fizzled out, really. There was no real commitment on either side, and then I heard he'd asked Chrissie out, so that was that.'

'And how did you feel when you heard that?'

'It didn't bother me. I didn't love Robbie, and I knew Chrissie was keen on him, because Eliza told me. I was quite glad they'd got together. There were no hard feelings and look how it's ended. They're engaged now.'

'Exactly.' She squeezed my hand. 'You see?'

'No,' I said. 'I don't see. What's that got to do with Nat and me?'

'If Nat had been seeing any other woman behind your back, would it have bothered you? Really?'

'Of course,' I said. 'He was my—' I stopped. I'd been about to say boyfriend, but he hadn't been really, had he? If anyone ever referred to him by that term, I'd quickly put them straight about it, and I'd made it clear to Nat from the start that it was going nowhere, that it was just a bit of fun.

If it had been some girl from the village, would I honestly have minded that much? I had to admit, I'd have shrugged it off, the way I had with Robbie.

'You think this was all about Georgia?' I sighed. 'You could be right.'

'I don't think it was *all* about Georgia,' she said. 'I think there might have been an element of Will in there.'

'Will?' What was she talking about? 'What's Will got to do with that?'

'Losing Nat meant losing your safety net.'

'My safety net?'

'You knew you and Nat would never really go anywhere. You knew, most importantly, that your heart would never belong to him. Nat was safe. Whereas our lovely, gentle Will was more dangerous than you could ever admit, because with Will, it wouldn't be a casual fling. It would be all or nothing, and you don't want to go down that road, do you, Lexi?'

A huge lump formed in my throat, making it difficult to speak. 'Can you blame me?' I managed. 'Look how relationships end! Look at my Dad, for God's sake!'

'Ah, yes. Gabriel.' She let go of my hand and stood up. 'Another coffee, I think.'

As she filled the kettle under the tap, I watched her curiously. She was so beautiful. Her dark brown, glossy hair, adorned with a bow of silvery lace, hung in curls around her shoulders. She was dressed simply in a black, ankle-length skirt, teamed with a silver-grey knitted jumper, yet she managed to look absolutely stunning. She was tiny — barely five feet tall — and very slender.

I paled as I suddenly remembered Nat's words. *Her face was in shadow. She was quite small, though, and slim. They were huddled together, talking. Looked quite intense.*

I trembled as she handed me my coffee and sat down again, smiling at me. Her expression changed as she no doubt recognised my distress.

'Lexi? What is it?'

'Was it you?' I whispered. After all, Nat hadn't been able to see her face. It was raining heavily. Anything was possible.

She sighed, then shook her head. 'You mean with your father that day? No, it wasn't me, Lexi. I promise you that.'

I'd been holding my breath for her answer and gasped for air, relieved beyond words. I believed her. 'So, who the hell was it?' I wondered aloud.

She sipped at her drink.

'Aren't you even surprised?' I asked suddenly. 'I mean, my dad's cheating on Eliza, and you don't even seem shocked. Why?'

'Because I know it's not true,' she said.

'How can you possibly know that?' I demanded.

'Well, really, Lexi, I'm surprised at you. This is Gabriel we're talking about. Of course I know it, and so should you.'

'You haven't heard how snappy he's been lately,' I said. 'He's hardly Mr Perfect.'

'There's no such thing as Mr Perfect,' she said. 'Nor Ms Perfect, for that matter. We all make mistakes. When things get on top of us, when we're hurt, or afraid, we sometimes do things we shouldn't. I'm quite sure that Gabriel's sorry for the way he's been behaving towards you all.'

I remembered his recent attempts to be extra nice to Eliza. His repeated apologies. The shame in his eyes. I'd assumed it was down to guilt. I realised that, somewhere in my mind, I'd built him up to be the ideal man, and when he hadn't behaved as I needed and expected him to, I'd knocked him from his pedestal with a speed that was shameful.

'When Eliza first moved to the village,' Rhiannon said, 'she heard those rumours about your father's so-called violent past, remember?'

'God, yeah. I remember.' I shuddered.

'She never believed it,' said Rhiannon. 'Not for one instant. She knew him, and she knew he wasn't the man they said he was. So, the question is, do you honestly believe he's the kind of man who'd betray Eliza, after everything they've been through?'

I put my head in my hands, unsure how she did it. Talking to Rhiannon really was like magic. Somehow, her words could make all the thick fog that had gathered in the mind disappear as if it had never been. The huge clouds that had hung over me for weeks, months even, seemed to scud away across the sky and evaporate.

Of course I didn't believe it. My dad loved Eliza. He'd always loved her. Okay, he'd behaved out of character lately, but there was no way he'd do the awful things I'd been accusing him of.

'What's wrong with me?' I pleaded. 'Why have I been so awful about him? How could I betray him like that?' My tears welled up again. 'He's always been there for me, always been the one I could rely on. I've really let him down, haven't I?'

'I think,' she said, 'that maybe it's just part of the process.'

'What process?'

'What you're discovering is what we all realise eventually. Allowing yourself to love is taking a gigantic leap of faith. I often say, the universe unfolds just as it should. I think events have conspired to bring you to this point, Lexi. This is the moment when you decide who you are, and what kind of life you want for yourself.'

'But what about Dad?' I said. 'Who was that woman? And what do I do about Will? I've hurt him so much.'

'When you know what it is you want,' she said softly, 'you'll know exactly what to do about everything.'

I gulped and wiped the tears away from my face. 'What's the second thing?'

'I'm sorry?'

'You said two things occurred to you. What was the second thing?'

She smiled. 'That even if everything you feared most came true, it's none of your business. If your father is cheating on Eliza, if Nat is lying to Georgia, it's nothing to do with you. You're not responsible for other people's lives, Lexi. Somehow, as a young child, seeing the way your parents suffered, you took the burden of other people's happiness on your shoulders. It's time to let that go and concentrate on yourself.' She rounded the table to me and kissed me gently. 'Go home, sweetheart,' she said. 'I think you might find some answers waiting for you there.'

Sniffing, I smiled at her gratefully. 'Thank you.'

I left her standing by the door, a wistful expression on her face. I could only hope that her own problems would be resolved soon. Rhiannon deserved happiness, more than most, whatever Derry thought.

Chapter 36

'Goodness! I can't believe you've finished that already. You *have* been busy.' Darcey's tone was admiring, but when Will turned around, she burst out laughing. 'I see you've taken up face painting, too. Aren't you the talented one!'

Will wiped his forehead with the back of his arm and put down the paintbrush. Joining Darcey in the middle of the room, he looked around, wishing he could feel some sense of satisfaction at a job well done. He'd emulsioned the entire men's toilet block in record time. He'd been putting off doing it, but somehow, that afternoon, it seemed an appropriate place to be. His life had just gone down the toilet, after all, and all his hopes and dreams had been well and truly flushed away, for good this time. He knew, without doubt, that there could be no coming back from it all. He wondered how he'd ever face Lexi again. Since she knew how he felt, things could never be the same between them.

'You must be worn out,' she said. 'Should you have done all this alone? You've not been well recently.'

'I'm fine,' he said. It was his stock answer, after all. 'They needed doing. I'll do the ladies' toilets tomorrow.'

'But it's the ball tomorrow night!'

'It won't take me that long. Besides, I'm sure you and Nat have everything in hand. You don't need me.'

She studied him, clearly curious. 'Has something happened, Will?'

'No, no. I suppose I'd better get inside and clean up.'

'I suppose you better had,' she agreed. 'Tell you what, get showered and changed, and I'll fix us something to eat. Mrs Woodrow's gone home, and Nat's gone out, so we may as well eat together.'

'I'm not hungry,' he admitted.

'Well, even so, you need to eat. You don't want to be ill again, especially not the day before our grand event. And, besides, I don't want to eat alone. Don't be mean. It might be the last chance we get. I'm leaving the day after tomorrow, don't forget.'

His eyes softened. 'So you are. I'll be sorry to see you go. Are you sure I can't change your mind?'

A shadow flitted across her face for just a moment. 'I'm afraid not. I've done all I can do here. The rest is up to you.'

A deep chill seeped through his skin and settled in his bones. It *was* all up to him. He knew that. He carried everything on his shoulders. Alone.

He bent to retrieve the brushes and paint tray, and the half empty drum of washable emulsion. He marvelled, briefly, at how easily he could carry them, when just days ago, he'd barely been able to support his own weight. It was amazing how quickly one's body recovered from illness, he thought. If only a heart could mend so easily.

'Spaghetti Bolognese okay?' Darcey asked, as they entered the house and headed down the corridor of the west wing.

'Sounds perfect,' he told her. 'I'll just nip in here,' he said, as they reached one of the staff cloakrooms. 'I'll wash the brushes and tray, then I'll dump this lot in my office until tomorrow.'

'No problem. Dinner should be ready in about thirty or forty minutes. Plenty of time for you to shower and change.'

She headed on towards the kitchen, and Will nipped into the cloakroom, spending ten minutes giving the brushes and tray a good soaking, before carrying everything to his office. He could leave it all there, just for the night. It would be quicker than carting it back to the storeroom.

He pushed everything into a corner and straightened, his eyes disobeying his orders and straying to the desk where, just hours ago, Lexi had sat. Where Lexi had kissed him. Where Lexi had given him hope that everything he'd ever wanted was finally within reach. He stood there, biting his lip, wondering what was going to happen next. How was he going to face her? How would she treat him? How the hell could they work together after this?

His gaze fell on an envelope, propped up against the telephone, and he frowned. That hadn't been there before, he was sure of it. *What now?*

He strolled over and picked it up, his heart thudding as he saw his name written on the front. He knew that writing. With shaky fingers, he tore open the envelope and pulled out the piece of paper within.

Dear Will

I'm so sorry. I should never have behaved the way I did today. Everything that happened was my fault entirely. I never put my brain into gear before I act, and this is the result. I never, ever meant to hurt you, and I hate the fact that I did.

Things have been really messed up lately. I've been dealing with a lot of stuff, and I think it's all got a bit much. I think, given everything that happened today, it's time for a new start. So, this is my official resignation. I have holiday entitlement which I haven't taken, so I'm taking it now. Four weeks, in lieu of my notice.

I don't want to drop you in it, Will, really I don't. But the truth is, you don't need me. Everything is in place for the ball, and you and Nat can sort everything else out. Darcey has left you in a good position, and I'm sure you can find another House Manager if you feel you need one.

Promise me you won't work too hard, though. You've taken on so much, and I'm afraid for your health. There has to be more to life than a house, Will, even one as beautiful as Kearton Hall. Take time for other things. Take time to enjoy your life. Take care of yourself.

I really am so sorry, but this truly is for the best, for both of us.

Lexi xx

As he absorbed the written words, something seemed to die inside Will. He felt his very essence ebbing from him. He had to sit down. His hands shook as he stared at the note, reading the words over and over again, drinking in every line, every word.

She was gone. She'd left him.

He turned his head, gazing out of the window at the stables, clutching the letter in his hand. Nat had said that Lexi didn't have a heart, but Will knew he was wrong. Lexi was capable of great love. She was just afraid to show it. He wondered why he'd ever believed he'd be the one to change that.

Well, it was over, and he was glad. He had nothing to offer her but hard work and dedication to a house that took every moment of his attention. She deserved better.

He had two great loves of his life, and he finally knew, with certainty, that to save them he had to fight to keep one and let the other one go. He crumpled the piece of paper in his hand and dropped it in the bin.

****

My mouth felt dry and my stomach fluttered with nerves as I opened the door to Whisperwood Farm. I'd left Rhiannon feeling determined and strong, but the closer I got to home, the more my courage ebbed away. As I walked into the kitchen, I actually felt sick. I was determined to get some answers, but would I want to hear them?

I knew something was different straight away. There was no sign of Amy, the twins, or Joe. Just Dad and Eliza. And they were sitting at the table, as if waiting for me. I briefly noticed that they were holding hands, which seemed a good start. Eliza's eyes were soft with compassion, and Dad's revealed anxiety. I had no doubt that my questions were about to be answered at last.

'Sit down, Lexi.' The fact that Eliza didn't jump up and offer me a drink meant whatever was going on was serious.

I swallowed and pulled out a chair.

'Rhiannon called,' said Dad. His voice sounded shaky and

uncertain. 'She said it was time we explained what was going on, and I think she's right.'

'So, she knows?' I said. 'I thought so.'

'You know what it's like,' said Eliza. 'Somehow, when you're carrying a heavy load, she's the one you unburden yourself to.'

'Don't I just,' I said. 'So, what's the heavy load *you've* been carrying?'

She turned to Dad, her face enquiring. He looked trapped and scared. She squeezed his hand reassuringly. 'Go on. It will be fine.'

He took a deep breath. 'Lexi, the day of the twins' party, I received a text message.'

'Yeah,' I said. 'Car accident insurance. Didn't believe that for a second.'

'You remember that?' He blinked. 'Well, anyway, the truth is, it was from your mother.'

Of all the things I'd thought he was going to say, that simply hadn't occurred to me. My mind whirled, as all the things that had happened started to make sense. His sudden snappiness, his obvious tension, and the woman in Whitby. Of course! Small and slender. My mother. If she'd had her hood down, Nat would have seen her red hair, and if he'd mentioned that, I just might have guessed, as unlikely as it was that she would come back after all this time.

How dare she make contact with my dad, of all people? After everything she'd done!

I realised they were watching me, waiting for my reaction. I didn't know what to say. I just stared at them.

'Are you all right, sweetheart?' Eliza squeezed my arm.

'So, you knew, too?' I said eventually.

'Not at first, no. Your dad was trying to deal with it alone,' she said, giving him a despairing look. 'As if!'

'I wanted to find out what she wanted first, and what she had planned. If she was back to stir up trouble, I didn't want her anywhere near you, or Eliza,' he said. 'But I couldn't keep it to myself. I was just getting stressed and making a mess of everything, and it wasn't fair on Eliza. We always said *no secrets*, and I couldn't break that promise. So I told her, and she told me to meet up with Zoe a few times, assess what the situation was. Then, well, we met her together.'

'You met my mum?' I asked, astonished.

Eliza nodded. 'Your dad really wanted my opinion. And, after everything that happened before, he didn't feel safe meeting her alone, in case — well—'

'In case she accused you of something else,' I finished.

'And besides,' he added, 'I really didn't trust my own judgment any more. Eliza's better at that than I am. I wanted to know if she'd really changed, or if she was up to something.'

'And what did you conclude?' I asked, my stomach churning as I waited for her verdict.

'I think she's genuine,' said Eliza gently. 'I think she just wants to make it up to you for everything that happened.'

I shook my head. 'She can't,' I said bitterly. 'She can never make that up to me.'

'Maybe not,' said Eliza. 'And I think she understands that, but she still wants to try.'

'Why didn't you tell me sooner?' I demanded. 'I've been worried sick, imagining all sorts.'

'Really?' He sounded puzzled. 'Until Rhiannon called, I hadn't realised you'd suspected anything was wrong.'

I couldn't help laughing. 'Oh, Dad,' I said, relieved that Rhiannon hadn't told him what I'd accused him of, 'you men really are clueless.'

He smiled. 'Maybe so. That's what we need our women for.' He kissed Eliza's cheek, then reached over and took my hand. 'Are you okay with this, Lexi? Maybe I should have told you earlier, but that day at the cottage, when we were moving out, you said you didn't want her to come back and spoil what we had, remember? Well, I didn't want that, either. I wanted to be sure she wasn't going to hurt you again. Can you understand that?'

'Of course I can,' I admitted. 'I'd have done the same to protect you. It's okay.' Actually, it was more than okay. It was a massive relief. Dad and Eliza were a solid unit, and Mum wasn't buried in some French graveyard. I felt as if a huge load had lifted from my shoulders.

'So, what do you want to do?' Dad watched me anxiously. I knew her coming back on the scene had to have really rocked him. It must have been like being hit with a sledgehammer. Poor Dad.

'You don't have to do anything you don't want to do,' Eliza assured me. 'This isn't a one-off opportunity. If you don't feel ready to face her yet, she can always come back another time when you *are* ready. This is entirely your decision.'

I gave her a grateful smile, but there was no decision to make. I was going to meet my mother.

Chapter 37

March had come in like a lion, but it seemed it had no intention of going out like a lamb. That last Saturday of the month, the rain lashed down and the skies were dark and menacing. I thought about the ball, as I sat in a café in Whitby, clutching a half empty cup of tea in my hand, as if it were a lifebelt. I hoped the weather wouldn't put people off going. The tickets were already paid for, of course, but it would be a shame if that grand marquee was half empty for the event, especially after all their hard work.

My thoughts drifted to Will. How had he reacted to my letter? Maybe he'd been relieved. It would have been awkward for him if I'd gone back to work, after all. I hoped he'd heaved a sigh of relief and put the whole thing out of his mind.

Liar. The word popped in my head, and I tried to push it away, but it kept screaming at me. *You don't want Will to put it out of his mind. You want him to miss you, to love you, to beg you to come back.*

Not wanting to hear it, I thought about the task in hand. God knows, that was enough to take my mind off any drama. Any moment now, I thought, looking at my watch. Any moment...

A hunched figure passed the window, scurrying along Church Street, head bowed against the driving rain. She wore a dark coat with the hood pulled over her head, and even as the question leapt into my mind, I got my answer, as she pushed open the café door and stepped inside, shrugging off her hood to reveal bright red hair.

I felt the blood drain from my body, as if Dracula himself had returned to Whitby and decided I'd make a tasty snack. Zoe Bailey. Or was it Zoe Appleton? Tiny, pale, and as attractive as ever. But she'd definitely aged. There were lines around her mouth and eyes to prove it.

As she stepped uncertainly towards me, I saw that she was shaking, her hand gripping the back of the chair opposite mine so tightly that her knuckles stood up in sharp points, the tightly stretched skin around them white and shiny. 'May I sit down, Lexi?' Her voice was quiet. I remembered her as being quite shrill. She was usually on the verge of hysteria. Now, she merely seemed weary.

I nodded, and she sat down, not even bothering to remove her sodden coat.

I gazed at her, taking in every detail of her face. She'd had her long hair cut into a bob. It suited her. Her face had filled out a little, and her body, although still slim, wasn't as stick thin as it had been the last time I saw her. She looked softer, somehow, like all the sharpness had been worn away. Seeing the anxiety in her eyes, my own anxiety began to ebb away. She couldn't hurt me any more, and she couldn't hurt my dad. What was there to be afraid of?

'Would you like a cup of tea?' A waitress appeared, and I ordered a pot of tea for two, seeing that my mother seemed incapable of speaking, suddenly. 'Do you still drink tea?' I asked, as the waitress left, and it occurred to me that I hadn't even checked.

She nodded. 'Yes. I still drink tea.'

We sat for a moment, neither of us apparently able to think of anything else to say. Then, just as I was thinking what a waste of time the meeting was turning out to be, she cleared her throat and began to fiddle with the button on her coat.

'I expect you're wondering what I'm doing here, after all this time.'

'It had crossed my mind, yes,' I said. 'If you've come back to cause bother, you've no chance. I'm not a kid any more, and I can take care of myself better now. And Dad's happy. He and

Eliza are mad about each other, they have twins, and we're a family. You can't touch him.'

She looked so sad that I almost regretted my statement, but I had to make things clear from the start. She had to know how we stood. Give my mother an inch, and she'd take a mile, as we'd learned to our cost many years ago.

'I'm not here to cause trouble,' she assured me. 'I met your father and his new wife. I can see how in love they are, and believe me, I'm delighted for him. It's wonderful that he's found so much happiness after everything I put him through.'

I watched her warily, unsure if she was genuine.

The waitress returned with our tea, and Mum smiled her thanks before saying to me, 'Shall I pour?'

I nodded. She seemed to be gathering her courage, as mine was fading away. What was she expecting from me?

'I can understand your suspicions,' she said, handing me my cup and saucer. 'After everything I did to you, I can't blame you in the slightest.'

Noticing the gleam of a wedding ring on her left hand, I took a deep breath. 'So,' I said, nodding at it in disgust, 'you married him, then?'

'What? Oh!' She glanced down at her hand and shook her head. 'It's not what you think. I am married, yes, but not to *him*.'

The way she said the word left me in no doubt that she'd seen him for what he was. Thank God. I eyed her anxiously. 'So, who then?' No doubt some other rich businessman who could buy her anything she wanted. What price had she paid that time?

She smiled, and the joy sparkled in her eyes. 'His name's Ron and, well, I suppose you could say we met through the refuge.'

'Refuge?' I put down my cup with a clatter. 'You were in a refuge?'

'What? No, no. I wasn't in one. I volunteered at one.'

I blinked. 'Volunteered? You?'

She took a sip of her tea, then replaced the cup in the saucer and folded her arms. 'I can see I'm going to have to start at the beginning. That would be best, wouldn't it?'

I sat quietly as she recounted her story to me. Evidently, it hadn't taken long for her to realise that no amount of jewellery or designer clothes was enough to compensate for life with the vicious and obnoxious Hugh Appleton. She'd had four months of misery in Paris, before gathering her courage to leave him. He'd never given her any money, so she'd had to wait until she could grab the opportunity to book a ticket back to England online, using his credit card. She was terrified he'd find out, but the last-minute flight was her only hope of escape. Arriving back in England, she'd been too scared to come back to Yorkshire, in case he tried to track her down, and had fled to an aunt's in Lincolnshire.

It wasn't long before the trauma of everything that had happened started to affect her, and her aunt made her see a doctor, who referred her to a counsellor. After almost a year in therapy, she'd felt stronger and had come to see the things that had gone wrong in her life, and the mess she'd made of everything. More than that, she'd begun to understand why she'd behaved as she had and had started to forgive herself for her behaviour. A vile childhood with uncaring, layabout parents wasn't her excuse, but it was a reason, and she wanted to start putting things right.

She'd volunteered at a local women's centre, who'd put her through various training courses in dealing with traumatised women — victims, just like her, of domestic violence. She'd then volunteered at a refuge, and, as her interest in its work grew, had decided to enrol at college, studying part time in a bid to be accepted into university, to study social work.

Ron was a fellow student. He'd been made redundant from his job and was seeking a new challenge, something that would really make a difference. The two of them had evidently befriended each other quite quickly, a friendship that turned to love. They'd married a few months ago and were working hard to achieve their degrees.

I couldn't believe it. I sat there, completely stunned, as she enthused about what they hoped to achieve, their passion for their studies, and the sense of fulfilment she'd got from working at the refuge. Was this really my mother? The woman whose only interest was shopping, handbag collecting and being a prize bitch? I couldn't take it all in, and after a while she stopped talking and flushed a little.

'Sorry. I've rambled on, haven't I? I suppose it must seem very boring to you.'

'Not at all,' I said quickly. 'It's just, well, you never used to care about anyone but yourself.' I supposed I shouldn't have said that, but it was the truth, after all. 'You've gone from being a wannabe Kim Kardashian to Princess Diana. It's all a bit weird.'

She laughed. 'I suppose it must seem so, from your point of view, but it was a gradual process. A slow awakening, as I looked around me and realised what was truly important. I thought about everything I'd lost, everything I'd thrown away. It was a very painful time, and I couldn't have got through it without professional help. The counselling was vital. I couldn't have moved on with my life without it. I had too much regret, for a start. Too much guilt. You, your poor father.' She shook her head as if embarrassed. 'I'm so sorry, Lexi. I can't even begin to tell you how sorry. '

I sat for a moment, trying to absorb everything she'd told me. I couldn't believe the change in her, but then, it had been a good few years and people *could* change. Move on. Especially when they'd been through such a traumatic time and had engaged with therapy.

I decided I believed she was genuine. And she'd married a student! I mean, she certainly hadn't married him for his money, had she?

I reached for her hand and squeezed it gently, and she looked up, tears welling in her eyes.

'You're alive,' I said, my voice breaking with emotion. 'That's what matters. Oh, Mum, you're *alive*!'

****

Dad was waiting for me in the car park by the harbour. I ran across the tarmac, dodging puddles, and as I scrambled into the car, he looked at me. 'Well?'

I nodded. 'All good, Dad. Let's go home.'

Eliza welcomed us home with lunch and a big hug. The twins were in their highchairs, hurling food at each other. Amy cantered happily through the hallway, telling Twinkle that he'd better stop refusing jumps or she'd get a new pony, and Joe was beside himself with excitement, waiting for Charlie to arrive home.

Catching Dad's eye, I wondered if I looked as contented and as thankful as he did. We had a beautiful family. Soon, we'd have a new home. Mum was alive and well and happy, so we didn't have to worry about her any longer. Things were good.

Charlie arrived home at around two, and the farmhouse descended into chaos. After giving him a welcoming hug, I made my escape and went upstairs, where I sat on my bed and thought about everything that had happened.

I'd sorted out something that had been hanging over me for what felt like forever — the situation with my mum. It felt strange to remember how we'd hugged as we left the café, how we'd promised to keep in touch, how she'd cried and told me how beautiful I was, and how proud she was of me.

It was even stranger to realise that I actually wanted to see her again. I wanted to meet her new husband. I wanted to know more about the new life she was living. If she was proud of me, well, I was oddly proud of her, too. I hadn't completely forgiven her, and I didn't fully trust her, but I wanted to, and that had to mean something, didn't it? We had something to work on, at least.

If only everything in my life could be resolved, I thought, as I huddled on my bed, my arms wrapped around my drawn-up knees. How did I sort it all out? What could I do to put things right? Where to start, even?

A tap on my bedroom door brought me out of my daydream.

'Can I come in?' Joe asked, peering in.

I smiled and nodded. 'Sure.'

He sank down onto the bed beside me, his eyes full of sadness. 'So, is it true?'

'Is what true?'

'You've resigned from your job. Really?'

'How did you know?'

'How do you think? My pal Will told me. I went round there this morning to get some of Charlie's favourite jam from the farm shop and bumped into him. Jesus, he gave me a fright. He looked ten years older. Of course, Will being Will, he said he was fine. But I wasn't having it. I marched him into the house and sat him down and made him tell me everything.'

I blushed. 'Everything?'

He turned a bit pink, too. 'Well, he was very discreet, but I caught the gist of it. So, my little Gingernut, what are you thinking, eh? What's your problem?'

I didn't know how to explain. So much had changed in the last few days. Talking to Rhiannon had started a process within me, somehow. Then, going back to the farm, seeing that Dad and Eliza were absolutely all right and realising that I'd had no need to worry about their relationship, because they loved each other and neither one of them would deliberately hurt the other. And finally, that morning, seeing my mother, making my peace with her. I'd listened, recognising a deeper truth when she'd told me how bitterly she regretted the way she'd treated my dad.

'He didn't deserve it,' she'd said sadly. 'It wasn't his fault. Any of it. I know he did everything he could to make me happy, but I couldn't *be* happy. Nothing could make me happy, because I didn't believe I deserved to be. I thought good things didn't happen to someone like me. Not really. So, if something good was within my grasp, I had to sabotage it, because I didn't think it was right that I should have it.' She shook her head. 'It's funny, you know. After everything that happened, it was your father that saved me.'

'Dad saved you? How?'

'When Hugh was beating me, telling me I was worthless, there was a huge part of me that believed him. But then, somehow, I kept remembering the way Gabriel had treated me. How he'd stood by me, supported me even when I'd broken his heart, and how, right 'til the end, when I'd lied and ruined his life, he begged me to stay with him so he could protect me. Acts of kindness that made me believe that, just maybe, I deserved better. He kept alive that little flame of hope, and because of him, I realised I *did* deserve better, and that I had to get out of that relationship. It took a while, but I started to finally forgive myself, and even love myself.'

She'd laughed, her nose wrinkling in a self-deprecating fashion. 'Sounds corny, doesn't it? But it's true, you know. If you can't love yourself, you really can't love someone else. And that's why, this time, I know my marriage will last. I'm not damaged any more, and I can give all my love to Ron, without fear of putting him through the same ordeal I put Gabriel through. I'm so glad your father's found someone who can give him the love he deserves.' She'd smiled at me, her eyes twinkling. 'Now we just have to find someone who deserves you.'

'Lexi?' Joe's voice coaxed me back into the moment, and I sighed, stretching my legs as I realised I was developing a cramp.

'Sorry. What?'

'I said, are you going to ask for your job back?' he said.

I shook my head. 'I shouldn't think Will's in any mood to take me back on.'

Joe ruffled my hair. 'You daft ha'porth. Will would forgive you for anything, put up with anything, as long as he could have you near. Don't you realise that by now? Jesus, all those months of you dating Nat, right under his own roof. Can you imagine what that did to him? Can't you see how much he loves you?'

For the second time in a few months, I found myself sobbing on Joe's shoulder, and he once again stroked my hair while making soothing noises, as I cried.

'There, there, love. It will be all right, you'll see.'

'But how can it be?' I wailed. 'Look how much I've hurt him already. This was exactly what I didn't want. How do I put it right? I just don't know what to do.'

'When you know what it is you want, you'll know what to do,' he said.

That was, more-or-less, exactly what Rhiannon had said, but it was easy for them. I was paralysed with fear. Will was the last person I'd wanted to hurt. The very last. I'd rather die than hurt him again.

I gasped suddenly and sat up, wiping away my tears.

'You okay, love?' said Joe.

I nodded. 'I will be, Joe. I've just figured out what I want. And now I know exactly what to do.'

Chapter 38

Will felt like an idiot. He had seriously contemplated not wearing his costume that evening, but as the host of the ball, it would look highly irregular if he appeared in ordinary clothes when everyone else had been instructed to come in fancy dress. He wished he'd selected any other costume than the one he was wearing. He could have ordered any number of costumes online, for God's sake. Why had he been so stupid? It felt like he'd set himself up somehow. Tempted fate.

He stood at the entrance to the marquee, smiling and nodding greetings at the guests as they showed their tickets to Gav and Dave, the two security guards he'd hired for the evening, almost wishing he'd been overcome by illness again. Any excuse to get out of this nightmare.

Inside the marquee, Derry and his band played a popular eighties tune, the music seeping through the fabric walls, as they waited for the place to fill up. He smiled, in spite of himself, as he recalled Derry's greeting to him when they'd all arrived at the Hall earlier that afternoon.

Pulling up in a decrepit old van, his bandmates had jumped out, carrying their instruments and whistling in awe at the sight of the house and marquee. Derry had scrambled out after them, trying to appear nonchalant, as if it was all old hat to him.

As Will had greeted them, Derry had said, oh-so-casually, 'Will, meet Cal, Den, Stu and Liam. Lads, this is my brother, Will.'

He'd had to fight to stay calm, after that little bombshell. It had been an amazing feeling, having Derry acknowledge him as his brother. He'd said nothing, not wanting to make a big deal of it and scare Derry off, but it had made his day.

Hearing the sound of applause from within, he left the security guards to it and entered the marquee, marvelling again at how beautiful it looked. The place was filling up nicely. He was relieved the rain had stopped, and even though the lawn was squelchy, the red carpet that led from the path to the marquee ensured there were no muddy stains inside.

Standing at the entrance, Will watched the boys performing on the stage at the far end of the marquee, feeling an odd sense of pride that his half-brother was talented enough to sing lead vocals in a band. He'd listened to them rehearse, awestruck at Derry's talent. So, not only was he extremely attractive, but he also had a great singing voice. Well, he must get that from his mother, because it certainly hadn't been from Sir Paul.

Nat wandered over to stand beside him.

'What do you think?' Will asked him.

Nat tutted. 'All right, I suppose.' He caught Will's eye and grinned sheepishly. 'Okay, he's good. They're all good. It's going to be a great night.'

Will's mood darkened immediately, but Nat didn't seem to notice.

He said suddenly, 'Are you sure it's okay, me bringing Georgia, I mean? I do appreciate it, Will. It's time Lexi and Georgia sorted this out. I know Georgia misses her.'

Will smiled. 'And that matters to you?'

'Yeah.' Nat grinned. 'Who'd have thought it, eh? But if Georgia's happy, I'm happy, and I know she'd feel so much better if we had Lexi's blessing. I just hope they don't have another row tonight and spoil the ball.'

Will's smile slipped, and he folded his arms, watching the band, though not really hearing them any longer. 'If it puts your mind at rest, Lexi's not coming tonight, so there won't be any scene.'

'Not coming!' Nat pulled on his arm, forcing Will to face him. 'What do you mean, she's not coming? Since when?'

'Since ... Since we had a difference of opinion, and she handed in her notice.'

'Lexi's resigned? I don't believe it. She wouldn't. She loves this place.'

Will didn't need anyone to tell him how much Kearton Hall meant to Lexi. The fact that she'd chosen to leave, rather than face him, said it all. 'I'm aware of that, but I assure you it's true. She's gone.'

'What really happened, Will? You can tell me.'

Will didn't answer. He stared over at the band as Derry began to sing a soulful version of Maroon 5's *She Will Be Loved*. Despite his best efforts, his breath caught in his throat as the lyrics of the chorus played over and over in his mind, and suddenly he realised he couldn't see Derry any longer.

The stage became a blur, and beside him Nat murmured, 'Christ, you really have got it bad, haven't you?'

'I could have loved her, you know,' Will said softly. 'If she'd only let me.'

'No *could have* about it,' said Nat, his voice uncharacteristically sympathetic. 'You already love her. You've loved her for ages. I'm sorry, Will. What happened between you? Why did she leave?'

Will couldn't answer, and Nat seemed to watch him for a moment, before saying, 'You told her, didn't you? You told her how you felt, and she got scared and ran. That's it, isn't it?'

Will nodded. He didn't feel it necessary to add that he'd leapt to a ridiculous conclusion before that and made a total idiot of himself. The details should, and would, remain private, if he had anything to do with it.

Nat sighed and put his arm around his shoulder. 'She's a fool. You could make her really happy, Will. I don't get what it is she wants.'

Will swallowed. 'She's afraid of being hurt. I understand that. Anyway, it's done now. Over.'

'Over?' Nat removed his arm and stared at his cousin, his face stern. 'Seriously? That's it, is it?'

'What do you want me to do?'

'William Boden-Kean, you've fought like a bloody tiger to keep this sodding house going for years. If you can fight like that for a house, are you seriously telling me that you're not going to do anything to get your woman?'

Will's heartbeat quickened. 'But she doesn't want—'

'*Make her want.* Tell her how you feel, and this time make her stay put and listen. She's scared of being hurt. Tell her you'll never hurt her, because you won't. I know you won't. She needs to know it, too. Give it your best bloody shot.'

'But if she says no...'

'Then at least you'll go down fighting, instead of standing here like some drip who doesn't believe he's worthy of her. You *are* worthy of her.'

Will shook his head. 'I'm not. I have nothing to offer her. Look at me. I'm not you, or Derry. All I am is the caretaker of this house. How can I expect her to bury herself here? Wear herself out with work and worry?'

Nat sighed. 'You just don't get it, do you? Lexi loves this house almost as much as you do. And almost as much as she loves you.'

Will's eyes widened. 'What on earth are you talking about? Lexi doesn't—'

'Will!'

He turned, his heart galloping when his gaze landed on Gabriel and Eliza walking towards him. They looked amazing, dressed as hippies, all headbands, psychedelic swirls and fringed waistcoats. In her hand, Eliza carried a tambourine, which she rattled every now and then for effect. Will couldn't help smiling, as Gabriel held up two fingers and said, 'Peace, Man.'

'What fantastic costumes,' he said. 'And what a great era to choose.'

'We decided that, after the last few months, we wanted to pay tribute to the time of peace and love,' said Eliza, glancing affectionately at Gabriel. 'But look at you! You look amazing!'

Gabriel watched him thoughtfully. 'I don't suppose you've come as Lord Kearton?'

Will felt his face start to burn. 'Er, yes. How did you know?'

They exchanged glances and Gabriel shrugged. 'Just a lucky guess.' He glanced at Nat. 'Nice costume. Huge effort there.'

'I haven't bloody changed yet,' said Nat, clearly outraged. 'I'm just about to go to Georgia's. I'm getting changed at her house.'

'How very nice for you both,' said Eliza coolly.

Nat tutted and glanced at Will. 'I'd better get off anyway. I'll be back in about an hour. Remember what I said, okay?'

Will frowned. Nothing Nat said had made any sense.

Eliza watched Nat leave, her mouth set. 'Huh. So, it's still on with him and Georgia then?'

'Seems they actually love each other,' said Will. 'He really cares about her, and that can only be a good thing, can't it?'

She eyed him for a moment, then smiled. 'I suppose so. Let's hope he takes care of her. I'm so looking forward to this. Are Rose and Flynn here yet?'

Before Will could answer, he heard a screech of, 'You bet your bottom dollar we are!'

'Good God.' Gabriel started laughing, and Will turned to see the extraordinary sight of the quiet, dignified Flynn wearing a white, rhinestone-covered jumpsuit, accompanied by Rose, wearing a black beehive wig, thick black eyeliner, and a bright pink mini dress that barely covered her modesty.

'My word,' Will murmured, as Eliza shook her tambourine in delight and shrieked with laughter.

'Elvis and Priscilla, I presume? You do know this is supposed to be celebrating four hundred years of *British* history?' said Gabriel.

'I told you so,' said Flynn, his face flushed with embarrassment. He sighed. 'She just wouldn't have it.'

'It *is* British history,' Rose protested. 'Elvis had a huge impact on this country. My mother says so, so it must be true.'

'She has a point,' said Will. 'Anyway, it's great to see you all here, and you all look spectacular. Thank you for making the effort.'

'God, Will,' said Rose admiringly, 'get you, with your pointy beard and your Musketeer boots. You look quite fanciable in that get up. Maybe you should think about growing a beard permanently.'

'He does look divine, doesn't he?' agreed Eliza.

'Too right. Are you Aramis, or Athos?'

'No, no. I'm … Never mind.' His voice trailed off as they all stood gaping at him. His face burned and he wished he was anywhere but here right now. He glanced down at his costume, especially made for him by a rather talented dressmaker in York. It would have been worth the effort, if Lexi had seen him dressed as her hero. Without her presence he felt stupid, standing there in a gold coat, high white collar with lace scallops, dark breeches, cape, high-heeled boots with bucket flaps, and feathered hat. The fake beard made him feel even more ridiculous, whatever Rose said. He couldn't help wondering, sadly, what Lexi would have thought of it.

'Jesus, who do we have here?' Rose cackled with laughter. 'Hell's bells, it's the Dowager Countess from *Downton Abbey*.'

'Do you mind?' Sophie's voice was indignant. 'Actually, I'm Queen Alexandra, and this is my husband, Edward the Seventh.'

Archie seemed pretty fed up, and Will sympathised. Fake beards were the very devil.

'You're too slim to be Edward the Seventh, Archie,' Gabriel said, winking mischievously at Eliza. 'I must say, I'm surprised. I wasn't expecting you to be quite so dignified, Sophie.'

'And why not, indeed? I can be very dignified, I'll have you know,' she said. 'Besides, as Sir William's personal solicitor,' she added, giving Will a gracious smile, 'Archie thought it only fitting that we come as something refined and elegant. Not like you lot. I mean, what the hell were you thinking? I'm surprised at *you*, Flynn, for a start.'

'Did you borrow that dress from Rhiannon?' said Rose sweetly.

Sophie glared at her. 'No, I didn't.' She flashed them a smug little smile. 'Although, she's going to be a bit put out, eh? I've out-Edwardian-ed the Edwardian lady herself. Serves her right for always dressing so ridiculously old fashioned.'

'Er, Sophie...' Gabriel's voice trailed off, and everyone turned to see what he was looking at.

'I don't believe it,' murmured Sophie in dismay. 'If that doesn't take the sodding biscuit.'

Will bit his lip, trying not to laugh. He stepped forward, holding out his hands to Rhiannon, who took them gratefully.

She looked absolutely stunning, though completely different.
Wearing a short, Union Jack dress, a ginger wig, and red platform
boots, she was barely recognisable as the elegant landlady of The
Hare and Moon, but she was a dead ringer for Geri Halliwell, aka
Ginger Spice. He'd been privileged to see Rhiannon's legs before,
but he doubted any of the others had, since she usually wore
ankle length skirts and dresses. She'd well and truly outdone
Sophie thist time.

'You look stunning,' he told her.

'Absolutely gorgeous,' agreed Eliza.

Rhiannon giggled. 'I thought I'd do something completely
unexpected.' She made a V sign with her fingers, and said, 'Girl
power!'

Sophie folded her arms. 'Red hair suits you, Rhiannon, as do
the red boots. So, scarlet's your colour. Imagine that.'

'Sophie, let's get a drink,' Archie said. He grasped her arm and
steered her towards the bar, nodding at Rhiannon apologetically.

'Darling, is Darcey here?' Rhiannon whispered in Will's ear.

'She's in the house getting ready. Why?'

She shook her head. 'It can wait.'

'Okay.' He wondered if he could steer her away to talk to her
privately. What Nat had said was ridiculous, of course, but he
couldn't help wondering. Why would he say something like that?
Lexi had made it clear she didn't want him. She'd even resigned.
It was all so confusing, and if anyone could help him make sense
of it all, it was Rhiannon.

He almost groaned in frustration as another whoop of delight
went up, and people started cheering and clapping. He turned
and, in spite of himself, started to laugh, as Charlie and Joe made
their grand entrance.

'Good grief.' He shook his head. 'I don't think you've quite
grasped the theme of this event.'

Charlie, resplendent in a long tunic, thick gold jewellery, black
wig and heavy makeup, blew him a kiss. Joe, handsome in a
Roman tunic, held up his hands and did a twirl.

'Antony and Cleopatra?' Rose tutted. 'What have they got to do
with British history? And you had a go at us for being Elvis and

Priscilla,' she said, nodding at Gabriel.

'We ain't Antony and Cleopatra,' said Charlie. 'We're Richard Burton and Elizabeth Taylor, and since he was Welsh, and she was English, you can't disqualify us.'

'It's not a competition,' said Will. 'Nothing to disqualify you from.'

'Ain't it? You mean there's no prize?' Charlie sounded dismayed. 'You never told me that, Joe.'

'Thought the chance to wear that costume would be reward enough,' Joe said, with a sly grin.

Charlie tutted, then his eyes widened as he beheld Will standing there, in all his seventeenth century glory. Rummaging in his robes, he brought out his glasses and perched them on his nose, which totally ruined the effect of his thick kohl eyeliner. 'Wow. You look fab. I could quite fancy you myself.'

'Er, thanks.' Will shuffled awkwardly, wishing he could just escape and head over to Whisperwood.

'Wait 'til Lexi clocks you,' Charlie continued, his face wreathed in smiles. 'She's gonna be thrilled to bits. Can't wait to see her face.'

Will looked up sharply. 'Lexi? She's coming?'

Eliza and Gabriel gave Charlie a pained look, and Joe nudged him in the ribs. He groaned. 'Sorry. I forgot it was a surprise. Well, yeah, she's coming. It doesn't matter now, anyway, 'cos here she is.'

Some part of Will was dimly aware that the string quartet had begun to play a waltz, and he wondered for a brief moment if he'd actually stepped into a fairy tale, as the most exquisite vision entered the marquee and glided towards him.

Her red hair had been swept up into a knot at the back of her head, leaving curls hanging at the sides of her face, in the style of a seventeenth century lady. She was wearing the most glorious green satin dress, and Will realised it was similar to the one worn by the Countess in the portrait they'd been given on loan. As Lexi reached his side, he fleetingly registered that she was wearing the brooch he'd given her for Christmas, that she was eyeing him rather nervously, and that she'd never looked more beautiful in her life.

He felt a stab of pain, longing to reach out to her, but searing doubt made him hesitate. It must mean something, surely, that she'd turned up for the ball, after everything that had happened? That, in spite of the fact that she associated William Kearton so closely with Will, she'd chosen to dress as his wife? It all had to matter, didn't it?

He swallowed. What if he'd got it wrong again? What if she rejected him? How could he bear it twice?

He knew everyone was waiting. He knew it was down to him to react, and for a moment he was frozen with fear. But Lexi would never be his if he didn't do something, and right here, right now, was his time. He knew he'd risk anything for her.

It felt as if the entire world had fallen silent. Will took a steadying breath, removed his hat, and gave a deep bow. After a moment, he straightened again and held out his hand to her, his heart pounding as she seemed to hesitate. Then she gave a low curtsey and took hold of his hand. Together, they swept onto the dance floor.

Chapter 39

I'd not realised Will could dance. I'd only seen him attempt it once, at the disastrous wedding of Rose's mother, and he'd not been that impressive. But that had been contemporary dancing, basically a free-for-all. This was ballroom dancing. A waltz, no less. This time, it was me who didn't know what on earth I was doing, but to my amazement, Will led me so assuredly, and guided me so smoothly, that he made it easy for me to follow his movements, and I quickly relaxed and let him take me wherever he wanted to go.

'I didn't know you could do this.' I said eventually, aware that we hadn't spoken a word to each other, and that he hadn't taken his eyes off me the whole time we were dancing.

'Boarding school,' he said. 'It was compulsory, and if you tell anyone that, I'll never forgive you.' His eyes crinkled in the corners, and I realised how calm he sounded, and how in control he appeared. In fact, I'd never known him to be so — well — masterful.

I glanced down at his costume, recognising it as a replica of the one worn by William Kearton in the Dobson portrait.

'Great minds think alike, eh?' Will's hand tightened a little on my waist, and I realised he wasn't as calm as he was making out. There was an unmistakable anxiety in his eyes, and I thought how much courage it must have taken for him to react the way he had upon my arrival, especially after the way I'd treated him.

My heartbeat quickened. He'd taken a leap of faith. For me. For love. 'You're so handsome,' I told him, meaning it. I felt quite breathless just looking at him.

He didn't tut or turn away or blush or do any of the things that Will normally did when someone gave him a compliment. Instead, he said quietly, 'We're not supposed to look at each other.'

'What?'

'When you waltz, you're not supposed to look at each other. My teacher would be having a fit now. Our head positions are all wrong.'

'I suppose they are,' I said. I had seen *Strictly*, after all. I wondered if I should tell him that Antony and Cleopatra were standing at the side of the dance floor, watching us and blubbing into their hankies. I decided, on balance, not to mention it.

'The thing is,' Will murmured, 'I can't *stop* looking at you. I've never seen anyone so beautiful in all my life.'

My stomach did a waltz all of its own. 'I can't stop looking at you either, Will.'

He suddenly drew me closer, and I felt his lips brush my ear. 'Lexi,' he whispered. 'I know you don't want to hear this, but I—'

'I'm sorry to cut in,' said a voice beside us.

'Then don't,' said Will, sounding irritated.

Weak-kneed, I turned my head, wondering who on earth had been so crass as to disturb us.

A man with close-cropped brown hair, and dressed in a black suit, stood at my side. I vaguely recognised him but couldn't think where from.

'I'm afraid we have a bit of a situation outside,' he said to Will.

'Are you serious?' Will looked aghast. 'Can't you deal with it yourself?'

The man pursed his lips and shook his head. 'In my experience, it's best to get clearance from the man in charge. And that, my friend, is you.'

Will's expression turned murderous. If I hadn't been so desperate for him to finish what he'd been about to tell me, I would have laughed. He released me from his hold and looked at me intently. 'Don't leave,' he instructed me. 'I swear, I'll be back before you know it.'

'It's okay,' I said. 'Do what you have to do.'

He held my gaze for a moment, then, with evident regret, he tore himself away and followed the man, who I'd just recognised as one of the security guards, out of the marquee.

I stumbled over to the nearest table and collapsed. No wonder seventeenth century women needed to fan themselves so frequently, what with all those masterful men in Musketeer boots striding round, being all commanding and masculine. Jeez!

****

Will couldn't believe it. 'Are you seriously telling me you called me out to deal with this?' he demanded.

The security guard who'd dragged him from the marquee sucked in his cheeks and let out a low whistle. 'No need to be so rude,' he said. 'We're only doing our job, aren't we, Gav?'

'Too right, Dave,' agreed his colleague, shaking his head. 'If she hasn't got a ticket, how can we let her in? You'd be the first to complain if we let all and sundry into that fancy do of yours, now wouldn't you? Be fair.'

Will rolled his eyes as Sophie tutted in disgust. 'Of course I have a ticket. It's in that bloody marquee with my husband. I only left because I needed to use the facilities.'

Gav shook his head. 'And how do we know that?'

'Are you serious?' Sophie glared at them. 'Look at me! I'm in fancy dress. I'm hardly likely to be out for a passing stroll in this get-up, am I?'

'You could be chancing your arm,' said Dave firmly. 'We see it all the time in this business, don't we, Gav?'

'We do, Dave. Frankly, this has been handled all wrong.' He shook his head at Will. 'In the clubs, they stamp people's hands, so if they go out and want to come back in, we can tell that they've paid. You haven't given us the facilities to stamp people's hands.'

'Well, of course I haven't,' said Will, shocked. 'I hardly think they'd appreciate that kind of treatment. It's not that sort of event, and they're not that sort of people.'

'Really?' Dave and Gav exchanged glances. 'You want to watch that, if you don't mind me saying so. You sound very elitist. Some of the most badly-behaved partygoers we've had dealings with have been *your sort of people.*'

Will rubbed the back of his head. 'I'm sorry, I really didn't mean it like that. Look, I can vouch for Sophie. She is most definitely a guest, so can you just let her through and let me get back to the ball?'

He heaved a sigh of relief when they nodded, then fought his impatience as Dave grabbed his arm. 'Hang on a minute. What do you want us to do the next time we catch someone without a ticket? Someone who insists they went outside to *use the facilities.*'

Will shrugged, desperate to get back to Lexi before she changed her mind and did a disappearing act. 'Just let anyone in.'

'Anyone?' They sounded incredulous.

'Anyone in fancy dress,' he relented. 'I don't care any more.'

Gav pulled a face. 'You're making a rod for your own back there, mate, but if you insist.'

'I do insist,' said Will firmly.

He took hold of Sophie's arm, and they turned back to the marquee before the security guards could interrogate them further.

As Sophie rushed off to tell Archie all about her distressing ordeal at the hands of two hooligans, Will's heart almost stopped as he spotted Lexi approaching. 'Where are you going? I'm done now, I've sorted the problem.'

'I'm just going to see what's keeping Darcey,' she reassured him. 'She may be having problems with her costume. She may need help to fasten it or something. I won't be long.'

'All right. But, Lexi…' His voice trailed off, and his eyes searched hers for signs that she understood.

She swallowed and nodded. 'I know. We'll talk. I promise.'

He stepped aside to let her pass. They *would* talk. He would see to it. She had to know that he'd never hurt her, and that he'd spend the rest of his life proving himself worthy of her, if only she'd let him.

'Problem sorted?' asked Rhiannon, as he reached the table. 'Lexi's just gone to find Darcey.'

Will nodded. 'I know. I saw her.'

Rhiannon beamed. Then her gaze fell on Bernie, and her smile dimmed. 'Everything okay, Bernie?'

'Yeah. Right as rain.' He took a sip of his pint and lapsed into silence.

'That's a very interesting look,' she tried again. 'Are you John Lennon?'

'Yeah.'

He looked mortified, and Will felt for him. He wondered why he'd agreed to a fancy dress ball. Although, thinking about Lexi, he was rather glad he had.

'Would I be right in thinking that we can expect Yoko any time now?' Rhiannon sounded sympathetic, and Will stared at them, puzzled. Was he missing something? Did Bernie have a girlfriend? Since when?

Bernie's face burned red, and Will decided it was time to change the subject. Thankfully, Derry's return to the stage provided the opportunity.

'The band's so good, isn't it? Derry can really sing. Did I tell you, he introduced me to the band members as his brother?'

'No!' Rhiannon eyes widened. 'That's wonderful! It seems he's finally starting to accept things.' She shrugged. 'Well, your side of things, at any rate. I'm afraid I have a long way to go before I can say he's forgiven me.'

'Still no better?'

'Not really.' Will could hear the pain in her voice. 'He dropped rather a bombshell on me today, actually. I almost didn't come tonight, but then I thought, if I stayed at home, I'd probably feel even worse, so…'

'What's he said?'

'He's going to live with my father.' Her voice was flat, but Will knew she was holding back an avalanche of emotions. She would see Derry going to live with his grandfather as the ultimate betrayal.

'I'm so sorry.' He wished he could take her pain away. 'It may only be temporary. He may get there and discover that you were right about your father. When he sees that for himself, he'll come home. I know it.'

'Perhaps.' She gave a tight smile. 'Anyway, enough of that. Tonight's a happy night. Lots of people are signing up for your friendship scheme. That's good news, isn't it?'

'Budge up, Will.'

He started at Nat's hand landing on his shoulder. Beside him, Georgia was obviously uncomfortable, and he tried to put his own nerves to one side as he realised how awkward the evening must be for her, given that she hadn't seen him since that fateful day at the stables.

'You look lovely, Georgia,' he said kindly. 'Great costume.'

She gave him a grateful smile. 'Thanks, Will.'

'See,' said Nat, nudging her with his usual lack of tact. 'Told you he'd be fine.'

'I'm glad you've turned up,' Will said. 'I have a surprise for you.'

Nat raised an eyebrow. 'For me? What is it?'

'You'll see soon enough,' Will promised him, smiling.

Nat seemed highly suspicious. His gaze fell upon Rhiannon and he gave her an insolent look. 'Ginger Spice, eh? Love the kinky red boots. Very apt for a scarlet woman.'

Rhiannon rolled her eyes. 'Yes, very droll. Sophie's already done the scarlet jokes, Nat. It's old news.'

She could have embarrassed him by pointing out that Nat and Georgia's costumes — Robin Hood and Maid Marion — did *not* fall within the brief for the theme of the evening. The fact that she didn't was typical Rhiannon. He wished Nat would see what a kind person she was.

He glanced around, hoping to catch sight of Lexi returning, and his eyes fell on a fair-haired woman walking through the marquee, gazing around her as if searching for someone.

He turned to Nat. 'Your surprise is here!'

Nat peered round. 'Where?'

'Over there. Look!'

Nat followed his gaze, and Will watched, surprised to see the colour drain from his cousin's face.

'Who's that?' Rhiannon peered across the marquee toward Will's surprise guest.

'Bloody hell,' murmured Nat. 'It's Rebecca!'

'Rebecca? Your sister?' Georgia turned her head, clearly anxious to see the new member of Nat's family.

'What the hell is she doing here?' Nat swallowed then glanced at Will. 'You invited her?'

'Of course,' he said, a little puzzled that his surprise evidently hadn't gone down as well as he'd hoped. 'I thought you'd love to see her. It's been months, after all.'

'I thought you got on with your sister?' said Georgia.

'I do, I just ... I won't be a minute. Need the loo.' Nat pushed back his chair, and as Will watched, baffled, he skirted around the edge of the marquee, undoubtedly avoiding Rebecca, and dashed outside.

'Well, how peculiar,' said Rhiannon.

Will smiled a welcome as his other cousin appeared at his side. 'Rebecca! I'm so glad you could make it.'

'Hello, Will. Wasn't sure I was going to, to be honest. This place doesn't exactly hold happy memories for me, what with Pa's bloody obsession with it, and all the rows it caused, but hey ho. A party's a party, when all's said and done, and besides, I haven't seen Nat for ages. Can't believe you've given him a job. What *can* have got into you? And into him, come to that. Never thought I'd see the day when he actually worked for a living.'

She gave a tinkling laugh, slipping into the chair recently occupied by her brother while throwing curious looks at the two women. 'Bloody hell, Will, you're spoilt for choice tonight. Which one's your girlfriend then?'

Will could barely breathe. What could he say to that? Not what he longed to say, that much was certain.

Luckily, Rhiannon seemed to take control. She reached out a hand to Rebecca, smiling warmly. 'Hello, I'm Rhiannon, an old friend of Will's. This is Bernie, Will's estate manager and good friend, and this,' she said, indicating Georgia, 'is your brother's girlfriend, Georgia.'

'Pleased to meet you,' said Georgia, nodding, with evident shyness, at the glamorous blonde.

'You and Nat?' Rebecca laughed. 'I can't believe it! You mean he's actually dating you? Properly? Like, taking you out and stuff? Not just shagging you senseless, then walking away as if you were worthless scum? Jesus, Will, what have you done to him?'

Georgia visibly bristled with indignation, and Will sighed. He'd forgotten how tactless Rebecca could be.

He gave Georgia a reassuring smile. 'They've been seeing each other for quite a while, and Nat is completely smitten, I assure you.'

'Fuck me, wonders will never cease,' said Rebecca, looking Georgia up and down with curious eyes.

Bernie sighed and stood up. 'Need another pint. Excuse me.'

'So, Will, tell me all about life as the new baronet,' said Rebecca. 'Bet you've got a queue of women gagging to be the new Lady Boden-Kean, haven't you?'

Rhiannon gave her a dazzling smile. 'I do love those earrings, Rebecca. Exquisite. Where *did* you get them?'

Chapter 40

I managed to get out of the marquee, in spite of being waylaid by Dad, Eliza, Rose and Woody, who were all in tears and couldn't tell me enough times how beautiful I looked, and how wonderful Will and I had been together on the dance floor, and how it was like Cinderella come to life.

After thanking them, and assuring them that, yes, I was coming back, and yes, I was going to sort things out with Will properly, I dodged between Meggie and Ben, who made an impressive Queen Victoria and John Brown, headed past the security guards, who eyed me very suspiciously, and rushed to the house, where another security guard, who'd been hired to patrol the outside of the house and grounds, grudgingly allowed me access to the Hall.

I could hear Buttons' mournful crying as I entered the west wing. Will had left him in the kitchen, not wanting him to find a way into the marquee, which he probably would have, somehow, in spite of the vigilance of the two security guards. I opened the kitchen door, and he bounded up to me, eager for a cuddle.

'Bless you, are you feeling abandoned?' I said, fondling his silky ears affectionately. 'It's just for a few hours, Buttons. Promise. Before you know it, this will all be over and life will be back to normal.'

Normal. What was normal any more, I wondered? I shivered, knowing that tonight was going to be the biggest night of my life. The night when I took that leap of faith. Will was so perfect, and

I'd never seen him look more handsome. His love for me was written all over his face, and he'd had the courage of his convictions, putting himself at risk again, after I'd already hurt him. It was my turn to step up.

I made sure Buttons had enough water, then turned to leave. Poor Darcey was probably going frantic in her room. I realised I hadn't even had the decency to ask her what she was wearing. Selfish. That was me. Thoroughly self-absorbed.

Buttons whimpered as I opened the door, and I sighed. 'Okay, you can come and find Darcey with me, but then you'll have to go back in here. Sorry, boy, but you can't go into the marquee.'

He needed no further invitation, bounding out of the door before I'd even finished speaking. He waited in the passage, and I laughed and headed upstairs to the upper north side, realising after a moment that I was humming the music Will and I had just waltzed to, and smiling to myself.

Reaching Darcey's room, I knocked twice, and when she didn't answer, I opened the door and peered round. Her suitcase was on the bed, and I felt a pang of sadness, realising that she would be leaving tomorrow. I would really miss her. I hoped she'd keep in touch with me, wherever she ended up.

Noticing a large, white floppy hat and a pair of sunglasses on the bed, I frowned. Was she going abroad? A long black wig was on the dressing table, and I stared at it, puzzled. Was that part of her costume? It seemed she'd changed her mind about wearing it.

'She must have gone down the other stairs,' I said to Buttons, who tilted his head, clearly agreeing with every word. 'Maybe she's already in the marquee. Come on then, back to the kitchen for you, I'm afraid.'

We headed downstairs, stopping halfway down the first flight, as Nat came bounding up towards us. He seemed agitated and was obviously concerned to bump into me.

'What are you doing up here?' I said. 'And what the hell are you wearing?'

He didn't give me a sarcastic retort, which was surprising. 'Just wondered where Darcey is. Still getting ready?'

I frowned. Why would he care? 'She's not in her room. We must have missed her. She probably went down the back stairs.'

'Oh, hell.' He ran a hand through his hair, looking stressed.

'What's the big deal? What's going on?'

'Nothing. Nothing.' He turned to go back downstairs. 'I have to see Georgia. Explain things to her. And Will.' He glanced up at me, his face ashen. 'God, what a mess. Looks like you're going to have your revenge, after all.'

I stared after him. I had no idea what he was talking about, but the odd thing was, I didn't particularly care. I had no interest in Nat's games. I didn't mind at all about him and Georgia. I wasn't even curious to know why he was searching for Darcey. All I could think about was getting back to Will, and in that moment I knew for sure. I was ready to make that leap of faith for him, and that was all that mattered.

I was about to follow Nat when an impulse suddenly took over. Winking at Buttons, I hurried down the last few stairs to the first floor landing, and headed to The Earl's Bedroom. It was stupid, but it felt important to see William Kearton — to tell him that Will had dressed in his honour, and I in Elinor's, and that the two of them hadn't been forgotten. A few more moments wouldn't make any difference.

I pushed open the door, and Buttons bounded ahead. We both stopped dead at the same time.

The hidden door in the panelling stood open. I stared at it, shocked, and stepped forward, noticing as I did so that there was a torch on the bed. But who knew about the room? No one, except for Will, Bernie and myself. Will and Bernie were both in the marquee. Someone else had clearly discovered it. But who? And how?

The answer to at least one of those questions came to me almost instantly. Nat. No wonder he'd looked so shifty. All that rubbish about searching for Darcey! But what had he been up to down there? Something to Will's disadvantage, I'd bet.

Without stopping to think about it, I grabbed the torch and flicked it on, telling Buttons to stay as I pushed on the oak beam and squeezed through the gap in the brickwork. It was a real struggle, considering the width of my dress. I had to turn sideways, hold my breath, and manoeuvre my skirts inch by inch until I was standing on the landing. I knew, deep down, that I should've changed first, but I was too impatient. Whatever Nat had done, I was going to spoil it for him. Was he hiding something down there? God, was he *stealing* from Will?

As I stepped forward, I almost screamed in fright as something brushed against me. I swung the torch, terrified, then leaned against the wall, panting in relief as I saw Buttons looking up at me, his tail wagging furiously. He seemed delighted to have finally been allowed into the secret place, and even though he'd disobeyed me, I had to admit I was quite pleased to have his company.

'Okay, you can come with me,' I said, 'but stay behind me and go slowly. No overtaking.'

Not that he had a choice. My skirts were so wide that they took up the entire width of the twisting stairway. I could only just get down there myself, so Buttons had no chance of passing me.

As we reached the bottom of the first flight of stairs, he barged into me. 'If you don't want to be sent back in disgrace, calm yourself down,' I whispered back at him, then stepped forward.

Without warning, the ground seemed to give way beneath my feet, and I found myself falling.

Buttons barked frantically.

Then there was only darkness.

****

'What time is it?' Will was growing increasingly agitated. Nat's mysterious disappearance, combined with Lexi's departure, had made him edgy.

'Nearly nine,' Bernie said, checking his watch, then draining his fourth glass of beer.

Will looked at him curiously. Something was troubling him, but what? And who was the mysterious Yoko that Rhiannon had mentioned?

'Bernie, would you accompany me to the bar?' Rhiannon's voice was gentle. Will watched, surprised, as Bernie, after a moment's hesitation, nodded and stumbled to his feet.

'Are those two at it?' demanded Rebecca, as Rhiannon and Bernie headed, arm in arm, towards the bar.

'Good grief, of course not!'

'Hmm. Rhiannon, how do I know that name? Jesus! Is that Rhiannon Bone? Ma told me all about her. Uncle Paul's dirty little secret.' Rebecca started to laugh. 'How come you're still friends with her? Nat's absolutely livid, and I can't say I blame him. She well and truly conned Uncle Paul there, didn't she? Getting herself knocked up, I mean. Mind you, serves him right, the randy old lizard.'

'Rebecca, if you don't mind—' began Will, but was cut off by someone calling his name.

'Will! Will, over here!'

He barely had time to register who was shouting across to him, before Rebecca's eyes widened in surprise and she squealed. 'Fuck me! Isn't that Darcey? What the hell is she doing here? Cooee! Darcey!'

Several heads turned, as her shrill call echoed round the marquee. Will watched in astonishment, as Darcey, having caught sight of his cousin waving her hand in the air, stopped dead in her tracks, turned quite white, then rushed back out of the marquee.

Within seconds, Bernie was running after her, with Rhiannon in pursuit.

'What the hell is going on?' Will murmured, turning to Rebecca as a sudden thought struck him. 'And how do you know Darcey?'

'Well, of course I know her. She used to go out with Nat,' said Rebecca, puzzled. 'At least, he shagged her when he felt like it, which constitutes a passionate courtship for Nat. No offence,' she added, giving Georgia a bored nod.

'She did what?' Will and Georgia exchanged incredulous glances.

Will's mind raced. What sort of cruel charade had the two of them been playing?

He pushed back his chair. 'I'm going to get to the bottom of this,' he said. 'Darcey and Nat have a lot of explaining to do.'

'I'm coming with you,' said Georgia. 'If he's been stringing me along all this time … Christ, I've been a fool. I want some answers.'

'Well, you're not leaving me out,' said Rebecca cheerfully. 'This party's turning out to be more fun than I thought.'

****

Will raced outside, his mind running through all the possibilities of why Nat and Darcey had lied to him all that time. He cursed as he collided with the two security guards.

'Blimey, there's more people out here than in the chuffing marquee,' said Gav.

'Sorry, can you get out of the way,' he said, pushing past the disapproving pair.

He headed for the gravel path, to find Nat surrounded by a stony-faced Georgia, an anxious-looking Darcey, and a highly amused Rebecca.

To one side, Rhiannon was gripping Bernie's arm, as if preventing him from moving forward, as Nat's sister drawled, 'I appear to have dropped you in it, Nat. You should have warned me your fling with Darcey was a secret.'

'Jesus, all we need is the cauldron,' he heard Nat mutter as he approached. 'Just back off, will you? This is between me and Will now.'

'What have you done, Nat?' Will didn't know what to think. Guilt was written all over both his cousin's and Darcey's faces.

'I'm sorry, Will.' Nat cast an apologetic glance at Georgia. 'And to you, too, Georgie. You've got to believe me, I was a different person back then. I've changed. You've changed me — both of you. It was a stupid thing to do. I've hated myself for ages, and we did try to put it right, didn't we, Darcey?'

'What the hell are you talking about?' Georgia sounded bewildered, and Will rubbed the back of his head, completely lost.

'Is it true? You and Nat?' Bernie demanded. His voice was

hoarse, and Will realised that he'd just solved the mystery of the mysterious Yoko.

'I think,' said Darcey miserably, 'that we'd better just tell everyone the truth, Nat.'

'Sounds like a good idea to me,' said Rhiannon.

Everyone stared at Nat. He looked thoroughly ashamed. 'I'm sorry,' he said. 'Rebecca's right. I did used to go out with Darcey. Well—'

'What he means by that,' said Darcey softly, 'is that I thought we were going out. In actual fact, I was just someone to pass the time with. What I thought was a blossoming relationship was a bit of fun to him.'

'I've apologised for that over and over again,' protested Nat.

'I know. I'm just explaining,' she said.

He sighed. 'Fair enough. We met in London, at a fundraising event for ECHOES, ironically.'

'So, you did actually work for ECHOES?' interrupted Will. 'That, at least, was true?'

Darcey looked offended. 'Of course it was true. My CV and references were completely authentic, I swear to you.'

'Well, that's something,' he muttered.

Nat gazed at Darcey with sympathy, as she hung her head. 'Anyway, true to form, I was a shit. We were having fun, but then Darcey's mother got ill, and I had no patience for that at all. I didn't stand by her, and when she went home to care for her mum, I basically dropped her. I'm not proud of the fact,' he said defensively. 'Like I said, I've changed now.'

Georgia put her hand to her mouth. 'So, all this time, you and her...'

'No! Never!' Nat sounded horrified. 'Tell her, Darcey, please.'

'Nothing has happened between myself and Nat since I arrived here,' she said. 'When he called me, asking me to do him a favour, I thought, maybe — well, maybe it was the start of something again. Then I arrived here, and I realised Nat was seeing Lexi. It quickly became clear that our arrangement was purely business. I blamed Lexi at first, I'm afraid. I was convinced she'd seduced him. I wasn't very kind to her. Then, when Nat betrayed her with

Georgia, I realised that's just who Nat is. *Was*,' she corrected herself quickly. 'I do think it's different with you, Georgia. In fact, I know it is. Nat loves you. He's told me so, and I believe him.'

'But what's this arrangement you mentioned?' Will said. 'Clearly, you were both working together to deceive me for some reason. What was it about?'

Darcey looked at him miserably. 'I'm really sorry, Will. When Nat called me, I was broke. I'd had a sort of breakdown after Mum died, and I'd given up my job. I was unemployed and trying to pick up the pieces of my life again. I was about to lose my home, and I didn't know what to do next. He offered me a temporary place to stay, a job, good salary, and a bonus if—' she swallowed 'If I could persuade you to sell the Hall to Grant's Hotels.'

'What?' Will shook his head. 'So, the whole interview was a set up? No wonder you took charge of shortlisting the candidates, Nat. I really am predictable, aren't I? You knew exactly who to choose, to make me think Darcey was the most suitable applicant.'

'Explains the building quote, an' all,' muttered Bernie. 'No wonder it were so high.'

'Of course!' Will couldn't believe Darcey had been so cruel. 'You got that firm in to give me an outrageously high quote, hoping I'd give in and sell up.'

'But then I changed my mind,' said Nat. 'I brought in another firm to put things right, didn't I?'

'We both felt terrible,' said Darcey, 'truly we did. I liked you immediately, Will, and really wanted to help you turn the Hall around. And Nat was wracked with guilt after you gave him a second chance.'

'But you didn't get on,' said Will. 'I had to lock you in the room together to make you sort things out. Or was that a lie, too?'

'No,' said Nat. 'Darcey was furious about Lexi, and I was angry that she'd expected us to pick up where we left off. Then, when I called in Marcus Leigh and Sons, after persuading her to get that fake building firm in, I made her look a complete idiot, and she was livid. Thought I was trying to stitch her up. Being locked in, forced to talk, was the turning point for us. I explained why I'd done what I did, and that I hated lying to you. She confessed she felt the same. We realised we both wanted the same thing, and we resolved to forget the past and work together to help you.'

'Huh,' said Bernie. 'As easy as that, eh? After he'd dumped you in Will's bed and made a complete fool of you, you just forgave him?'

'Yes,' said Darcey, eyeing him steadily. 'I did. Because, the truth is, once I realised I didn't love him, none of it seemed important any more. And I knew I didn't love him, because I loved someone else. Even though that someone else is too ashamed to admit that we're in a relationship.'

Bernie's face was scarlet as everyone turned to him.

'Why don't you tell her what you told me?' said Rhiannon gently, nudging him.

Bernie cleared his throat. 'It's not that I'm ashamed of you,' he murmured. 'How could I be? You're beautiful. Far too good for the likes of me. I'm too old for you, and that's what everyone will say.'

'Do you really think I care what everyone else says?' demanded Darcey tearfully. 'You were willing to let me move away, rather than tell everyone we were together. That's all I care about.'

'So, you and Darcey...' Will's voice trailed off. How hadn't he picked up on that? Bernie had been like a father to him, and he hadn't even noticed that his closest friend had fallen in love. Well, that explained all the trips to other country houses together, he supposed. 'You handed in your notice because of Bernie?'

'How can I stay here,' she said with a sob, 'when he thinks our relationship is some dirty little secret?'

In an instant, Bernie was at her side, gathering her in his arms. 'I don't think that,' he said, stroking her hair. 'But look at me. Look at you. There's nigh on twenty-five years between us. I'm nearly sixty, for God's sake. Have you any idea how much gossip there was about Sir Paul and Rhiannon here? The things they said…' His voice trailed off, and he shrugged at Rhiannon apologetically. 'Sorry. No offence meant.'

'I rather think,' said Rhiannon, 'that the gossip was more because Sir Paul was married at the time, and because, well, he was lord of the manor. People had a very fixed idea about the way he should have behaved. People round here love you, Bernie, and I can only imagine that they will be as delighted as I am that you've found true happiness with someone who clearly adores you. Love is ageless,' she finished. 'You should take a chance. Really, what have you got to lose?'

'I don't want people pitying her,' said Bernie.

'Pitying me!' Darcey's eyes widened. 'They'll envy me. I'm loved by the most wonderful, kind, interesting person I've ever met. I *am* loved, aren't I?'

Bernie looked down at her, his eyes bright with tears. 'You're loved, all right. But are you sure this is what you want?'

'More than anything in the world,' she said. 'I don't want to leave here. This place feels like home — these people have become my family. But if you don't want me, I *will* go, Bernie. That's how strongly I feel about you.'

He hugged her to him. 'You don't have to go,' he told her. 'You'll never have to leave here again.'

'Well, this is all lovely,' said Rebecca, 'but are you seriously expecting us to believe that you've turned over a new leaf, Nat? That you're actually in love with this Georgia, and that you want to work for a living? Because, I have to say, it sounds jolly unlikely to me.'

'I've never had a purpose in my life before,' said Nat, taking hold of Georgia's hand, 'but now I do. Georgie means the world to me, and so does Will. And this place — I get it now, Becks. What Pa felt, I mean. I don't know. It gets to you, somehow. I just wanted to make it up to Will and make this place pay its way. That's all.' He gave an embarrassed laugh. 'We both felt bloody awful about the whole business, didn't we, Darcey? We've even been poring over old maps, trying to figure out where the earl could have hidden his treasure.'

'The treasure!' Darcey suddenly squealed in excitement. 'That's what I was coming to tell you! I finally found it. At least, I'm absolutely sure I have. There's an old chest down there, and from what I could see when I swung the torch around, no one's been down there for God knows how long. It has to be the treasure, doesn't it?'

Nat's eyes widened. 'Was it where you thought?'

'Sort of, but there was this other bit. Nicholas Owen was a genius. I mean, talk about a triple bluff … Oh, I'll simply have to show you all. It's so exciting.'

'So, that's what you've been doing?' said Bernie, astounded. 'Treasure hunting? No wonder you're still not in costume. So much for our John and Yoko act.'

Will felt a sudden anxiety. 'Darcey, did you see Lexi in the house?'

She shook her head. 'No. Should I have done?'

'She was trying to find you. Thought you might need some help with your costume.'

'I saw her upstairs just before I came out here,' Nat said. 'I was trying to find Darcey — tip her off that Rebecca had turned up and warn her to stay out of the way. Lexi told me Darcey wasn't there. But that was ages ago. She was right behind me.'

'What on earth can she be doing?' said Darcey.

Will rubbed the back of his head. She wouldn't, would she? She wouldn't go home and leave him? He'd insisted they had to talk. Had he frightened her off again?

'She wouldn't have gone in The Earl's Bedroom, would she?' said Nat suddenly. 'I mean, you did shut the door, right?'

'What door?' Will looked from one to the other of them, as they exchanged knowing glances.

'Will…' Darcey's voice was shaky. 'I've just thought of something awful. I was so excited, I left the passage door open. And, oh, no! I didn't replace the trap door!'

'What are you talking about?' Will said, but just as suddenly, he realised what she was trying to tell him.

Giving a strangled cry, he turned and ran towards the house.

'Where on earth are we going?' he heard Rebecca call, as they all ran after him.

'To stop Lexi,' he gasped. 'Please, God, don't let us be too late.'

****

I'd no idea how long I'd been lying in the darkness. It could have been minutes or hours. I wasn't even sure it was still Saturday. The blackness swirled around me, pressing down on me, until I could hardly breathe. The pain crushed me, and I felt increasingly nauseated, the cold, stone floor rough against my cheek. My eyes closed. I just wanted to block everything out, to sleep, but a little voice kept urging me to stay awake, that I mustn't give in to the darkness.

I thought of Dad and Eliza, Amy and the twins, Joe and Charlie. As my thoughts became ever more confused, I hung onto the image of Will's face, and tears rolled down my cheeks as I realised that, out of everyone, it was the thought of never seeing him again that was the most painful of all.

I knew I had to do something. I couldn't just lie there waiting for death.

Taking a deep breath, I gathered my courage and tried to roll over. A scream echoed around that brick coffin. The world swung, then the darkness descended again.

Some movement brought me back. I could hear breathing, feel something wriggling beside me. Was it a rat? There was a whimper, and a dry tongue licked my face.

Buttons. How had he got in there? Had he fallen, or had he jumped?

I opened my eyes, and the darkness smothered me. Black shapes formed, looming over me and then disappearing again. I cringed in fear, then cried out in pain. I was in hell.

I shivered, the cold of the brick tomb seeping into my bones. There was another whimper, then a warm shape curled up against me, as if determined to keep me from freezing.

Let me sleep, Buttons, I pleaded in my mind, as the dizziness and pain overwhelmed me, but he wouldn't. Each time I let the blackness carry me away, he would nudge me awake, back into a world of fear and nausea and agonising discomfort. My scalp prickled in fear as I realised that I was, in effect, buried alive. I was going to die here. No one would come.

Dimly, I was aware of Buttons whimpering softly and nuzzling my face. But it was no use. I was beyond help. I closed my eyes, unable to stay awake any longer, and as Buttons licked my cheek, I took comfort from the fact that at least I wasn't going to die alone.

'Lexi?'

A soft, gentle voice. A warm hand stroking my forehead.

'Pass me that torch. Careful.'

Pain, searing through me. The world swirling, carrying me away, as if I were nothing more than a speck of dust in a whirlwind. A scream, echoing through my head.

'Don't move her. We have to get help.'

'She needs an ambulance. Run back upstairs, tell them we need help to get her out of here.'

A yelp. Buttons. Someone was hurting Buttons.

'Lexi?' That voice again. Soft, soothing. Full of love and concern.

'Don't worry, we'll get you out of here. Help's on its way.'

'This is all my fault. How could I have been so stupid?'

'You weren't to know, love. We need to go back up, make room for the paramedics.'

'My poor baby.'

'She'll be all right, Gabriel. Just stay calm.'

'Did you get through?'

'An ambulance is on its way.'

The world stopped spinning quite so quickly. I groaned as the pain in my shoulder and arm intensified. My head was pounding. Where was I?

'Don't move, sweetheart, don't move.'

My eyes flickered open, and I knew I'd died. 'William?'

Green eyes, bright with tears, looked down at me. Above a neat, pointed beard, soft lips trembled with emotion.

'I've never heard her call you that before.'

'She thinks you're Lord Kearton.'

'It's me. It's Will.'

'The treasure.'

'It doesn't matter, Lexi. Don't worry about anything.'

'No, the treasure. The real treasure. Rhiannon said...' What had Rhiannon said? I couldn't remember any more. 'It hurts. I'm scared.'

'Don't be scared. I swear to you, you're going to be all right. Trust me.'

I was going to be all right. Will had said so. But the blackness was descending again.

'Just breathe into this, Lexi. It will take the edge off the pain.' Another voice. Calm. Reassuring. Something was on my face. I found suddenly that I could breathe properly again. The world seemed to be singing to me. There was a rushing sound in my head. The earth spun again, but in a rather pleasant way. The pain was there, but it was as if it was standing apart from me, somehow.

'Careful, careful.'

'Please don't hurt her. Please...'

'She'll be all right, Will.'

Dimly, I felt someone squeeze my hand. Someone murmured *I love you*. I think — maybe — it was me.

Chapter 41

'I'm sure I'm up to going home today,' I said. 'I feel so much better already.'

'You heard the doctor,' said Eliza sternly. 'One more night. You've had a rough time of it, and they want to make sure your concussion is healing.'

'Not to mention your fractured clavicle and ribs.' Dad shook his head, sinking into the chair by the side of my bed and burying his head in his hands. 'God, Lexi, you frightened the life out of me.'

'I scared myself a bit, too,' I admitted. I still felt a tremor of fear whenever I remembered bits and pieces of what had happened the previous evening. I couldn't remember it all, which Dad said was to be expected. I was concussed and would have been drifting in and out of consciousness.

He'd been more worried about that than the broken collarbone and fractured ribs, although it was those two conditions that were causing me the most discomfort and inconvenience. My left arm was strapped up, and I would have to return to the hospital at a later date to check that the break was healing satisfactorily. I was in for a long period of rest and recuperation, as well as physiotherapy and a bucket load of painkillers. Dad said it could take up to four months to heal properly, which meant I wouldn't be returning to work any time soon. Not that I had a job to return to. I had, after all, given in my notice.

I smiled to myself. Somehow, I didn't think Will was going to hold me to that.

A nurse pushed open the door of my room, smiling as her gaze landed on where I sat up, chatting. 'You're looking much brighter this evening,' she told me. 'You had us quite worried last night. Are you up to any more visitors?'

'I have more?'

She rolled her eyes. 'Do you have more? There's a waiting room full of people out there, all begging to be allowed in. I've told them, it's two to a bed, but they're practically offering me bribes. You're a very popular young lady.' She grinned. 'So, do you want to see them?'

'Yes, please.'

'We'll wait outside,' said Eliza.

The nurse shook her head at them. 'You're in a single room. You won't be disturbing other patients. I won't tell if you don't,' she whispered.

'Can I have a word with you outside?' Dad stood and followed her out of the room.

Eliza smiled. 'He's checking you're really okay. He's been worried sick. You should have seen him last night when they were getting you into the ambulance. Thank God for Flynn, blinding him with science. I was useless. All I could do was cry.' She shook her head. 'When I think of you all alone down there, all that time...'

I twisted the sheet between my fingers, not wanting to remember. I glanced up as the door was pushed open, glad of the distraction when a crowd of people shuffled in. I checked through them, eager to see a shock of thick brown hair and a pair of green eyes, but Will wasn't there. I tried to push down the sense of disappointment, and managed a smile as Charlie, Joe, Rose, Flynn, and Georgia gathered round my bed. They held out photographs to me.

'What are these?' I asked, as pictures of tulips, gerberas, lilies, roses and God knows what else, flashed before my eyes.

'We all got you flowers,' said Charlie, 'and then, can you believe it, we were informed you can't bring flowers into a hospital any more. The world's gone mad.'

'So, we all took photos,' said Rose. 'And then Joe printed them off for you.'

'There's loads,' I said. 'Whose flowerbeds did you raid?'

'There's some from Sophie and Archie, too,' said Eliza. 'And Fuchsia and Pandora.'

'And Tally, and Chrissie and Robbie, and Meggie and Ben,' added Charlie.

'And Rhiannon and Derry,' said Rose. 'And Woody, and Eddie, and all the girls from Lightweights. And a massive one from Darcey and Bernie. Poor Darcey's absolutely mortified. She's blaming herself. Mind you, Bernie's doing his best to comfort her,' she added with a wink.

'And these,' said Joe, holding up a photograph of a huge bouquet tied with satin ribbon, 'are from your mum.'

'My mum?' I looked at Eliza, who nodded and smiled. 'Your dad called her last night to tell her what had happened. She sent you her love, and she's going to come and see you at the weekend.'

'At the farm?' I eyed her nervously. 'Is that okay?'

'Of course it's okay. We've told her she's welcome to bring her husband, too. That's if it's all right with you, of course.'

'It is,' I said. 'I just don't want to upset Dad.'

'Believe me,' she said softly, 'your dad's so happy that you're all right, he's willing to do anything. Besides, it's a start, isn't it? And we have to start somewhere.'

'Time to build bridges,' said Joe. 'It will take time, but it will be worth it. I just hope she doesn't get hay fever. It's like living in Covent Garden Flower Market at the moment.'

'How are you feeling, pet?' Rose stroked my forehead, pushing tendrils of hair away from my eyes. 'By, you gave us the fright of our lives. Flynn said you looked as rough as a badger's arse when they found you.'

'I don't think those were my exact words,' Flynn protested.

'Well, as good as. What a bloody ordeal. I don't know. Mind you, it's not every day you find treasure that's been hidden for hundreds of years. Quite exciting.'

'It was real,' I murmured. 'I knew it. But I still don't understand how Darcey found it.'

'It's quite a story,' said Georgia. 'But I think it's best if Will tells you everything.'

'Where *is* Will?' I said, feeling hurt that he wasn't around. He'd been with me at the hospital last night. I remembered seeing his anxious face, through a haze of gas and air and morphine. I'd been quite convinced for a short period of time that I'd been visited by the ghost of William Kearton, until I remembered Will had been in costume. How had I forgotten that? I thought of my own dress, which was probably torn and filthy now. What a shame.

'He's on his way,' said Charlie.

'He had to be somewhere,' said Eliza, not looking at me. 'He won't be long.'

I was pretty sure they were keeping something from me, but just then Dad came back in the room with a big smile on his face, evidently reassured that I wasn't about to keel over and die, and announced that Will had arrived and was pacing up and down outside. They all decided it was time they cleared out and left us to it. I was promptly smothered in careful kisses, and Dad and Eliza promised they'd be back to collect me the next day to take me home, and everyone said they loved me, and Georgia blew me a kiss, which I returned, and the door closed and all was silent.

I sat waiting, plucking at the bedding with nervous fingers. The minutes ticked by, then just as I was thinking he'd gone home, the door opened and he stood there, watching me uncertainly.

'Will.' I so wanted to hold out my arms to him, but obviously that was impossible. Instead I stretched out one hand, carefully, nervously, and he stepped forward and took hold of it with equal tentativeness.

'I was so worried about you,' he said softly.

'I know. I remember your voice last night, telling me that I was going to be all right. I believed you.'

'You did?'

'Yes, of course I did. I trust you.'

He sat carefully on the edge of the bed. 'Do you remember much about what happened?'

'It's a bit blurry and confused,' I admitted. 'I just remember thinking I was going to die. I was in so much pain, and it was so cold.' I stared at him, suddenly scared. 'Buttons! He was with me. He tried to keep me warm and conscious, I'm sure of it. God, is he all right?'

He nodded. 'He will be. I've just come from the vet's, that's why I'm a bit late. I wanted to see how he was doing for myself, and to thank him for taking care of you for me. He's fractured his pelvis, and he's feeling a bit sorry for himself, but the vet thinks he's going to be all right.'

'Poor Buttons,' I said tearfully. 'He did it for me, I'm sure of it. He saw me fall, so he knew the trap door was there. He must have jumped in to try to help me. All that time he was comforting me, and he must have been in agony.'

'He certainly made plenty of noise when we were getting him out,' Will admitted.

'I don't remember hearing it,' I said.

'Well, you were in and out of consciousness. I'm not surprised.' He shook his head. 'I was so scared, Lexi. I thought — I thought I'd lost you all over again.'

'I still don't know exactly what happened,' I said. 'How did Darcey know where the treasure was? And,' I added, remembering my conviction that Nat was the culprit, 'was Nat in on it?'

Will rubbed his thumb over the back of my hand, gazing down at it as he seemed to consider what to say. 'I suppose he was,' he said. 'But it's nothing sinister, I promise, although I can understand why it would appear that way.' He looked at me apologetically. 'When he first arrived, he was sure he could persuade me to sell the estate. When I wouldn't play ball, he needed a Plan B. He admitted to me that he manipulated you into believing that employing a House Manager was your idea, but that he'd actually planned it for a while. He had someone in mind, you see. Someone who would try to persuade me that the Hall could never pay its way, and I'd be better off turning it over to that hotel chain he kept banging on about. An ex-girlfriend, in fact. Darcey.'

'Nat and Darcey? You have to be kidding me? Are you telling me it was all a big fat lie, right from the start?'

He squeezed my hand. 'Shh. Let me explain, and don't get yourself all worked up.'

If it hadn't been for the dull pain in my shoulder, and the fact that I'd not long since taken some painkillers, I might well have got worked up, seeing the way he looked at me, and the way he was holding my hand. Sadly, anything remotely romantic seemed a very long way away. 'Well, go on, then,' I said. 'I want to know everything.'

Softly, he explained the plan that Nat and Darcey had come up with. I listened, stunned, as he recounted how devious and manipulative they'd been. 'And then Nat changed his mind. Unfortunately, Darcey wouldn't leave. He tried to persuade her to go, but she wouldn't. She said she loved it here, and she'd fallen head over heels for Bernie.' He smiled as he added that last bit.

'I know!' I hadn't believed it at first, when Eliza had told me that morning. 'I'm glad she loves him, because it's been obvious for ages that Bernie adores her. But do you really believe Nat changed his mind?'

'I do. I would never have let him stay, if I hadn't thought he meant it when he told me that day that he wanted to help me make Kearton Hall pay its way. I made him promise to be kind to you, but I couldn't just throw him out and leave him with nothing. Besides, if there was any chance that he meant what he said about the Hall mattering to him, I had to build on that. He's my cousin, and I love him. I wanted him to stay. I wanted him to care. I'm sorry I hurt you.'

'It's okay,' I said. 'I understand why you did it. I think I got a bit blinded by my mistrust of Nat. I'm glad he didn't let you down in the end. And I understand why you backed away from me, too. I'm sorry, Will.'

'For what?'

'For what happened the other day. For hurting you so badly. I was an idiot.'

'It's all right,' he said. 'I understand. You don't want to be hurt.

I get that.'

'No, it's not that, at all.' I tried to sit up straight and winced with pain.

'Do you need anything? Shall I get a nurse?'

'No, no. I'm all right. Just this bloody shoulder. It will heal.' I assured him. 'Things do heal, eventually. Did Dad tell you I met my mother?'

He stared at me. 'Your mother? When?'

I smiled. 'It was all rather unexpected. You know when I said I had things on my mind, things at home? Well...'

I told him it all, holding nothing back, even my suspicions about poor Dad.

'That's wonderful, Lexi,' he said, when I'd finished. 'I'm so happy for you.'

I knew he was, too, and given that his own mother hadn't been anywhere near him for years, that was pretty big of him. But what else would I expect from Will?

'You never told me,' I reminded him, 'about how they found the treasure?'

He smiled. 'Well, do you remember that night when Nat planted Darcey in my bed?'

I blushed, remembering the effect the discovery had had on me. 'Yeah. I remember.'

'Well, after all that business, I locked them in the sitting room together and made them sort out their differences. It seems...' His face suddenly turned scarlet. 'It seems, er, that Nat told Darcey that he'd only done it to shake us up. You and me, I mean. He decided we were made for each other, and it was time we knew it. He thought hearing that I'd been in bed with another woman might make you realise that you cared for me. Stupid idea.'

'Not as stupid as you might think,' I admitted. 'It worked. I saw you together. It broke my heart.'

He stared at me. 'What?'

'Carry on with the story,' I said. 'We'll come to that in a minute.'

He hesitated, then cleared his throat. 'Er, well, apparently, when Darcey heard the reason he'd done it, she started to see another side to Nat. It seems she agreed with him. About us, I mean. Anyway, by then, Darcey was completely smitten with Bernie, and was well and truly over Nat. She also admitted to him that she didn't want to leave the Hall because she cared about everyone in it, and wanted to help turn it around. They made a pact to work together, to help in any way they could. Nat had said, jokingly, that the best help would be to find the treasure, and Darcey took it seriously. They started studying old floor plans of the place, and Darcey visited other stately homes known to have priest holes and other hiding places, looking for ideas. I still think they wouldn't have found it, though, if it hadn't been for Bernie.'

'Bernie?'

'He told Darcey about the secret in The Earl's Bedroom. He was so apologetic when he confessed to me, but Darcey had been going on about needing a big attraction to draw people to the Hall, and he was so smitten with her, he confided in her about the secret I'd told him. Darcey told Nat, and they made a thorough examination of the place, at every opportunity they had, convinced that must be where the treasure was hidden.'

'Why didn't they tell us?' I said indignantly. 'We could have helped.'

'Darcey didn't want to get Bernie in trouble with me,' he said. 'And they didn't confide in you because ... Because they both agreed that you were too loyal to me and wouldn't keep it a secret from me.'

'Well,' I admitted, 'they're probably right.'

He squeezed my hand, smiling. 'Unfortunately, they couldn't find anything, and when they saw the tunnel was blocked, they came to the conclusion that perhaps it was behind the wall, and they'd never find it. But Darcey badly wanted to make it up to me before she left, for everything she'd done behind my back. As I said, she'd been researching Owen's work, and had seen examples of priest holes created under landings, and it occurred to her that the passageway would be the ideal spot for a hiding place, because anyone finding that entrance would be so intent on following the tunnel, they wouldn't give much thought to searching for another hidden room. So she decided to give it one last shot. She had to wait until everyone was at the ball to try to find it. When she did, she was so excited that she quite forgot to replace the trap door, and just ran back to the marquee to tell me. Unfortunately, she got waylaid when Rebecca spotted her and recognised her, and, well, you ended up lying down there for all that time. I'm so sorry, Lexi. I can't bear that you were hurt. I'd do anything to protect you. You have to know that.'

'I do know that.'

'Do you? Really?'

'Of course I do. You don't get it, do you? All this time, you've been sure that I was afraid of getting hurt. It wasn't that. I was afraid that *I'd* be the one to hurt you.'

'What?' He looked at me, startled. 'Why would you think that?'

'I don't know. Genetics? The way my mum treated my dad. God, Will, you've no idea how bad it was. I thought, what if I grew up to be that person, too? I was always scared I would become like her. I didn't ever want to do to any man what she did to Dad. It was only as I sat talking to her in Whitby that I started to understand her. She wasn't mad, or bad. She just didn't expect any better from life. She thought Dad was too good for her, and she made that her reality. Well, I don't want that for me.'

'You don't?'

'No. I have to believe that I deserve to be happy, too. I always thought — I don't know — that I'd done something bad. Something wrong. Because Mum didn't want me, and she wasn't happy, and I couldn't make Dad happy, either. It was Eliza who healed him, not me. Then Mum told me something. She said, the memory of Dad's kindness towards her kept that little flame of hope alive in her; a tiny spark that told her she deserved to be loved. I realised you've done the same for me. You've always made me feel safe, and cared about and valued, Will. That's what gives me hope that I can be happy, and that I can make you happy, too.'

I shook my head, hoping that he understood what I meant. 'Deep down, I always knew you were the one. I just couldn't bring myself to admit it, because, of all the people in this world, you're the last one I'd want to hurt. The very last. What I finally realised was that I could never treat you the way Mum treated Dad, because the truth is, I'd rather die than hurt you.' I sighed. 'I wasted so much time with Nat, Robbie, and even Derry. They were safe, you see, because I didn't love them. But you...'

'What about me?' He pulled at the hospital blanket, seeming unable to meet my gaze.

I stroked his face, ignoring the twinge of pain as I leaned forward slightly. 'I can't help myself,' I said. 'I've tried everything I can, but it's no good. I can't stop myself from loving you, Will. And the truth is, I don't *want* to stop myself any more. I want to love you. I want to love you heart, body and soul. And I want you to love me in return.'

The silence hung between us for a moment. He sat completely still, and I wondered what he was thinking. Then slowly he turned to me, and my heart contracted, as I saw the first tears I'd ever seen him cry roll slowly down his cheek.

My hand cupped the back of his neck, and he shuffled closer until our foreheads touched. Then I gently kissed away his tears, knowing that he was my forever love, and I would never, ever hurt him again.

Chapter 42

'Mind the steps. Be careful.'

I laughed, seeing the expression of concern on Will's face. 'I'm fine, stop worrying. I can walk up some steps by myself.'

It's still early days,' he said. 'We don't want to do anything to delay the healing process.'

'Too right we don't,' I agreed. 'Have you any idea how frustrating it is to be strapped up like this?'

'I can imagine,' he said. 'Not being able to hold a knife and fork properly, struggling to dress yourself...'

'I was thinking more of the fact that you and I can't get up close and personal,' I told him. 'I can't wait to show you exactly how much I love you.'

He flushed but laughed. 'Well, I have to admit, I'm looking forward to that day, too,' he admitted. 'In fact, I can't stop thinking about it. But it will be worth waiting for, I promise you that.'

'I'm counting on it,' I said, wrapping my good arm around his neck and kissing him gently on the lips. As always, he responded immediately, and for a few moments, I think we both quite forgot where we were, or that we weren't alone.

'All right, you two, enough already. Children present,' Eliza said, but she was smiling.

I grinned at her, feeling a bit bashful, but too happy to really care. I took hold of Will's hand, and he squeezed it gently.

'Are you ready for this?' he asked Amy, who nodded in excitement.

'Bloody hell,' said Rose, 'what are we waiting for? Are you going to cut a ribbon, or something?'

Will threw open the door and waved everyone inside. 'Welcome to you all, the first VIP guests of the newly reopened Kearton Hall.'

Everyone clapped, and we all hurried into the Great Hall, where the first warden was waiting for us, to relay any information we required about the room.

'Ooh, it's gorgeous in here,' said Eliza. She nudged Dad, laughing. 'Maybe we could have portraits of us painted to hang in our new house.'

'God forbid,' he muttered. 'Although, I think there should be one of Will up here now, don't you agree, Lexi?'

'You're absolutely right,' I said, wondering why I hadn't considered it before. 'The Fourteenth Baronet deserves his place on the wall.'

'To echo your father,' said Will, 'God forbid.'

Sophie and Archie gazed up at the portraits of the Boden-Kean ancestors, and Sophie cooed about how important she felt, knowing that her husband was the personal solicitor to such a noble family, which made both Will and Archie flush with embarrassment.

Joe and Charlie wandered off to examine the portraits in the Inner Hall, and we smiled as we heard their astonished declarations that they'd never have believed how good-looking Sir Paul used to be. Meanwhile, Dad, Eliza and Amy, along with Rose and Flynn, got very excited by the Georgian Room, with its display of smuggling artefacts and information about the Sixth Baronet.

Nat and Georgia came strolling into the hallway, arm in arm.

'How's Buttons?' I said immediately.

'Looking much brighter,' Georgia said, smiling. 'He's a bit fed up having to be confined for a while, but it will soon pass.'

'And Woody's spoiling him rotten,' added Nat. 'By the time she's through, he'll probably be faking his injuries, just to stay with her.'

'I must go and see him,' I said.

'In a moment,' Will promised. 'There's something else I want you to see first.'

'Really? What's that?'

'Haven't you told her yet?' Nat asked.

Will shook his head, and I eyed them all suspiciously. 'Told me what? What are you up to?'

'About our new exhibit,' Nat said, grinning. 'It's pretty special.'

'What new exhibit?' I said.

'I'm going to show you, if I can get a word in edgeways,' said Will. 'Can you keep everyone else occupied down here, while I take her upstairs?'

'Of course. Leave it with us,' Nat said.

'Oh, Lexi, you're going to love it,' Georgia promised.

Will took my hand and led me carefully up the stairs, reminding me, as if I needed reminding, that I'd had a nasty injury and had to be careful. We climbed to the first floor and halted as Darcey and Bernie came out of The Earl's Bedroom.

'How are you, Lexi?'

I smiled. 'Honestly, Darcey, you don't have to ask me every time you see me. I'm doing fine. Look, it was an accident. Stop worrying about it, okay?'

She nodded. 'I'd hug you, if I could, but I daren't.'

'Best not,' I agreed. 'What were you doing in The Earl's Bedroom, anyway? I hope you weren't testing out William's bed!'

I laughed at their shocked expressions, then winced in pain, which I supposed served me right.

'We'll leave you to it,' said Bernie. 'Got a long afternoon ahead of us, choosing new curtains. Can't wait.' He rolled his eyes, but his smile was a dead giveaway.

They walked away murmuring to each other, and I looked at Will. 'Are they moving in together?'

'They are. I'm letting them have the gatehouse. It needs some decorating and cleaning up, but they're both very excited about the prospect of living there. Best of all, it frees Bernie's cottage up. Chrissie and Robbie are going to rent it. You can't begin to imagine how happy they looked when they came to sign the tenancy agreement.'

'I bet I *can* imagine!' I laughed, delighted that my friends were finally going to have the home they'd dreamed of. 'So, what are we doing here, anyway?' I said, nodding at the bedroom door.

'Why don't you see for yourself?' He opened it, and I stepped inside, feeling a sudden tremor as I remembered the last time I'd been in this room.

Taking my hand, he led me through into the adjoining dressing room, and I looked around, astonished. Two mannequins stood opposite the door, wearing familiar costumes. I looked at him questioningly.

'I thought it would make a nice touch,' he said. 'Meggie very kindly had them cleaned, then repaired them both. They were rather the worse for wear after what happened, but they look as good as new, don't they? Of course, if you don't want your costume on display, I'll remove it. I just thought…'

'What *is* this?' I asked, eyeing the space curiously.

He smiled. 'Can't you see?'

I gazed up at the wall and shivered suddenly, as I noticed a portrait I'd only seen in a photograph before. 'William and Margaret Kearton,' I said quietly. I gasped as my eyes fell upon a smaller painting, hanging on the wall opposite. A young couple smiled back at me. This was no stylised portrait. This revealed their true faces, and they were both beautiful. The man's arms were around the woman's waist, and their faces were alight with happiness and love. I would know those green eyes anywhere. I turned to Will, feeling a sudden excitement. 'Is that—?'

'William and Elinor,' he confirmed. A faint flush of pink spread across his face. 'Everyone who's seen it has remarked that they can now see the resemblance between him and me. I kind of see it myself now.'

'I told you,' I said. 'I saw it straight away. He's gorgeous.'

He grinned, looking bashful. 'Well, I wouldn't go that far, but they both look very happy, don't they?'

I gazed up at them, feeling a warm glow spread through my body. 'They do. Where did you find this? I haven't seen it before.'

'You won't have,' he said. 'It was rolled up and hidden in a chest for almost four hundred years, in a room under some stairs.'

I looked round sharply, wincing as the pain in my ribs and shoulder reminded me that I shouldn't do stupid things like that. 'It was in that room? You mean — you mean, *this* was the Third Earl's treasure?' I looked back at it. It wasn't in the usual style of painting from that era. It certainly wasn't a Van Dyck, or even a Johnson. 'Who painted it? Is it very valuable?'

'That's the thing,' said Will, putting his arm carefully around my waist. 'It was painted by Margaret Kearton, and I don't think it's worth much in terms of money, but to William, it was evidently priceless. It survived intact down there all those years. Luckily, the chamber wasn't damp, and there was no sunlight, obviously. Plus, the temperature would have stayed pretty constant down there. Even so, I think it's something of a miracle, which makes you think, doesn't it?'

'So that's what he considered worth hiding from the Parliamentarians,' I said, astonished. 'You said it was just the usual stuff, when I asked what he'd stashed away. I thought you meant coins and jewellery.'

He shook his head. 'I just wanted to surprise you. I wanted you to discover it for yourself and feel the same amazement that I felt when I found it. This painting's not all he'd hidden. These were inside a leather bag in the chest. Look.' He led me over to a display cabinet, and I peered at some sheets of paper that were spread out under the glass.

'What are they?' I peered closer, trying to read the tiny, faded writing.

'We've copied key lines from them and put the words up on those information boards,' he said, nodding at the wall beside the cabinet. 'Read them.'

I began to read, but within seconds I had my hand to my mouth, swallowing down a sob. 'Love letters!'

'Between William and Elinor, going back to well before their engagement. It seems they loved each other for years, but Elinor's father wanted to keep her safe, and thought he was doing the best thing for her by marrying her off to a protestant landowner. He hoped that would allay any doubts people had about the family's religious beliefs and give Elinor some protection. In an increasingly paranoid and dangerous world, he put his love for his child above his faith.'

I thought about my dad and was certain he'd have done the same for me. It seemed Elinor and I had both been blessed with very loving fathers. Even so, I was glad she'd been able to marry the real love of her life.

'After his death, William and Elinor were able to marry at last, with the blessing of her brother who was one of William's closest friends,' Will continued. 'As we know, the marriage was to be a short one, but from reading these letters it's clear it was a very loving one, too. So much so that, in a house full of treasures, the only things William considered worth saving from Cromwell's men were the portrait of the two of them — painted by the sister he adored — these love letters, and his wife's Rosary beads, which, as you can see, we also have on display.' He nodded to another card on the wall. 'I thought that quote from the Bible was rather appropriate.'

Tearfully, I read the quotation from Corinthians 13. *And now abideth faith, hope, love, these three; but the greatest of these is love.*

'Oh, Will.' I blinked away the tears, not entirely successfully, as he held me to him. 'It's so sad,' I said eventually. 'They all died so young.'

'I know,' he soothed. 'I know.'

'They could have had such a happy life,' I said, looking up at him through blurry eyes. 'Not just William and Elinor, but poor Margaret, too.'

'Which is why this room will be a tribute to all three of them,' he promised. 'Their story will be here for all to see, and they'll never be forgotten.' He tucked a strand of my hair behind my ear. 'The whole focus of this house will change. It will be about love, and faith, and hope.' He smiled down at me. 'We have big plans. Nat's going to apply for a licence to hold weddings here. It's going to be a happy house. A place where people can make their promises to be together forever. And we're going to open up the priest holes and passageway in The Earl's Bedroom.

Obviously, we're going to have to make it safer to get down there, but it should be shown, shouldn't it? People should know what true love, and true faith, really are.'

I nodded, thinking it sounded amazing. There was just one thing that jarred, but how could I bring it up now?

'And as for the shoot,' Will continued, 'that's been abandoned.'

My head shot up. How did he *know*? 'Really?'

'Really. It's not what we're about. I can't imagine what I was thinking.'

'You're a really fabulous person, Will,' I said. 'Do you know that?'

'It wasn't just down to me,' he said, bashfully. 'I talked it over with Nat and Bernie. We all agreed it wasn't something we wanted to pursue. We have other priorities now.'

'Love changes everything, doesn't it?' I said, awestruck.

'It really does.' He hesitated, then said, 'I have something else to tell you. I've arranged a meeting with Archie and John. We're going to start negotiations to set up the Kearton Hall Preservation Trust. If things go according to plan, they'll be two of the trustees, and I shall hand the house into their safe keeping.'

I stepped back, shocked. 'But why? After everything you said!'

'Because I know now what's really important to me. Do you remember that day I took you to Scarborough Castle?'

'Of course I do.'

'We went to see Anne Bronte's grave, and I said it was sad that she was buried so far away from her family. I said that people were more important than places, yet I'd lost sight of that myself, somewhere along the way. The fact is, however much I love this house, *you're* the love of my life, Lexi. My father always told me that I was a failure, and I was terrified that, by handing the Hall over, I'd prove him right. I thought I had to show everyone that I could do it on my own, that I wouldn't let my ancestors down. But when I saw these things, it was as if William was trying to tell me what really matters. Where our real treasure lies. I realised I didn't have to prove anything to anyone. All I have to do is put you first and make you happy. Darcey and Archie are right. The Trust will safeguard the house's future, and it's not as if much will change. We'll still own the rest of the estate, still run the place. The Hall will still be my home, and, maybe one day—' he hesitated, his anxiety apparent, '—maybe one day...'

My eyes widened. 'Are you asking me to move in with you, Sir William?'

'I think, maybe, I'm asking a lot more than that,' he murmured. When I didn't reply, he held up his hands. 'Sorry. Is it too soon? It's just that, it feels—'

He didn't get the chance to complete his sentence, as my lips met his, and his words were buried within a long, lingering kiss.

'I think you've done it again,' I said eventually. 'You always seem to know what I want, without me having to say a single word. You don't have to ask. The answer's yes.'

His smile flooded the room. 'You belong in this house, Lexi. You always have. I think the house knows it, too. Just imagine it. One day, it will be a real family home again, with children running up and down the stairs, and sliding down the bannisters, giving Woody a heart attack.'

'Great! So it's okay for me to invite Amy and the twins over?' I teased.

His face flushed, and I laughed. 'Joking.' I rested my head on his chest and sighed. 'It's all going to be okay, isn't it? We're going to be happy.'

'We are,' he promised, kissing the top of my head. 'We have everything we could possibly want. Each other.'

'There is just one more thing,' I said, a moment later, as we turned to leave the room.

'Anything,' he promised.

'Well, it seems to me that what this house is lacking is a portrait of the Fourteenth Baronet. And I do feel that I couldn't possibly settle here until that situation is rectified.'

Will surveyed me thoughtfully. 'Hmm. You're right. And I think it also needs a portrait of the future Lady Boden-Kean. So, how about we both sit for portraits as a joint engagement present?'

'Oh, hell,' I said. 'That backfired on me, didn't it?'

'I think it did,' he agreed, closing the door behind us, and pulling me gently into his arms.

It's odd, but for one brief moment, I could have sworn I heard a sigh of pleasure coming from behind that door. But I expect it was just the floorboards settling. Old houses do creak an awful lot, you know…

And now abideth faith, hope, love, these three; but the greatest of these is love.

The End

To find out more about Sharon Booth
and to sign up to her newsletter
visit her website
www.sharonboothwriter.com

Acknowledgements

My thanks must, as always, go to my family and friends, who have been so supportive throughout this. I couldn't do half the things I do without the help and encouragement of my husband, whose faith in me is truly awe-inspiring. Thank you, Steve.

To my lovely fellow Write Romantics, who are always around to comfort me when I need to pour out my worries and doubts, encourage me when I feel like giving up, and cheer when things are going well, massive thanks. It's such a fantastic group to belong to, and I know we all feel the benefit of having such a tight and supportive network. Thank you so much, Alex, Deirdre, Helen P, Helen R, Jackie, Jo, Julie, Lynne, and Rachael. You know how much I love you all!

Thanks also to my beta readers, Julie and Alex, whose comments and thoughts really gave me cause to rethink the book and led to me changing quite a lot! I was appalled at the time, but they were right. I'm very glad they're such tough taskmasters.

I owe a huge debt of gratitude to JB Editing Services, who did sterling work as always, editing and proofreading my manuscript, and to the wonderful Berni Stevens for the cover design.

I also must mention Sarah and Karen, who gave me permission (or rather, begged me) to include two certain characters in the book. I hope you approve! And to Irene, Sandra, Caz, Jacquie, (and Jacquie's mum!) and all the other ladies at MGP, who are so lovely about my writing — thank you!

I've had a lot of fun writing and researching this novel. Special thanks to my daughter, Jemma, who took me, not once, but twice, to Burton Agnes Hall in East Yorkshire, so that I could absorb the very special atmosphere of a stately home. In my mind, Burton Agnes Hall became Kearton Hall, and if any readers want to know what Kearton Hall looks like, head to this beautiful Elizabethan house near Driffield and you'll find out. I also went to Scarborough Castle, to discover more about its role in the Civil War and immerse myself in the character and history of the place. My lovely husband accompanied me, and we had a fantastic day

Finally, I must add that, although Nicholas Owen was a real person, and did indeed create the most amazing priest holes and hiding places, there is, as far as I'm aware, no evidence that he ever built tunnels or passageways. I took liberties there, I'm afraid. On the other hand, the man was a genius and a marvel, so who knows what may yet be discovered…

Sharon xx

More from Sharon Booth

There Must Be an Angel (Kearton Bay Book 1)

When Eliza Jarvis discovers her property show presenter husband, Harry, has been expanding his portfolio with tabloid darling Melody Bird, her perfect life crumbles around her ears.

Before you can say *Pensioner Barbie* she's in a stolen car, heading to the North Yorkshire coastal village of Kearton Bay in search of the father she never knew, with only her three-year-old daughter and a family-sized bag of Maltesers for company.

Ignoring the pleas of her uncle, chat show presenter Joe Hollingsworth, Eliza determines to find the man who abandoned her mother and discover the reason he left them to their fate. All she has to go on is his name – Raphael – but in such a small place there can't be more than one angel, can there?

Gabriel Bailey may have the name of an angel but he's not feeling very blessed. In fact, the way his life's been going he doesn't see how things can get much worse. Then Eliza arrives with her flash car and designer clothes, reminding him of things he'd rather forget, and he realises that if he's to have any kind of peace she's one person he must avoid at all costs.

But with the help of a beautiful Wiccan landlady, and a quirky pink-haired café owner, Eliza is soon on the trail of her missing angel, and her investigations lead her straight into Gabriel's path.

As her search takes her deeper into the heart of his family, Eliza begins to realise that she's in danger of hurting those she cares about deeply. Is her quest worth it?

And is the angel she's seeking really the one she's meant to find?

A Kiss from a Rose (Kearton Bay Book 2)

Rose Maclean's new beginning in Kearton Bay didn't go quite as expected, but now she has a new career and things finally seem to be improving.
But Rose's life never runs smoothly for long. With money tight, space in her tiny flat at a premium, and her eldest daughter, Fuschia, behaving even more strangely than usual, the last thing she needs is to spend more time with her mother. Mrs Maclean is straight-talking and hard to please, but when she becomes the unexpected victim of a crime, Rose has no choice but to take her into her already cramped home.
Reduced to sleeping on the sofa, dealing with her mother's barbed comments, and worrying endlessly about her teenage daughters, Rose is desperately in need of something good to happen.
Flynn Pennington-Rhys is the quiet man of Kearton Bay. He lives alone in a large, elegant house, and works as a GP in the village. Thoughtful, reliable, but a bit of a loner, Flynn is the last person Rose expected to fall for. Then a drunken kiss at a wedding sets them on a path that neither could have predicted.
But Flynn has his own issues to deal with, and when events take an unexpected turn, it seems Rose may not be able to rely on him, after all.
Will the quiet man come through for her? Will her daughters ever sort themselves out? And will Rose ever get her bedroom back from her mother, or is she destined to spend the rest of her life on the sofa?